Atomic Dreams
at the
Red Tiki Lounge

10th Anniversary Special Edition

S.P. Grogan

Atomic Dreams
at the
Red Tiki Lounge

Art by Brad "Tiki Shark" Parker

Addison & Highsmith

Addison & Highsmith Publishers

Las Vegas ◊ Chicago ◊ Palm Beach

Published in the United States of America by
Histria Books
7181 N. Hualapai Way, Ste. 130-86
Las Vegas, NV 89166 USA
HistriaBooks.com

Addison & Highsmith is an imprint of Histria Books. Titles published under the imprints of Histria Books are distributed worldwide.

Library of Congress Control Number: 2014919497

ISBN 978-1-59211-293-7 (softbound)
ISBN 978-0-98011-646-5 (hardcover)
ISBN 978-1-59211-358-3 (eBook)

Dedication

Still to the crazies
the wild and weird
the fun-loving
those with never-grow up mind set
those who still chase rainbows
to those who enjoy watching
the Pu'u 'Ō'ō lava flow at midnight

Pamela
Abbas
Tiki Shark Parker

also to those fun-crazies
those Cre8tives
who play with Shellfish
in the celluloid sand

Hunter Hopewell
James Hopewell

Hopewell came to believe that when he saw these shadow-mist devil sharks swirling around someone's head that person would in the future die a violent death.

Part One
Hunter Hopewell

1

November, 1943
Choiseul Island, the South Pacific, held by the Imperial
Japanese Army

O nce again his gaze is fixed upon the hideous face of the blood spattered statue falling towards him. As if trying to ward off some diabolical creature, he raises his hands in a futile gesture. Too late: embracing the crush of stone he experiences the terror of his death, as he has so many times before in this recurring nightmare.

He hears shouting. *Corpsman! Corpsman! Over here!*

In another unsettling dream — perhaps the same — in a swirling fog atop a mountain precipice, he is caught in an invisible tug of war between the statue, moving with plodding steps, no longer stone of reddish-brown but dark as a bottomless pit. The statue pulls at his arm as to his opposite side does a beautiful woman with black flowing hair, her bronze face haloed in orange fi re. Be strong, my warrior, he hears the whisper of a female's lullaby voice, calming his mind, bringing him back to vague consciousness.

Tinny sounds he hears, odd in their mixing, intensified into the pounding of waves. In the background, muffled explosions, whistling screams followed by quaking, ground-jarring thumps; the pop, pop, pop of small arms fire, the staccato rat-tat-tat of a spitting machine gun. Dazed, he finds himself jerking his limbs on a field stretcher, then an awkward lifting. He guessed they had tied him down on the deck of that torpedo boat, the one designated for the rendezvous to bring them off the island.

His next sensation, like a rough thrown skipping rock, was the war craft bouncing to the rolling of the ocean and the vibration of the high-octane motor, easing him back into his unconscious stupor, from which he wakes to a fog when the shaking and roaring falls off .

He tries to move but cannot. His head hurts.

The war's over for you, says a man's gentle voice. Strange. In his misty vision, through slits of swollen eyes, swirls a shadow, so much like a small dark-gray shark, circling around the head of the man who spoke.

Another voice. — *My God, Mister Kennedy, is he still alive? Are those his brains?*

— *That young marine died in my bunk this morning. This guy's still breathing; he deserves our best.*

Soon he feels himself rising, lifted by many hands. And then… *what do I feel?*

In and out of a dark landscape of memories, real or not, he senses the vibrations of airplane engines. A quieting descends upon his soul; all around him and within, an infinite silent blackness. No, not quite true. He could sense a pinprick of light, at first far distant, growing as it moves towards him into a broiling fire wherein swirls the visions of that bloody statue from the pagan cemetery. The woman now stands to the statue's side beckoning him. She is so lovely, so desirable, so real, he tries to reach out his hand to touch her. The statue lurches between them, keeping them apart; an icy touch from the stone, he knows not how, it burns. He sees in the empty eyes of that crimson face — unholy violence. *How can I see this if I'm dead? Can the dead dream?*

Excerpt from Major General R. Geiger's after-action report —

Set up by the upper command the diversion by the United States Marines, 2nd Parachute Battalion, was to convince the Japanese in believing the upcoming invasion of Bougainville would take place on the island's east side. The raid seemed to be successful, up until the ambush. Forty marines accompanied by a French-speaking coast watcher and his administrative U.S. Navy liaison were trapped and forced to make a stand in an ancient native cemetery and religious meeting ground. Three marines and the advisor liaison, Naval Commander Hunter Hopewell, were seriously injured, with one marine later succumbing to his wounds.

2

Dirt had been his last taste.

My mouth feels like it's stuffed with cotton.

His crusted eyelids opened to an antiseptic room and the feeling of being cocooned, swaddled tight within a metal bed, everything pale alabaster in color. A nurse had been tucking in his sheets, and her movement must have brought him conscious.

So, he was not dead.

His dry tongue slurred out his question: "Where am I?"

"Aiea Naval Hospital, Honolulu," she replied, startled.

"Don't move. I'll find your doctor."

He could not move, though he tried. *What happened to me?*

Two men entered both doctor-looking in their white garb and stethoscopes, followed by several nurses rushing in to stare with expressions of... wonderment... disbelief?

"Commander Hopewell, welcome back from the dead," said the older of the two medical men.

The Commander — *that's who I am* — replied in a low raspy wheeze, "Yes, I was dead," to him the truth as he had dreamed. His comment elicited titters and laughter from the medical audience surrounding his bed. They thought he had made a joke.

Both doctors began probing, first delicately at his head, and he felt tingle sensations above his eyebrows as they unwrapped bandages, murmuring 'hmm-mm' and 'yes, yes.'

Nurses assisted in the turning and adjusting of his body as he felt pokes to his arms and legs. *Wait!*

"I can't feel my left arm." With a fearful glance he discovered his arm lay there, though unmoving despite any effort. He pushed out a deep sigh. *Thank God, I have not lost my arm.*

"Yes, your arm sustained some injury," offered the younger physician, a bit cavalier, as if any answer would be solace. "The surgeons here did major reconstructive. It should be responding, and still might. Nerve damage, you know. We know little about nerve connections." If that was an apology for the profession's failure to bring him whole again, the doc would gain no absolution from this patient.

"Commander, do you remember how you were injured?"

Searching disjointed memories, he did recall and his eyes widened. All in the room saw a man facing a relived terror.

"The ambush."

He said no more to a disappointed audience and would not do so until he made his formal report to the proper authorities, to his O.S.S. superiors. Commander Hunter Hopewell harbored secrets that still might fall into enemy hands.

Without warning, a stabbing sensation seared through his mind, flinging pain like a hundred ice pick stabs into the head wound and forcing out a yelp of agony.

A nurse rushed out, returning with an injection of morphine.

Very shortly, and like a tidal flow surging through his blood, he felt the opiate relax all tension and he drifted off on a soothing cloud. But behind the cloud lurked a nightmare of the ambush, first of the many subconscious haunting visions which would plague him in the months to come as the need for pain relief led to a drug dependency. This night, in unsettling slumber, he saw a monster tiki destroying Honolulu, and he felt weak and helpless to protect the beautiful and mysterious woman standing next to him. Hunter learned too late that morphine was named after the Greek god Morpheus, the deity of dreams.

In his nightmare, as the giant tiki destroyed Honolulu, he felt weak and helpless to protect the beautiful and mysterious woman and screamed awake, sweating, praying for any chance to save her and the city.

3

Three years later, early July, 1946
Red Tiki Lounge and Bar, Honolulu, Hawai'i.

Crashing cymbal music and a cannon-fire drum beat woke Hunter Hopewell from his dark reverie. He pulled his far-away stare out of the deep depths of the glass of liquor and downed the last of this liquid medicine. Waving for a refill, he took in the chaotic scene through glazed eyes.

Laughter came easy to this night's crowd in the Red Tiki Lounge and Bar. Only eight months previously the Japanese Empire, decimated by Allied revenge, had capitulated aboard the battleship *U.S.S. Missouri* in Tokyo Bay. The U.S. military already had begun mothballing their war fleets and downsizing their armed forces. Honolulu, the largest city in the Hawaiian Island chain, situated on O'ahu, offered the last port of escapism before departure to the States and the return to civilian life and uncertain responsibilities.

With all evil now forgotten, those who had partied like there was no tomorrow now celebrated even more ardently since they had their tomorrows and were going home alive. Tonight, the Red Tiki patrons, lubricated with shots and beer or sweet cocktails and entranced by the pounding of the tom-toms, the snarl of slack-key guitar and the flash-strumming of ukuleles, believed that morality could be postponed, however briefly.

Over on the dance floor several couples were jump jiving to the five piece band *K and the Dogg Men*. Its members were stylish zoot suiter Hawaiians who, as they bounced out fast jungle rhythms or big band melodies, began removing perspiration drenched layers of clothes, so that by the early morning hours they jammed bare chested which, in turn, brought in the night ladies to seek respite from their horizontal trade. As such, by talent and reputation, the musicians never greeted the morning sun alone nor went to bed without companionship, if they so chose.

The Red Tiki consisted of three semi-open rooms, all dedicated and named within the last few years. On the wall of the bar, paneled in dark wood, its floor strewn with peanut shells, a posted sign declared, the '*Pyle One On*' Bar, in memory to roving newspaperman Ernie Pyle, friend to foxhole dwellers from Normandy beaches to the Pacific where he took a bullet on Ie Shima island, off Okinawa, in April of 1945. The dance floor was appropriately dubbed the '*In the Mood*' Room after the song composed by officer-band leader Glen Miller, missing in action, 1944, somewhere over the English Channel. Here, up to twenty-five couples could hug-glide or turn the floor over to the gyrating ambidextrous when a swing tune brought out the jitterbug crazies. K and the Dogg Men seemed unworldly in offering a musical catalogue repertoire, which usually won any Stump the Band challenges, from *Nu'a O Ka Palai* [The Ground is Strewn] to *Donald Duck in Nutzi Land*.

If someone were to define the Red Tiki's decor there would be several apt descriptions, such as 'beach bum simplistic' or 'tsunami trash'. Definitely, Hawaiian yard sale came to mind, for hung from walls and various parts of the cluttered ceiling were fish nets adorned with glass ball net floats interlaced with dried out starfish and puffer fish puffed. A mounted swordfish graced the entrance to the dance floor, its spear point impaling a dozen discarded or purloined nurses' brassieres and one girdle.

Near one wall in the bar, patrons stood reading thumb tacked bar napkins or writing their own missives for posting to the unofficial Red Tiki jungle message board, a mid-ocean way station for those seeking lost buddies or misplaced girlfriends.

Elsewhere displayed, a framed pre-war travel poster of a winging Pan Am Clipper, captioned: *Enjoy the Orient*. Tongue-in-cheek during the war years, now left intact, perhaps in hopes that the message might soon be back in vogue to capture tourist dollars.

And no lounge tour would be complete without noticing above the bar a reef-broken longboard from friend Duke Kahanamoku, Olympic medal swimmer and pioneer surfing enthusiast, prominently situated there to the bar's betterment and political goodwill, for at this time, Duke was the Sheriff of Honolulu.

So, out on the town, those in the know grabbed beach sun at the Royal Hawaiian and maybe caught Ray Kinney vocalizing with Don McDarmid's

Orchestra who were this month performing at the Kewalo Inn, but invariably, in quest of lust or love, flirting or heat dancing in an inebriated fog, later to be called unforgettable memories, one closed the night out at the Red Tiki Lounge and Bar, town of Honolulu, islands of Hawai'i,

American Territory.

No wonder, Matson Ship Lines had written in an early 1941 travel brochure:

Everyone passing through the islands must pat the 'Red Tiki' statue for the luck of good fortune, and while you're there an island beverage inside the famous Red Tiki Lounge and Bar wouldn't hurt either.

DEAD MAN'S
CHEST

Tiki Shark's view of the Red Tiki bar regulars

4

Over at the main bar, where serious drinkers were knocking back the half-priced rum specials, fifty cents a glass, Hunter Hopewell hunched on his elbows lost in the drink before him. He was not your usual alkie, dependent on a haze to make it through the days. He required stimulant to rid himself of the pain and nightmares of his combat wound. The doctors could boast of their repair job but were yet unable to find the cause of the headaches.

With such tribulation, women at first glance found the outer casing attractive, a young man in his late twenties with tousled unkempt hair, a war-matured face, even distinguished, narrow and rectangular, rugged with two day old beard growth. It was when one looked close and saw the sea-blue eyes surrounded by redness, saw in his expression that goofy smile of the bar fly, that women steered clear and sought out more receptive conquests. Hunter, in his self-numbness, paid the opposite sex little attention except for two women who tormented him, one in his unsettled dreams and the other, somewhere in the bar this night.

Hunter slung his groggy view around the crowd. Above his head the heavy fog of cigarette smoke wafted upwards to the teak rafters before being pushed around in swirling clouds by the chain-cranked, squeaking ceiling palm fans. The smoke and spilt beer odors mingled with the perfumed sweat of the working girls, the fragrance of hair pomade of the mulatto dockworkers, and the cologne aftershave of the sailors, airmen, and army soldiers, the majority sporting Hawaiian Aloha shirts and enjoying their first or last hours of leave.

Such partying generated brisk business to the bathrooms, where *Kane* and *Wahine*, their slatted bamboo doors swinging back and forth like rushing turnstiles at an amusement park, effused from the stalls their own smell mix of urine and vomit. This final, suffocating concoction inhaled, by all who entered, hit the newcomers hard like a typhoon gust, but they quickly tolerated it as their senses adapted, for visitors knew by word-of-mouth and marquee billing that they were privileged to be entering one of mankind's great social watering holes, boasting a Pacific Rim reputation for its strutting and rutting.

It was one of these mating rituals that finally caught Hunter's attention. The drunken leering, pawing attitude of several sailors had moved from rough flirtation to hit the wall of the woman's firm response, "I said, 'no thanks' several times, fellows. Please take the hint."

More physical pressing against her had escalated into a shouting match with the woman finger pointing, her tongue spewing less common curses, more rapier thrust exclamations of 'I don't think so, shit toad' and 'go grab your own ankles, bum fucker.' Hunter knew the woman well. They had a relationship, nothing sexual, more an estranged business partnership. Secrets were held between them. The young lady being harassed was Judith 'Tommi' Chen, the Honolulu businesswoman, bookkeeper for Lyle Sheftel, owner of the Red Tiki.

"Come on, girlie, let's go dance," said one of the drunk sailors, more demand than request, as he tried to grab at her arm, and missed.

"Well, Heggen's ugly, but I'm more the wild man lover," another sailor pushed in.

She did not diffuse the situation, more egged it up a notch.

"Go have your fun somewhere else. Or are you out to prove you won the war, one last conquest?"

Their boisterous teasing quickly then turned ugly.

"You Japs did lose. We're more men than you'd ever deserve."

"Sometimes I wonder, if you didn't have the bomb, if the outcome would be much different." Hunter, hearing this barb, gave his own crooked smile. *Yep, that's Tommi, feisty, in your face.*

"Slant eyes," mumbled a third sailor, and the sailors closed as a pack, dark anger fomenting in their minds some sexual punishment against the young woman.

Another 'slant eye', more menacing, stepped into the tension. Before them stood Mister Manaa, the Māori doorman and bouncer of the Red Tiki.

"I think you gentlemen have had enough. I think you should pay your tab and call it a night." His voice bore steady menace, as he turned in such a way that his shoulders and girth formed a muscle barricade between the rowdies and Tommi Chen.

The sailors coalesced into a fighting unit but then the band stopped playing, and though wasted by drink, they were not so stupid drunk as to fail to notice that the odds of battle in the bar had shifted against them.

They grumbled, puffed their chests, pushed chairs around roughly, and departed, the last of them, the sailor called 'Heggen', cursing out the best parting shot he could muster, "You'll be sorry."

The band struck up the calypso tune "Rum and Coca Cola", stressing the lyrics, *'workin' for the Yankee dolla'.* The levity and dancing resumed.

Tommi hovering, half way between contemptuous and smug, paused to reconnoiter her surroundings, not wanting to stand out by this tussle, wishing to again be low key, for unobtrusive had served her well these last years of war, first year of peace.

She spotted Hunter Hopewell at his regular bar spot staring back at her in his own stupor, and she thought, '*Good, right where I want him.*'

Hunter returned to his drinking, throwing off his own silent comment: '*It was those sailors who needed protection, not her. Damn woman is the most dangerous Jap in the entire islands. Even with this fucked up war over.*'

5

Honolulu, Hawai'i 3 a.m.

Having been deftly ejected from the Red Tiki Lounge, the befuddled sailors believed they had been rudely mistreated. The incident festered. Angered still by the young woman's emasculating tongue and forced to exit with hustled shoves by the no-nonsense bouncer they did not see themselves in the wrong by not taking her no as a firm 'no'.

Reinforced with more liquor, they decided to resort to petty revenge. The Red Tiki Lounge and Bar must suffer, and that is why they returned, with a last minute plan for vandalism.

Their attempt at silence was broken by drunken coughs and suppressed chortles, hands over their mouths, at this late night lark. They were going to steal the tiki of the Red Tiki, the bar's tourist landmark, the good luck totem for all who entered. It would not be an easy task; the statue was massive, near eight feet tall.

Two of the sailors, experienced stevedores, motioned the crane truck backing up to come just so far. Already, two other sailors had swaddled the massive statue in a canvas tarp tied with rope. The hook clasp tightened as the crane grunted at the load and the statue broke free of its concrete pedestal.

"Look at that," came a whispered shout from one of the sloshed culprits. It was sailor Heggen, the most drunk of them all.

"What?" asked one of the co-conspirators as his hand signals motioned the hefted load over to the flatbed truck where two other enlisted men were waiting to tie down their prize.

"I could have sworn the damn ghoul's face moved."

"Have another slug at the bottle, Heggen, maybe our new good luck charm will start singing 'Anchor's Away'."

"And it wasn't a smile; it kinda sneered at me."

"Get in the truck and don't throw up."

Loaded with their cargo, the two trucks moved off quietly from the Red Tiki heading toward one of the dry docks where their ship had just been flushed out with a clean bill of health for its final sea voyage.

Several blocks away, the convoy turned toward the docks of Pearl, passing the Honolulu *Star-Bulletin* newspaper truck off-loading the early morning edition at Sammy Nimoro's newsstand. The streets at this before dawn hour might bear produce trucks delivering fruit and vegetables for the daily markets, but Sammy thought it unusual to see military trucks loaded with sailors waving and laughing and having a binge party good time. Sammy cut the strings to the bundle of newspapers with the July 2 headlines: "Operation Crossroads — Success at Bikini Atoll" — "Chiang Kai-shek launches new attacks on Communist Chinese forces of Mao Zedong" — "Boxer Jack Johnson Killed in Auto Accident."

"MP's gonna git you," said Sammy aloud but to himself as the trucks rushed past.

At Pier Gate 3, the sentry waved them through after receiving a bottle of good bourbon to look the other way. Close by, civilian custodian Quan Lee, on his night shift of dumping trash from the maintenance sheds, watched the bottle transaction and the trucks moving past.

After two hours of crane work and dolly shoving and sliding, they could be satisfied with their work. Their sacrificial totem stood near the bow of the de-commissioned destroyer minesweeper, the *USS Southard*. The stone figurehead would remain hidden under the canvas tarp and would not be displayed until their vessel had cleared port for the open ocean.

As the final covering was tied down securely, Sailor Heggen, posted to the Southard's last cruise, said aloud to no one in particular, "This stone feels real warm."

"Jeez, why not, asshole, summer nights around here drip heat."

"Doesn't feel right, you know, when they say 'stone-cold' — ."

"If you want a hot rock, just wait; our tin can is going to get the best fireworks send-off in the world, and have this buddy boy along to kiss Davy Jones's ass."

"Just saying; didn't feel burning to the touch back at the Red Tiki."

"God, Heggen, we're finished here, go sleep it off!"

They paid little attention to the tiki statue thereafter, and when late in the morning the ship eased out of Pearl Harbor with its unusual cargo, the salvage transport crew working under the heat of the summer sun never did discover that the thrumming vibrations coming from *USS Southard's* oil burning engines were not the same as those coming from the stone tiki god. When the ship sailed away from the shores and reefs of Hawai'i, there was a brief shimmering, mirage-like, when an invisible boundary was breached; releasing an ethereal message, a cry upon the wind, climbing towards the sky, and higher still to the reach of the heavens, a warning, that on this day all was not right with the world.

From the frivolity of drunks amazing events, beyond all normal understanding, were put into motion, so...

Do not discredit or curse those things that you know nothing of.

Against the pyrotechnics display of fire and brimstone, amid the geysers of explosive lava in a massive new eruption of the volcano known as Kīlauea, she walked naked from the magma caldera, awakened from a long, slumbering repose, to take human form again, in the likeness of the young native woman, so long ago sacrificed to appease her wrath. The fearful worshipers had acted in ignorance for they did not really know her temperament, or the source of her immortality. Yes, such deity spirits do exist beyond the pale. She was earth-eater, the creator of new soil... the birth mother of what is called Earth.

And in the miasma of those unseen forces that released her and brought her forth a woman ...she held desires.

Pele the goddess.

The night the stolen stone statue began its journey across the sea, an angry tremor rose from the bowels of the earth and sought release. The sailors of the *USS Southard*, by their petty theft, had initiated a collision course with disastrous consequences. The balance of harmony between the spirit world and the earthly world of mankind had been broken.

Pele had been sent to repair the damage, regain the balance, before it was too late.

Around the goddess swirled the frothy mantle of wind and lightening that heightened her power while she walked the surface, an unworldly storm that vainly tried to hold in check the fire of her soul.

Before her rose a wraith, a spirit, a shape shifter to do her will.

"Kama Pua'a," she invoked.

From sparking lava came substance, and with snorting squeals a large pig appeared and ran down the slope to escape the heat and cooling pahoehoe lava. Long ago, this spirit creature was once her lover transformed, from man to ash and thence into the cursed form of a swine when he made Pele angry. She was not a goddess to toy with.

"Go. Find my warrior."

Kama Pua'a obeyed with squeals and snorts and disappeared into a racing swirl of black dust.

6

Lyle Sheftel, the owner of the Red Tiki Lounge and Bar, was taking his ritual morning walk on the wet sands of Waikiki Beach. He fit the part of a bar owner: in his early forties, not tall, but not short either as his stature showed off a wrestler's triangle girth of muscles, his mop of greased black wavy hair, topping a face pock-marked from childhood scarlet fever. His Chicago twang came out gravelly after years of cigars and backroom smoke from too many all-night poker games. He seemed out of place for the islands, but these days everything was out of place, everyone disconnected from their roots.

Today, he took his time watching the early morning swimmers and surfers, eyeing the incoming waves, ever the opportunist, for the odd cast-off salvage debris, more certain to find dead fish or water-logged coconuts, smelling the salt air, before turning inland to let the fresh aromas of dew on the plumeria and orchids clean his senses. Before long, such fresh perfumed air would be overwhelmed by the morning-after bar smells when he opened the front door and began the hosing clean-up.

He stopped with a lurch.

"Holy Mother!"

The owner of the Red Tiki stood looking at the empty pedestal, stricken first by shock, then curses, and finally grief. His lucky totem, stolen. His head shook with anger and frustration. With a weak hand he tapped the empty spot where the tiki once stood, and found no relief, no comfort, a man violated by theft.

How would his business now fare? In that regard, he should not have been worried, yet... Lyle Sheftel ran a great hooch and hoofer joint. Everyone said so. But he was indeed worried; what action to take? He furled his brow with intent. Good business owners are decision makers. His mind settled on those people who might have the talents to discover the thieves and recover his giant amulet: His bookkeeper, Tommi Chen, with fingers in a myriad of lucrative pies. The hepster artist, Tiki Shark, who had the gossip pulse of the street people.

And he would enlist Hunter Hopewell, the Red Tiki's number one barfly, the ex-Navy Commander, the wounded warrior sidelined to be an investigator for the Judge Advocate's Honolulu office, now beached. Although as a newly minted civilian the man was barely making ends meet in his one-man private investigations office. Sheftel had heard, from Tommi Chen, that Hunter had once been a highly efficient navy investigator. That was good enough for him.

Yes, before he called the police and risked the bad publicity, even ridicule from his competitors, he would launch his own search. This might be a kidnapping, the statue being held for ransom. Above all, he wanted first to recover the tiki and next exact revenge, Chicago-style, with crowbar or baseball bat.

Sheftel knew how to find Hunter Hopewell: just pound on the ceiling of the bar with a broom handle, for Hopewell slept in a two room apartment-office right above the Red Tiki. Up side stairs against the outside building, a badly scrawled sign above the door announced: *Hopewell Investigations.* Not the best location, as a fledgling private eye for hire, for attracting clients or inspiring the confidence by decor. The bedroom consisted of a discarded metal frame hospital bed, a small dresser, and a wash basin. For his physical bathroom needs he had to go downstairs and use the bar's facilities. His office, again minimal, held a battered army surplus desk with two chairs and one filing cabinet, missing the lower drawer. He worked, when he had a client, outside of his office. If he required a telephone, the bar phone became his answering service.

7

Thump. Thump. Thump.

Hunter sensed his downstairs alarm clock banging on his floor. He struggled out of one of those dreams that seemed to come and go, like a haunting. His headache seemed worse, more so than his usual hangover. He laid in bed, going back in his mind to when he woke up in the hospital and the nearly eight months of treatment, and of course, the doctors. His one eye finally opened, blood-shot, as he re-lived the terror of medicine's attempt at healing.

The day after he had regained consciousness, he was propped up, his body infused with a haze of I.V. dripping drugs. He had been slurping lukewarm beef broth when the two doctors, this time without their following of acolytes, returned for another examination.

The older of the two spoke first. "I'm Dr. Gerald Lundell, and this is Doctor Henry Heimlich. He's traveling back to the States from a stint in the China Theatre. I'm lucky to have him help even for a short duration. I can assure you that you are in good hands."

Hunter saw a kindly, grey-haired practitioner who resembled actor Lionel Barrymore playing wisdom spouting Dr. Gillespie in the *Dr. Kildare* movies, his voice a soft baritone one might hear on a day time radio soap opera, sponsored by Colgate.

Hunter's memory, from the damage lost due to his wound, he supposed, had improved; he had begun to recall snippets of past events, before being transferred to the war zone. *When was that?* Back in 1942, I think. There was the last time he had been in a movie theater: Washington, D.C., with two weeks at liberty before he shipped out. *Funny, I can't put a name to the face of the woman I invited out that night.* Barely, did he see her face; did they laugh? They must have. That first-run movie was the Hope-Crosby *Road to Zanzibar.*

Hunter dismissed, in his humble opinion, the other doctor as a fledgling associate, too eager, lacking a clinical bedside style, and prayed that 'the kid' in the white smock had not swung a scalpel anywhere near him.

"We do need to know how your injuries occurred," said Dr.

Lundell, his tone cautious, "to make sure we have not missed a symptom, physically or even, as they call it now, psychological, from possible brain damage. The nurses have been hearing you shout in your sleep. I'm guessing there are deeper issues we surgeons may not have the ability to heal."

The doctor let Hunter absorb the broad perspective and its suggestion: if he wanted to heal, a confession as to how he got here and what was bothering him would be welcomed in the diagnosis.

Doctor Lundell, offering a weak smile, continued to espouse his prepared speech.

"Let me start first on what our response was when you arrived at the hospital. Maybe, back up earlier, even to those on first response who saw you in the mobile medical tent in the Solomons before your airlift evacuation." Doctor Lundell pointed to the top of Hunter's bandaged head.

"I'm the chief neurosurgeon here at Aiea. Never had I seen a soldier — pardon me, or navy, brought in with their skull cracked open, a big chunk missing, and the outer neural dura tissue layer peeled back to where we could visibly see the frontal and parietal lobes. And, I might add, have the patient live, or better yet be cognitive and alert." Hunter felt his stomach juices sour. Maybe he had been dead.

"You were gravely wounded," Doctor Heimlich gave his observation. "Under any other circumstances, you would have died on the battlefield." The doctor failed miserably at bedside manner. He tried to recover with a quick diagnosis.

"Must have started with the field corpsman who reached you first. He dumped Sulfanilamide directly into the open wound, found the skull bone, washed it off, and wrapped it in bandage and placed it on your stretcher. What he did not do was try to put the bone back on, cover your brain and bandage it."

"You know, son," said Doctor Lundell, reasserting himself into the conversation, "since Doctor Harvey Cushing pioneered brain surgery and even with his work in World War I, our medical responses to combat head injuries have still been primitive. Sadly, it takes a new bloody world war and too many patient sufferers to advance medicine. You are not only a test case; you certainly will be in a future edition of JAMA." Hunter gave the doctor a blank look.

"The Journal of the American Medical Association."

"And don't forget this penicillin?" added Doctor Heimlich, looking pleased with the story so far, and Hunter wondering if this young doc might be positioning himself to gain a co-authorship byline to any such research paper published.

"Penicillin, what's that?"

"That's an odd thing in the telling," said Doctor Lundell,

"When injected, it definitely does seem to ward off jungle infections at the critical time. I've seen little field study data on this medicine; it is a type of germ-killing bacteria, developed from mold called Penicillium. A bacteriologist by the name of Fleming discovered the spores in the 1920's but it's not been commercialized until recently by the drug manufacturer Pfizer.

"They only started a fermentation process two years ago, 1941. I read somewhere that any supplies they made in mass quantities were allocated towards the European Theater for the Second Front, whenever that's going to happen."

Doctor Heimlich rushed into conversation as an eager novice physician with a researcher's curiosity, tinged with suspicion or was it jealousy? The doctor talk was tiring Hunter.

"There's no penicillin in this hospital," explained Doctor Heimlich. "None in the entire Pacific Theater, but somehow you received two injections of this mold juice when you were put on the P.T. boat for extraction to Bougainville. And two more doses on the flight here to Honolulu. How and why these sailors got their hands on this 'wonder drug' is just baffling."

"Most assuredly," affirmed Doctor Lundell, "through channels we have made our own demands for supplies of this Penicillum medicine. Squeaky wheel and all that. If, as with your case, the results against battlefield infection are quantifiable, the patient mortality might be significantly reduced."

Commander Hunter Hopewell knew he wanted only one answer.

"So, how did you put my head back together?"

The doctors exchanged glances of awkward guilt.

"We really haven't finished buttoning you up," said Doctor Heimlich, matter-of-factly.

"You still have," Doctor Lundell wandered far afield from the clinical approach, "if I can use the word properly, you still have 'debris' scattered on your brain. In fact, one might say your brain has been coated with a fine layer of dust and smatterings of this debris. We have been letting it breathe, frankly, trying to figure out the best way to 'vacuum up' before rebuilding the skull."

Hopewell's heart beat out anxiety like a bass drum.

"You mean my skull is open for all to see inside! Goddam that! Sew me up and get me out of here!"

"Calm down," Doctor Lundell, patted Hunter's sheet covered leg. "Here's what we need to do. First, finish the cleaning up of this 'debris'. Second, put in a metal plate, and then we will put on your broken skull pieces around the plate, and then add in some other living skull bone, that we believe will in time grow over and adhere to your existing bone. Basically, a reverse craniotomy. You may merely have a bump after healing, perhaps micro bald spots you could comb over."

Hunter felt a constriction in his chest, a tightening in breathing.

"You are going to put a steel plate in my head like patching a battleship?"

"In such a severe wound, there are risks of course, we won't candy coat your situation. We are using the latest techniques. I believe the skull bones will fuse together, and you will heal, and be once again a productive member of society."

"Except for a useless left arm." Hunter could move his fingers, but not his upper arm. Strangely, though, the muscles didn't seem to have atrophied; rather, they were hard as rock.

Their Hippocratic Oath, or its fudged variations, required the doctor prior to surgery to be upbeat even in regard to Hunter's new found handicap.

"There's a baseball player," said the senior physician, "named Pete Gray, lost his right arm. Heard he is a record bunter."

"Yeah, and I heard he can't hit a curve ball. Besides, I play scratch golf. You know of any one-armed Bobby Jones players on the course?"

"Lord Nelson," chimed in Heimlich. "He had only one arm and won sea battles."

"Yeah, but too many medals got him sniped dead. Me, at least, I will start with one medal, The Purple Heart. Maybe I'll be lucky on my next tour of duty." Hunter was not humored as he tried to raise his left arm. Little movement. "Wait a minute; you said other bones would go on my head. Where's that coming from? Somewhere else? My left arm? You aren't going to experiment on me like a Frankenstein?"

"No, no. We will take live tissue and bone from cadavers."

"Dead people?"

"It's a new technique of transplanting. Published studies seem to say it works in most cases."

"Most cases? Am I in a hospital under your care, or am I lab rat in a teaching school?"

"By your chart and background file," said Doctor Lundell, wondering if being too upfront and technical might not have been the best approach, "it says we are dealing with a bright young man, product of East Coast Ivy League college, a naval officer, field assigned as an intelligence officer from one of those thrown together military alphabets, something called the Office of Strategic Services. I'd expect you can handle cold hard facts, blunt truths. Being a military man, that's correct, isn't it?"

Fearing the worst, Hunter could only mutter.

"Yeah, we Navy boys can take the shit. Alive but a one arm spastic."

"No, perhaps not. You have been under constant observation. We've seen none of this. But you were, are, severely injured. When they brought you in, you were unconscious with definite brain trauma. That is why your awakening was both a surprise and some sort of miracle."

Hunter tried to recall a distant dream but only the lilting voice whispered in his mind. "Be strong, my warrior."

Doctor Lundell was still speaking. "Here is the crux of the matter. We must perform one last operation to clear this 'debris' and I must understand its source, it's composition. You see, you were wounded in that raid on Choiseul Island. I have been told where your battle took place, this ambush, was all sand composition, and yet what we found in our first inspection inside your skull were microscopic strands of silica, long strands, less than 0.5 millimeters round, but with several of the strands six inches long.

"Isn't sand made of silica?"

"Yes, but not the type to be found on that island; it's truly a quest mystery for the forensic scientist. I sent some samples over to the Geology Department at the Bishop Museum. They laughed, saying the stuff can be found all over the Hawaiian Islands, but not in the Solomon Islands chain where ancient volcanic rock has been worn down. This silicate was created by molten volcanic material windblown into these fine glass strands. I need to know where and how you picked it up."

"Picked up what?"

"What the locals here in the islands call 'Pele's Hair'."

Thump. Thump. Thump.

"I hear you, Sheftel! I'm up!" Three years later as Hunter swung his feet to the cold wood floor in his small garret apartment, he removed from the forefront of thoughts of this remembered conversation with his doctors, but the continuing fear remained. And this day brought it harshly home. His headache was of pin-prick pains, as if the debris, those Pele's hairs, were still poking his brain; and worse, if that could be the case, he felt his side, under his armpit where his skin was hard, just like his left arm. Whatever he had, whatever residual damage from his war injury, it seemed to be spreading, like a cancer.

Former Naval Commander Hunter Hopewell, a man troubled, facing his own personal internal demons stared at Tiki Shark's drawing and wondered at the meaning. What prophecy is this to unfold?

8

Mid-afternoon, after the lunch crowd eased off , Sheftel held his strategy meeting in the lounge's third room, the small restaurant with its six booths and ten tables covered in red checkerboard table cloths, real cotton. The kitchen operated with a four burner propane gas stove, and to save money, two other cooking elements were fully used: an electrical hot plate, and a grill that Sheftel had received in trade for a marine sergeant's bar tab. The marine had hoped to take it home to the States as a war souvenir, but it had failed rules and regs for being too unconventional. Like a BBQ only smaller, table top size, something called a *hibachi*, had been picked up in a cave on Okinawa. It worked well enough for the little spam/pineapple finger food appetizers called *pupus* by locals, grilled for Happy Hour. Though the Red Tiki might have a dive hangout feel, their menu could match any top hotel restaurant along the Waikiki beach with delectable offerings like Blue Pacific Mahimahi in Ti Leaves — cooked in coconut milk ($3.75) or a Nui Nui Cut of Parker Ranch Prime Rib ($4.75).

Off in a corner of the restaurant in one of the red vinyl booths sat Sheftel and the three members of his problem solving team, each with secrets, each with a black cloud of depression hovering, muted anger carved into their faces, each for a different reason.

Sheftel groused and banged the table top and set the meeting's agenda.

"They stole my damn Tiki. How'd they do it? I know the thing must weigh over 400 pounds." Known to all island citizens, the missing tiki statue, daubed red and gigantic at nine feet tall, was the logo and mascot for the establishment, standing at the entrance as official mute greeter to incoming patrons. Sheftel's rant continued, "Thieves in the night... brazen crooks. They should be shot. Where did it go? Who could have taken it?"

Lyle Sheftel up till this morning had thought the world would continue to spin his way. The Red Tiki drinking and entertainment emporium had become a must-see tourist haunt and military hang-out during the war years. Everyone entering who was someone, and all those wannabes, had passed by the tiki, patting the stone sentinel for good luck, for there were those who believed ardently in such voodoo and mumbo jumbo of fate and chance, Sheftel being one of them. Religiously and daily he gave his customary pat to secure fortuitous blessings as he opened the doors for business. He had his reasons. His dream of a comfortable livelihood was under threat. In this postwar economy revenues looked uncertain. The 'Last Party' boom of departing military was sloughing off due to downsizing of the armed forces. The bar also faced new competition as patrons might gravitate toward a fresh and spruced up knock-off of the Red Tiki. To mollify his ulceric distress, he lambasted to the three, his lucky totem must be found and returned, the good karma re-asserted.

Another morose voice at the table spoke out: "I know my creative spirit is flushed down the crapper." The young man speaking, known as 'Tiki Shark', sported a scraggly fuzzed beard and paint stained fingers. Nervously, he grabbed his Coke bottle, slurped through a straw and wailed in lamentation like a keening mourner. "The Mighty Red Tiki was my friend, more important, my muse. Its spirit watched over me." Around seventeen years of age, the boy was a vagabond street artist who sat evenings at an open-air booth — a rickety chair and a small table — on the sidewalk towards the front of the Red Tiki, where he sold his garish, cartoonish paintings. For the bar owner the mobile art gallery was an unexpected blessing as it kept the waiting customers amused and distracted from boredom and grumbles when on the busy nights crowds lined the crushed coral sidewalk. They stood impatiently under an arc of lighted torches, queuing up to the door, waiting to be granted entry by the ex-New Zealand military policeman who flavored the place as the bar's Māori bouncer. Manaakitanga, known in the bar as Mister Manaa like a Mister Moto, held the power to select those so favored and accept them into the inner sanctum of earthy pleasures. And, any who caused trouble he'd dispatch with a swift kick or shove out the door those undesirables who wore out their welcome. The most recent incident, just last night, unbeknownst to them all, had been the catalyst towards the large tiki's theft.

Sheftel, seeing the kid outside each night, formed a loose bond with this wayward free spirit, accepting him not as the usual homeless bum, but in the bar owner's mind, the kid hustler had the makings of a gutsy entrepreneur, fighting for survival, like Sheftel himself in his earlier days as a numbers runner and scrapper from the streets of Chicago. Those sitting at the table only knew the kid as 'Tiki Shark', from his scrawled art work signature. No one ever asked his real name. His creations of bright swatches of colors splashed on canvas or driftwood, usually featured some version of a Tiki god. Occasionally, when he was zapped out from unknown substances, mostly reefer smoke, out from his distorted imagination sprang mysterious Polynesian-styled creatures: lagoon monsters, erotic maidens dancing with Menehune dwarfs and more sinister, black demon sharks that swam in the air far from the sea, circling the heads of the accursed. Tiki Shark's creations were strange and unusual, rainbow splashes of exaggerated art like Disney's *Fantasia* when stoned on the good stuff .

And, embedded in most of his conversations about any subject, whether upbeat or down, fitting with his look and character, Tiki Shark interjected his trademark expression, "Wowie."

"What am I going to do?" In dramatic defeat, the artist dropped his sketch book onto the table top. "Wowie," he said with deflated spirit. "This is probably my last drawing. Like Van Gogh should I sacrifice a body part to regain my creativity?"

Two of those at the table, Tommi and Lyle, knew that Tiki Shark was harmless and of good nature, the other, Hunter Hopewell, was a naval commander recently discharged from the service, a good paying Red Tiki customer. He thought he knew a secret about Tiki Shark. It usually took several drinks under Hunter's belt, but whether true or not, when snockered, Hopewell believed the boy when high as a kite, unknown to himself, was some kind of artistic fortune teller — a seer, a prophet, that what his paint brush dabbed and stroked on canvas must be guided by the spirit world. For, to Hunter, it seemed that after Tiki Shark's completed a new artwork, not all the time but often, it followed that something coincidental happened. That his art suggested future acts; and when interpreted and reviewed by said officer through the lens of his cocktail glass, such incidents did not necessarily bode well. Former Naval Commander Hunter Hopewell, a man troubled, facing his own personal internal demons stared at Tiki Shark's drawing and wondered at the meaning. *What prophecy is this to unfold?*

Next to Hopewell, a delicate hand picked up the artwork and Tommi Chen asked, "What are these? I can tell one creature is a ten-story tiki god fighting this other creature which seems to be a giant lizard spouting fire, or is that a dragon?"

"I don't even remember painting this — must have been in the middle of the night last night, like I was sleep walking, but at my easel. Wasn't it a dark and stormy night? I thought I heard thunder but didn't smell any rain."

"No bad weather last night; it was starry, a very starry night," said the woman. "And in the midst of this battle of monster giants, you have a woman casually sunbathing on a beach, playing a ukulele, oblivious to it all."

"Perhaps she signifies apathy of the coming disaster," mulled Hopewell, downing his liquor and motioning to the waitress for another round.

"Hell with your giant tiki fighting imaginary lizard monsters, I want my property back, and in one piece." Sheftel set imploring eyes on the woman. "You're good at this, Tommi, you know, the scrounging, the finding of needful things. No questions asked."

Judith 'Tommi' Chen actually did believe she might know who stole tiki god.

"Last night, you might remember, there was a work gang of sailors in here, drinking near the dance floor ogling the talent. Heavy drinkers, boasting they were going to tow off some ship and let it be blown up. Their last cruise. Muscled up Navy, just the type to know where to find a crane truck and a flatbed for heavy lifting."

"I think I remember them. Didn't they get kicked out?"

"Miss Chen, with her usual finesse, had them deep-sixed."

Hunter displayed a slight sarcastic smile.

"They were making asses of themselves." Tommi did not let on to Lyle that she had set them up after they tried to force her to join them for a 'private' party, and when she declined, they resorted to racist swearing. So, she baited them, got them riled up, and Bouncer Manaa assisted in their departure. If that were the cause and effect, she smiled that she might have just created a business opportunity for some quick cash.

"By God, that's great news," beamed Sheftel. "Think you can track it down?"

"Well…" Her trademark response was crafted to leave the unsaid hanging. She would wait out the bar owner's deliberation and mental math calculations. How much was that hunk of stone really worth to him?

Last night, she did remember the incident well. She could not help going on the verbal offensive when those plastered lunkheads came up empty-handed in their bid for her affections and called her 'a loser piece of ass like her yellow slant eye brothers'. This sloppy harangue had happened occasionally over the last four years, depending on the social environment in which she placed herself. Most times she avoided confrontation she with a well-rehearsed response, beginning with a fake, singsong Asian dialect.

'I'm Judy Chen, I'm Chinese. I am citizen of one of America's allied partners. God Bless President Harry S. Truman and Generalissimo Chiang Kai-shek. I lost my parents when the Japs bombed Shanghai. Please have some respect.' Even the blind drunks usually slunk away ashamed and, yes, stupid. They knew she was Asian but could never figure out the 'oriental' eyes angle, even after there was a full spread in *Life Magazine*, early in the war, on how to identify the enemy: the ability to define Korean, Chinese, and those 'slant-eyes' in her own home country, Japan.

She had begun daydreaming about the past when Hopewell nudged her back to reality. He knew many of her tradecraft secrets and, when alone together, called her 'Tommi', not with affection but, from her viewpoint, a taunting disgust, perhaps still racially motivated from those days of Japs vs. Yankees. She could accept his smoldering; she held her own resentments and inward anger, not so much against people in general but definitely hatred against American foreign policy. Her parents had been killed at Nagasaki by one single American bomb, an atomic bomb.

"Did you hear what Lyle was offering?"

"What?" Her dreams of the embittered past fled, and the noise of the Red Tiki Lounge returned.

"I am willing to give you," said Sheftel, still dickering in his cash-register brain, "$300 for the location of the statue, and $400 for its safe return."

Without hesitation, one of her quirks, she countered.

"$500. I point you in the right direction. Another $500 when it's back in front of your door."

The bar owner mulled it over. $1,000 out of his pocket equaled two hours of good bar business on a Friday or Saturday night, and for what, the purported mystical totem of good fortune? Yes. Having good luck was worth a thousand bucks.

"Okay, deal. I presume it goes into your accounting book?"

"Always." Tommi pulled a small black book from her inside jacket pocket and made a notation.

Just then, a naval officer, the uniform baggy on his thin frame, approached them, his wire rim glasses, his central facial feature, peering out from under his military cap, with his head balanced by ears sticking straight out. To those at the table, he came across more like a timid office bookkeeper than a Navy man with a combat ribbon. But then, the war made unsure boys into callous men. He saluted.

"Commander Hopewell?"

"At ease," responded Hunter, slightly buzzed. "I've been out of the service since the first of the year. Just a civvie looking for a way home." Not true. In his fragmented mind, Hopewell had no sudden urge to re-enter the unknown world back wherever, back in what would be the new American normalcy. To himself he thought, *Thank you, but no, the Red Tiki, and its ingredients provide a better comfort zone.*

"Admiral Nimitz personally said I was to contact you. I'm doing some research on the war, mostly collecting personal experiences. I was assigned as a Navy Historian in the Solomon Islands campaign. I wish I had run into you then."

"Can we skip to what you want before I say 'no'?" responded Hopewell, brusque, disillusioned with the past, loath towards tomorrows.

"The Admiral heard some stories especially about the Australian coast watchers you were involved with and said you might find the time to tell me."

"No, I'm all out of stories. The war does that to us — the need to forget."

"I understand but the Admiral said if you didn't have time, there was a doctor over at the Aiea Hospital, Dr. Lundell, who could be ordered to open his files to me." The current naval officer smiled. Hunter Hopewell, ex-naval officer and former patient of that hospital, did not smile.

"Okay, okay. I'll answer one or two questions. That's all."

The officer historian pulled out a small dictation notepad.

"No, let's go over to the bar where only you and I can hear."

"Hey, I'd like to hear," laughed Tiki Shark. "I never got close to the war zone. Wouldn't want to, too dangerous, I heard."

"So, would I," acknowledged Sheftel. "Hopewell is one of these big, strong, silent drinkers, looks in the glass with those far-away eyes. He says nothing when you know there is a world of shit inside."

Tommi's interest was piqued as well. She knew Hopewell as an occasional business associate (not by her wish), but she really didn't know the man himself. Any insight might give her an advantage.

"Yes, let's hear a few yarns," she grabbed on Hunter's arm as if restraining him from any thought of escape. His left forearm, the useless one that now moved slightly, felt like rock. That surprised her. A withered limb should be frail and degenerative.

She recovered quickly, "We got time before we go off hunting a wandering tiki. Pull up a chair, sailor. What did you say your name was? Let's all be good and friendly tonight."

He did pull up a chair and sat down, with a genuine grin as he poised his pencil over his writing pad, looking at them all, anticipating. His gaze fell on Hunter Hopewell.

"I'm Lieutenant Commander Michener. But since I'm also getting out of the service, the name's James Michener. Jim works."

"Welcome, Jim, to the Red Tiki Lounge and Confessional. Okay, Hunter," said Tommi, the devil in her charm, "the stage is yours. Better make this good, I bet Jim here is a good critic of whoppers."

Once more experimenting on fruity rum drinks and using Hunter as the most accessible taster of choice; soused Hunter confirmed to himself; yes, Lyle, the Red Tiki bar owner, did indeed look like Dracula.

9

L ater that evening, Hunter was sitting at the end of the bar, working on his descent into inebriation served with a dash of oblivion. One of those brief rain cells passing through the neighborhood rattled the corrugated tin overhang attached to the Lounge where customers could sit outside if they so wished. Hunter tried to recall if he had put out the buckets to catch the two identified leaks in his small apartment-office located above his head on the second floor, a convenient living accommodation for the perpetually thirsty. Of recent, his business, unlike the pummeling rain outside, was less than slow, more like a dripping faucet of commerce.

His present drinking, as if he needed a reason, had much to do with the rambling mutterings he had unloaded earlier in the evening on the surprised then disconcerted audience while the Navy historian Michener scribbled away. The alcohol haze, a common escape of these last several months, had too easily loosened his tongue and he was angry with himself for allowing his true emotions to surface around new acquaintances.

12-year-old Scotch was usually Ex-Commander Hunter Hopewell's preferred shot of numbness, but tonight Lyle had been once more experimenting on fruity rum drinks and using Hunter as the most accessible taster of choice; since these test drinks were gratis for being the guinea pig, how could one say no to the advancement of social sciences? And most startling as the drinks were poured and judgment rendered, to Hopewell's strange and glazed look, the pourer began to resemble that film actor, what's his name, Bela Lugosi, who plays Count Dracula in the movies. Yes, Hopewell mumbled confirmation to himself, *Sheftel did indeed look like Dracula wearing a Hawaiian shirt and mixing cocktails.*

"Doesn't he look like Count Dracula?" Hopewell threw the question at Tiki Shark, who sat next to him drinking a ginger ale, likewise on the house, while sketching with pen and ink, one of the waitresses he had goo-goo eyes for and who, to his pain, ignored his existence. He openly daydreamed of the bar girl, imaging her as the Island Mona Lisa, to convince her of his sincere ardor. Being young as he was and with little tread wear on his heart his forlorn romances came and went like the endless tide. Last week, he was in love with the lei maker who cruised through the bar selling her orchids to the guys trying to impress the tight bloused girls looking for a swing partner. Tiki Shark was a doomed romantic.

"Something new tonight?" Tiki Shark looked first to Hunter then asked Sheftel as to the concoction being stirred, shaken, and poured.

"It's something I've been working on. I call it an *Atomic Zombie*. One drink will blow your world apart."

"What's in it?" Tiki Shark, under age, asked with childlike curiosity.

The bartender shoved over a Red Tiki napkin with scribbled ingredients.

1 oz pineapple juice

1 tsp sugar

1 oz orange juice

1 oz lime juice

½ oz apricot brandy

2 oz light rum

1 oz dark rum

Mix in Collins glass with ice

½ oz the highest octane rum drizzled on top

Pineapple slice, sprig of mint, cherry

For the bold crazies, pour two Atomic Zombies into a Tiki drinking bowl and add dry ice

"He's going to patent this drink like that one he did a couple a years ago," snickered Hunter, knowing that would set Sheftel off, who never in his life tried to copyright or otherwise protect his drink inventions for marketing purposes. Now, the scuttlebutt from transient sailors said there were two bar owners on the West Coast claiming to be the cocktail's inventors.

"What was that drink you invented way back when, sometime in the late '30's?" Hopewell and everyone knew it was one of the bar's bestselling fru-fru sips.

"Maitai," grumped Sheftel, grouchy as anticipated. "The bastard, heard about me when I was tending bar at the Saint Francis Hotel in San Francisco. He came in and asked me the mixes, and he watched me make a dozen. And damn if they're not on his drink menu six months later. And damn it, I hear he's now planning on opening a second bar and restaurant over here this fall. Damn the bastard." Sheftel put another drink in front of Hopewell and watched the ex-Navy man take a swallow, but not before, as the art required, gargle swilling the liquid around in his mouth, puckering his face with his verdict. "Ah." And a loopy smile gave approval.

"What bastard?" asked Tiki Shark.

"Rob Roy?" Hopewell ventured a guess.

"No, dammit, it's still an Atomic Zombie."

"Oh. Isn't Bela Lugosi a zombie?" Hunter nibbled at his drink's pineapple slice.

Tiki Shark, looking up from his drawing: "The bastard is a zombie?"

"No, the bar guy's name is Gannt. Calls himself Donn Beach and his place Don the Beachcomber. He and another guy, Victorwhatshisname, and his restaurant is Trader Victor's, something like that. Both have California places that look like palm thatch lean-to's… want customers to think they're on the beach in Tahiti. But they're actually a knock-off of my place. Yeah, maybe a little bit better constructed, you know, because of the mainland building codes. But no live-life-hard personality like I went through, like the Red Tiki shows off, no hurricane raw. Now that the war's over, Donn Beach wants to open a joint in Honolulu and push me out."

A 'who's on first' three-way exchange began:

"Don the Zombie?"

"Don the Beachcomber."

"You look like Count Dracula the zombie."

"Dracula is a vampire. Zombies are dead people walking around."

"Walking around dead?"

"And they eat people and turn them into the living dead like them."

"Walking around dead? That's the most stupid thing I heard. Who'd believe that?"

"Hollywood for one. Abbot and Costello were chased by zombies. Come to think about it, they were chased by the Mummy, the Werewolf and your Count Dracula."

"Our man Sheftel looks like Count Dracula and he's mixing a Zombie. Is drinking a Zombie like eating a zombie? Will I become a zombie?"

Dumb bar silence, the low limit of this wandering dialogue having been reached.

"Are you going to tell us another war story tonight?" Tiki Shark finally queried, and Sheftel looked up, both willing to hear a reprise of combat blood and gore, since there were no more stories in the daily papers. Hopewell's recounting earlier this evening had indeed risen to worthy adventures, and scribe Michener seemed to like them.

"No," said Hopewell looking deep into the drink before him and returning into his wet melancholia. "No. No more stories."

He thought back, not happy with either his stories, or his life.

10

To this scribe Michener, and to his listening audience, Hunter only told bits and pieces, and when it came to his being wounded in the pagan cemetery, he glossed that over, fooling no one, he knew, for all at the table were aware that he had been horribly damaged, the mental scars still apparent the more he drank.

Certain parts of Hunter's storytelling he mentally redacted from his verbal recollections for personal and security reasons mainly related to his clandestine job. Let them make Hunter Hopewell a man of mystery, but there is nothing much to it. The Office of Strategic Services — O.S.S. — put together by 'Wild Bill' Donovan had recruited him out of Yale in his first year of law school. He had joined the Navy R.O.T.C and they pushed up his commission to active duty. He was hoping to go into the elite club that could be found in the European war theatre, but that didn't work out because, being from Colorado on a baseball scholarship, he lacked private school spit and polish and looked too third generation WASPish. Another demerit: he spoke no foreign languages, so by 1943 he was posted first to English-speaking India and then directed by the O.S.S. station chief to Australia. Here his assignment, somewhat covert but essentially bureaucratic field auditing, was to help coordinate the Allied-Navy intra-agency communication with the volunteer coast watchers scattered in the enemy-controlled islands, risking their lives to gather intel on Jap movements [never 'Japanese', they were all 'Japs', spoken always with bitter damning descriptive racial epithets against the 'Yellow Peril'].

One story he would not tell, not out of embarrassment but because of the truth that it caused him to start drinking, took place in January of 1943. Hunter found himself in the Guadalcanal war zone hanging around the headquarters of the 25th Infantry Division. His coast watcher contact was trying to locate him, travelling beachside in a native canoe, paddling through enemy lines with information on where enemy barges were landing with reinforcement troops, the Jap goal being to recapture the airfield the American troops had held tenuously since their island invasion.

One afternoon of jungle swelter, Commander Hopewell stumbled back into field headquarters, his clothes disheveled, breathing heavily, his forehead bleeding. Only two staff clerks were present, and one ran for a medic. The other clerk, a private with the stitched name on his uniform, *J. Jones*, asked what happened. Hunter didn't think he would blurt it out but his adrenalin was over-charged and the words spilled from his mouth.

"I went out to take a shit in the slit trench latrine and was squatting there and, by God, all of sudden, a Jap soldier with a bayonet rifle comes running into the clearing right at me, trying to stick me, and I'm in this duck waddle, dodging and weaving, bare-assed, pants and underwear down at my ankles. The Jap is weak, a starved skeleton, and we go tussling with the rifle. Finally, I got around behind him, and used his own rifle across his chest, squeezing, puffing the air out of him; he starts making these gagging coughs, and then I bring the rifle up to his neck and strangle him. For good measure I bayonet him, four or five times, maybe. [*Goddam*, he swore to himself, *and wouldn't you be crying at the same time?*]. I'm looking down at the corpse and there in his pocket are photos of a woman and child, his family. I'm alone in the world. No family. But he has a family and like me they are going to find themselves alone. I caused their sorrow. I have killed, not at great distance but in a death hug against another human. This war is a big fuck-up! I will not pick up a gun even if ordered. I can't take another life."

Private Jones stuck a glass of hooch in his face and he chugged down the heat. The Captain's personal stash, purloined for good cause, said the private, accepting that they would bond over his secret and Hunter's. The latter took the proffered refilled glass. The bite, it was Scotch, never felt so sweet. He swore he needed that strength to temper his shock at a man's death caused by his own hand.

Moments later the headquarters tent filled with a medic and curious soldiers. They asked for the story. By that time the drink had warmed him away from what had happened and the images were secreted into the deep recesses of forgetfulness. Sniper shot at me was his story, and to those who had been under extreme battlefield conditions for the last several months, such a tale was inconsequential. Snipers were the mosquitoes of the day.

The next day, the coast watcher showed up and Hunter condensed his reconnaissance information into one of his concise, mimeograph forms, and then boarded a destroyer to report that more amphibious Jap landings were expected. After that, he never went back to Guadalcanal. *I hope*, Hunter thought sadly, *that Private Jones never turns my confession into some dirty joke to be told at future bridge parties. That sort of reality is no joke for me.*

That story Hunter would take to his grave, later rather than sooner he prayed, and so now, under the influence, he gave a rambling interview (the same given to the doctors at Aiea Naval Hospital prior to his skull surgery), to his private audience, for the benefit of this wannabe Navy historian, one Jim Michener, with an attentive mixed audience of Tommi, cute but too serious, Sheftel the grouchy bar owner and Tiki Shark, an innocent kid in a sick world. Not bosom buddies, but the only people that could so far tolerate Hunter Hopewell in their lives.

11

Hunter gave his small audience a smattering of war vignettes, telling stories of the related patrols and campaigns he personally knew about, never casting himself the hero, just a stand-off observer.

Michener asked where the others at the table always skirted the subject. "And how you were wounded?"

He tried to take the injury and shambles of his life and make light.

"We were caught in an ambush, mortar rounds coming right down on top of us; the Japs had triangulated the range. They blew me up. And a large stone tiki fell on me. What they told me later was that this torpedo boat, PT-59, evacuated us and I, as the most grievously wounded, was airlifted back to Honolulu. In that rescue I lived and a young Marine died." *I do not tell my listeners about my dreams nor that I saw this black shark cloud circling above the PT boat's commander; for I know now, much later, from Tiki Shark's prophesied drawings, that anytime I see a ghost shark image encircling a person's head it means a violent death will someday follow.*

Another secret of my craziness to be left untold.

"Glad you survived," said Michener.

"So am I, I think."

"I like that coast watcher story you told, different from other war stories." Michener added a note on his writing pad.

"Hey, they were the true heroes, out there by themselves with only a few native guides against battalions of enemy," agreed Hopewell, sipping on a fresh cocktail, this one with a small umbrella sticking out. "They saved a lot of downed allied pilots. When they came in from the jungle and you cleaned them up, they had this animalistic swagger. Most female army nurses who'd grown tired of all the cocky soldier boys trying to hit on them, they'd see one of these coast watchers, them all having accents, Australian or one of these French or Dutch rubber plantation owners, and go all gaga, knights in shining armor sort of romance for a nurse."

Michener made another scribbled note.

"What are you going to do with all these stories you're writing down," asked Tiki Shark, feeling camaraderie towards a fellow creative type.

"Not sure. Just writing down stories, maybe compile them later."

"Well," offered Judy Chen aka Tommi, "if you hang around the Red Tiki long enough you will get all the wild tales of the South Pacific for sure."

"Yeah, hell, stick around, Michener." Sheftel saw a potential long term customer. "You should take notes on Hawaii. I've got a few stories to tell. Like the time..."

Interrupting the owner, a wave of laughter rolled loudly from the bar and was rippling towards them when in a rushed blur, a large pig charged out of the rain into the restaurant, oinking loudly. Dashing into the restaurant area, surprising to all, the pig trotted up to Hunter and in a quick darting action, pressed his slobbering snout on Hopewell's pant leg with glances exchanged between man and beast. Then, turning away with much scrambling fanfare of avoiding several bar staffers making feeble, lunging grabs, the pig made a squealing exit.

Someone from the bar shouted out, "Well, Sheftel, we know your Kailua pork tonight will be fresh!" And the patrons of the Red Tiki dissolved into hysterical guffaws, not understanding that Kama Pua'a, the pig, tracking the heavy scent borne of otherworld mysticism, had finally rooted out the man it had been tasked to discover: *Pele's champion.*

12

I'm surprised to see you here, Commander," said Dr. Lundell, looking up from his work of packing assorted medical files into boxes.

"Not as much as I am," suggested Hunter, seeing no place that he could sit, if an invitation had been offered. Boxes were piled everywhere, most taped shut. "And it's ex-Commander, now alive and retired with full medical discharge and benefits, thanks to you on both counts, though the monthly stipend barely covers my bar bill."

"And how is your pain management going?"

"Not bad. Took me six months to heal from your surgery, surviving with a liberal dose of pain killers, then another six months after I went cold turkey to kick the morphine addiction. Today, it's alcohol, preferably 12 years old and bonded, that helps me to forget the war and assorted nightmares. Besides those complications, I'm floating free from gainful responsibilities."

Dr. Lundell continued his packing while carrying on a conversation with an old patient he considered a friend.

"I thought the Navy gave you a cushy job while waiting for your discharge papers? Are you still doing that?"

"No, but it did start me on a new career: investigations, finding missing persons. The Navy JAG [Office of Judge Advocate General] assigned me a small squad to ferret out AWOLers who wanted to hide in the islands with their mama-sans. I did the tracking, my guys beat in the doors. Then the war ended and my job, so I thought, until I had a roadmap to a new life for the mentally erratic, I would try the gumshoe route, you know, a regular Phillip Marlowe type shamus."

"You're a private detective?"

"Rarely, but I'm new in the game. My talent seems to be writing the best of flowery reports for a client, if and when I have any. But my deductive reasoning is short of brilliant; for example, it looks to me like you're shutting up the hospital."

"All the wounded are being sent stateside. Patients want to be treated in hometown facilities. I hear this is going to be some sort of military office building. No more patients."

"I assume this means no more Dr. 'Heinrich Himmler' Heimlich.

Good riddance. He treated me like a guinea pig, a pin cushion repository for hypo needles."

"Oh, my young associate left quite a while ago. And, I believe the feeling was mutual. He did not consider you one of his favorite patients, especially for that awkward incident in the ward the day when the patient in the bed next to you started choking on his lunch, started convulsing, and you started screaming at the sailor, grabbed him from behind in a bear hug, and popped a partially eaten prune right into Dr. Heimlich's face. He's going to remember that the rest of his life."

"I learned that technique from killing Japs." Hunter's voice was distant and bitter.

Doctor Lundell allowed the man's anger to fade by giving a wistful look to his boxed-up life. "I will be the last to leave by the end of the week."

Hunter regained the momentum to his visit. "Well, I'm lucky I caught you then. Consider me your final victim. You know my medical files: hell, you wrote and made medical history with my body. I need a physical, but I don't want to go and see or hand over my records to any of these local sawbones who might find an excuse to re-open my brain for their own demented pleasure."

"I'm honored. You were indeed a remarkable case. Did your headaches come back? Those bad dreams?"

"Alcohol only dulls the headaches. Passing out brings on the nightmares. No escape, it seems. But something new has come up. You know about the hardness in my arm?"

"Yes, still a mystery to us. We thought calcification, but no, it's not that. The hardened muscles seemed impervious to any medication; your left arm was like concrete. Is that still the case?"

"Yes, about the same. I have a little more movement, can move my fingers, but the arm muscles remain stiff. And now this — it's odd, if not downright scary — but my upper thigh is tight as a brick, like my left arm."

Doctor Lundell stopped what he was doing, the inquisitiveness of his profession heightened. He walked over and tapped on Hunter's leg.

"Good grief. Whatever is happening, whatever it is, it's travelling, progressing."

"Is it paralysis?"

"I don't think so, but perhaps we need to get you into a V.A. hospital and run tests."

"No more hospitals, no more doctors. They'll stick me under a microscope." He took a deep breath. "There's one more thing happening to me that I can't explain."

"What's that?"

Hunter prolonged the silence for dramatic effect. He glanced around, his eyes on the closed door. They were alone.

"My"... and he pointed to his crotch, slightly embarrassed, "well, *it* is like my hip and my arm: hard, but with the joystick it's longer and bigger than I thought it was when, you know, I was naturally excited. I still have piss flow that works. Started happening, showing this week and I feel somehow embarrassed to have a torpedo instead of a popgun. I've had to get some bandage tape and cotton gauze; wrap the gauze first to avoid rubbing abrasion and then the tape around me, like to make sure it is pressed against my body; if not, you would see a horizontal flagpole, more like a factory chimney. As it is, the damn thing wants to peek out above my belt line and take no prisoners!"

The doctor's jaw dropped opened. He thought he had heard about all the strangest ills of the world. This was a new one.

"Easiest explanation: do you have the clap?"

"No, of course not, and from the training films I know the symptoms. No, my body is failing at the same time I am going mentally bonkers. Three nights ago this tourist tiki we have out in front of the bar, I mean, where my office is located upstairs from the bar, someone stole it. Before that, every time I passed by that statue, I could have sworn it gave me a wicked smile that no one else could see. Now, it's gone, and last night my nightmares suddenly went vividly as big as a drive-in movie screen — and this tiki statue was the main star. And there's an attractive girl in the story. But when I wake up in cold sweat, for the life of me, I can't remember any of the dream's plot, like it happened but didn't happen. But then the hard-on started."

"Drop your trousers," commanded the doctor. After a quick examination, with many 'hmmf's' and 'aah's', the diagnosis was troubling to both. "You seem to have a condition of priapism, constant erection. Is it painful?"

"No. How can I get it to go away?"

"I have heard that a person might develop this condition from a spinal cord injury; here it might go back to your head damage. Not sexual, more neurological. I can't readily explain it without a full workup."

"Like I said, no more tests. Any pills you can give me?"

"Not that I'm aware of… Have you tried to see if an ejaculation might provide relief?"

"Hey, doc, call me old fashioned but I'm not a one man, one hand show; I need a little womanly passion."

"Ok, not the remedy I would write out as a prescription, but yes, sexual intercourse might be the best experiment I can suggest. It would take pressure off the blood concentration. But with all these other events, your arm, your upper leg, all taken together, I have concern. It's like you're suddenly turning into a rock, becoming a living statue." He laughed, but his patient found no mirth in the diagnosis.

13

Was he just glad to see me, or real glad to see me?

Tommi did not know how to take Hunter's look. The guy walked towards her with this huge bulge in his pants. She could never recall this much excitement in him? And was she the cause of the obvious? Certainly Sheftel and Tiki Shark would not have the quirkiness to notice what a woman sometimes is drawn to see with satisfaction that her looks and tease might produce below-the-belt response, but she felt confused: she and Hopewell had never before connected in the romantic sense.

For nearly a year and a half now, they had each held their own in an abrasive business partnership based in part, she had to admit, on mutual dependency and blackmail. Skin color and ethnicity only deepened the mutual distrust between the former wartime enemies.

Since their first meeting they had hustled to find ways to use each other for their own agendas. Hunter, digging into her Japanese heritage, discovered she was not an American citizen and thus an alien, subject to deportation if he decided to blow the whistle. He held that over her head as he began to realize she did have a network of friends and associates who could assist in his investigative assignments. Under this cloud, the *White Chrysanthemum Marriage-Divorce Services* which she owned and was one of her business fronts for her own nefarious dealings, became compromised and Hunter pressured her to give up the names of servicemen who were hiding out. His stature among JAG colleagues rose as his apprehension rate skyrocketed to a point where the word got out that perhaps it was best for Navy men to turn themselves in, avoid dishonorable discharges, and just be shipped home leaving the girlfriend behind.

Tommi could not tolerate this economic handcuffing. It vexed her that first subtle, then blatant, attempts to bribe him did not work. It was oddly refreshing to realize that she may have actually found an honest man, yet she resented the fact this virtue could interfere with her various clandestine enterprises. Dogging him in a false effort to be a supportive friend, several weeks later she found the chink in his polished armor. So simple a solution. She sent to his BOQ residence a case of top shelf scotch. At that time he was not talkative about his war experience but she had heard through a hospital orderly, that he had been severely wounded and had these headaches where he saw visions. Delusions. 'Evil specter fish' sightings or 'death sharks', he had called them. She accepted such statements as post deliriums. Once, when walking together he had mentioned his shark fantasy while pointing out a man they saw on the street. A week later, she heard the fellow ended up shot to death in a bar fight. To her, only coincidence.

The answer was to pickle him into ineffectiveness, but it worked too well. Soon, his JAG superiors got fed up with his descending fog and the dark mood swings; consequently, his discharge papers were rushed through and he was let loose upon the streets of Honolulu… not good for her interests since, in his destitute financial circumstances, he decided to fall back on his key asset, Tommi aka Judith Chen, forcing her to set him up in a business where he might employ his very iffy skills at intelligence gathering. At this point Tommi needed to keep him close so she could watch over him, but give him misdirection; let him handle the cheap divorce cases she heard about, so he did not interfere with her more lucrative activities.

In March of 1946, she herself underwent a serious catharsis.

News of home traveled slow in these confused times and through her aunt and uncle, who were released from their Arizona detention camp, she learned that her parents were dead, had been killed by Americans. Events of the closing days of the war were murky at best. On August 9th, 1945, her parents left their home and journeyed by train into the Urakami Valley to the city of Nagasaki to lodge a protest with the military authorities who demanded all professors at the university must begin to teach classes to the male students on how to use bamboo bayonets, and for the women, the best methods to kill themselves before the invading Americans would rape them. The invasion of the Japanese homeland expected in the Spring of 1946 never happened; instead a bitter peace slammed Japan like a tsunami when the airplane Superfortress known as *Bockscar* dropped the second atomic bomb cored with plutonium on Nagasaki, incinerating, searing and radiating to death 70,000 people, Tomoe 'Tommi' Jingu's parents among them. Their home in the nearby mountains was left unscathed.

Tommi's heart went cold at the news. She swore revenge but lacked for follow through… Whom could she fasten her anger upon? She could not hate the civilians of Hawai'i, mostly Asian like herself, and could not despise all the haoles (white people) because in her dealings with them she found that most were decent. So she came to hate the policies of the United States government, and anything she could do to take advantage of and to damage that target was fair game.

That left her with the strange irony of her relationship with Hunter Hopewell, ex-government military person. Once when he was deep in the cups, she heard him rant against the killing horrors of war, yet just before she decided she had found a person of like minds, he babbled about the dirty Japs starting it all, trying to kill him, and the chasm between them widened.

Now he stood before her with one giant hard-on, and with the opposite of a leering expression, he said almost painfully,

"You called this meeting?"

So much for the urges she mistakenly thought emanated from a sexually needy male. Was this the disappointment of a vague *what if...*? She gave a deadpan response as if nothing could toy with her emotions.

"I found the Red Tiki's tiki."

"I knew you could," yelped lounge owner Sheftel, "Never had a doubt. Okay, where do we go pick it up? Did they arrest the scum?"

"Do you have a tugboat?" Tommi would enjoy this conversation, realizing she'd never get the bartender to cough up their negotiated fee, even with half of the job solved.

"What?"

"It's at sea. Like in sailing away. Bon Voyage to your tiki."

Hopewell saw that Sheftel might have a coronary.

"Okay, Miss Chen, the whole story?" Hopewell grumbled, uncomfortable, adjusting his trousers under the table. Tommi looked at him from a new perspective. *I never considered that he might be abnormally well-endowed.* For a moment she tried to visualize but, given her audience, realized it would be best to focus on what she did know for certain.

"What my people found is that a group of boozed-up sailors, as I suspected from this bar, stole your overweight good-luck tiki charm in retaliation for being kicked out of this fine establishment. They loaded it on the *USS Southard*, a rusty tub bucket destroyer-minesweeper, which set sail two days ago for a rendezvous in the South Pacific."

"Rendezvous?" Hopewell, sober so far for the day, shifted into his interrogator mode.

"The *Southard* has been decommissioned. It is being sailed or towed down to a place called Bikini Atoll where it will be a target ship."

Tiki Shark's eyes stretched. He was literate and could read headlines, though usually did so only on his way to the comics pages.

"That's where they just set off the atomic bomb; they're doing a whole bunch of testing."

Tommi concurred.

"Sometime near the end of July they plan to detonate an underwater atomic bomb. And from what I learned, your red tiki along with the *USS Southard* will be vaporized at the Bikini Atoll or sunk by an immense tidal wave."

14

Sheftel felt as if a close, wealthy relative had died without leaving him a dime.

"What am I gonna do? It brought me all the luck, making money at least, ever since I bought the place."

Something chewed into Hopewell's curiosity. You take things for granted then one day, a question pops up unexpected.

He had to ask, "Lyle, where in the first place did you get your red tiki doorman?"

"I've always had it. Came with the building… sort of."

"Sort of?" asked Tommi.

"Well, yeah, the red Tiki used to be in a church."

Tiki Shark coughed up his Coke. "A church? You desecrated a church?"

"Naw," said the bar owner, off ended that someone thought he had no scruples. "It's like this. There use to be an old church here on this spot. A small one, and it burned down a couple hundred years ago, and all that was left was this back wall made out of old coral rock. When I bought the lot and jerry-rigged together the bar and lounge out of surplus, bricks, shipping crates and lumber, I decided to tear down the wall, but that's what was both strange and really started my good luck. The outer wall was a false one and there was actually another wall behind that, sort of a chamber and sitting there on the ground was this huge black stone tiki idol — the same one you saw sitting out front. It was all covered with dirt, old vines and glass hair."

Hopewell braced himself straight.

"Glass hair? What do you mean?"

"You know, the stuff the volcano sometimes throws off. Our red tiki had it all over. I kept the back wall, you can see it in the kitchen, and had the work crew pull the statue out and cleaned up and stuck it out in front. Gave the place its name."

Hopewell did not know what to think. He never gave the entryway greeter much notice since he was usually in a hurry to reach a drink. Tommi saw only a marketing gimmick.

"You know it did look kinda old," said Tiki Shark. "I bet you had a real authentic tiki god figure, not just some native knock-off carving for turn-of-the century tourists. When the missionaries came to the islands preaching baby Jesus and the God Jehovah of damnation, some of the islanders didn't convert immediately. Some probably even clung to their gods longer than anyone ever thought, like hiding them from the parsons and priests, secretly still worshipping the old deities."

"You mean that thing might be worth a lot of money? Of course I wouldn't sell it, with the luck and all that." Sheftel's mercenary mind grinded away. "But I wonder how much I could get for it?"

Money had no relevance to Tiki Shark's way of life, basic sustenance worked fine for him, so he shouldn't have been so glib in his response.

"Oh, I'd think a museum or some big antique dealer might pay you like a hundred thousand dollars if it was pre-Cook Discovery, you know before 1798. Quite rare. One-of-a-kind stuff ." Tiki Shark did have the smarts on ancient Hawaiian art even though what dripped from his own paintbrush onto canvas tumbled out more as frenzied cartoons, island crazy art, like what might be expected from artist Paul Gauguin after smoking evil weed or Modigliani after downing a bottle of true wormwood absinthe.

The four of them, in silent thoughts, were sharing a new appreciation to the stolen tiki. Hunter waved over Mister Manaa, the Māori bouncer, who at this lax time of day was sitting with the newly hired piano player, a young guy named Martin Denny, joking, both of them making animal sounds as Denny hunched over the keyboard tickling out jazzy notes seeking a jungle theme to match the lounge decor. The approaching mid-week Happy Hour required more subdued background music, easy on the worn down, after work crowd.

"Manaa," questioned Hunter. "Do you know much about tikis?"

"You're talkin' about our tiki dast got ripped off ?"

"Yeah, that and in general. You know about what is a tiki?"

"Yeah, part of our Māori heritage. 'Tiki', our old people story, means 'First Man'. Not Hawaiian word. Here the word is 'ki'i'.

The story likewise held Tommi's interest. To Sheftel she asked, "Was your tiki always painted red?"

The bar owner looked sheepish and guilty.

"Well, when I did start cleaning it up, the base had all this dark rust color. And I guessed, hell, maybe they held sacrifices like with pigs and goats, and that was dried blood. So the idea struck me, it might be a better draw if it was painted blood red, you know, suggesting human sacrifices."

"Ancient Hawaiians didn't have goats," explained Tiki Shark, "until the white explorers showed up. Probably what you saw was dried up human sacrifice blood."

Manaa chimed in. "Strange taboos still alive. Once or twice a year believers throw blood on the damn thing. Burn incense. Have ta hose it off."

Hunter found himself a little more intrigued.

"You two know your tiki lore; okay, do you know what kind of ancient god our tiki is?"

"Not sure," said Manaa. "If Māori the face does resemble Tūmatauenga."

"Although I called it my muse," Tiki Shark's opinion, "I saw a drawing of this type of statue up in the Bishop Museum, and they have a feathered image of the same god: Kū-ka-ili-moku.

"And, both meaning?" pushed Hunter.

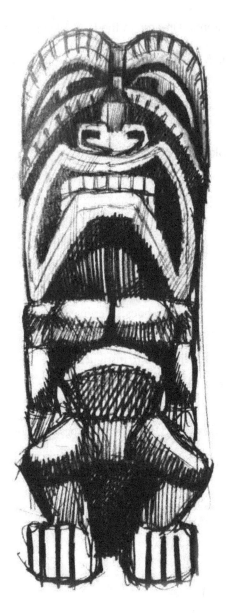

"Kū, the Hawaiian God of War" said Tiki Shark, and Manaa nodded confirmation to the Māori myth translation, adding, "It is only god of all the islands requiring human sacrifice."

15

Bar noise faded fast to sudden silence, replaced with lusty wolf whistles.

"Would you look at that?" There was only one object, other than loose cash on the bar that could pull the owner of the Red Tiki away from a discussion about a statue perhaps worth untold wealth. At the door of the Red Tiki stood an extremely ravishing young lady, and like in an aura she stood out, almost as if she glowed.

They all looked up to the entrance, each taken aback in gawking surprise. Tommi, less the business mogul, more the woman and snippy critic to her sex, said to those around her, "Lyle, finally looks like your place is becoming a class act." The bar owner was mentally salivating. Tiki Shark had instantly found a new muse, a new Mona Lisa, and quickly he went to his sketch pad, inspired, intoning reverence for the human form: "That is the most beautiful woman I have ever seen."

The bar went quiet; the new piano player, the kid named Denny, stopped making his jungle noise plinking, and switched to a low melodious Hawaiian love ballad, *'Kuu Ipo i ka Hee Pue One'; Here, please listen; Here, your lover is here; She came last night; We delighted in the forest.'*

Manaa saw something others did not see, that the very young woman wore a sarong of deep ocean blue, walking barefoot, her waist length black hair tied up in plumeria flowers; not only was she beauty unadorned, but she was pure Polynesian and not of blood mixed by sailors, whalers or missionaries — in her dark skin a pureness, truly rare in the Pacific. Unblemished Polynesian.

Hunter Hopewell saw the woman that he had seen before. In his dreams. In his nightmares.

He was stunned, and more so as the young girl walked right up to him, parting a sea of customers in the bar. She spoke to him softly in words he could not understand. In his dreams he did not understand either when she talked to him, though somehow he did comprehend. But that was a dream, and no doubt here, this woman was of flesh and blood, of heat, desire, mystery, with soft brown eyes looking into his own, moon-size in wonder.

"Not good on dialects," said Manaa, "she speaks kinda Tahitian, maybe Micronesian. Not pidgin speak. Not today's Hawaiian words."

The girl, who could be no more than eighteen, repeated her words her eyes riveted on Hunter, which annoyed and miffed Tommi.

"Well, anyone want to try for a translation? We at least know she's talking only to tall, dark and handsome here." Tommi spoke with sarcasm, tinged with, *what? Jealousy? Bull shit*, she dismissed such thoughts.

Manaa's guess: "I think she is saying to Mr. Hopewell, "Come with me, I need your help.""

Shaking his head from his rude staring, Sheftel agreed.

"If anything, her body language is saying that, especially her pointing at him, then at the door." That was so obvious. Couldn't she stay, hoped Sheftel? What a draw she could be. How do you say 'waitress' in Tahiti speak?

Hunter Hopewell looked to those around the table, gave a weak smile, shrugged and followed the young woman out the door. *What's a guy to do? After all I am a detective of sorts; I help people.*

The front door closed, and everyone woke from their startled awe of what had just occurred.

"She probably is from a Tonga lua'u troupe, a dancer," offered Manaa, not believing it for a second, "and she lost her friends in the big city?"

"'The Come Hither Look' gets you guys every time", snapped Tommi as she waved an empty glass at Sheftel. Maybe a double was in order.

"I want to paint her," moaned Tiki Shark, "She's the Madonna of the Islands, a goddess."

Youth had never spoken so true.

A blue glow painted the way for their slow steps into a clearing bathed in an orange-red, shimmering, and Hunter could see a rocky pool surrounded by flowery lushness. In this garden stood a giant stone tiki, and before it the girl sat, waiting for Hunter's unsure arrival.

16

After walking two blocks at her side, asking questions to which she answered little, and of that nothing he could understand, he felt like a child or a rat following the Pied Piper, clueless as to the purpose yet strangely, mysteriously conditioned to follow the girl. When she kept pointing beyond the city to the hills, he realized they needed transportation. She perhaps could handle trekking for miles barefoot, but his current pastime as bar jockey meant panting huff s of exertion.

The taxi he grabbed dropped them off at a gravel road in the foothills, the driver complaining that he could go no further. An uphill road with switchbacks looked uninviting as did the setting sun and lengthening shadows. Certainly, Hunter wondered with developing trepidation: they weren't going traipsing around in the dark, were they? Where was she taking him?

Two vehicles travelling uphill, one a small utility, passed them by, even as Hunter made exaggerated efforts to flag them down. How did an older haole with a young island girl look anyway but guilty of something lewd? While she watched his thumbing she continued to walk up the mountainous, rutted road, he following. Finally, at the sound of a car approaching, she walked into the road, stood in the glare of oncoming headlights, and pulled her sarong down to her waist.

The whipping cloud of dust signaled that the vehicle had been brake stomped; when it came to a halt, Hunter saw a beat-up and dented 1942 Packard Clipper. Slightly shocked, thinking he had seen somewhere before a version of this girl's effective traffic stopping ploy, Hunter moved quickly to help her into the back seat, while her breasts, small and firm, remained uncovered. For the sake of whatever decorum still existed, Hunter sat in the front seat, readjusted upward the driver's rear-view mirror, turned the man's head to the front view, clamped shut the man's open mouth, and told his ride, "Up the hill, please, and no peeking."

Thirty minutes of bumps and swerves later, the road took a sharp turn across a ridgeline, and the girl gave a shout.

Believing he understood, the driver stopped and, in looking back, was disappointed: The sarong had reclaimed its prizes, and the girl exited without saying a word. She quickly moved off, barely visible in the falling evening, onto a vine covered trail, Hunter hustling to follow.

He could not explain even to himself what happened after a few minutes of walking. Covering clouds met a rising ground fog, bringing coolness to the warm night, and yet, with no stars visible, a blue glow painted the way for their slow steps into a clearing bathed in an orange-red, shimmering, and Hunter could see a rocky pool surrounded by flowery lushness.

In this garden stood a giant stone tiki, and before it the girl sat, waiting for Hunter's unsure arrival.

The tiki was not the bar's stolen statue; this was something entirely different, the carved face almost — not smiling — more pleased? And it looked — what? — not at all weathered by time and then elements — as if newly created.

The girl motioned Hunter to her side and he complied.

Silence stretched between them as if their thoughts would be carried on the sounds of the night: bass-throated frogs, squawking parrots, the water in melodious tones tumbling over the moss and rocks… the language of Mother Earth.

She leaned over and kissed him, tender touching of her lips as a butterfly might caress, growing into more firm searching, moist wandering, tender probing of her tongue. He responded; how could he not? Their embrace became a slow fall against the soft green carpet both of them intensifying their hold on each other… and… Hunter Hopewell fell into a dream unlike any before.

17

Burning, his whole body ached with fire. The rolling and sweating coupling yielded pleasure and pain in equal measure. Ever since she had walked into the bar his self-consciousness about his rigid shaft, being a fossilized Priapus, seemed forgotten, but now her guttural scream caused him guilt. He was unable to stop as the mounting beast, though cursing himself for claiming… each jamming plunge, an untouched woman. How could that be? A pure body writhing with a travelled mind experienced in hungry demands, and between them both the sex peaked without heart-pledged commitment.

The entwined bodies slid away each carrying the other's cooling juices, panting sighs, frayed nerve endings and questions asked ever since the Garden of Eden.

— *Are you now complete?* — she asked, her own smile of inner satisfaction after so many eons deprived. He heard no voice aloud except as thought in his easing mind, and answered in the same silent conversation.

— *Yes* — his own comfort, a warm limp feeling.

— *Did I hurt you?* — her next question that should have been his.

— *That was to be my concern-*

— *The pain comes from the First Man. It is to be expected.* —

— *Yes, if you say so, I guess it seems I am the first.* —

— *And from a new god.* —

— *What?* - His sublime feeling plopped away.

— *Your body has been consecrated as a god and you have been called to help all gods.-*

— *What?* —

— *In the war of your people, one of our gods when destroyed joined with you and lives within you.* —

He sat up and removed his hand from her abdomen where his fingers had been playing in her wetness. Did she mean the ambush at Choisuel Island? That statue that fell on him was a god? He gave his memories a hard look: that tiki in the cemetery did have the same construction as the stolen red tiki — similar to the tiki that loomed above the couple in repose next to the pool in the too-good-to-be true garden. He realized the commonality: none had any scrapes and cuts from a sculptor's mallet and chisel.

— *What are you saying?* — He was not so much upset as lost in a bewilderment that she might have the explanation to all his nightmare pain.

— *Times have become troubled. Your people have created a devil wind that has torn sky boundaries between our world and yours. If the heavens are not repaired then those gods who do not like your kind are ready to enter and destroy.*

— *Help me here. What are you saying?* —

—*The god you call by many names. Ares, Kartikeya, Anhur, Tohil,*

'*Oro. Many names, but one spirit was captured to contain the destruction of all life. By the wish of my brother and sister gods I turned Kū to stone, with the power of earth that I command. I then bound him with my hair and hid him away from all eyes. Now this evil god has been taken from my power, and if it mates with your wind devil, the God of War and Death and Destruction shall become alive and unstoppable, and those who oppose him shall die horribly and the rest of mankind, your people, shall become slaves. And he shall have the power to defeat all gods who enter from our world wishing to do justice and right. And from his body he might create his own children and raise them to be as powerful as he.* —

Her words soaked in. He tried to disbelieve; this was a dream, was it not?

— *Are you saying our Red Tiki that was stolen, that was placed on a ship, going somewhere, that was a real god, captured in stone?* —

— *Yes, and if it comes alive, he will be the most powerful of gods, and dispense Death to all those who oppose him and your people will become enslaved, and he will have passage to our world and all gods will have to pay him homage or be destroyed. When the heavens wage war no one is safe* — She paused in a silence of sorrow. — *Any children born of man, of gods, and even between man and gods shall be especially cruelly treated. He will put upon them a curse that they shall never know their parents, never understand love or the quiet times of peace.* —

—*This coming alive, do you mean by the blasts of our atomic bombs? That will make this stone statue — Kū — come alive?*-

—The devil wind has torn into our world and if it were to burn over a stone god, such a god would have extraordinary strength. And all gods would come forward to begin to war against this god and many would die. It cannot happen. You have been chosen. You are the only god now walking the earth, the only one with a human heart that can hold goodness and love. —

— I am not a god. — To himself he thought: *If anything, I am a washed out... drunk.*

— By the time you fight Kū you will be an earth-created god. —

Now, in the mist of this dream, he was alert. The foreknowledge of danger had that effect.

— I am definitely sick. —

— I will make you well and you defeat Kū. —

— How can you heal me? —

— You have an empty heart, but Love and Fire will repair the damage. —

— And if it does not work? —

— You will take the place where Kū once stood, stone and silent until the world of your people ends, and then become dust. And I will go and seek another champion if it is not too late. —

Hunter Hopewell did not know what was real and what was not. All she had said seemed a pebble of possibility. Why not? The unknown might indeed offer alternative answers, a secondary world where all imagination might live, where all religious deities might be less created of superstition and exist in some form of truth.

— How can I be sure? I feel like I am in a dream. We do not speak the same language. I want to be healed, be a better man, but I am no Superman.

She pulled him against her, and again he felt his body temperature rising, saw flames within her eyes; her carbon-black hair between his fingers became glassy threads waving in a rising breeze. He could have sworn the tiki above them had changed its expression to a devilish grin, and from nowhere a large hog ambled into the glen, snorted, and plopped down to watch them.

She whispered in his ear.

— I shall help as I can but first I have needs that only you, my champion, a half-god, can satisfy. —

He was overwhelmed by a new wave of passion and entered her with all his strength, listening to her rising moans, and when a flaming explosion, like an ammunition dump blowing up, swept through him, his eyes opened within this reality: a dream which was not a dream. As they became one, his mind opened to feel her concern, to understand this threat to all living things, and as he felt the earth shake, he knew it did so troubled and turbulent.

In the morning when he awoke, alone, no Garden of Eden, but tilled sugar cane fields for his pillow, he discovered he could budge his left arm, rock hard still but with a better range of motion. And he discovered his once priapic engorged penis, with satisfied warmth lingering, had retreated to normalcy.

Soon, a genuine smile graced a calm face. For the first time in years, as he began his trek back to the city he realized his constant headache was gone.

18

Tommi, in a foul mood, nevertheless devoted this new day to community service, planning for her last stop to be the Red Tiki. Among the low-key good deeds that she accomplished for the Japanese-American community was her post-war contribution collection campaign. With the help of her employees, she smartly placed large mason jars with slits cut in the tin tops in major tourist restaurants and assorted stores to collect funds, the hand scrawled labels saying "Help Our Brave Wounded Soldiers, sponsored by: Hawai'i Hospital Benevolent Association," though this charitable fundraising organization did not exist. As expected, the generous and sympathetic public gave as they could not fully realizing that their dollar bills and loose change went towards carrying for Japanese wounded veterans. In fairness to both sides, funds were distributed through the soldiers' parents, the needy being either those returning in shame to their Japanese homeland or the Nisei, second generation Japanese-Americans who served bravely in Italy in the all-Nisei 442nd Regimental Combat Team of the U.S. Armed Forces.

For example, Tommi was helping the Inouye family, living in Honolulu, who were awaiting the return of their son Daniel who having lost an arm in the Italian war zone, was still hospitalized abroad. Funds were being set aside to help him return to the University, the goal to find a new vocation since the boy was no longer able to become a surgeon as he once dreamed of being.

In another instance, a few donor dollars mingling with her own went quietly to the Hiroshima and Nagasaki Relief Organizations, designated to be spent open-ended for new patients, who suddenly were appearing at hospitals with a strange medical diagnosis just now coming to the attention of the world: radiation sickness. She knew little of the affliction, but felt for the victims suffering from this horrible invisible malady.

In today's collection she counted $27.52 out of the glass jar at the Red Tiki, where she found that Sheftel's dark mood matched her own. "What's up?" She questioned, knowing she'd sooner than later hear the whole story.

"Received a letter. This restaurant owner Donn Beach is heading this way. Wants to visit with me. I know what he wants. Wants to buy me out and convert the Red Tiki to one of his stamped out *Don the Beachcomber* plastic tacky places. I'm not going to sell. But, if I don't, then he'll open up a copycat place and drive me out of business."

"It can't be as dismal as that?"

"I could fight him, but how? And with what? With my good luck totem sailing away to its doom, and like the statue I'm gonna be sunk."

Tommi couldn't give him comfort as the obvious seemed apparent, one large statue over the horizon gone for good.

"But business, by the on-sheet bookkeeping, looks great." Tommi knew Lyle skimmed a little from the till for his rainy day fund. She could make the books balance and he praised her accounting work. Besides, being part of the scene at the Red Tiki was like being center point at the largest switchboard in the Pacific, the perfect listening post to all types of intelligence that she would sift and separate and turn to her advantage — as long as she kept her nemesis, Hunter Hopewell, in liquid ineffectiveness.

"Hi, guys, beautiful day." Tiki Shark greeted them with a grin, his blue bird of happiness warbling.

"Who says so?" Sheftel barked.

"Sold my drawing, the one with the two giant monsters fighting. $10 bucks." Believing good fortune deserves feeding the mouth of the dragon, he dropped fifty cents into Tommi's wounded soldier gifting jar. She thanked him on behalf of all wounded soldiers.

Sheftel wasn't giving up trying to gather everyone nearby under his storm cloud.

"And who was crazy enough to buy it? You can't put that dragon scrawling up in your living room."

Tiki Shark could only see the world as his for the taking.

"Some soldier in the Signal Corps. Said he had a buddy in the Signal Corps who drew comic strips back in New York City. He's going to send it to him." Tiki Shark went rooting in his pants pocket for a torn piece of paper. 'The artist in New York -name is Stanley Lee.' The soldier who bought it told me I should send him some of my drawings, maybe the comic guy might buy more. Comics! Who would have thought?"

Sheftel's opinions today came narrow and closed minded to his black mood. "Comics? They're only good for a newspaper, and only on Sunday. No future in comics."

"Good for you, Tiki," said Tommi, who saw her bad karma fading. She could never stay mad; maybe to get even, but ingrained anger did not suit her temperament. "We all need something good to happen to us."

"Well, it looks like 'very good' happened to him," said the young artist, pointing at Hunter Hopewell, who was just then entering the bar.

Even Sheftel edged a smile to his face.

"Of all things I can spot, is a guy who got lucky."

Tommi's mood again went sour.

Hunter approached. Although there was no longer a bulge in his trousers, his gait was still strange and stiff . She tried to define his look of — what? *Satisfaction by exhaustion*, Tommi considered, *but no, not with his creased frown?*

To the three of them sitting there, Hunter Hopewell said without prologue, "I'm going after the Red Tiki." He spoke in a voice strange to them, rumbling deep with purpose. Fixing his eyes on Tommi, all serious in expression, his back straighter than usual, he added, "And I am going to need your help."

Part Two

Tommi Chen

19

L ike a disease she had, Tommi caught all of owner Sheftel's negative moodiness. Her cure: not hard liquor, but the cook's famed pineapple upside down cake. Well, yes she admitted, the dessert was heavily laced with rum.

Here in the restaurant she looked up to see before her the amateur naval historian Jimmy Michener. In his hand he held a well filled notepad with scrap paper insertions, folded tabs and pencil scratchings. Tommi, seeing a man who could not be blamed for anything, cut him slack and voiced civility as a guest might deserve.

"Seems like now you have the makings of several good stories." She usurped his opening line of inquiry, having watched him work the Red Tiki, squeezing out morsels of war stories. She actually admired talent. He was good at his work like an inquisitive Westbrook Pegler, the columnist, or a fact-digging Walter Winchell. Tommi nevertheless had been keeping her distance. Let the man write his war stories, just keep her out of them.

"I did not realize," said Michener, casting his eyes to take in his surroundings, "that the Red Tiki Lounge was the fount of human experiences. I'm on my second notepad."

Tommi agreed with her own insight. "What the Red Tiki is, after one absorbs a few drinks, is a confessional." She swung her arm around the room, taking in the early evening's patrons: the boisterous and the serious, the morose slobbery and the off -key vocalists, peanut shell shuckers, and even a few men receiving silent pats on backs, acknowledged the smiles of their new made friends, for they sat coping with new realities, using crutches in place of a missing leg, or with their only arm hoisting their always filled glass.

"This place, a confessional," Michener mused. "Yes, I see that."

She could see that as the recording observer, Michener allowed the hazy and raucous bar scene to burn into his mind, filing it away for future use.

Tommi enlarged on her own interpretation of what she saw.

"All these soldier and navy boys are heading home, to a world that has changed. They want to unload their worst memories, the bloody battles they survived, or embellish their service record if their tour of duty was boring. They don't want to take back their horror, or their mortal insignificance to their loved ones. They want to find the courage or the lie to face a home front that might not fully appreciate them. From their perspective, they saved the world… what do they say, 'Saved the World for Democracy'. The Red Tiki here is a temple for absolving sins, cleansing and uplifting spirits."

"Very profound, Miss Chen. In talking to your Commander Hopewell, it seems like he came out of his foxhole still an agnostic, still dealing with his demons." He gave her a gentle look.

She recalled the source of her muted anger. "He is not my Commander, but yes, there are some here who have not yet found salvation. Some who might never recover from their own personal hell." Tommi began to think of Hunter Hopewell and his demons, even those she had helped to create.

Michener saw her contemplation, serious introspection caught unaware. He pounced.

"And how do you, Miss Chen, fit into this irreligious tabernacle? What is your war story? What circumstances of fate brought you to the Red Tiki that I might jot down? Even a sanitized version, or a lie that from your lips I am certain would be entertaining."

Her guard went up instantly, behind a forced demure glance.

If only I did enter the confessional, she wondered, would it absolve my desire for revenge? No, I am not ready to dole out sacramental forgiveness.

Still, she laughed.

"Officer Jim, I am but a simple bookkeeper. My company does the books for the Red Tiki Lounge. Mr. Sheftel is grateful that I can balance his books and he most often listens to my business suggestions, and, to my benefit, occasionally the Lounge comps me a drink or as you see, dinner on the house. I am here to help, and yes, sometimes, if it suits me to smile and accept a drink from a lonely serviceman. But that's seldom. Business is my focus, it's my survival."

"That could be a human-interest story. Local makes good."

"You should stay here longer and meet more of the Hawaiian people. Listen to the tales of their proud history. They deserve someone to tell their story. This war caused many Hawaiians to suffer as much as on your battlefields. I am unimportant."

"Why do I get the feeling the high priestess of the Red Tiki is sitting next to me, very attractive I might add, but nevertheless the true proselytizer for this congregation."

This time she gave no response to his comment but eased him on to talk about himself, his future plans, his dreams. He began an enthusiastic monologue. She was an adept listener. For the last five years of a World War in the Pacific, playing the quiet, barely noticed and seemingly helpless young woman gave her many opportunities, most taken advantage of, to the benefit of her pocket book, or better said, to her many bank accounts.

If only this Navy person, Jimmy Michener, heading stateside for processing out of the service, his head stuffed with war stories, if he only knew the truth behind this seemingly diminutive owner of J. Chen Bookkeeping Services, he could have written a best-seller.

20

Her birth name was Tomoe Jingu and she was born in a three room house in the foothills, near the base of Mt. Kompira on the Japanese island of Kyushu. Her parents were college professors who believed in free-thinking and women's right to vote, and were staunchly opposed to the country's increasingly militaristic and nationalistic jingoism. In 1939, on a Christian missionary scholarship, she found herself at the University of California, Berkeley, studying at their College of Commerce. She aspired to master an understanding of the western democratic approach to capitalist business and Keynesian macroeconomics, and to someday become an educator like her parents. In California, she stayed with an aunt and uncle who ran a restaurant across the bridge in San Francisco, and she worked summers and holidays on their small farm in the Alameda County countryside to supply the restaurant's kitchen with fresh vegetables.

Her world changed in 1941. With war clouds looming, her parents begged her to come home. Duty and honor to her family, proper Japanese traits ingrained in her character prompted the girl known as Tommi by her classmates to put her honor studies on hold and abandon her hectic social life of cheering at Cal Bruin football games, the social whirlwind of being a beloved and accepted sorority sister. To herself, she swore she would not sacrifice her American addiction to hot dogs, Lucky Strikes, and ample use of rouge and eye shadow. Yet she knew what post feudal conservative Japan was like where politicians recently had legislated priority marriages for those women with large hip bones who could bear many children.

By duty to family, she continued to say herself, *I shall obey my parents' wishes, but that does not mean I must leave behind all the things that make me feel beautiful and wanted.*

Preparing to come home, her bobbed hair growing out, Tommi gave away her Lana Turner tight sweaters that always drew men's stares. As best as she might try, she could not hide her attractiveness even after this back-to-basics makeover. Her clothing still was occidental; she owned no kimono. As she boarded her ship in San Francisco, her attire had not quite achieved the look of the demure and subservient Japanese woman; instead, more she bore the neutral color fashion taste of designer Elizabeth Arden, with tailored suits or her blouses with exaggerated shoulder padding like actress Carole Lombard wore.

For all this effort towards her homecoming, she got only as far as Honolulu. In early December she arrived on the *S.S. Lurline* of the Matson Lines to be directed by the unanticipated hand of fate. Even now, five years later, in 1946 with the war ended, even to those who knew her at the Red Tiki or to the historian novice Jim Michener, she could not tell anyone her enormous secret: Tommi had been a Japanese spy.

21

On December 6th, 1941, Tomoe 'Tommi' Jingu walked into the Japanese Consulate Office for transit approvals to board her homeward bound Japanese merchant-passenger ship. Odd. She found the offices and the staff employees in nervous agitation, and found herself getting the run-around, even though she was closely questioned by Vice Consul Okuda and another unassuming man, quickly introduced as Mr. Morim.

"Tell us about where you come from, who are your parents, what did you do in California?" And a casual if not strange question: "What do you think about this oil embargo that President Roosevelt placed on Japan?"

"I do not like it," said Tomoe Jingu, showing deferential respect with bowed head to those of superior rank. It was an uncomfortable feeling to return to the diminished world of a Japanese woman. Still, she was a well-read woman. She told them, "Economic blackmail never solved political foreign policy issues. Japan is forced now to find energy resources to run their ships and for their steel factories like importing from the Dutch East Indies." They nodded their heads and told her to return the next day at 8 a.m., sharp.

She arrived promptly at 8:00 a.m., the morning of December 7th, 1941.

At first, she was escorted to the proper passport document office. Within moments of her arrival, shouting began and office workers ran to the windows while others hurried away, fast walking past her, their arms loaded with files. When Tommi asked what the excitement was, a secretary rushing past gasped in horror, "We are bombing the fleet at Pearl Harbor! Our Empire must have been attacked by the Americans!"

Within this melee, and Tommi's unheard cries to stamp her passport, 'please let me reach my ship,' her arm was grabbed and she was dragged along by Mr. Morim, who pulled her into a side office.

"I did not expect this day, but yes, Sunday, I see it now. They would not be expecting an attack today." He paced nervously and then gave her a quick appraisal. "You are a true Japanese, are you not? You are loyal to our homeland? We need you this moment to be strong, to be a hero. Your parents will be proud."

At the mention of her parents, she voiced alarm: she only wanted to reach her ship and go home. He dismissed her needs with a flurry of waving gestures, pointing towards the windows.

"We are now at war. All our shipping in port will be seized.

No one can get out of Hawai'i, not now until we are victorious or negotiate a favorable truce. But if you were to help us quickly, the Consul can make you an employee. The Americans will certainly detain us. We are assuming they must exchange us for their own ambassadorial staff in Tokyo, under house arrest. This may take months but it will happen. If you want to get home you must help us."

She flustered and stammered in crisis. What was she to do?

Though she had developed American mannerisms, spoke the language well with little accent, and enjoyed the popular habits of an adopted country where her aunt and uncle maintained residence, she finally gave a slow, hesitant nod in agreement. At heart, and by birth, she was her parents' child and a Japanese citizen. That truth gave her answer.

"What do you want me to do?"

Morim was a spy, the top Japanese spy in Hawai'i. His real name was Takeo Yoshikawa, a naval reserve ensign, who since March, 1941, had spent all his time gathering intelligence on military installations in the American territorial Hawaiian Islands, where his reports led the Japanese Imperial Fleet to target Wheeler and Hickam airfields and U.S. naval ships at anchorage in Pearl Harbor.

Window casements rattled. Both of them could hear the success of his clandestine endeavors by the propeller whine of passing aircraft, those of Japan, for the moment holding hostage the violent skies.

She followed him as he left the office and sprinted down the hallway. She viewed piles of papers being torched, the smoke filling the seldom used chimney. Outside in a side yard as she passed the consulate windows, she could see a bonfire of burning boxes and documents.

Over his shoulder, seeing her wide-eyed surprise, Morim threw out staccato remarks, "The consulate will destroy their records. I need to get rid of my secret documents that are not here but I dare not leave or I go from being a consulate employee to perhaps being caught on the outside. I would be shot or hung. These Americans would grant me no honor to die by *hara kiri*.

"I need you and one of my contacts to retrieve my files and bring them here."

Morim opened an office door and shouted authoritatively to several consulate employees who were smashing radio equipment.

"Konchi, stop your work; prepare several employment documents plus another passport for this young lady, immediately. Give her official paperwork as a secretary of the consulate. Second, give her an American passport: she has family in California, use that address, but let's give her a Chinese-American cover. Pick an appropriate name with good fortune attached." He gave her a shrug. "For the Americans in this town, Chinese, not Japanese, will be the preferable rice dish in these days to come."

Thus, Judith Chen, Chinese-American citizen, was born amid the destruction of coded documents at the Japanese Consulate on December 7, 1941.

A taxi driven by a Japanese-Hawaiian local named John Mikami, under Morim's instructions, drove her to the spy's cottage where they both loaded up sealed boxes into the trunk of the cab.

A block away from their destination, the driver slammed on the brakes. They could see the Honolulu police had thrown up a cordon around the consulate. Mikami walked to one side of the building where he could be seen from the windows and returned with a package that had been thrown down to him, including new i.d. cards-passport for one Judith Chen. "No one is allowed in or out," said Mikami as they drove off. "We must carry out the second part of our assignment alone. We must not fail."

22

The taxi climbed into the mountainside Alewa Heights section of Honolulu to the *Shuncho ro* [Spring Tide] Restaurant on Makanani Drive. Tommi gasped at the view. No wonder Mr. Morim chose this spot as his central location to gather intelligence. The panorama took in Ford Island, now obscured by black smoke. Planes with Rising Sun emblems darted among a growing number of anti-aircraft shells peppering the skies. The Americans were waking up. A plane trailing black smoke caught fire and spiraled toward the ground.

Tommi said a quick prayer for the pilot, and extended a please be safe wish for all the young men down at the harbor, many dying in sinking ships. She did not realize that this phase of the battle was the second and final air attack from the Kido Butai Task Force.

Entering *Shuncho ro*, a Japanese-styled tea house, the two of them walked past the restaurant employees and sleepy-eyed geishas, all now fully awake, who were watching the battle unfold below them only six miles away. The owner, a native from Japan's Shikoku Island, escorted them to the building's second floor where, from a hidden panel in one of the geishas' entertainment rooms, they retrieved a wireless radio set and a wooden box tied shut with hemp rope.

This new 'luggage' was jammed into the trunk and covered with a University of Hawaii logo blanket.

"We can't drive back into town with all these documents," said Makimi, beginning to look nervous, twitching at the continuing harbor explosions. "We must destroy them."

"No," Tommi surprised herself with this sudden courage. "Mr. Morim wanted these papers. See if you can find a way to approach the Consulate safely. Devise a plan and I will help you get them inside. Meanwhile, there are sugar cane fields below. Let's hide everything somewhere safe. I'll stand guard until you return."

Tommi had never heard the military adage spoken by historic generals, 'all great battlefield plans do not survive the first cannon fire.' This day, the fog of war would lay heavy across Oahu, disrupting all lives.

She waited in the sugar cane field until near dark. Tomoe Jingu sat down in the middle of the field, chewed on cane stalks, and considered her options. If she were caught with more than one passport in hand she had good reason to assume the authorities definitely would execute her on the spot. She could not use her Japanese documents until she knew she could safely enter the Consulate. She must become the American-Chinese student, Judith Chen.

When her ride failed to appear she knew something was wrong. Having no assurance as to the taxi driver's loyalty not to sell her out for his own leniency, she took protective measures.

In the growing dusk, she moved all the boxes and the radio to another spot, across the road from the sugar cane, to what looked like an abandoned field worker's station. In the rotting debris she hid everything under a fallen wall. Next, she hiked a mile back to the *Shuncho ro* Restaurant and let them hide her for two days as the momentous events of the outside world ran their tragic and brutal course.

The owner of the restaurant returned with what news he could garner, and for the Japanese living on the islands it was as to be expected. They were all judged deceptive criminals and spies.

Tommi soon learned that the F.B.I. had scooped up cab driver John Makimi before he even made it back to the Consulate. If she were to hope for an exit strategy at the Consulate, nothing was forthcoming.

Years later, she would discover that the Japanese Consul and his senior diplomats were placed incommunicado for a week, then hustled aboard a ship to San Diego, and on to an internment camp in Arizona. Two years later they would be repatriated back to

Japan. Morim/Yoshikawa, the spy, and the driver Makimi were among those detained and carted off. Tommi came to realize that wherever the Consulate staff were being shipped off to she was most fortunate not to have made it back to join them.

Early in the new week, the F.B.I. came to visit the occupants of the *Shuncho ro* Restaurant, who had wisely shuttered their doors. It would be an invitation to vandalism if they looked too happy.

Names were taken, and since it was expected they were all

Japanese, for this Tommi used her *Tomoe Jingu* passport. With the anger of superiority, of revenge, and looking for anything illicit, the F.B.I. thoroughly trashed the restaurant, but nothing sinister was found. When the F.B.I. departed, all the employees knew the government agents would be back to arrest them, simply because the restaurant owner and the geishas represented too openly a culture now anathema to all decent Americans.

Tommi knew she needed to depart quickly and locate a better hide-out until she could decide on a survival plan. At an outside market while buying basic food staples for the restaurant staff, and under the alias 'Judith Chen,' she was accosted by U.S. Army soldiers on patrol, out looking for saboteurs. They scrutinized her false passport, looked into her eyes. An idea of deceit materialized when she realized the stressed-out, uniformed boys playing grown-ups could not tell Chinese from Japanese. Under martial law, these were dangerous times for Asians to be walking around Honolulu, facing everywhere itchy-trigger-finger soldiers with 'shoot on sight' orders. Analyzing the situation with calm versus panic, her college-honed intuitive thinking kicking in, and after balancing all the facts, she decided her best option would be to hide in plain sight.

Judith Chen on December 10th went to the University of Hawai'i in Mānoa to register for the next semester. Because of both the attack and the holidays, the university was closed for two months. Perfect. She stayed on campus, learning all nuances of pretending to be a long term student. She found pleasure in scamming the system, easily dressing the part of the college student where empty dormitory rooms provided shelter. She made friends of the kitchen staff for food and ingratiated herself with the business/economics professor in the College of Arts and Science Department who found her bright and well enough educated to give her a trial test as an unpaid Teaching Assistant when classes resumed.

For college she was transfer student Judith Chen, her parents killed in Singapore by the Japanese. Those who knew the 'eyes' never probed deeper with their suspicions since there was an underlying them versus us syndrome at the beginning of 1942, that being the white race against anyone of Asian ancestry.

In case it happened that someone on the street would dare challenge her and ask why did she look of Japanese ancestry with a Chinese name, she planned her retort: 'My Chinese mother was raped by a Japanese soldier in the Japan-Qing War. Which bloodline would you answer to?' Of course, she laughed at her inside joke, for had that been true, her age on that event date would have made her 56 years of age. It never came to that and she found a comfortable security net in the great melting pot of oriental cultures that made up Hawai'i.

A week after she had installed herself on the U.H. Mānoa campus, she borrowed a car on the excuse of a doctor appointment and drove back into the hills to locate the hidden boxes. Her initial thought was that this stash of documents was too explosive to be left lying around, and perhaps the taxi driver had been correct and everything should be turned to ash and cinders.

As usual, it was a warm day. She brought along a sandwich and an orange. The smoke had dissipated over Pearl Harbor. The newspapers, screaming for revenge, now under tight wartime censorship said 500 sailors had been killed at Pearl Harbor, whereas according to street gossip, the real numbers were up towards 1,500 dead Americans. She had mixed feelings as she thought about it, actually little feelings at all. Surviving was her only mantra. *I shall survive, do what I must.*

Back in a campus atmosphere, she easily fit with the American ways, even adopting the Hawaiian attitude of being laid back in nonchalance. Still, her true identity was Japanese and what citizen could not be proud hearing war news of the quick expansion of Japan's Greater East Asia Co-Prosperity

Sphere [*Hakkō ichiu* — 'all the world under one roof']. Certainly, she mused in hope, all sides could reasonably come to some agreement that would let America and Japan have defined boundaries and economic spheres of influence in the Pacific.

In a picnic mood, her world stabilizing, Tommi sat on the stoop of the derelict field workers' shack and systematically began sifting through each box. She made two major discoveries.

23

One box held a filing system listing hundreds of names, Japanese names with addresses. Surprisingly, none were set in code; perhaps it was the arrogance of a 'you can't catch me' spy. With these documents she had uncovered the Island network of all who supported Japan's imperial aspirations. Beyond gaining a web of agents to advance her country's war effort, she now held in her hands, unbeknownst to those in the file, a cadre of contacts, who could, first and foremost, aid her. She should never be wanting again. In time of war, information sourcing was the coin of the realm.

But it got better. The next to last box held a padded envelope stuffed with $12,000 in American currency. Yes, with Christmas so close, this must be her gift from those favorable gods who inhabit Hawai'i. Had they singled her out for some greater purpose? Laughing, doing her own small dance of good fortune, she shouted: *Thank you, spirit gods. I shall be worthy!* Not that she believed in any ancient deities, but, okay, she could agree to accept this ordained windfall.

From 1942 to 1945, Judith Chen became not one of the greatest espionage agents in the annals of Japanese intelligence, but instead one of the wealthiest black marketers in the Hawaiian Islands chain and within the Allied South Pacific Command. Her rousing success came to an abrupt end, however, in June of 1945 when her organization was uncovered; she was not arrested nor was her business destroyed, but it was co-opted and manipulated against her will.

Her grating nemesis at the time: Commander Hunter Hopewell.

When her network had been unmasked, when he was the Navy's top troubleshooting investigator in Hawai'i, the first words out of Commander Hopewell's mouth surprised her,

"The gods sent me, and you are mine."

Before she met Hunter Hopewell at war's end, back then in early 1942, with her list of Morim/Yoshikawa's contacts she moved judiciously to establish her bona fides as the successor to the spy's information flow. Many in the card file were mere workers in subservient roles like auto mechanics, maids or janitors. Figuring they were not really spies themselves, these people saw no harm in helping the mother country as long as they avoided any significant risk. With little coercion, they responded to her prodding and supplied her snippets of gossip and word on any unusual events tied to the American military presence on Oahu. It was up to her to weave the broad mosaic that could become extremely valuable, such as knowing troop deployment destinations. At first she was enthused to be part of the war effort, on the side of her parents and her homeland, but her first and only attempt to… spy came to nothing and soured her against the intelligence officers within the Japanese Imperial Navy staff.

In late May, 1942, a Japanese shoe shine boy overheard a customer asking a buddy. "was the stuff on JN-25 any good?" Later the same week, a cruiser captain asked the pro shop at the Waialae Country Club to store his golf clubs for at least two months, saying he was taking his boys and going spear fishing up north. Why would a heavy cruiser steam off by itself into the empty ocean north of the Islands unless it was part of a fleet? And finally, what could explain the unbelievably quick Pearl Harbor entry and departure of the carrier U.S.S Yorktown, sailing on May 30 after round-the-clock repairs, so soon after arriving from a sea battle, that she heard through sources, had occurred far south in the Coral Sea? As Tommi reviewed all the snatches of information and pieced them together she concluded that a major naval sortie was in motion, but going where?

On June 1st she climbed a ridgeline up in the Koʻolau Mountains near the village of Kaneohe and conveyed with her wireless the possibilities of an American action to the receiving radio beacons of Japan Naval Intelligence via their relay link station on Wake Island. Officers on that end were quite skeptical if not arrogant; even if the guarded responses were cryptic and short, nevertheless they struck her as rude. That their original spy, now detained, had entrusted his network to a woman seemed an inexcusable lapse in judgment. Certainly, to them, she must be incompetent, for they knew without doubt from eyewitness accounts of their pilots that the USS Yorktown had been sunk with horrible loss of life in the Coral Sea battle.

Furthermore, although surprised by the reference to their secret navy codes known as JN-25, they assured her that she needn't worry; the codes had recently been changed and were infallible against being broken by the enemy. Their sign-off said it would not matter in the coming days, an allusion to her that the Imperial Navy was likewise on the high seas. A great chance for fresh espionage was lost by the Japanese. With this cavalier slap delivered by shortwave she was dismissed as trivial to the impending collision in which Imperial strength on the high seas, as they saw it, would prevail in the anticipated battle to end all battles and drive the Americans from the Pacific, from Hawaii, back to the west coast of the United States.

Tommi's assessment of her own worth as an intelligence agent was confirmed when the American military, under wartime censorship, released highlights of a great sea victory over the Japanese fleet, June 2nd to 4th, near a speck of island in the mid Pacific, aptly called Midway. By this time, her pride of knowing she had guessed correctly was pushed aside as she had to study for semester final exams at UH, with the extra load of being a Teaching Assistant.

In this atmosphere of learning and political chatter, she found a new cause, being easily drawn to the plight of the Japanese citizens stranded in Hawai'i and those Japanese-Americans who felt the full brunt of island martial law. On the mainland, American citizens who happened to be of Japanese ancestry were being rounded up and shipped to remote internment camps in California and throughout the Southwest. To Tommi's ears they sounded more like prison camps. Under President Franklin Roosevelt's Executive Order 9066 in February, 1942, Tommi's aunt and uncle, were among the 100,000 U.S. citizens on the West Coast forcibly removed by armed soldiers and police. They lost their restaurant and farm to a white man, in response to the racial fears of those times, who changed the eatery name to something more American like 'Uncle Sam's Café,' and continued making a profit.

The pressure was on to do the same round-up in the Hawaiian Islands, but how does a government remove an entire population of Japanese-Americans, 150,000 strong, who made up one third of the islands' population? In Hawaii, according to the military way of thinking, if you couldn't imprison the traitorous populace, you could bluntly ostracize, belittle, and harass them, impeding their daily livelihood so as to remove the perceived threat. These stories of mental and physical subjugation were not pretty.

Here, Tommi found her backbone to fight the enemy on her terms. Under such dire circumstances she was inspired to set up a Community Chest style support effort for the Japanese population. She cajoled those in her card file system to help set up a food bank; she convinced Japanese-American lawyers, even liberal litigators like the fledgling ACLU, to fight against prejudicial laws and discrimination. All this she accomplished under the radar as an incognito volunteer of sorts, and her success led to new supportive friendships having nothing to do with the agenda of the Japanese imperialists and Prime Minister Tojo. All this activity opened her horizons to greater economic opportunities, likewise revealing her character flaw: the desire to make money as a measurement of her self-worth — not such a bad fault, she rationalized.

Her ventures started small, like her barter co-op using war ration coupons as tradable currency of which she took a mere mark-up of five percent commission, followed by her delivery service, employing Filipino refugees, that supplied liquor and cigarettes to sailors stuck aboard ships in port, which taught her the fine art of spreading dollars under the table.

By mid-1945 she had graduated from the university with a Business major, rare for a woman in those times, in a society that even now was laying off the Rosie the Riveters and sending them home to the kitchen. Tommi had put aside her student persona, opened a small office offering bookkeeping services as her public cover, and was doing quite well for herself. She had lost interest in how the war was going, could care less who was winning, except to sense it would be over soon as the Americans moved toward Okinawa and the main homeland islands. She prayed her parents would stay out of the cities, which seemed to be targets for the high altitude B-29 Superfortress bombers deploying incendiaries to spread fiery carpets of death.

Preparing for a termination to hostilities… peace in her time… she started up another small clandestine operation, and here is where she met Hunter Hopewell, under less than amiable terms.

'Tommi'
Tomoe Jingu also known as Judith Chen
"I will survive."

24

Jimmy Michener would make a great investigative reporter.

In the space of a week, he had cajoled and wheedled and lubricated Hunter, teasing out of him the story of how he and Tommi had come to meet. Michener had noted their surface interchanges, as he could see, was not outright bitter hatred, more a mutual antipathy, like swallowed icky-tasting cough syrup, disliked but medicinal.

He pulled out his notepad.

"All my sources are confidential," he stressed to Hunter having caught him alone one afternoon, as usual at the bar in the Red Tiki. Pencil poised. "I just find it interesting how two people, different in ethnic and cultural backgrounds, can work together, so soon after the war.

"No, I'm not going to tell you that story," said Hunter, and then he did.

Commander Hopewell and his six man flying squad were based out of the JAG office, and known and feared among the locals as the Heart Breakers for their assigned role to be out looking for AWOL sailors who jumped ship for a varied of reasons: fear of dying bloody or drowned in a torpedoed ship; or homesick but not really wanting to go back home; and more often than not, falling in drunk love with a hoochie-koochie dime-a-dance sort of saloon girl and being taken for a ride until his shore pay ran out. While the naïve soldier/sailor believed they were a romantic couple forever, the floozy quickly moved her wiggle onto the next chum bait.

"Yeah, maybe one out of a thousand was the real thing," admitted Hunter in his dialogue with Michener, still reluctant to believe in any of that mushy love crap. Seeing too many bad ends — heartbroken young kids, heading back to their ships in a depressed stupor — his own heart had hardened.

Hunter's job was sleaze law enforcement in which his squad tried to get the wayward boys into the brig and back to their ships before they stepped up to the altar. It could get more complex. If one of the girls got pregnant, she would start trolling for a sailor with a future and a bankroll and get him into bed, call him 'Cuddles,' make him think with his dick, and then send him a note a month or so later, the reverse of a Dear John letter, more like 'make our kid legitimate and take care of me while you are at it.' Shit work, but at that point in his life, Hunter's body and mind felt equally shitty.

"It was July of 1945," he told Michener, "a month before my out-patient medical discharge from the service. The idea appealed to me of staying with the JAG as a civilian employee while working toward a law degree in night classes, when I started noticing a pattern in the investigative files."

Michener scribbled fast as Hunter mumbled away.

According to Hunter, with the war winding down, there was a growing list of war bride requests, which needed to be investigated as to true claims, and some of the footwork fell into his lap. Many of these applications, he soon discovered, seemed to be written in the same hand, and the petitioners were being represented by one particular attorney, already on file as being highly respected in the community, but when the war began, he had been on the Army-FBI watch list. The lawyer was an American citizen but of Japanese ancestry. More recently, there were rumors floating around that many of his clients might be under the sponsorship of the criminal black market ilk, those selling military stores that seemed to fall off convoy supply trucks or foodstuff that had gotten lost in the commissary records.

Further digging and a few polite inquiries of several of these lady 'war brides' revealed that there was a printed business card posted in bars all across town (yes, one in the Red Tiki), offering marital legal services: White Chrysanthemum Marriage-Divorce Services, the business owned by one J. Chen. To Hunter, that name struck a bell, or rather a carillon tower full of ringing. There was a J. Chen Shipping & Forwarders, holding an approved military contract that provided a valuable service to married officers and family members to ship their furniture allowance of personal property back home, and if any military personnel, from private/ensign up, had more war souvenir trinkets than allowed by duffle bag size regulations, they could be brought together en masse and container shipped back to the States.

Both businesses seemed legit, totally proper and tied up

Legally with no filed complaints, which bothered Hopewell.

Maybe too much finesse in the execution of services, like greasing palms to the right level of authority in order to skirt the minefields of triplicate paperwork for quick transit out of a still active war zone. One person, J. Chen, signed all the manifests as "corporate secretary." Coincidence?

"Was this 'J. Chen' our Judy Chen", asked Michener replacing the stub of his pencil, with a new number 2.

"Hey, I'm telling this story." Hunter glanced around, half-shouting, dramatically pointing. "Hey, my glass is empty!" Refreshed and reinforced with another iced tumbler, he continued.

"No doubt I needed to pay a call on this J. Chen, the secretary, and have her tell me who the head boss is. I wanted that man."

Tracking her down, however, was not so easy. He heard she operated a bookkeeping service as one Judith Chen, staffed by a few female pencil pushing scribe types but she was never on the premises herself. Finding her invisible, he came to believe she did indeed hold all the secrets and that intrigued him.

"I was forced to set a trap." Hunter smiled dumbly at some memory of his past brilliance.

He had the Honolulu Police spring one of the more prominent hookers from jail and sent her to the White Chrysanthemum as a potential client. The ploy didn't work. The pigeon met with a perky secretary who took all the information and said she would be in contact. The same no-show occurred at the stake-out where Hopewell assigned a couple of his squad members to sit on the J. Chen Shipping location. Two Asian guys worked a freight receiving desk and in the warehouse, but no J. Chen, no Judith Chen.

"The first attempt failed, but nothing can stop me when I put my mind to the puzzle."

From his dusty legal experience sprung a light bulb of ingenuity: another ruse. A large bill for state corporate taxes was mailed to J. Chen Shipping, demanding that the owner appear for an appointment at the Revenue Department office on a specific date and time. He was waiting outside the government building when this very attractive young lady, early twenties, came waltzing in.

"I thought she was quite the looker," said Hunter with a staring pause, "before I came to discover what she was like under the brown silk skin — a conniving personality."

Hunter lost himself in a reverie about those past days.

Having interviewed a lot of war bride applicants who dressed for modest appeal to impress and investigator, it was pleasant to see a woman dress effectively, using her clothes to help argue her case.

Neither frumpy by any means, nor like a military man might come to expect, a girl out boozing the town. With the wartime rubber shortage barely over, Hopewell could see she wore no girdle, and her shoes were open-toed with wooden heels. Her understated beige pleated skirt hung mid-calf while a bright, floral patterned short-sleeve blouse completed the look. Her black hair, definitely long and flowing, had been tied in a bun. No, not like a salaried office secretary, Hunter wondered if she was the girlfriend of the business owner. A very fascinating woman, and to this day she still was he had to admit.

Michener brought him back from his daydream. "And this is where you confronted her?"

"No. Though all this was highly suspicious, instead of bracing her there in the Revenue Department, I decided I could be the cowboy lawman of the Old West, track the rustler, give her freedom of the trail, loosen the reins and see where she might lead; find her hide-out."

Following the script he had written, the Revenue people apologized profusely for the incorrect mailing, and the interview ended. He decided to apply his novice talent at shadowing on the street, a basic education learned from the one or two off — the book clients who required him to do motel window peeks to trap their philandering officer husbands. So thinking himself clever and invisible, he watched this Miss Chen exit the office building, definitely upbeat for having overcome governmental red tape.

A healthy walk later, he trailed her into Chinatown to 115 North Hotel Street, where she entered a side door of the Wo Fat Restaurant. He waited a few minutes, then ambled over and read the building's tenant register. Listed upstairs, above the restaurant, he saw it: J. Chen Bookkeeping Services.

"My brain cells click. She's definitely the front person, or she is the owner, and definitely running the service like this to help facilitate her people. You see, all her clients were probably Orientals, but is what she doing, illegal? Perhaps, perhaps not. But back then, I just had this feeling she's conning the system, helping Asian dolls hook up with a better life back in the States. Maybe a little smuggling on the side."

His story continued. Not knowing what to do next, Hunter ended up buying a bowl of chop suey, eyes on the door. Anyway, he had nothing better to do until cocktail hour.

An hour and half later she was on the move again, this time by taxi. 'Damn,' he thought, 'this will start costing me,' but he followed, deeply intrigued. She exited the cab in the industrial district of warehouses, most of them one-story wooden buildings, but several nailed together in scrap metal Quonset hut design. This wasn't her shipping office. John Chase Fabrics reads a small sign above a door, everything downplayed and unobtrusive. Facing another wait, he pulled out a silver flask.

"The J.C. initials used with her businesses must have spiked your curiosity?"

"Yes," said Hunter, engrossed in his own telling, but wondering if he had already told this part of the story before. His mind now foggy. "Something struck me when I was on stake-out. Could Mr. Chase be a real person, or was this another J. Chen business. Seemed a stretch; women do not run the show. And this was a young girl, with an air of confidence in style and presence. How could she be the brains? I thought maybe the girl's mother runs all these businesses? I have to admit, like the sailfish drawn to the flashy coloring of the lure, snap! — I was hooked for answers."

25

ithin fifteen minutes something seemed wrong. Hunter spotted two men, a Mutt and Jeff team, both Chinese by their looks, and not warehouse workers as you would expect in this district, but wearing pretty sharp clothes, summer business suits without ties. Two things caught his attention: one, they also seemed to be also casing the building where Miss Chen had entered. Second, and shocking to his psyche, above one of the men, the taller of the two, he saw this swirling cloud, of darkness, of form — of, if he could believe what he saw, they are circling black sharks. He shook his head in disbelief but the dark sight remained; it was beyond the impossible yet seemed physically real. Twice before he had seen such circling sharks: off Choiseul Island above the head of that Commander Kennedy who saved his life by rescue and his savior by providing the supply of Penicillin. Turned out his rich dad was some big government mucky-muck who pulled strings to protect his boy by sending him a package of experimental medicines no one else could obtain.

He'd seen those devil sharks one other time in a drawing by the artist called Tiki Shark, working an outside stall over by the Red Tiki Lounge. The kid said that in his paintings, black sharks which swam in air currents were god-warning devil demons who carried a curse as dark as their color. If they circled you, it meant you would come to a bad end, violently, and not in an accident, but by man, or by an angry god. Hunter Hopewell did not then believe such bull, but now, a year later, and with his continuing headaches, nightmare dreams and visions, he was not so certain, and albeit hesitantly, was prepared to accept there are things mysterious and unexplained, and accepting this altered world possibility did cause him to question his sanity.

Shaking his head to clear the fog and refocus on his stakeout, Hunter watched the two Chinese hoodlums — he knew the type — as they approached the factory door and slid in effortlessly. The demon sharks followed.

Hunter was at the crossroads: with his bad war experiences he didn't really have a taste for danger. What should he do?

He followed them in.

There were nondescript front offices, and, he assumed, this was some sort of manufacturing in back for whatever "fabrics" means. He heard shouting coming from behind a door, a man and woman yelling, in English, not Chinese. As he cautiously edged closer to the altercation, he realized again: *I am no hero, and I am unarmed. Shit.*

Peering in, he was surprised to see about twenty women, all Asian, standing away from what looked to be a work area of sewing machines and metal fabrication equipment. The women showed fear, certainly intimidated as the tall man (with the halo of sharks — can't everyone see them too?) waved a very nasty looking fish-gutting knife. In front of the cowering women stood Judith Chen, unafraid and angry, yelling at both men; some of her words could, as they say, make a sailor blush.

In any language Hunter didn't need a translation to understand what was going down: it's the older-than-dirt protection shakedown racket. They were demanding: Pay us a small weekly insurance fee and nothing will happen to your little factory. These small time hustlers might be part of a tong gang or moonlighting on their own. It's against the law, and damn, in some interpretation of naval regulations, he was an official card-carrying officer, capable of making arrests, even if that was a bit of a stretch. In reality, he could only apprehend and incarcerate Navy personnel. But it was too late for such speculations; the women workers noted his silent entrance, and their widening eyes foiled his stealth approach. What more could he do but the obvious.

"I think you gentlemen need to leave," he said in a deep voice, trying to sound menacing, but they made no move towards the exit. Instead, they turned on him.

"Not your business, sailor boy. Get lost." The smaller man flashed Hunter a feral grin, implying that the two-against-one odds did not favor his health and safety.

"Last chance. I do have reinforcements coming."

"None that we saw with you hanging outside." Well, that gambit didn't work and now the knife holder moved at a leisurely pace away from the victims towards the presumed rescuer. Hunter broke a sweat to this predicament.

Thunk.

The woman he would come to know as Judith Chen, also known as Tommi, slammed what looked like a scabbard sword flat side down on the tall thug's hand, sending the knife skittering under a work bench. From nowhere a second, third, several swords appeared and began flailing away at the men, forcing them to duck, hands over heads. They were not being seriously injured but the flat sides of the sword casings wielded by at least ten women pounding on them like screaming harpies would be bruising. Nevertheless, the thugs were still dangerous and they still out-numbered the commander; hitting them with his fists would mean getting in too close. So, Hunter shattered a wooden chair over the tall Chinaman, sending him sprawling and unconscious; Judith Chen then took a large coffee urn to the other man's head — *Clunk!* — with the same satisfying results.

Hunter stared at the women, focusing hard on the fake Chinese businesswoman who was really Japanese. From personal experience, he distrusted any Japanese and felt he should spout officialdom, but instead, he smiled at her in celebration of their first joint victory, and, not knowing why, said, "The gods have sent me and you are mine." *Why did I say that?*

As the worker bees grabbed rope to tie up the failed extortionists, his eyes took in the surroundings and he tried to process what he saw. Some women had been sitting at ancient Singer sewing machines, while others probably stood at some sort of assembly line indeed cutting fabric. At the end of one long table where he observed two small buckets, one filled with dirt, the other... what?

"Cow blood," said Judith Chen sensing his curiosity. "Some of our customers demand gritty realism."

Hunter held up an example of the finished product. *A Japanese flag with the Rising Sun symbol.*

Over in a corner the women had piled the weapons that saved all; he now recognized them as Japanese swords.

Judith Chen continued her guided tour like a shopkeeper showing off her prized wares.

"The *nihontō* is a samurai sword, the smaller of the three is the accompanying dagger, *tanto*, and these are Japanese naval swords, *kai gunto*."

Hundreds of them were stuck in large vats of dirt that she didn't need to explain. "The aging process?"

"To be sold as if right off the battlefield." Miss Chen was not confessing to a crime: if anything, she was proud. "There is an unbelievable demand for war souvenirs, and not all the American soldiers or sailors were in the midst of the fighting. And we are talking about thousands who are heading home without a good story to tell. I merely supply the props for their valiant wartime deeds." Now, that tone in her was slightly condescending and bitter.

Hunter had to ask. "Where did you get all these swords? Straight from a Jap — pardon me — factory in Tokyo?"

"I'm Chinese."

"And I'm Joe DiMaggio." Her lie might have worked well on others; she in turn expressed her savvy.

"And who are you, really?"

"Commander Hunter Hopewell, Investigator, Judge Advocate General's Office. And as soon as I can figure it out, you probably are in trouble."

"For being a capitalist? For voting the Democrat ticket in my first national election? The swords, by the way, are actually from a Milwaukee plant. I have a partner on those."

26

O ne of the men on the floor gave out a small groan.

She looked at Hunter with a scrutiny that spoke years of character study and he felt naked, with all his foibles showing.

Seeking to change the direction of her prying stare, he gestured toward the two thugs.

"Well, what are we going to do about your friends here? I could probably throw them in the city jail, but then you'd have to file a complaint." He gave her factory a wide gaze. "And I don't think you need any city police detectives to come calling."

"These jokers have been by before," she said, dismissing them with a wave of her hand, scum that they were. "I would, however, expect them to return, more violent, more destructive, with a few more of their associates in tow. There needs to be a message sent. A permanent solution to maintain my business as it is." She was thinking aloud, actually soliciting his opinion before she gave hers.

"And — ? If we aren't going to jail them, then an alternative of throwing them in the bay tied to one of your sewing machines is not my solution. I'm not into violence."

"Surprised me."

"Lethal, that is. I've been too closely acquainted with death to have him or his buddy go swimming with the bottom feeders. Too bad you can't banish them to some deserted isle."

Strange: a glow rose up from her chin and blossomed into to a coquettish smile that nearly absorbed Hunter's consciousness.

"No, but I can export them."

Hunter Hopewell, paragon of law and order, did not know why he was willing to add kidnapping and 'exporting' to his lifetime list of sins he should someday seek forgiveness for. That day, he now guesses, he was just bored, halfway sober, perhaps a little intrigued to see what Judith Chen had in mind, and distracted by a growing desire to launch a full background check on this young woman and all her entangled enterprises.

They loaded the two gagged and tied up punks into the back of a small J. Chase Fabrics delivery truck and soon were at the docks where another warehouse was situated; this one he had some knowledge of, her J. Chen Shipping and Forwarding office. Two burly stevedores, Filipinos, squat as blocks of muscle, took over the received 'freight packages'. To satisfy his ego, he had to sound like some sort of customs official.

"And what are you going to do? Not turn them into fish food, I hope?"

"Could be better for them, but no," explained Chen, kicking one of the prone captives. "Appropriately, the word here is 'shanghaied.' I have some empty freight containers heading to China for cargo. I can arrange to have their suits removed and have them inducted into the warlord army of Chiang Kai-shek. Give them better field experience at how to be brutal, if they survive."

This is one hard, play-for-keeps business woman, Hunter marveled as he spoke to her strategy.

"And all the Honolulu low-lifes might wonder where they disappeared to, might actually fear this J. Chen operation, but won't know who the head boss is, because you like it that way… low key and unobtrusive, as I found out while trying to locate you."

"Precisely. There is a symmetry of justice here that I sense you comprehend, that the rule of law is flexible."

Hunter pinched his temples to stem the tide of pain coming on. Within arms' reach they exchanged unblinking eye-contact, exploring motives, defining attributes, wondering.

Judith Chen broke the introspection with light banter.

"From that Bogart movie, are you going to say, 'this is the beginning of a beautiful friendship'?"

As to supposed friendship, he did not answer, choosing instead to start poking around the scattered and stacked crates to see if he could nail her for illegal contraband.

The tall crook, having recovered, began trying to break his bonds, while screaming through the gag about what he would do to them once freed. The other Chinese hood, also conscious, knew the score, a one-way slow boat to China, so to speak, and already had pissed in his pants. Hunter Hopewell discovered a new theorem on this eye-opening afternoon: when bad guys are unconscious, the black tiki-looking sharks go into some sort of disappearing hibernation, if that's any solace to the damned. To Judith Chen he pointed out the 'exportees' awaiting their new crated home.

"The tall one there, in his new line of soldiering, I know he will be killed. Of that I am certain." That's how they met, two years past: Hunter, who could vaguely foresee future events, and Tommie, who was hoping to alter the course of coming events to suit her personal desire for retribution.

27

I t was with total confidence in her plan for revenge that Tommi could say with airy aplomb, "Do you want the bomb?"

"What are you talking about, miss?"

Tommi listened for an accent but there was none, though she knew he spoke fluent Ukrainian and a smattering of Russian, the heritage of his ancestors.

The two of them were sitting in the dining room of the Moana Hotel facing Waikiki Beach. Out the window she could see swimmers and sunbathers. Back in 1942, this beach bristled with barbed wire and edgy, armed soldiers, anticipating the invasion that never came. This might be her last visit to the Moana restaurant. She heard they were already talking about building an addition to the hotel, demolishing the restaurant. Thousands of military personnel who had passed through Hawai'i onto the battlefields, currently heading towards military separation centers might be future returning tourists. Already, the newspapers talked of 'post-war boom', something Tommi was eager to take advantage of, but not before she purged her anger.

Today at the Moana restaurant, July 15th, 1946, observers might jump to the conclusion that the two of them were on afternoon date; he looking gentlemanly, in his late thirties, sporting a casual Aloha shirt, she in demure flowered blouse and beige skirt. In fact she had enticed him to this tête-à-tête with a telephone call for a late afternoon cocktail, suggesting she might have some furniture design work for a new home she was contemplating. He owned a small woodworking and craftsman shop catering to hotel room restoration after drunken shore leaves and the occasional custom work on the new homes that were being built up towards Diamond Head.

Tommi Chen, however, knew that beneath the facade of Hawaiian businessman and dues-paying member of the Honolulu Chamber of Commerce, Mr. Peter Baran was a Russian spy.

For her purposes of revenge against the American government, Tommi required his services, and in a hurry, so she would pull no punches.

"Your family name is Barisnikov. Your grandfather, a Ukrainian, was one of those farm laborers indentured by Czar Alexander I and sent to the islands to work the sugar cane plantations. When the contracts expired, your grandfather decided warm weather trumped Eastern European winters. And your father, who worked in the fields alongside his father, grew to hate the colonial ways of the capitalist exploiters like the Doles and the Libby's. He became active in organizing all the ethnic field workers, from the Portuguese to the Filipinos. At the same time he embraced the Soviet doctrine of shared wealth and workers' rights. The worker ethic might have been strong in your family but when you came along you were smart enough to figure out a new angle, and more power to you; the boy known as Pyotr became Peter, Barisnikov anglicized to Baran. Your skill at woodworking led you to become a respectable member of society… albeit a closet communist, especially after the little recruiting visit paid by an officer of the NKVD or their special section of military counterintelligence, tied into the Navy's RKKF. I believe that was in July, 1941. What button on they pushed I can't guess, unless it was love for the motherland after the Nazis launched Operation Barbarossa and conquered your ancestral Ukrainian home. Family is always strong motivation, I know that so well. It is known now [she did not reveal it was thanks to an informative talk with an inebriated Hopewell] that the Soviets' Japanese spy cell run by the German Richard Sorge in Tokyo had predicted the attack date of Barbarossa but was dismissed by Stalin's advisors. So when Sorge learned from his sources that Japan would attack American interests somewhere in the Pacific by year's end 1941, there was a rush to have a spy in place who could report on American fleet movements as well as garner any tidbits on Japanese war plans."

Peter Baran maintained his composure with slow sips to his cocktail. Visually casing the room, he saw empty tables around him, his privacy protected. Certainly, he accepted, this was a ploy of the F.B.I. to entrap him into becoming a double agent. What else? His mind was racing. Shocked denial was his best cover, but she seemed to have pertinent facts on him. What compounded the problem was that this Miss Judith Chen (call me 'Tommi') held him enthralled, a young, eye-catching beauty, her lilting voice easy on the ears, enticing. At 37, he was not old at all, believed himself attractive to the ladies, and squared his back; perhaps two could play the game of betrayal and seduction.

"You are a great story teller, Miss Chen, but I see no facts to this accusation, merely speculative smoke."

"How about if I tell you, one of your early and most successful assignments was when you ratted out Nazi spy Bernie Kuehn, here in Honolulu."

Baran did actually choke on his drink, and brought a napkin to his mouth. *How in the world did she... unless she was F.B.I.? But how could they know?*

"I don't know what you are talking about?" A weak response, he knew.

"Let's try this: Kuehn was a buddy of Nazi Propaganda Minister Goebbels. In fact, Kuehn's 17 year old daughter was one of Goebbel's mistresses. Anyway, Goebbels sent Bernie and his family here to Hawaii in 1935 to spy and help out their Axis partners, the Japanese. Your spy, Richard Sorge, in Tokyo, learned there was a German spy based on Honolulu. In the late 1930's this was neither priority nor valuable information since Germany and the Soviet Union had signed a non-aggression pact which the Deutschland betrayed with their invasion of Russia, and since patriotic Russians despised the Japanese, this going back to their naval defeat at Japanese hands in 1904 [at this point Tommi smiled, knowing the victory in the naval battle of Tsushima was one of the great Japanese victories in the Russo-Sino War] you were tasked on uncovering this network."

Baran had to join her in savoring a job well done, without revealing his involvement. He still did not understand her agenda. Warily, he shrugged his shoulders, looked out the window, not seeing tourists but sensing the heat of the day, and he replied, "Bernard Otto Kuehn was an inept spy, so I heard. He employed his whole family in this espionage business; his wife ran a beauty shop to pick-up gossip, his daughter dated servicemen, and Kuehn even had his young son dress up in a Navy uniform and walk the waterfront making patriotic friends to gain information."

She nodded. "Sooner than later he would be easy to discover, somewhat like yourself, and please, I mean no offense. Living beyond his means, sloppy at transmitting information via radio, occasional visits from messengers posing as sailors passing through the islands." Tommi misdirected as to exactly how she had discovered Peter Baran's secret life. Her own leads came from the old card fi le of spymaster Takeo Yoshikawa.

Besides spying on the American military, he kept tabs on spies and alleged spies of all nationalities. On the card marked, with the initials, B.J.O.K., Kuehn's card, was a notation dated, *November, 1941... K thinks he is being followed. Not police. Man named Baran. Why? Need follow-up.* But there was to be no follow up; Pearl Harbor was attacked the next month, and shortly thereafter Yoshikawa was yanked off to a detention camp.

From liquored up and loose-lipped Hopewell she had gained the following historic tidbit which she relayed, matter-of-factly.

"The Kuehn family, on December 7th, were still sending information to the Japanese, but the U.S. war-paranoids were now focused on anyone like us, the slant-eyes. Someone tipped off the FBI to start watching the Kuehns and by February, 1942, they were all arrested. To avoid a firing squad, Kuehn started squawking like a cockatoo, and gave up German and Japanese spy networks, but knew nothing of any Russian espionage.

"Who made the anonymous call fingering Kuehn? You as the source would be my guess. [Tommi had her own source having directed one of her Hawaiian student graduates to gain employment at Baran's furniture store, which he did as an upholsterer, grateful for the paying war-time job]. And you are still reporting on U.S. ship movements but, I sense, more importantly, your Kremlin bosses want all you can get on these atomic bomb tests, because they are in our backyard, and since they don't have a bomb, or so far the makings of one, then you would receive the Order of Lenin, and if you were to photograph an atomic bomb up close, maybe sabotage it — give the Yankees a black eye — or who knows, perhaps steal one... I mean, why should the Americans be the only nuclear world power?"

"Again, a very nice story, but I am a businessman who makes furniture. What would I do with an atomic bomb? And how could one possibly 'steal' a bomb, as you suggest?" Within the denial of guilt, the door of 'what if's' eased open. She had him sniffing the bait.

"Cards on the table. I am not an American, and not Chinese, as you, I believe, recognized immediately. What is important is I do not like the American government and wish to hurt them. Why, that is my personal business. I have found an opportunity to do so without pulling out a gun and shooting a bunch of soldiers at the PX.

"In three days, my associates and I are going to fly to this Bikini Atoll; and slip onto a derelict ship they are using in their tests, to retrieve something that was taken from us. The object is large, so we are prepared to lift something heavy and store it on the plane we are obtaining. We could lift a bomb just as easily if someone could get close and do so a few days before the thing is to be set off. My people can't, or being American patriots won't, help steal a bomb for you. As I see it, you need to bring along your own crew, preferably no more than eight, and certainly, since the next test is underwater, deep diving equipment might be useful. Maybe I can also secure these new shallow diving snorkel tanks I keep hearing about. Scuba, they call it. And find an underwater camera, if you are only going to take photos. Or, a small amount of explosives if you are going to wreak public relations havoc by sabotage.

"That's all I can provide, the prize and the method to get to it. Everything else is your plan, not mine."

"And where would a simple businessman, owner of Baran Furniture and Upholstery Repair, gain a crew able to steal, and perhaps do damage so violently, if necessary?"

"Violence will be unnecessary if you get in and out quickly. As to your own group of culprits, I suggest you look to that Russian fishing trawler sitting in the harbor. I have noted it certainly has a lot of electronic gear in its masts. It would be my guess that it is one of your spy ships ready to set off to monitor the testing, as close as they will be allowed. And crewed by Russian sailors who I am sure are rough and mean enough for your purposes."

"Interesting observations. Shall we do dinner and talk more?"

Her goal was not his; in her personal life, she protected herself from slugs and leeches. "No, thank you. I will need to know by tomorrow if you are coming along. And if you feel this is some kind of set-up, think again; why would I want to fly you several thousands of miles only to arrest you on a small island chain, when, if I were a government agent, I would have done so before you bought me a drink, with what I have conveyed I know, circumstantial as it might be." She rose and sought his hand in a friendly gesture. "Goodbye, Mr. Baran. Let your mind wander to striking a great coup for Mother Russia and the Ukrainian people. Feel how proud your parents and your grandfather would be of your accomplishment. And knowing your sense of commerce, think what you might be paid to bring back one U.S. atomic bomb. That is temptation hard to refuse."

"And this mythical trip, you can get us to the bomb range before they explode the next bomb, in plenty of time?" No further veil of innocence; avarice was reeling him in.

"My partner in this adventure is acquiring our transportation as we speak."

Part Three

Pele

28

Chrissy Iolani giggled and ran with her girlfriends to catch up with the rest of the school's field trip consisting of classmates and teacher. The girls, all in their school uniforms, were caught up in the good-natured gossip about Chrissy's new relationship with Danny Gonzalez, teasing her to confirm that she and Danny had been necking only this morning behind the Kamehameha school building before class.

In her off ended shouts of 'not true' Chrissy denied such an event took place when in fact the deep kisses, the thrilling press of eager bodies, the mutual arousal were fresh in her blushing memory. She contained her excitement in front of her girlfriends, praying Danny could get his uncle's car this weekend. Her mind ran with the marvelous possibilities; with child-like eagerness she was wishing they would together find a dark sugar cane road, listen to the music of 'Hawaii Calls' on the radio, and let the passion take its course to the perfect gift for her upcoming high school commencement, to experience her own private version of graduation, from child to woman.

The day trip led by her geography teacher, took the class to visit Volcanoes National Park, founded in 1916. They would leave their rickety school bus to make a closer, inspection of the surrounding landmarks upon the slopes of the Kilauea volcano, including the smoking yet quiet Halemaumau Crater, walking in ancient cave-like lava tubes, observing the diverse flora and fauna, and discussing geology and the formation of Hawai'i by volcanic action.

As in most teaching of young adults, information flowed in and out of their attention span, with a few tidbits lodged in their developing minds. Finding a large amount of flowing lava would have gained their awe, but this year, most volcanic activity lay dormant or hidden as streams of lava flowed through underground vents to the ocean near Kaimū Bay, venting steam as fire met the sea.

The crowded bus emptied and the chattering kids followed their instructor through a copse of salt-stained palm trees towards the barren rough terrain of the lava field formed in the 1924 major Kilauea eruption. Just as the next lesson was to begin, a large noise rose above nearby pounding waves and from out of the underbrush charged a herd of pigs, setting the students into startled and panicked scrambling.

Most wild island pigs are scrawny and small, but among the animal attackers stood out one large pig, hog-sized, wiry and pink, and whereas the other pigs were merely a distraction, not especially dangerous, this massive pig had purpose.

Chrissy ran with the others, laughing at the melee, but in a glance over her shoulder, she noticed a pig actually chasing her, and she ran faster, out into the open towards the steaming ocean. Concern became fear, but she believed all would be well as the pig would not follow her onto the sun-baked rock.

Catching her breath, she turned to find the large pig had stopped, its head swaying back and forth. She could hear her friends and companions shouting but could not see them. This had been a lark. When the pig retreated she would rejoin them and there would be a good story to tell.

Craack. A noise not identified caught her attention. Turning in a circle, she realized she had come close to the ocean. The rotten-egg smell of sulfur arose from the nearby steam, blowing over her, blinding.

Craack. The moving lava, deep beneath the spot where she stood, had cut out a shelf under her feet, unseen, and with sudden collapse an entire section of hardened lava crashed into the boiling water.

No, no, she screamed, as the heat hit her. Clawing her way to the water's surface, she screamed, but the hissing of steam hid her cries. Thoughts of how could she make shore and safety quickly faded for the temperature around her rose above human endurance and the scalding began.

There, ahead of her, coming towards her, a rescuer. Where had this person, a young woman, come from? This girl was not one of her classmates, as she shot towards her, swim strokes knifed seamlessly through the water, her long black hair flowing as a dark wave, seeming unafraid of the fiery lava's endless onslaught as molten rock cooled into new earth. Chrissy, within the churning cauldron, felt a lulling warmth; she reached out to touch the girl but found herself pulled into an enraptured embrace, a fragrant kiss to her mouth, and as Chrissy closed her eyes and felt her body being drawn down into the depths, the young girl whispered into Chrissy Iolani's mind, into her last living thoughts: '*thank you, child, for your sacrifice.*'

29

Y ou want to borrow the *Island Clipper?*"

"Well, how about as a rental? I see four of these sitting around idle," said Hunter, waving his arm around the small basin, "and I could use one for a quick, short jaunt and the *Island* looks like it's in the best shape."

They were standing at the dock edge looking at two tethered

flying boats, bobbing lightly to the passing shallow wake of small craft, and two other of the Boeing 314A flying boats which had been winched up a recovery ramp sitting like quiet giants, their propeller mounts under tarp for protection. Hunter, in his old Navy uniform, played the role of a procuring officer to a vague agency of the U.S. government that needed a plane quickly for a classified mission. His subterfuge had led him into this conversation with Pan American Airways Regional District Manager and sometimes chief pilot, Christopher Philip Lang.

They both stared at the silent *Island Clipper*, the tail marked with its identification, NC18613-27. The two men bore opposite emotions, the chief pilot melancholy, Hunter eager as a dealmaker, now understanding what could make Tommi relish her life of shady commerce.

During the war, the U.S. Navy and the Army Air Corps had impressed into military service the Clipper airplanes operated by Pan American Airways. Stripped of passenger comforts, the flying boats became bare-walled supply and troop carriers beneficial because of the plane's long range capabilities.

"It is my understanding," stated Hopewell, knowing the answer, "that Pan Am has basically mothballed the Clipper fleet; that they will be sold off for shorter runs or maybe scrapped or cannibalized for parts."

"Yeah, that's true," admitted executive Lang, somewhat disheartened, being a tenured pilot from the China run. "Our Clippers are now obsolete, some say, less safe than what I hear these new Lockheed Constellation long route haulers will be. Hell, I hear that there might be a future where those German Me-262 Swallows, that came out in '44, might be engineered to someday have an airplane carry passengers using jet engines, going over 250 knots. Unbelievable but, hey, my Dad didn't believe a plane could fly the Atlantic, and Lindbergh overcame that impossibility, and now Lindbergh's an advisor for us at Pan Am, so maybe he'll get us the latest."

Hopewell began pressing.

"The *Island Clipper* is just sitting here; the Navy has released it, but Pan Am doesn't seem to want it, so a quick trip carrying a heavy cargo could be arranged. Correct?" He paused, not looking at this corporation executive, who seemed unsure of his own employment future. "Not only lease the plane for a week," Hopewell continued, "but perhaps hire a consultant to provide all the needed pre-flight maintenance and red tape clearances? Perhaps even someone who might like a cash contract as the pilot?" Hopewell looked out into the harbor, inhaling the water's pungent fish and ship oil smells, avoiding Lang's eyes, letting the suggestion hang there.

He could see, across the bay, salvage crews with crane derricks still pulling up unexploded ordinance from the harbor's shallow bottom, residual yet deadly reminders of the December 7th attack five years earlier. Just that long ago, he mused, a world was torn apart for geo-political reasons now so vague, greed or power or both. He had never had a taste for either the uniform or the battles that had been thrust upon him. Maybe this rescue of a statue would be his last battle, the consideration of 'saving the world' still a disbelieved notion, not yet an accepted fact in his mind.

The pilot overcame his nostalgia and went for the bottom line.

"Everything's in limbo but possible, I guess," replied Lang, his mood buoyed, sensing an economic enterprise that might be advantageous to his pocketbook. "You'll need to crew the ship. Normal crew was 11 but maybe you could do with less, a pilot, co-pilot, navigation, flight engineer, maintenance. Yeah, I might be interested, if the bucks are good. My job here will be ending soon."

"How about you provide pilot and navigation only? No need to over-staff . Quick trip. Cargo haul only. I will be supplied with a co-pilot/mechanic of sorts." That's what Tommi had told him, and besides, she had committed to providing some front-end funding for the trip until lounge owner Sheftel could help cover some of the costs. This recovery operation would make the Red Tiki a very expensive statue, and Hunter would not have taken one step for its retrieval if it weren't for the dream-like sexual intercession of the young Hawaiian girl, calling herself Pele, and asking him to help as the whole world's existence depended on his actions. He would have ignored the wild story of war gods on the loose and the destruction of mankind, but his whole body seem to be effused with a gloaming spirit, not a malaise of evil, but an overwhelming euphoria of clarity, that what the young girl had told him was indeed the truth, no matter how improbable the story.

He was not in control; instead there was an invisible force giving him direction toward an unknown outcome. Two conflicting concerns faced him. First, Hunter did not feel like any one's champion, and he intended to make that case again when he next saw this child-woman of Polynesia, if somehow and some way he could communicate to her. Second, he was scared for each day he felt parts of his body harden. He was turning into something non-human.

Pele at the party; but she was not a goddess to toy with.

30

I n the heady post-war winding down of military affairs, the 'going away' — back to the mainland — parties at the Red Tiki, now sans tiki, would have been legendary, if anyone could remember much of the festivities, the morning after. Such an occasion was this night known as the 'Rescue Our Tiki' sendoff, which brought together all concerned plus a few supportive fans of the tiki's presumed totem magic. Other parties added to the evening's crowded and boisterous atmosphere. Friends of Jim Michener gathered to send him back to the States. Sheftel worked the bar but kept an eye on Jimmy's table crowd. His hope was that if Michener ever wrote down the tales and histories which Sheftel and Tiki Shark had spent the last several weeks recounting to the naval writer about Hawai'i, at least Sheftel's name might be spelled correctly, and better yet, the Red Tiki Lounge and Bar would somehow, like Mark Twain's tour of the islands in 1866, gain larger prominence as a landmark tourist destination from a witty paragraph or two. Sheftel, through his own life struggles, seldom mentioned, and of dubious repute, had grown to realize that to achieve success, beyond being the chief bottle washer and overseer of the till, a bar owner had to be the shill, the hands-on barker and promoter.

On this special night, and to cover the recent influx of thirsty crowds, Sheftel begrudgingly had added one more bartender, a twenty-one year old kid, calling himself 'Dutch' after the knuckleball pitcher Dutch Leonard, even sporting a Dutch tattoo on his arm to cement his wartime nickname among his navy construction buddies. The kid had run ship commissaries for the Seabees and was willing to work bargain wages. "I need to make extra money,' said Dutch, "I plan to go to the University of Detroit, maybe apply for that new G.I. Bill," referring to the 1944 federal legislation providing an assortment of benefits for the returning serviceman, from college tuition and board to low-cost home mortgages. Dutch speculated that maybe someday he'd buy one of those $8,000 Levittown starter homes. To Sheftel, the young man did the job well enough, and talked smart, so he sent him over to Michener's table to keep everyone happy with a free pitcher of beer. Sometimes gratis reaps surprising dividends, but they better spell my name right.

Over on the dance floor and up on stage, unique jam sessions kept the sounds flowing with a mixture of jive jump and Hawaiian slack-key serenades. Hilo Hattie, the singer/actress, dubbed the Sophie Tucker of Polynesia, flaunted an exaggerated hula while singing one of her signature songs, "The Cockeyed Mayor of Kaunakakai", featured in a Betty Grable — Victor Mature movie, *Song of the Islands*. This was a send-off for her as well, her cruise ship departing two days hence to commence a year-long mainland junket of the supper club circuit, as everything Hawaiian, in 1946, seemed to be the new craze. After that she would move on to Hollywood to take another bit singing role in a slapstick movie. Among those accompanying her music and comedy shtick was the house band with two other musicians, the youngster piano player Martin Denny and a slack guitar player by the name of Gabby Pahinui, a part-time city sanitation worker.

To round off the local celebrities in the mix, sittng at a table with buddies was probably the most famous of the locals, Duke Kahanamoku, Olympic swimming champion and movie star in his own right with 20 movie credits from 1922-1933, including one film with B-Western up-and-comer John Wayne, another Duke. At this point in his life, Duke K. was serving his fourth term as Sheriff of Honolulu City and County, and the Red Tiki was one of his favorite off-hours hang-outs, a place where sinners and saints could meet on neutral turf with everyone having fun, as it should be. All firearms respectfully asked for and checked at the door by the hefty bouncer, Mister Manaa.

"Who's that solo guy watching the band?" shouted Tiki Shark over the festivities.

Sheftel was busy pouring multiple drinks and setting them out on the serving tray for his night shift waitress, a dish-mop haired floozy named Brenda, whose freckled breasts overflowed her stained blouse. Brenda made her harried impatience known to all by shouting insults to her regulars, bustling her hips through the crowd as she aimed toward a table of thirsty customers who were rising vocally to the sloshing point.

"Don't remind me," said the octopus, assembly-line drink slinging Sheftel. "I told you he was coming. Don the Beachcomber himself."

"He gonna buy you out?" Tiki Shark, at the bar, nursing a grape soda pop.

"Or open across the street, who knows? Said he was on vacation to visit all the islands but still wants to visit with me in about a week. I can tell he's on a location scouting mission. I'm getting my damn ulcer kicking up a storm trying to guess his strategy. Wish I had my lucky tiki to pat."

"He sure is watching Mr. Denny play; think he's going to steal your musicians away?"

"Probably."

"Why don't you just have a showdown, divide up the business on the islands?"

"What, dueling pistols at 30 feet?"

"Naw, you know, more civilized. A dart game. Shoot pool. I don't know, maybe cut a deck of cards, high card takes

Honolulu, loser gets Maui. Nothing happening over there."

Sheftel stared at the kid, shaking his head, again accepting the fact that the world of cutthroat business would never be the young artist's forte.

"You're loco. Risk my whole business on the flip of a card? I play poker, I know the odds of the blind draw." Sheftel hustled into the bar well to fill another waitress order.

As much as he growled and cursed, Sheftel had to believe the possibility that superstitions held merit, and why not, better than nothing if he could be immersed in the glow of good fortune to save his business. It was now costing him an arm and a leg to rent some damn airplane to go hop scotching across the ocean in this wild search, with any results perhaps already too late, but so be it. The return of this red tiki, *his* red tiki, Sheftel kept telling himself, might through some mysterious mumbo jumbo solve this Beachcomber problem and the chain's intrusive goal of restaurant-bar expansion. And if he could not stop a mimicking island-themed hang-out, perhaps he could sell his tiki for the big bucks — for his a monsoon rainy-day fund — and take early retirement, though that was not what he really wanted to do. No, above all, he needed his tiki back to ward off evil spirits, including other restaurateurs.

Tiki Shark, with soda pop in hand, walked over and casually threw himself down in a chair, uninvited though not dismissed, at a table with Tommi and

Hunter, quickly noticing that ex-Commander Hopewell was employing his best investigative demeanor to question their new flight passenger, a Mr. Baran. Black hair greased back from his puffy face, the man was certainly no recent war-weary veteran, but a civilian of some sort, Tiki Shark observed. Viewing everyone as a potential art critic, the artist concluded that the guest was a businessman who thought too much of himself.

As Hunter asked his questions, Tiki Shark noted that Baran's brief responses and smiles were directed more to Miss Chen. Somehow, he felt off ended by the man's attempt at flirtation with a woman Tiki Shark admired, sadly for him, from afar. Still, being an artist and expert on the nuances of body language, Tiki Shark sensed in body mannerisms the strained tension existing between Tommi and Hunter, more so tonight than usual. On other occasions he clearly saw how the two of them unconsciously found positions of close proximity. Now for some reason they were standing off as their tense postures suggested strained emotions. So many interesting dynamics in play with those three sitting at the table, noted Tiki Shark, like circling predators, like angry goblins dancing, and the young artist pulled out his sketchpad to capture that wild image.

To the on-going conversation the businessman responded, "Yes, I will provide the work gang to load and secure your statue."

"And the cost to us?" asked Hopewell. Since he had just met Baran, he sought to understand this new wrinkle of the offer put forth.

"Miss Chen and I have reached a business accommodation; I owe her for past services, and this can be the easiest method of repayment."

"And these workers are...?"

"Six of them will join our trip. I know of a ship that is in port for a couple of weeks and the captain would find this subcontract work beneficial in keeping his crew occupied. These men can earn extra money rather than throwing away their pay or even making an unplanned visit to the city jail for some indiscretion."

"Okay, if Tommi is vouching for you and your services are free, I can't say no." He looked to Baran and then to Tommi, waiting for one of them to blurt out the answers to unasked questions that boggled his mind. Something was not right; who was this guy? Hunter had never heard about him, and what was his real relationship with Tommi, business or personal? Baran was older, but did that matter? *Whatever their side deal, it doesn't matter to me, for all that I care… how can I object, I who am not in his right mind with strange unspoken conversations from a strange young girl, agreeing to find the red tiki, some sort of war god? Find the tiki, save the world, no problem.*

"How many do we have going altogether?" Hunter asked Tommi.

"Let's see. You, me, your pilot and navigator, Mr. Baran and his six. I have two of my people joining us; one of them has flying experience, small planes and transports. He'll sit second seat as co-pilot. The other has some mechanical experience and will help with refueling for the return trip."

She paused, looking hard at Hunter. "They are both Japanese, if that bothers you?"

"We're all now buddy-buddy, right?" Hunter finished it off with light sarcasm, "So long as they get the job done." His comment surprised him; was it over for him, the war and its enemies, those propagandized animosities, memories of ugly death, himself seared by grave wounds?

Was the previous hate really buried and new allies formed? He seriously wondered how he felt and what gave him pause in his old attitudes. Had making love to a bronze-skinned woman, the girl calling herself *Pele*, humanized him? By the taste of burning lips and fused bodies, was the color of skin now inconsequential? He shook his head at these unsettling and heated musings and replaced them with mental math.

"That's thirteen in our party. "Then, there are weight load considerations, like the barrels of aviation fuel for the return flight, knowing we won't find a gas pump in the middle of the South Pacific. Any other equipment?"

Without mention to Hunter, Tommi had calculated weight load of the *Clipper's* flight back to Honolulu. With a full fuel tank, and a 400 pound statue aboard, there was a max cargo allowance of 9,700 lbs. available, the exact weight of a Fat Man atomic bomb like the one dropped on Hiroshima and of similar dimensions to the one, she hoped, the Russians might steal. The airplane would be right at its limits, a dangerous situation, which left Tommi definitely concerned. Perhaps she could talk Baran into stealing only the triggering mechanism. At any rate, her priorities had changed: the bomb came first, the statue second, if at all.

She returned from her musing to Hunter's question.

"Mr. Baran will be supplying deep diving equipment if necessary, and a small size lift, pallets, ropes, and a collapsible boat with outboard that can be reinforced to carry heavy weight. Everything for lifting and securing something heavy like this statue." *Or even a Sherman tank, or a bomb,* she pondered to herself. "Also, not counting the plane's life rafts, three small inflatable runabouts of our own with quiet motors. We will need these for scouting out the location of the statue on the *USS Southard* in the atoll among all the other derelict target ships. We will stay in contact using that new radio system I got hold of, they call the units 'handie talkies'." She looked to Baran and received his nodding agreement.

Above all they were in a rush. The atomic bomb test would likely take place on July 27th according to her sources (cleaning people in the Operation Crossroads Honolulu staging area), and their flight plan had them at the Bikini Atoll early on the night of the 24th, leaving a two day window, just enough to carry out their plans. Tommi and Hunter in two collapsible rafts would seek out the USS Southard to set up the statue's move. Baran and his group to arrive with the barge boat to take off the statue. That was the story she explained in strategy to Hunter. In truth, Baran and his group would go off immediately to reconnoiter the bomb's location, not the statue's. She would keep Hunter distracted by sending him first to do surveillance on the headquarters of the Operation Crossroads command. By the time he returned, the bomb's fate would have been decided, whether stolen or sabotaged, and there would still be time remaining to likewise extract the statue, perhaps. On this trip, her desire for revenge might trump promises and friendships.

Yes, if she could, she would honor the agreement with Sheftel. She continued to worry quietly about the bomb and statue and their combined weight for the Island Clipper. It would take a long path of acceleration to gain the proper lift. The sea could not be choppy. And there was the fuel required for the return trip. If the extra weight, ate into the fuel reserve, she had a back-up plan of landing at the Kamakaiwi Airfield on Howland Island, an abandoned Naval Air Station. Her military quartermaster sources informed her that hundreds of barrels of aviation fuel had been left in fuel tank farms to rust and leak. How typical of the wealthy and wasteful American government, and what serendipity for us, she calculated.

Tommi excelled at logistical planning and felt comfortable with this operation. So what was driving her direct participation in this dangerous trip? It would be so simple to stay back on Oahu, be only the middleman, and collect a fee. She felt within herself an undercurrent of uncertainty as to what she really wanted from this adventure. Wealth and revenge held much value, but the anticipated satisfaction already seemed empty and they had yet to take flight.

Also it seemed to her that Hunter was on his own hurried deadline. Unsettling to herself, she felt confused about Hopewell's sudden urge to launch this crusade for a stone monument that any local sculptor could easily knock off with a replacement. She saw something new in him, intensity, like an explosive fire from fuse to brilliance, and she didn't know if his revitalization was in her best interests. For two years she'd had him under control, alcohol-anesthetized, but now she was mystified as to what was driving him, knowing only that this 'born again Hunter' all began with an unfamiliar girl showing up. Chafing, she moved back to the logistics at hand.

"I'll start a master list of passengers and our equipment."

"I'll get you a total weight of what my people will be bringing," offered Baran with his best, most amiable expression.

"Hey, don't forget me," chimed in Tiki Shark.

"You're not going," said Hunter.

"Yeah, but you need documentation. I am the artist of the expedition."

"This could be dangerous," Tommi, gave him a smile of genuine concern. It was a dangerous trip, she even believed, if not foolhardy.

"I missed serving my country in time of need, at least let me serve the Red Tiki Lounge & Bar. It's my home away from home, after all."

"Sorry, buddy," Hunter gave the boy a brotherly pat, "it's a 2,500 mile flight, anything can go wrong. You have a future as a famous artist. You don't need to take chances."

Tiki Shark began to pout; then, looking away from those he thought were his friends, he saw that angel-like face in the crowd.

"Well, Commander Hopewell, I think you are taking chances yourself."

They all followed the youth's gaze to the very young and striking girl walking towards them.

31

W ho's the hot dish?" Baran's earthy appraisal put the ax to any future physical interest Tommi might have had in this Soviet spy; the man, she affirmed, was a basic lout. Still, she had to put in her dig.

"She is Commander Hopewell's latest fling." Tommi knew nothing about any previous romances the man might have had, but derived a minimal pleasure in seeing Hunter wince.

Tiki Shark put in his two bits. "She seems to be pure Hawaiian, doesn't speak any American. Very strange that she targeted you, Commander. Where did you guys go the last time?" The insinuation was a lame joke ignored.

His question to Hunter remained hanging, as Hopewell felt those urges of a drawing power flooding his mind. *Was all that she said true?* Her presence reinforced an unreal dream he sensed in which he was only a small part of a larger puzzle. To 'capture' a statue before it might come alive, before Hunter himself might become stone: who would believe such a tale?

At least they would communicate between minds, silently, not permitting everyone else to join in.

Not so. She focused on the table, blew a chewing gum bubble while they stared, and popped it with great pleasure before she spoke. "Hi, geezers, what's the show? Great band sounds. Do you be-bop the floor, Hunter, honey? Or are you a dead hoofer?"

They were dumbstruck. Furniture mogul Baran heated to the teenager's perky sexuality. Tiki Shark wondered if he could talk her into posing nude; and Tommi noticed that the girl had dropped the luau sarong persona from her last bar visit, fooling them all it seemed, and now had bounced to life as some type of nubile bobbysoxer. The girl wore a tight white blouse hanging over a pleated skirt, her hair in a stacked, braided bun, drawing one's gaze to her long neck and flawless skin. Her shoes were white and brown pumps, and seemed new. The girl took in Tommi's appraisal.

"Went shopping today. Bought killer-diller stuff. Had to pack for the trip."

"Trip?" cried several voices at once.

"I'm coming along. Hunter says I am a... it's a big word... 'cultural representative'; that I know my Polynesian lore."

Tommi exploded. "You can't be serious, Hopewell. We can't take this... adolescent with us."

Both women exchanged examining stares before the girl spoke, very crisply, hardly the immaturity of a high school girl. "Ease up and don't flip your wig. Do you all know how to handle the tiki, to avoid the wrath of the gods; how to properly chant the spells, wrap the tiki in Ti leaves and O'o nuku'umu feathers to give it a safe journey? Besides, Hunter and I have reached an understanding. Isn't that so, baby?"

All Hunter could say was, "What's happened? You've changed... your personality... You are so... modern."

"Modern, that is a good word. For you to be successful I had to understand your world; no reason to dwell among the ancients. Just required finding a knowing spirit of these times."

Baran finally overcame his nasty thoughts and rose to act the gentleman.

"I don't think we've met. I'm Peter Baran, and you are?"

"Please call me Pele." They shook hands, and Baran looked to his hand, extremely warm, tingling. A good feeling, he thought.

"Pele? Like the goddess of volcanoes here in the islands?"

"Earth and power, one and the same, that's me, buta little out of sorts; all this 'modern' is wacky stuff." She turned back to Hunter. "Letting you know as Pele travels far from the security of her earth home, like over water, her power can weaken, and she may become vulnerable." She actually fluttered her eyelashes at him. "You will have to be my hero, my champion."

Incredulous towards this crazy girl, Tommi spoke firmly. "I still say she can't come."

Hunter understood that he was being led on this journey, to an unknown future, with the path set before him, with no say, no control. It was so implausible;

who would believe him? He touched his hardened leg, now feeling a numbness in his side. He accepted his fate, for he had no choice.

Hunter gave Tommi a look of sincerity that she had seldom seen in him, a truth in pain.

"I trusted you with making these trip arrangements; trust me on this."

She did not have time to answer, for Pele spoke with a giggling laugh.

"Come on, big daddy, let's try some of this dancing. Isn't that a Benny Goodman song? I haven't danced in… well, not with shoes on." And she laughed again, pulling the surprised Hunter from the table, leaving the rest unsure of this coquette who had just steamrolled over them, and bounced away.

"Is she for real?" A valid question from Baran.

"I don't know what is going on," answered Tommi. "She is — different — today. There's more to this, but I don't know what."

"As long as it doesn't interfere with our plans," Baran's voice took an ominous tone, a warning inference.

"What plans?" Tiki Shark took a noisy slurp from the last of his soda pop.

"Nothing," fidgeted Baran. "I just want to help recover your statue and get paid."

"Paid? I thought Tommi paid you?"

"Figuratively speaking, yes. We are talking job satisfaction."

Tiki Shark felt the conversation die away, especially so when another surprise visitor approached their table.

"Miss Jingu, excuse me… Miss Chen. And how are you doing? I hear you are mounting a rescue attempt to bring back our island tiki mascot. Good aloha if you do that. Also, good *kouun*. That's the word, is it not, Miss Chen?

Tommi glanced up, not so much in concern, but cautious to her own plans. Nothing must go wrong.

Tiki Shark's vision of Duke Kahanamoku surfing — "If anything I

can say, his sidewalk art is always a wonderful conversation piece."

32

She made the introductions.

"Gentlemen, let me present our illustrious Honolulu Sheriff,
Duke Kahanamoku. I believe, Sheriff, you probably know Peter
Baran from all the Community Chest projects he supports."

"Indeed I do."

"And our resident artist, Tiki Shark."

"Yes, our island's true hip cat. I am fortunate to have one of Mr. Shark's paintings hanging on my den wall near my bar, even if the caricature of myself surfing seems to have changed me into some sort of scaly sea creature on a souped up motor powered surf board. As if there will ever be any water motorcycles. If anything I can say, Tiki Shark's sidewalk art is always a wonderful conversation piece. May I sit down and join you?"

Uncomfortable with being in close proximity to a municipal police presence, even though the Duke's position was more honorary than gun-toting, both Baran and Tiki Shark took the intervening moment to say goodbye with excuses for their quick exits, the furniture store owner off to gain an early night's rest, so he said, and Tiki to return to his booth out in front of the bar to see if he could sell his creations to the lounge patrons who might have misplaced their artistic propriety in these late hours.

Once settled, the Sheriff got to the point.

"I need a favor, and one from someone who can get hard jobs accomplished quickly... Miss Jingu."

Tommi did not flinch, nor did she deny. The war was over, buried secrets were bound to become porous and percolate to the surface. Certainly a worldly man such as Duke Kahanamoku, with his local contacts and access to police records, could have heard enough scuttlebutt to put two and two together about her earlier amateur career in black market dealings, and, to a lesser extent, espionage.

"And how may I help? I am but a simple business woman, a bookkeeper."

"And if that is so, I was but a simple beach bum with a piece of wood to ride the Waikiki waves to the amusement of haole tourists."

Yes, they were both none such.

He continued, "I have heard, from many sources, that you are the obtainer of goods. Several of those contacts say that you are able to pick up surplus war materials that the military no longer needs and at cut rates. Here is my problem. I will be leaving next week on a goodwill tour to California. Seems they are trying to start up a West Coast Surfing Association, something like that, and want me to give a few pep talks. Put on a demonstration. Challenge me to see if I can stand up on one of those short boards they're experimenting with. Damn problem is I am getting too old and the waters off Santa Monica, and worse south of San Francisco, are freezing. I don't need pneumonia at my age. So, I've read where some high altitude pilots wore some sort of rubber or elastic covering to keep their heads and upper body warm, somehow insulating, keep the body heat in.

"Miss Jingu, or rather Miss Chen, I need you to find me upper body covering gear that can keep the cold water out, and better yet have your girls from J. Chase Fabrics make me something to my size. I will compensate accordingly, but not too much out of pocket."

"You realize I am leaving the day after tomorrow to rescue Lyle's statue for its overblown sentimental value?"

"Even if you are absent you do have, do you not, a warehouse full of seamstresses and workers that could help me?"

He seemed to have his own wired grapevine. No one, except Hunter Hopewell, knew of her tie-in with J. Chase Fabrics. She gave over to that thought. Maybe Duke had talked to Hunter, seeing if he had the military connections to get this headgear he wanted to go surfing in, and maybe

Hunter thought she could take care of the request. Hunter gains quid pro quo with the local Sheriff : yes, possible, she considered, that does build bridges within the local constabulary, friendships that in the future would help a gumshoe detective like Hunter Hopewell. She didn't know if she should be angry at Hunter for leading the Sheriff right to her for sourcing, or if she was pleased that he had confidence in her abilities.

All good feelings slipped away as she saw this Pele girl putting the clutches on Hunter as Gabby Pahinui eased out a slow dance on the slack key guitar, and someone lowered the ceiling lights.

"Yes, Sheriff, I will make an extraordinary effort to either find or design what you are looking for."

"Mahalo. Just make sure it fits me like a glove. And perhaps someday I can reciprocate and give you some help."

"Yes, perhaps someday," said Tommi, thinking to herself that what she really wanted at the moment was to borrow a service revolver from Sheriff Duke Kahanamoku and clip the snuggling couple on the dance floor.

It was one-thirty in the morning and the Red Tiki Lounge and Bar was going through its final clean-out of empty bottles and repulsive debris. Any surviving patrons had an hour earlier stumbled out to various endgames of street-side vomit or quickie orgasms with blurred strangers.

Lyle Sheftel was doing his cash register count and closeout when he heard the thumping from above, and could well explain the sound. Muted gasps interrupted by loud squeaky springs and the jumping slams of the metal bed against the wood floor reverberated down from the offices and small apartment of Hopewell Investigations.

Lucky bastard, thought Sheftel with a smirk of lechery, the guy has everything going for him. Hunter Hopewell has caught the world and is riding it like a bucking bronco. There was more truth in that thought than the bartender could ever imagine.

33

Tommi and Hunter stood watching as the last of their equipment was loaded onto the *Island Clipper* and Tommi's two Japanese 'employees' boarded.

Pointing to one of the Japanese men, Hunter asked, "What about this Sad Sack? What's his story?"

"War's over but not for him."

"Is he going to be dangerous? I'm not taking a chance. This trip is crazy as it is."

"Pilot Shigeru Mori, once a lieutenant, is only a threat to himself. He flew a Zero off the carrier *Hiryu* in your Battle of Midway. A pretty silent guy, all to himself. What he's willing to tell me is that he is ashamed that he did not die for the glory of the Emperor. Apparently he could not protect the bombers he was sent to escort for an attack on the aircraft carrier USS Yorktown; he then decided to crash his plane into the carrier, but he was shot down; his plane pancaked into the sea, he survived, knocked unconscious; and woke up in the ocean as his plane started to sink. After two days floating he was picked up by an American cruiser and sent to Pearl."

"And how did you get a hold of him for your devious purposes?" Hunter did offer a smile, a compliment that surprised her. She just could not let him stay in a good mood.

"I bribed one of your people to bring me a list of prisoners that were being interrogated."

"Bribed one of my flying squad?" His anger flared at such a betrayal.

"No, not your team of cowboys, but within your Intelligence Section." She gave him back her own smile. "Men, a long way from home, have weakness of the flesh and of the craps games."

"So, why did you pick this Mori? "

"Access let me know which prisoners were going to mainland POW camps, and more importantly, intelligence reports let me know their pre-war and combat skills. Those who had value to me were mislaid off the prisoner tally lists and by bureaucratic error released on work detail parole from the Hickham stockades. Mori as a pilot, his value lies in knowing about flying all types of planes, and I needed someone who could make unscheduled cargo runs inter-island. I scrounged up an old DC-3, and Japanese military pilots are — those still alive — excellent at night flying. He has been a great help, but still has this death-wish, says he's lost face for living and is disgraced. He has no desire to go back to Japan. On this trip he will prove useful to us as plane mechanic or pilot relief in the cockpit."

Hopewell did admire her pluck, her ability to make the best of the limitations of her sex, but as much as he wanted to treat her decently, and the more he tried to adjust his attitude, the more she liked to grate and rattle his chain.

"Okay, that's your call. You keep your two buddies under control and let's get this crate in the air."

Hunter expected death at any moment as the lumbering *Clipper* took most of the outer harbor waters to gain aerodynamic lift. Because of the morning darkness he could only sense the plane heading for the seawall where the racing out-flowing tide met the choppy ocean waves which, if hit at the wrong angle, could bounce them like a laundry washboard and plant them nose first into a whitecap. Wet and dead.

He felt the surging engines, gritted his teeth to the shaking vibrations.

In an instant they were over the stone barrier, rising up over small boats with running lights leaving harbor security to seek the deep water fishing grounds before the sun edged the horizon for the new day. In a slow arc, the plane made a sweeping turn and flew southwest slowly gaining altitude, and thank god, none of the tied-in cargo shifted or broke loose. Their filed flight plan had them scheduled to land in Guam, but with a slight change in compass heading, two hundred miles out they would approach the Marshall Islands and the Ralik Chain, a group of small islands, more rock escarpments barely above the water line, consisting of eroded volcanic calderas, one being the Bikini Atoll.

The Island Clipper in pre-war configuration

Before undertaking this adventure, Hunter had double checked on all the statistics on his ride he now hunched in. The *Island Clipper* was a work horse airplane. With the Boeing Model 314A the *Island Clipper* provided a 4,100 miles flying range, and Bikini Atoll fell into that reachable radius.

In peacetime, pre-1941, flying on the Island Clipper, 77 passengers would experience first-class luxury comfort with a crew of eleven. In its heyday of modern 1939-41 travel, the Pan Am Airways route, for example, could get a passenger one way from San Francisco to Hong Kong and would make the trip in six days. The cost: $670. San Francisco to Honolulu was 19hours. To the specs for this adventure, the wartime conversion of the *Clipper* was exactly what the tiki recovery team sought. The passenger seating from the forward galley back had been years earlier ripped out to ferry either soldiers or military equipment, and one passenger door enlarged to accept the fit and weight of a jeep, heavy stone statue, or — as Tommi and Baran knew — a Fat Man type atomic bomb.

The netted cargo of Mr. Peter Baran's complement had been loaded the night before. The Pan Am ground crew serviced the plane and, topping off the fuel tanks, packed the hold for the return flight with pallets of aviation fuel barrels, 4,000 U.S. gallons, under the supervision of pilot Captain Lang and his navigator-engineer, introduced only as Spenser, a grizzled, bearded-man, two arms full of nautical tattoos. Enough fuel had been computed by Spenser to bring them back to these islands with a slim margin of safety. No detours, however, said Spenser, and he laughed at his black humor before disappearing into his forward cubbyhole.

Likewise, pilots and navigator were located at the front of the plane, on the second level up by a stairway in the nose, and with a mimic salute to the old seafaring days of the wind sailing Flying Dutchman clippers, the airplane cockpit in the Pan Am *Clippers* was called 'the bridge'.

For all, it had been an awkward departure. Baran's fellow passengers gave Hunter a worried pause. They were a rough looking lot who kept to themselves at the back of the plane, sitting in bolted down metal chairs or lounging on the stored and softer heavy-duty rubber rafts.

The whispers among their clique Hunter recognized as a Slavic tongue, guessing it was Russian. He accepted on the surface, at least, that they were all allies from the same world war. This could not be said of Tommi's two companions, both Japanese, each with unknown agendas. She had given Shigeru Mori a moniker since his real name was dead to the world; he became, simply, 'Shiggy'. Introduced as the co-pilot and dressed in civilian khaki garb, he would sit second seat next to Captain Lang. Because of the language barrier, his words were limited to the occasional '*hai*' and non-committal grunts with intent focus on all cockpit gauges, as if he were just learning how to fly. Hopefully, Hunter prayed, he was merely re-acquainting himself with the control mechanisms, ready to step up in case of an emergency.

The other man, introduced as Ishiro Honda, aka 'Ish,' found his own corner in the open cargo hold. Quite skinny, rickety and undernourished, he boarded the plane carrying 16 mm camera equipment and immediately began shooting film footage when allowed; the 'Russians' cursed him away, indicating no photo work in their direction and their desire for anonymity bothered Hunter even more. Tommi, not forthcoming as to her intent, must have decided to document this adventure for some future celluloid matinee, though he caught a glimpse when Baran made a quick hand expression to his 'workers', a silent finger slash across the throat, to indicate that this raw film footage might not see the inside of a darkroom.

34

Of them all, in this air transit, Pele drew the most attention. The Russian men, watching her wander the cargo floor, exhibited blatant carnal lust. This she ignored, ignored them totally, an insult to their masculinity which drove them into a leering caucus of dirty jokes, as Hunter presumed, of what might be possible with this young girl in their hands. Keeping control of the situation might not be within his power and he had no idea what he ought, as tacit leader, to do if an incident occurred.

Tommi gave Pele, who was not paying any attention to her either, a surly look followed by the best condemnation stare to Hunter as if to say, 'how could you cradle rob?' He could only throw back a weak smile. They would inhabit the close quarters of the passenger compartment for at least four flying days, coming and going, where bunk beds could be folded out from the walls, privacy provided only by curtain dividers, so an unspoken truce fell into place between Hunter and Tommi, so that at least aloud Tommi would avoid making snide comments about the girl. As they soared among the clouds, Tommi sensed a new development in Pele's demeanor towards her boyfriend. They had indeed been an odd couple, but Pele began to seem less goo-goo, kissy face, as soon as the plane took flight. Not stand-offish or distant, but now treating the ex-Commander with, what was it, *tender respect?* Even looking up to him, deferring to his direction… indeed not as the lover but the leader of the expedition. And just when Tommi thought she had Pele dissected as a male-crazy nympho with a father figure crush, the girl would go from silly innocent schoolgirl to high priestess of Delphi.

Pele, oblivious to all these random stares, even ignored the airplane bouncing on the air currents, and the loud vibrations of the four powerful 1,600 horsepower Wright Twin Cyclone propeller-driven engines. She curled up in a chair in the passenger compartment, and seemed to hide any anxiety of flying, burying herself deeply into current copies of *Photoplay* and *Movie Screen* magazines, along with a single *Time* Magazine, 1946 May, which happened to feature designer Elizabeth Arden as that week's cover story.

To no one in particular, Pele spoke, not looking up from her perusing, "Do you think I am like Gene Tierney playing Laura in '*Leave Her To Heaven*'?"

Hunter had no idea. Finally Tommi, having seen the film six months earlier at the Bijou on Market Street in Honolulu, smiled in light single-drip sarcasm, "Only, my dear, if you act insanely jealous with murderous intent, and I see no opportunity or event here that could make you that jealous." She shot a tart gotcha look to Hunter Hopewell.

Pele then looked up, at Baran who was napping nearby, then at both Tommi and Hunter, and replied sweetly, "But I can be oh so murderous." Her smile matched her words. She put down her movie magazine, picked up a comic book, turned to page one and quickly became deeply engrossed. Tommi stretched to read the title, "Superman Vs the Mad Nazi Scientists."

Tommi, strolling past Hunter, finally had to express amazement in a whispered voice.

"What is with this child-woman you've latched onto? What is your story, Hopewell?"

"It's a long story, mostly confusing, and…"

If he were about to try the unbelievable truth out on her, he had no chance, as one of the Russians unleashed a loud, expletive shout, and came forward to retrieve Baran, gesticulating wildly with a revolver in his hand; as Baran followed the man out, first Hunter and then Tommi went hustling back to the cargo area at the back of the plane.

"Whoa!" yelled Hunter. "Whoa, point that thing down." He tried a litany of negative words before landing on 'Nyet! Nyet!" The Russian pointed the gun at some of the packed cargo, as Baran made his way to the location, himself angry and out of sorts.

"Seems like we have a stowaway. My fellow saw movement in that container there." He took the pistol away from his man, but in turn aimed at the target. "Come out, before we begin putting live rounds into cargo that may be dangerous for all of us."

With a lump of movement, Tiki Shark poked his head out, and chirped plaintively, "Don't shoot; it's just me!"

The Russians exchanged words, Baran gave back the pistol, and the armed man returned to his angry buddies, all throwing off dagger glares at Tiki Shark, at Hunter and at Tommi.

Said Baran in a cutting tone, "My man wanted to throw you out the plane, but I told him we were all friends. Correct?"

"Yes, yes." Tiki Shark sweated his fear, though the cargo space was chilly from their altitude. "Yes. Friends. Amigos. Comrades; that's it. Comrades."

After this excitement there was a settling down of passenger nerves and a return to their 'first-class' cabin chairs. Tommi and Hunter chastised Tiki Shark for his careless behavior, but such reproaches held no weight considering they were out over open ocean and one could not be sent to their room without supper.

Only Pele gave the young artist a supportive smile and told them, looking at Hunter, "I have a boar pig, Kamapua'a, whom I cherish for his desire to serve me. You have a seer who can create parchment drawings of the beyond but can't see himself. Who calls himself, *mano kanaka* or *Ukanipo* [shark god of Hawai'i]. Such lesser gods will protect us." She smiled again at Tiki Shark and resumed her reading, playing with her hair to see if it might roll and fold into another movie star look.

Tommi whined out, surrendering to her exasperation.

"What part of 'crazy' am I not getting here?"

35

From time to time, pilot Lang or the engineer Spenser would wander through with a nod or a short conversation as they inspected the plane and stretched their legs. Hunter had to bring in Tommi to bolster a story plausible to the flight crew as an explanation for this long distance trip to the lower boundaries of the South Pacific: to acquire new technology products to replace electronic vacuum tubes. Mechanically minded people like the flight crew knew that the technology of the war was pushing the industrial world towards jet propulsion-type planes and new gizmos for a few wealthy homes, like an entertainment box called tele-vision. These coming newfangled inventions required sources of power and connectivity to transfer data quickly.

Tommi, at a dock-side meeting while they were loading up *the Island Clipper*, let it be known to the pilot and engineer that while the cover story was to retrieve the stone door greeter for the Red Tiki Lounge (most drinking scene regulars of Honolulu haunts were now aware of the theft), the true mission was to land near Bikini Atoll to rendezvous with two Army electronics technicians from the Baker test section of Operation Crossroads, and pick up crates of 'surplus' electronic gear, with an unusual name of 'transistors', that would otherwise be destroyed. There was a growing market for these goods, explained Tommi, at high mark-up resale to Japanese firms who were shifting from war production materials, no longer an option, into whatever a consumer, American or Asian, might be willing to buy. Small radios without power cords required this 'transistor,' and she showed them what looked to be a cumbersome prototype, casually nodding her head in the direction of the two 'mysterious' Japanese passengers, both of whom looked thin and frail. She hinted that Ish and Shiggy were coming along to verify the quality and viability of these cut-rate transistors, while the Russians were supposedly hired as stevedores for the toil of heavy lifting and loading.

Pilot Lang, whether he believed the story or not, gave a shrug of acceptance, happy with the hefty upfront fee for flying passengers to and from safely. For those who loved to take to the skies, Lang would hardly have refused the opportunity.

The wide world of the South Pacific and Asia still ran to the rough and tumble, as he well knew. On his own, back in the 1930's when the *Clippers* made the Far East runs, he had ferried across the Pacific in unmarked containers small shipments of jade and early dynasty porcelain, spoils out of the ashes of the Chinese civil war, seeking new homes.

Hunter could only look upon Tommi's two Japanese passenger acquaintances and, under his breath where no one could hear, whisper harshly, "Those guys are P.O.W.s!" He knew the gaunt look well; he had once strangled a starving Japanese soldier on Guadalcanal who looked just like the 'pilot'. The resemblance haunted him and made him uneasy.

"Repatriated. They are only trying to get home. And they have talents we might need. They help us and I buy them a freighter ticket back to Tokyo."

"What's with the camera equipment guy?"

"Ishirō? Ish? Not sure yet. He said he was good. And film footage might have value." She was thinking of filming a stolen atomic bomb for blackmail purposes. Hunter knew her too well.

"Don't get any bright ideas for sticking around to film the bomb blast. We're going to be long gone with our red tiki before the 26th."

To her view, if the bomb could not be grabbed there was that photoplay opportunity.

"Film of the fifth atomic blast in history would be worth a small fortune. All reporters on the atoll will be under military quarantine censorship, probably for at least a week. Lowell Thomas [famed journalist] would pay top dollar to get a jump on the competition."

"Jeez, woman," said Hunter exasperated at her mercenary zeal, "You'd probably have sold film of the bombing of Pearl Harbor, from the Japanese pilot's perspective."

"And Movietone would have paid a pretty penny too, without batting an eye."

36

The *Island Clipper* lumbered on through the day towards another night and their island destination. The galley had been stocked sufficiently and, as punishment for his sneaking on board, Tiki Shark found himself tasked to serve simultaneously as cook, steward and K.P. Breakfast had been hot coffee (hot plates were working) and something Hunter had seen before, Army issued Spam, sliced, and wrapped around cooked egg and rice with some green veggie-looking strip ['*nori*' said Tommi, she but did not explain]. Pele had two of the small servings while the Russians gobbled up sizable platefuls, again saying little, but drinking vodka like water at every meal. Lunch had been cold ham sandwiches and Coca-Cola. Dinner consisted of heated foil-wrapped pork chops and pineapple stirred into steaming white rice.

It was after dinner that a new crisis reared its ugly head. The Russians were restless and back to shouting, pointing fingers at their companions and up to the front of the plane at the paying passengers. Baran translated their displeasure.

"They are accusing someone of drinking up all their vodka."

"I don't drink," Tiki Shark immediately retorted, proclaiming his innocence.

"I am a scotch man myself," was Hunter's deadpan answer to such a ridiculous accusation. "Besides, if you've noticed, we've stayed clear of the tail of the plane."

"We need them sober anyway. You need to keep them under control, Baran," said Tommi. "And they need to get some rest if we are soon landing in the dark to start this operation."

Baran, taking unkindly to being bossed by a woman, stalked off to calm his underlings.

Wondering without guessing who might have been hitting the Russian crew's vodka, Tommi and Tiki Shark gave a cold stare to the resident lush.

"No, not me. Look." Hunter went rummaging in a canvas knapsack he had squirreled away under a pile of Mae West life jackets. He pulled out a bottle of good scotch.

The bottle was empty.

"No, no," came Hopewell's fainthearted cry. He dug further to pull out a second bottle — empty — and a third, the same. In anguish, his body tensed. His crutch for steady nerves gone, he felt weak and nauseous, empty inside as his bottles. Without looking at the others he followed Baran, hoping beyond hope the Russians had overlooked some of their own hooch.

"If he needed three bottles of liquor to weather this trip," said Tiki Shark, not flippant and not as a joke, "The Commander must have fallen into his own personal hell."

"A long night and day ahead for this job and chances of his having withdrawal tremors over the next few days will indeed be hell on him, and on us." Tommi had no idea how she should act or respond to his alcoholic need, which she herself had encouraged.

Tiki Shark had picked up one of the empty fifths that Hunter had flung aside in his sobered despair.

"Hey, look at this. The tax label wrapping on the scotch cap. The seal isn't broken."

Both of them checked the other two bottles: empty yet unopened. They slowly turned to Pele, who had been ignoring the recent conversations, her eyes focused outside, absorbing the sight of a black universe full of stars and constellations.

"To use his strength he must be clean in body and spirit." Pele said, turning towards the two. "I care for him, to save us. Are you his friends? Do you not care for him?" Her eyes had rested on Tommi, drilling her deep with this accusation, one that Tommi could not answer.

Part Four

The Bomb

37

Tempers strained, after dinner, Baran, Hunter and Tommi held a war council. The passengers, all of them, were to try and sleep, as they would be arriving in the vicinity of the target (11.5833° N, 165.3833°E), Bikini Atoll, at about 2 a.m., the date July 24th. The strategy was to come in low, and with a clear and calm ocean anticipated, land on gentle swells and taxi to within a mile of the atoll before launching the rubber boats. They had agreed that the first trip in was to be stealth reconnaissance to locate the *USS Southard* and the statue. They'd brought with them their own invasion flotilla: four small rafts with outboard motors and one 10 man raft requiring assemblage, with a wooden slat floor designed to carry heavy equipment, unknown — Hunter, the 'bomb package' assumed to weigh 15,000 pounds plus. The heavy raft would be adequate though it would sit low in the water, and a jerry rigged lifting cradle had been engineered to ease the 'package' into the plane.

It was their plan that on the initial scouting trip they would go in different directions: Baran and four of his crew would travel in stealth, within the lagoon, counterclockwise in search of the ship and, being heavy, would enter from the atoll mouth near Eneu island (Tommi knew the Russians would immediately head to the bomb's location); Tiki Shark was drafted to escort Tommi and Pele using the direct approach in a smaller raft, one easy to scrape over the reef, their entry point halfway a land spit between Namu and Bikini Island itself. Finally, Hunter, in his old navy field uniform, in a third raft, would search out the central command headquarters or otherwise gather the latest scuttlebutt on Operations Crossroads. The two Japanese friends of Tommi's, Shiggy and Ish, would stay behind with two Russian sailors, and with Pilot Lang and Engineer Spenser, would begin the arduous fire brigade line of pouring the jerry cans of aviation fuel into the plane for the return trip.

The timetable agreed to: first day of the operation, the 24th, gain their bearings in morning's darkness, then return to the *Clipper*; second day, on the night of the

25th into dawn of the 26th, make the snatch. With the bomb's detonation three days off, set for the morning of the 27th, they expected that any sort of security for the abandoned and derelict ships would be lax and spotty. Those on duty would be attending to the observers as they set led into their viewing bunkers on off shore ships and fine-tuned their cameras, optical telescopes and measuring equipment, with no activity at the detonation site, that being under radio controlled guidance from afar. This particular fireworks show, by the U.S. government, was being called 'Baker', according to Tommi's sources within the military bases back on Oahu. "Able" had been the plane-dropped bomb on July 1st. Many more tests were to follow.

In case for some reason in the process of searching for the statue they were discovered, they had manufactured international press credentials and would explain that they were trying to get close to shoot their own film of the underwater atomic explosion. Hunter was set to step in flashing his expired Navy investigative badge and take charge if anyone became detained for unwarranted intrusion. Yes, the cover story and backup extraction plan were thin, but it could provide confusion among the authorities for enough time to slip away and back to the *Clipper*. After all, who would believe they flew all this way just to steal a stone statue because they were asked to do so by a bar owner, urged on by a ditzy teen-ager tagging along just for kicks, with a lusty crush on an older man, proudly boasting of her semblance to a goddess? The absurdity of it all weighed heavily in Hunter's mind, as well as the possible danger, now knowing that some of the Russians were armed. And strangely, for reasons which he could not then fathom, the Russians were carrying helmeted diving equipment and a bulky water-proofed camera, saying it would be part of their cover, that of last minute underwater fixes on leaking ships. Was he fearful for the success of the operation? The palsy of his trembling hands was not imaginary, but for what reason?

The plane and its passengers were bouncing towards midnight. Darkness enveloped all the nooks and crannies of the *Clipper* and everyone not at the bridge controls began to slip off into slumber to the propellers' throbbing lullaby. The Japanese co-pilot was now flying the craft as Captain Lang and navigator-engineer Spenser slept on a four-hour short shift in the crew quarters.

Before trying to find his own sleep to stop his growing shakes, Hunter recalled another strange event of the day. Tommi, when she seemed to have time on her hands and was not staring out the window at the great blue expanse above and below, busied herself with sewing. Hunter found this amusing, since he did not see her as domestic, and he had to inquire.

"See this material, it is called neoprene. Made by DuPont. The military bought up the manufacturing plant when your war started, the object being to replace rubber where exports from the Dutch East Indies were blocked."

"Blocked by your people," Hunter said as a comeback. "So this is that synthetic rubber stuff ?" He picked up the material; it felt like rubber, elastic and light in weight.

"Instead of a rubber replacement it became an entirely different product. I believe that there could be a lot of commercial applications. I found a whole warehouse stacked with sheets of what you call 'this stuff '. One just needs a product and a moulding extruder and there you go, instant whatever."

"And this Halloween outfit you are sewing on?"

"My second prototype. This is an entire suit, for the water."

"Water gets in between two layers, and a body warming occurs, which helps for swimming in frigid water or at great depths. I made a helmet cap and neoprene shirt for your buddy, Duke K, for some surfing demonstrations he's conducting along the California coast. He's going to give me a report back."

Hunter took from her lap what looked to be a pullover rubber poncho shirt.

"And you think this will provide protection?"

"We shall see. More experimenting is required, perhaps different densities for underwater compression. As you well know, I am a woman to grasp many opportunities." She eyed him. "I don't need a man in my life to be accomplished."

"Well, this new suit is too small for the Duke."

"I made it for you. As an experimental guinea pig you will do fine."

"You know my measurements?"

"You are an easy read."

"I don't plan on going anywhere wet and cold."

She laughed. "This is for when maybe you get pulled in over your head and sink down into the abyss."

What could he say after that?

Now, thinking back on that exchange, as he felt the plane's engines thunder on, knowing they would be descending within two hours, Hunter Hopewell wondered if he was entering the crest of the abyss.

He dreamed of Tommi's warning: saw a gurgling pool of fiery lava circling at his feet and rising to lap around his neck, sensed the abyss, and the terror of finality, until a sharp nudging brought him groggily into sweaty, cold consciousness. His head beat in tune to the plane's heavy engines thrumming.

Later, suddenly awake, Tiki Shark leaned into his face and whispered in his ear,

"When I was trying to find a place to hide yesterday, I ran across two small, unmarked crates. I looked inside one box. *Dynamite*. What do we need explosives for?"

38

Everyone tended to their assigned tasks, their ears popping as the Island Clipper began its descent, sensing a loss in speed, knowing, perhaps dreading that the ocean runway was fast approaching. From Tommi's J. Chase Fabrics manufacturing shop everyone donned appropriate clothes for the operation. The Russians looked like Navy yard workers in overalls and jeans and denim blue shirts. The women and Tiki Shark would attempt to look non-descript in naval tan khakis, while Hunter eased back into his officer's uniform; unworn for a year, it had required tailoring, to let out the waist and shoulders. Strange. Where he thought he had lost weight during his hospital stay, his old clothes barely fit: a tightness of the fabric, as if he had somehow expanded.

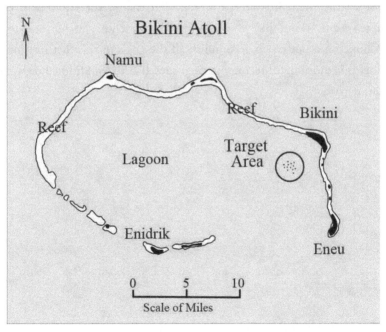

Tommi thought Hunter looked, what's the right word, 'regal' in uniform. In their earlier confrontational meetings he was the Authority of the hated government. However, this morning, presently on her side at least in this adventure, she began to see him as a fellow traveler and, with this Pele girl's fawning over him, began to notice the masculinity showcased in the uniform. She saw, and was surprised, as his eyes met hers, that they seemed intent, yes, he had the shakes, but they seemed less noticeable as he grimaced towards the mission, stretching his stiff arms, anxious.

Those occupants of the plane remaining behind and those of the three boats synched their watches and checked out their communication gear. They would be employing the new Signal Corps radio transceiver called a 'handie-talkie'[later called 'walkie talkies']. Because these had been introduced in the last year of the war by corporate Motorola to be an improvement over the back-carried radio units, they were still not in general circulation and Tommi felt fortunate for having gained a crate of them in a midnight sale from a warehouse clerk with slippery fingers. The radios were somewhat cumbersome AM devices using high voltage dry cell batteries with a range of 1mile over land and 3 miles over water. She had to give a quick demonstration on how they worked and warned everyone to avoid being immersing them in water. Everyone felt that if the equipment did not perform to specifications, they would rely on their watches, with set times to return to the Clipper and not try to accomplish all the goals in this first mission. After all, besides this morning of reconnoitering, they had two additional days. Locate, get it out, depart.

39

Earthshine on July 25th, more than the crescent moon dipping above the horizon, gave light enough to paint the wave crests with reflective silver slices, and in the distance the reefs put forth warnings with a noisy carpet of white foam. The Russians had gone off on their wide swing to the lagoon entrance while the two smaller rafts made their way to the sandy spit of land between islands Namu and Bikini. Here they beached, and at the edge of the landing hauled and skidded their rafts to the quieter and calmer side of the atoll. They maintained silence because even at this unnamed spot of sand they could see by its bulk shape an unmanned monitoring bunker only a hundred yards away. Noise or seismic sensors might be operating.

They were ready to launch again into the lagoon, with Hunter off to ferret out information from any military presence and Tommi, Pele and Tiki Shark to search out the *USS Southard*.

"Che'!" Tommi's long suppressed Japanese surfaced with her surprise. *Damn!* She passed over the binoculars she had brought along to Hunter.

"I see about thirty or more black shapes out there."

"That's the target zone. They look to be in a wide circle, probably with the bomb below whatever ship is in the center." He passed off the glasses to Tiki Shark who added his two cents.

"How are we going to find one ship among this cursed fleet?"

"Start on the outside and look only at all the smaller vessels.

I am guessing they want to test the bomb impact against the largest vessels, and those will be closer into the detonation range. When you find it, get back to the *Clipper* as soon as possible. We'll take the statue out tomorrow night."

"Ja, mein fuhrer," Tommi replied. "As if we have not discussed our strategies thoroughly." She was more nervous, knowing the Russians were going to make for the center of the circle of vessels, to steal or sabotage. She had not prepared herself for the final scenario of her revenge; what would be Hunter's reaction to the

Russians showing up with a bomb? She accepted that Baran might have to use threat and muscle if necessary, and demanded of him pledges: nothing more than strong arm; no extreme violence. Perhaps she was being a little naïve about what this prize meant to the communists, but the scales of justice as she saw them would be balanced.

Trying not to dwell on what might come to pass, staring into the darkness, she saw Pele dancing in the sand. The young girl then ran to Hunter and kissed him deeply before he launched his raft into the water and started the small outboard motor. Tommi almost thought she saw the couple glowing in their embrace, but dismissed it as the moon appeared beneath low clouds before dipping out of sight. It was an ocean night nowhere black as pitch as one might expect, for defused light played everywhere, wisps of phosphorescent organic strands on the ocean current and a billion plus blinking stars pinpricking the canopy above.

"She is of the land," said Tiki Shark.

"What?" Tommi had been staring at the odd couple.

"Pele is the mother of the earth. When we were flying above the water didn't you see she was lethargic and quiet. The sea is the domain of Pele's brother, Ka-moho-ali'i the shark god, or her water sister, Nāmaka. Now she is back on land, as little as this reef is, and I'm guessing, she has re-charged her batteries."

Tommi feigned disinterest to the nonsense. "Come on, Tiki, let's get this inner tube launched. And go get that girl — and she is no mother of anything. Childish tart, most certain, I will give her that." She wanted to say 'bitch,' but caught herself, realizing her tongue was about to mouth 'witch', not knowing if one or both were the apt description, and wondering why she felt such animosity.

40

Baran could not believe his good fortune. An hour after they had left the *Island Clipper*, with four strong sailors as his crew, their awkward, barge-like raft had reached the landing craft, LSM-60, identified by heavy cabling that held the bomb, which was dangling somewhere below in the murkiness. As early as they had arrived in the darkness, they were hoping to find the site deserted and it was, yet bright with working lights, running on batteries, attached to the landing craft railings and pointing down into the water's deep blue. They could not see the bomb; one of the crew would have to be deployed as the helmeted diver.

Baran set his men to work and at the same time answered the cautious fear of his crew about the silence within the lagoon.

"They are not expecting anyone. And they are Americans. They come to work at proper capitalist office times." To himself, he was somewhat disappointed, for he had hoped they had not yet lowered the bomb into place since there were still two days to go before the planned explosion. If that had been the case, they would have come back the next night and tried to cut the cables and disarm the radio activator on the detonator. What he could see, or rather could not see, was the bomb somewhere beneath the water. His Plan B was not too much of a concern. He would use, with the cables cut from the landing craft, the sea to tug-drift the bomb out of the lagoon to the plane, and there, if they could not load it easily, sink the bomb in a hidden location until the Soviet intelligence trawler, whence he had gained his crew, could make rendezvous to retrieve the prize. Baran, confident, would adapt to make his plan work, and tomorrow night steal America's atomic bomb. All would be apparent when they showed up at the plane with their 'souvenir'.

Baran could care less about retrieving the statue for the Red Tiki Lounge. From this moment on, he would be in charge, not this weak Japanese girl.

First things first: the bomb.

"Let's get down there," he commanded. A tarp was pulled back to reveal the diving gear, one crate of dynamite with waterproofed electrical timer, and several military grade M-1s with ammunition. Baran came prepared for any eventuality and no one was going to stop him.

After one hour of looking, Tiki Shark, peering through the binoculars, pointed as if he had spotted a breaching Moby Dick.

"Thar she blows." The motorized raft headed towards what was definitely a destroyer-sized ship. During the previous hour they had passed by several larger ships: the German heavy cruiser *Prinz Eugen*, the Japanese battleship *Nagato,* and the Lexington-class aircraft carrier *Saratoga*, still floating after being damaged in the Able bomb test on July 1st. Tiki Shark saw marked floats indicating where submarines had been sunk to test the blast effects since the Baker bomb would detonate underwater.

As they circled their quarry, and identified the name on the stern as the *Southard*, Tommi turned the rubber skiff around to return to the *Clipper*.

"No, we can't leave," said Pele, her first words during this lagoon trip. "I do not see Kū aboard. Did you say he was supposed to be placed at the front?"

"I don't see the statue, Tommi," Tiki Shark agreed and pointed at ship's bow. "It would be a shame if we boarded it with everyone ready to move it, and it wasn't there."

She fretted at the situation but knew they were right.

"Okay, we board for a quick search. I will let Hunter know when we find it; then we go back."

"Yeah, not a problem," said Tiki Shark. "Besides, I don't see anyone around."

Tommi had noticed. For what was going to be happening in a few days, she thought it odd, no guards patrolling, no distant bustling sounds pre-reveille from the atoll's islands. Where she should be elated that all was going to plan, the feeling of discomfort rose instead.

41

Hunter covered his raft with a camouflage tarp, walked up the sandy beach to find a packed roadway, and started a nonchalant walk toward the few lights he could see a half mile ahead. Earlier, back on the *Clipper*, he thought he might find the officers' club on Bikini called the "Crossed Spikes" where even if it was shut tight as a drum this early in the darkened morning hours perhaps he'd be able to bribe a night watchman for a bottle of good scotch. Now, for some strange reason, he felt no urge to drown all his pains and anxieties. Mysteriously, if that was it, all hunger for alcohol and its cures felt... absent. When did that feeling happen? He laughingly accepted, not really believing, that it was probably in that last kiss from Pele. She tasted of heat, searing. In fact, since then he felt awake and alert, strong, and he stiffened his back feeling good, yet hearing a seam in his shirt tear slightly. From his muscles? Hardly, just lack of wear, he decided, and he trudged on, his smile ratcheting up his temperament. This was an adventure of the oddities.

After only a few hundred feet, as he passed by several concrete bunkers guessing they were some type of remote monitoring stations, he began to slow his jaunt, coming to the realization that Bikini Island was a ghost town. Even the open air officers' club he finally saw had the shutdown feel. There must be people around, somewhere. In the distance he could see ships of various sizes being launched, LSTs, whalers, and the small cutters naval officers used. Surprisingly, they were all moving away from the shore. Far in the distance, where it looked like star pips on the ocean, out there barely seen on the horizon, he concluded, there ought to be anchored the task force for the Baker test of Operation Crossroads. Unbeknownst to them both, he and Baran had the same thought that perhaps with daylight the navy and army personnel and the cadre of scientists would return to resume their scheduled work.

Somebody was coming towards him: three men in military garb, one with a carbine slung from his shoulder.

"Hold on," the armed military policeman shouted, not in anger or with the power of his weapon, but a mere challenge of sorts. "Who are you, and why aren't you at the evac dock?"

Evac as in Evacuation? Hopewell responded to this shore patrol with his prepared identity.

"Commander Hopewell, Intel Instat, JTFI Command, assigned to Admiral Blandy direct. I was assigned to make surprise field inspections, make sure that during the night everything on the island was sealed up." He held in his breath. He had flashed his expired I.D. badge, hoping the dawning sun in their eyes would keep them from closer inspection.

"Well, now," laughed one of the other men, dressed not Navy but in U.S. Army field khaki. "Guess you're going to be on the last cutter out with us. We're supposed to be the ones shutting and sealing the Baker test stations prior to the countdown." On closer inspection, Hopewell saw that the man who'd been speaking was an officer; at his casual tone the armed enlisted man relaxed.

Countdown? Hunter froze. Did that mean…

The other military man, a brother Army officer, held out his hand and Hunter accepted the handshake, trying not to let confusion cloud his expression.

"I'm Dr. David Bradley, and this is my esteemed colleague and senior, Colonel and Dr. Stafford Warren. Dr. Warren here is Chief of Radiologic Safety Section for the Task Force. Skipping the alphabet soup, the task force calls us RadSafe, but most of the grunts call us medical observers the 'Geiger men'.

Hunter, recoiling to a feared truth, had to get hold of himself and learn the on-the-ground situation quickly.

"Mind if I walk with you all a ways, before heading back?" Hunter sought to move the conversation forward to his head pounding shock. "I don't get the chance to talk with you… 'Geiger men', especially on what you hope to discover, I mean, in the scientific vein. I know we military intel people just want to understand how to survive, and yes, figure out counter measures. I mean after two Japanese cities got obliterated (Hunter flashed in his mind on Tommi's sadness at the loss of her parents), it is apparent that if there is an atomic war there will be no place to hide."

"That's an astute observation, Commander," said Dr. Bradley. "'No place to hide', I guess that's what we are really seeking to determine."

"Yes, do join us in our final prep stroll," said Dr. Warren.

"When you get back stateside, who knows, *Life* Magazine might want to interview you, some story like — 'I was the last man on Bikini before it became uninhabitable.'"

Their path led towards one of the monitoring bunkers facing the lagoon.

"I don't understand. You mean, afterwards, we won't be able to ever return to this atoll?"

"Oh, I don't know if I'd go that far," began Dr. Bradley lecturing, definitely a college medical professor in a previous life. "But this bomb, they call it 'Helen of Bikini', which we will be testing this morning is plutonium fission, and beyond expecting the gamma ray exposure rads similar to what we picked up with the Able test, a plutonium explosion might show us different characteristics, as yet unseen. My colleague believes there might be an increase in alpha emitters, highly more dangerous, and something we might not be able to quantify with the Geiger equipment we've developed so far. Shows you the rush of technology sometimes moves faster than we are prepared for."

The four of them, with the guard trailing, arrived at the bunker. Doctors Warren and Bradley entered, with a slight nod to Hunter, "You don't mind if we leave you outside? Rules and Regs, you know."

"Totally understand."

Hopewell turned to the guard, who raised his own question first. Now the protection of his VIPs had given him an uneasy break. The navy military policeman lit a quick cigarette, offering one to Hunter, who declined.

"Do you think any of this radioactive stuff, this plu… tone… e… um, will be worse than the Hirosh bomb? I mean on the Able test they had a whole navy squadron washing down the decks of the ships that survived and I heard scuttlebutt that these Geiger counters were still beeping off the scales. We have 42,000 sailors and soldiers either off shore here on a hundred ships or sitting over on Kwajalein. We're all going to be okay?"

The navy guard had Hunter's concerns, and then some. But he put on his brave officer front.

"Yeah, if the government says we're safe, we are." Even Hunter did not buy that sack of shit. He was anxious to get away, to flee back to the Clipper, steer clear forever of the Southwest Pacific. The U.S. Government did not know it but they were going to kill him unless he made his escape. Trying to go with the scientists here would blow his cover, and would not help Tommi and the others to flee. That dawning realization that he had to get to his radio pronto, gather in his own forces and make a hasty retreat suddenly became his number one priority. Damn the statue of the Red Tiki Lounge.

Matter-of-factly he asked. "You know, I just got posted here about three days ago. I heard our explosion was set for the 27th, and here it is the 24th…"

"Hell, where you've been? Oh, sorry, sir." The sailor M.P. blew out smoke as he laughed. "It is a little bit confusing I must say. Just like many of newbies who show up, you forget we're in a different time zone. International Date Line stuff . It's the 25th today, not the 24th if you were in Hawai'i. In fact, it was going to be held on the 27th. They forecasted a heavy storm in a couple days so they moved up the shoot by 48 hours. Today is the day."

Time zone change. Of course, Hunter wanted to kick himself; *how stupid, the simple mistakes that might get him blown up, irradiated to bloodied jelly.* Just then, the two Geiger-men doctors exited the bunker.

"Well, I don't want to keep you all," said Hunter, trying to mask his urgency. "Think I'll finish my inspection and make it back to the last water taxi. Say, when was the H-hour countdown? I heard several different times, one from the Officer of the Watch aboard my ship, and one when I landed here an hour ago."

"Think it was around 9 or 10 a.m.," said Dr. Bradley, not sure himself.

"The posting said maybe as late as 11 a.m.," offered Dr. Warren.

"Excuse me, sirs," offered the military policeman. "I believe it was 9:30 a.m. Heard we all had to be off island no later than 6 a.m., that's in half an hour."

"Must be right if he says so," laughed Dr. Bradley. "Only one more monitor to check. Say — Commander — ." Hunter was moving away from them. "I don't see your rad film badge. Everyone must be wearing one today."

"The badge?" He then noted each of the other men did have a sort of flat square like a political campaign button but more like a swatch of movie projector type film.

"It's a dosimeter measuring badge. More than 0.1 per cent of roentgen per day makes Jack an unhealthy boy," quipped Doctor Bradley.

"Well, that's our current thinking. After today, I think, there will be a surprise for us all," intoned Dr. Warren, definitely serious with concerns.

Hunter shrugged. "Must have left my badge aboard ship."

"Well, I carry a few around just because this does happen. Don't forget to register your badge number with your ship's O.D. Which ship you stationed on?"

As his mind could not recall any ships in the assembled task force, Hunter tried to parry the answer.

"I did have a scientific question, maybe just fear mongering. Some citizens in Hawai'i wondered if an atomic bomb blast could destroy the atmosphere, what did I hear — 'tear apart the heavens.'" That's what Pele told him. Hunter started again to move away.

"Hiroshima proved such a possibility in the troposphere for naught," said Dr. Warren.

"Though," countered Dr. Bradley. "the genie of the atom has been uncorked. We just don't know what it means for the human race."

Before the doctor's words ended, Hunter had turned a corner past a silent Quonset hut, and took off running.

42

The flowering sun etched the eastern sky's call to morning. Blackness over the last hour had faded in the lagoon as Tommi made her way carefully along the side deck passage toward the bow of the *USS Southard*. Tiki Shark took the lead, avoiding the various carved out holes left by the mounted gun salvagers, while close behind, Pele… eager to be reunited with her stone tiki, pushed the artist adventurer along.

A clicking noise from Tommi's handie-talkie radio broke the silence: a voice muffled by static. She had earlier discovered that chattering radio waves from other sources bounced around the lagoon causing distortion. Believing the voice heard was that of Hunter Hopewell she responded with her own acknowledging click and, speaking in a false baritone voice, the code word 'Op 1'. A static voice came back at her, indistinguishable, and before she could try again came the distraction that had led to this foray onto the ship.

"Here he is!" cried Pele.

Stumbling over cables, Tommi arrived to find Tiki Shark pulling off a tarpaulin. The statue had been laid down near the forward gun turret.

"They were probably trying to hide it from the admirals who would have just chucked it overboard as not meeting seafaring standards." The covering came off. "Behold, the red tiki."

The expression on the carved stone figure looked menacing, a look Tommi could not recall seeing before, but then she never really gave it much thought nor went in for the patting of the belly or feet for good luck. She believed in making her own good fortune and today's remained to be seen.

"The terrible god Kū," cursed Pele. Within the tepid tropical morning, Tommi could not see but sensed the girl Pele throwing off an icy stare of hatred at the silent form on the ship's deck. "I hope we are not too late to save your people and save peace for the gods."

Tommi dismissed the girl's hocus pocus mumbo jumbo. It was wearing. "The world will return to normal, and I am sure there will be drinks on the house, once your stone voodoo king is reacquainted with his pedestal in front of the Red Tiki Lounge."

Her radio chirped with another static call. If she could not hear Hunter, perhaps he could hear her and she let him know they were aboard the *Southard*. She gave out her location using several of the larger ships as a bearing, letting him know the minesweeper-destroyer was on the farthest outer circle of the sacrificial ships, one of those farthest from the bull's-eye target center. As if that mattered, thought Tommi. In two days, now they had located the statue, and if all went according to the plan, they would be long gone.

"What's that noise?"

They all listened. Two noises. A small whirring in the distance. Tommi realized Hunter was motoring his raft full speed towards them. The other noise? Closer. A squawking gull?

"Over here," called Tiki, directing her to the other side of the ship. A bleating goat, standing on hay, in a small pen, a water can barely in reach. Minimal food supplies.

"Poor baby," said Tiki, patting the nervous animal. "They're going to roast the critter, just for their stupid tests."

Hunter was shouting on the far side, and Tommi walked back over, as a panting Hunter ran down the deck towards her, his face disturbed, by an anger she had never seen before in him.

"The bomb! The explosion is today! Not two days from now!

Let's get out of here!"

"How much time do we have?" Tommi responded, not panicked, just trying to get her actions organized. She remembered her conspiracy. *Baran*!

"I don't know, maybe two-three hours." He moved around her with a glance to the stone tiki, no longer a priority. Lives were at stake, their own.

"I am not leaving Kū," came Pele's defiant shout.

"Oh, yes, you are," and Hunter lunged towards her in determination, giving Tommi a quick chance at the radio.

"Ops 3. Do you receive?"

Static, but then a squelched voice.

"Ops 1. You are clear."

"Ops 3, abandon your position. Your target is hot today. I repeat, your target is hot. Sometime this morning. Baran, leave immediately."

"You're kidding. We are taking photos."

"Now, immediate, or you will glow in the dark… or just be hot ash." Tommi wondered if radio technicians from the task force were picking this up, wondering who was talking, with a voice sounding female.

Hunter was approaching, carrying a kicking Pele over his shoulder.

"No, it can't be", came Tommi's gasp, noticing Hunter's change, he looking Charles Atlas brawny. Tiki Shark was right behind, dragging a reluctant billy goat, the bleating mixing with what Tommi accepted were ancient Hawaiian curses from the young girl.

"Did you get a hold of Baran and his people?" Hunter looking around. "Where is he?"

A siren whined across the lagoon. More sirens answered in the far distance, barely heard, from ships of the task force out of range, waiting to bear witness.

"Good God, we're out of time! We'll never get over the reef and out of here in time." He looked frantic, and finally, Tommi joined him in fear.

"What can we do?"

Hunter threw worried glances in all directions.

"Need to take deep cover in the ship. That will protect us from a direct blast. And we need to pray that this ship can ride the blast tsunami." He looked to a ship hatch. "This way."

"You cannot let the sky be torn!" shouted Pele. "He will live!"

"Too late, for the torn part." And Hunter led them hurriedly into the bowels of the ship. He took them to the aft crew berthing, pushed them down into a back corner, and started piling mattresses on top of them. "Just stay here, I will be right back."

Tommi anguished.

"Where are you going?"

Hunter was surprised, off guard. Was this sincerity, real concern?

"We've got to get Baran in here." He took away her radio.

"Where's he coming from? I'll direct him."

"From the bomb; he's coming from the bomb."

The statement hit Hunter like a bullet, and then the realization hit. Of course, they're Russians. They would want to take a look at the bomb. For Mother Russia. Spies. He gave Tommi an angry stare.

"You knew?"

Her silence was affirmation, and Hunter turned and ran, for what, to save a nest of spies?

He guessed he had little time before the blast. He reached the bow of the ship and yelled into the radio while fast scanning the lagoon, searching for them.

"Baran, you have to take shelter now! We are on the *Southard*. If you are near here head to us!"

Static, then a reply.

"We are going back to the plane!"

Hopewell cursed and clicked his response.

"You'll never make it." There, he saw them, with their raft bouncing and lumbering. Instead of exiting the lagoon where they had entered near Eneu Island he saw Baran and his people going the opposite direction. He must have realized the lagoon entrance was too far to reach; even Bikini Island where Hunter had come from was over 3 miles away. No time. Their raft shot straight toward the lagoon sand bar where Hunter and Tommi had beached earlier. Hunter yelled again at the inert gizmo in his hand. "Your craft is too heavy. You aren't going to clear the reef. There is a bunker where you are headed. Break in and hide in there, that will offer some protection."

The last thing Hunter needed to do, if time was left, was to secure his own or Tommi's raft. They needed a raft to escape the lagoon, to return to the *Clipper*, and a raft had to survive. By its rope, he began hauling his raft up to the deck. His new-found strength served finally a good purpose.

How fortunate, merciful in retrospect, that he stood at the stern, angled away from ground zero, and had just pulled the raft over the chain railing... when the world changed... forever.

43

Tommi screamed, her fears real. The survivors inside the ship, and they were survivors, heard no explosion, but a gonging punch of a sound wave, followed in an instant by brutal tugging of the ship, which rose, tore its anchor and like a skyrocketing elevator, the *Southard* rode a gigantic wave bow first. They all fell against the wall, now the floor, as they reached nearly 90 degrees, straight up. Tommi accepted that with one more degree in the uppermost listing, the ship would breach over onto her back, or turn turtle, and they would drown in a watery tomb, all her hopes and dreams washed away. Her last thoughts were to be not a prayer but, 'Sorry I deceived you, Hunter.'

All military, and all observers, including a large press contingent, foreign dignitaries, and yes, even a Russian military guest in attendance, recorded their private views of what the future of hell now looked like. It was a horrendous vision.

At 8:30 am (they were all wrong as to time), the Helen of Bikini plutonium bomb of the Baker Test detonated. There was no heated blast and sound wave as in the July Able test. Baker exploded underwater. The LSM-60 ground zero ship vaporized. The blast, like an exploding hot gas bubble, hit the sea floor and the air simultaneously. There would be no mushroom cloud; instead a huge water dome emitted skyward at 2,500 feet per second, later confirmed by the awe-struck scientists with their cameras filming, watching their measuring devices. A chimney column formed of churned sand and water and rose 6,000 feet, 2,000 feet wide, the top looking like a garden head of cauliflower, dirty white and ugly. All this happened within four milliseconds.

In the next second, the dome at the top, all two million tons of highly radioactive water, collapsed in on itself back into the lagoon, while the base of the frothy circular chimney moved out in a supersonic hydraulic shock of water pressure to greet the ghost fleet. Within the next eight seconds ten vessels sank in this immediate rolling blast wave and all vessels were washed over by wave or water spray, effused with intense alpha emitters and gamma ray radiation, making them uninhabitable, a fact the scientists would not discover until a month later, weeks after attempts at scrubbing decontamination by hundreds of vulnerable sailor crews had no effect.

Blanketed loosely under the raft, Hunter Hopewell found himself riding the roller coaster, clinging against the engulfing wave rush that nearly tore the small boat from his hands. As the Southard moved upward towards its apex, Hunter had the never-again view of looking under a geyser of foam before it rained back down upon him. But in that instant, between the billowing skyward bomb blast and the untouched surrounding blue sky with fluffy clouds of a beautiful morning, he saw something else, like a shimmering, a barely visible ragged line against the sky, and he thought, this is what the heavens — or another dimension perhaps — might look like if rent and torn.

Within that moment, his reasoning mind was betrayed by his eye, because he believed he saw a dark thing... something... out of nowhere, pulling aside with talon claws the miasma fabric of sky, crawling out... and taking wing, upward, away from the atoll, a mere speck of blowback dust on any focused camera lens. Vanished.

And then the angry cloud above him dumped an ocean upon his frail refuge, suffocating him into blackness.

44

The *Southard* did not glide back down the trough on the giant wave's backside, but rather fell, at least two hundred feet, plunging bow first before returning to the boiling swells, righting itself with side to side twisting. Everything that had been loose was flung as debris missiles through the wardroom and berthing bunks and only by the fortuitous foresight of Hunter burying them in mattresses were they protected, limited to light bruising.

Not all escaped so easily. A plaque once secured on the wall fell off to strike the top of the frantic mewling goat, concussing the creature into a dazed silence. Tiki Shark picked up the handmade, hand-scratched iron plaque to read: "*Exec H. Wouk + ensign 1st N. Rolla + crew survived Typhoon Ida — 15 Sept 45*"

"Well, guys," said Tiki Shark saluting the past crew, "Your ship just made it through an Atomic Tornado."

"Not quite," shouted Tommi, jumping to her feet. "This ship is settling. It's sinking."

Tiki now felt the slight listing and pulled Pele to her feet. They followed Tommi to make their escape and arrived on deck to see the cloud, still hovering, but having expended its energy, slowly misting into a rainy fog.

"Tiki! Here's Hunter. He's hurt!" She was at the stern, pulling on the raft to shove it off him, and did so with Tiki's help.

"Holy Buddha," came Tommi's startled reaction on seeing the man lying on the deck.

"Jesus H. Christ," Tiki echoed.

The man, Hunter Hopewell, was —

"He's scaly," Tiki saw cracked skin, but cracked in a design pattern, like overlapping leaves.

"The ocean bottom has sandblasted him!" Tommi had to believe that and then took in the whole scene. The blast had stripped him near naked, his clothes in tatters. There was more about his body — it had grown somehow, muscular, bronzed. What was he — was this what radiation poisoning did to the human body? She stammered out her concern. "Is he — ?" Alive or dead? No, please, a silent prayer, not dead.

"He has become one of us." Pele looked down on the form, and nodded a grim pleasure. "He will help us." Hunter groaned in a gurgling breath.

Tommi turned in rage on this siren sprite who had bugged her ever since she had entered the Red Tiki Lounge. "Damare! [Shut up!] You crazy kook — you — Bukkorosu! [I'll kill you!]" She even balled her fists and made one step in the girl's direction.

"You will not live if you touch me," said Pele, in a calm tone that only further enraged Tommi, and she took another step, but stopped when she heard Tiki's yell over-lap the hanging threats of violence.

"Double Jesus H. — You gotta see our red tiki!"

"It's destroyed? Good riddance!"

"No, Tommi," Tiki's voiced went into a dramatic strained scream. "It's alive!" As it was once shouted in that old horror movie, *Frankenstein*, 1931.

What? Tommi ran awkwardly through the passageway to the bow of the ship, balancing against the increased listing.

She saw no carved blooded statue.

Laying on the steel deck bow of the sinking *USS Southard* was a man, tall and large in breadth, deep brown in color — just the size and stature of what she saw in Hunter's transformation. Except this unconscious man was entirely naked, and in Tommi's shock of unknowing, she was sane enough to take in the view that the man was proportioned more than well. No small fig leaf for this guy, a palmetto leaf was more like it.

"The war god Kū has come to destroy," came Pele's cruel and odd observation.

"Wowie." Tiki Shark drawled out the word, seeing and not believing.

"We have to get out of here." They all turned to see Hunter standing, weaving to the ship's shifting. Tommi's mind, one step short of being unhinged, in that fraction of a second, before madness might descend, stared unabashedly at both men in turn. They looked identical, but the man on the deck had long black, stringy hair and was oily and smooth skinned while Hunter stood sand-scaly, rough, increased in girth, ripped out of his clothes, hips bulging from his boxer shorts, now too small, and she remembered when Hunter was in the Red Tiki Lounge with a hard-on in his pants. Daring to match that memory against the naked man, she could only wail out the double entendre which summed up the world in general: "What the fuck?!" Overwhelmed by this new reality, she fainted.

Part Five

KŪ

45

A spray of water, and the bouncing of the raft, brought her conscious. She leaned over the side of the raft and vomited. They were all crammed together. Pele sat back near Hunter, who directed the tiller on a wide open motor throttle, not at race craft speed but fast enough en route to the atoll's shoal, towards where they had first entered in the dark. The statue, now the live man, his head lolling, semi-comatose, half dressed in a loose fitting naval shirt and khaki shorts, stretched across the entire middle of the raft. Under him, trussed up, was the goat, looking miserable, if such animals displayed human expressions.

"I couldn't leave Billy to be dissected by lab quacks," Tiki Shark shrugged as he bailed out water with a large Folger's coffee can. "We have a leak somewhere, plus what comes in over the gunwales."

Tommi wanted to doubt her last memories. "Wha — -."

"Do you want the short or long version," offered Tiki Shark. "I asked all the questions that might eat away at your sanity. I can't wait to get to a sketch pad. I've got a wild imagination, but this all slips beyond reality into shit-hot fantasy but real life stuff, you know." He paused. "Well, yes, it really does."

"Give me a version that might just keep me out of a mental hospital."

"Alright, but let's go right for the loony tune story, and you can decide what to believe or not believe."

"I hope I'm just a passing tourist in someone else's nightmare."

Tiki Shark relayed his story in bursts while continuing to bail water over the side.

"Our young lady here is *actually* Pele, not just some kid named for a Hawaiian goddess, but her in the flesh, the main goddess of all goddesses when it comes to creating earth."

Immediately, Tiki put his hand to Tommi's mouth with a 'shussh' as she started to say something. "My story, however wild, go with me for a few minutes."

Out went another swoosh of the ocean. It seemed the rubber raft was filling faster than the can could empty it.

"She *is* Mother Earth. There are no other main gods around: they are all up at Olympus or Valhalla, playing god politics or out hiking cloud mountains or playing bocce ball. Who knows? And do you think the real Mr. God is around? Pele won't say much. Says He put up this blank canvas, but let them do the paint mixing and splashing, you know, creating mankind and all the animals. If you think about it, doesn't it seem right that we are all mixed up in colors, languages, and strange types of beasts with no rhyme or reason? Take the platypus for example and those dinosaur fossils. My guess is they didn't work out for some god's big plan of a zoo."

"Tiki, stay on track. What do we have here and now?"

"Okay, you're right, I did ask some far out questions, but you know, if you can ask a god, or goddess, what are the real answers about what you've been told in school, it was worth a shot." He noticed her hard stare.

"So, man does unto man and the gods give them their space on what we call Earth and everything's okay, except now we've gone and split the atom and are shooting off big kablooey bombs. And dropping an A bomb does something to all the balance, throws off the Yin and Yang between worlds. The bad gods and, what Pele told me, the nasty gods and their minions are bored because the good gods have them under control on their side of the heavenly fence, up there somewhere, but these bad gods can use an atomic bomb blast, its disruption of the lower cosmos, and slip over to our world. They didn't with the first bomb, the New Mexico blast, but that let them know they could, and the first boogie devil god came over with the Hiroshima bomb. Pele tells me with each of these heaven-rips, where the bad guys are coming through, she's trying to slip in her brothers and sisters to help. Unfortunately, she says, most of them have limited powers. They're minor gods. The big gods don't want to show up, yet. They want us to take care of this as our own problem we created."

Tommi was going to get through the 'loony tune' version just by remembering how Tiki Shark's art work exaggerated Polynesian folk art, and was so way out there — in baseball vernacular it would be *far out in left field* — and this was perhaps him creating a faery tale from his own misplaced brain cells. She gave him a fake nod that she was buying into what she had so far heard and tried to ask a reasonable question to the unreasoning.

"So, maybe, by my bomb count, there could be five evil spirits let loose on the planet?"

"Pele said there are those from the heavens, and there are those that man is creating."

"We are doing what?"

"This bomb spin-off, this radiation, is doing its own evil juju. Pele doesn't know the science, but she hears from her brother and sister, who are ocean dweller gods; they told her of seeing strange new beasts. Atomic-type beasts."

"Oh, Tiki, what are you telling me? That we have to bring in the United States military to beat them back to their own side, to where, some dimension we call heaven? Believe me, I carry no faith in that government, and they will never be the heroes in any story I hear."

Tiki pointed at Hunter, who was staring towards the approaching shoal and land spit with its monitoring bunker.

"Gods don't like government types either; they caused this ripped sky mess. But what about him?"

"Who? Hunter? What?"

"According to Pele, he's the one who is going to fight and defeat the evil from heaven's hell bringers."

"Hunter? Are you kidding?"

"Hey, just remember, I am the minstrel bard of this myth. Pele says Hunter is now a demi-god."

Tommi began to laugh out loud at the ridiculous stupidity of it all, but caught herself, this tall tale was only half told.

"What about him?" She gestured toward the native-looking man, who, she realized, had partially opened his eyes and focused them on her. That felt creepy; she felt odd, like his stare might undress her, might make her want to undress.

Tiki continued, the water up past his ankles. She felt the sides of the raft, flabby, deflating.

"This is where it gets really dicey in the story telling; even I have a few issues with Pele's rules of this game. Seems like no good, super big shot gods want to come over to help us."

"Except Pele, correct?"

"According to her telling, they told her she had to come over and take care of Kū, the war god, her responsibility. It was she who found a way to encase him in lava and stick him inside a tiki statue. She can't kill Kū, he can't kill her; they have equal power, but they can fight by proxy. Hunter versus Kū. Good armies against bad armies. But I think there's more to this than Pele is telling me, telling us."

"This guy here, definitely a six foot man, I'd say, was hidden in a nine foot stone tiki, whatever he is or came from, which I don't believe this nightmare at all, you know, because in any fight he would murder Hunter."

"My exact thoughts. Hunter is an armchair alkie navy man, probably signed up before he was drafted. Navy ROTC to avoid hard basic training. I don't think he would know his way around a firing range. He's just not a fighting hero. And I am his friend. I don't want to see Pele sacrifice him to make some point. These gods need to send in the high-powered cavalry throwing lightning bolts."

Tommi, regardless of whether she was hearing truth or fiction, did worry about Pele, whom she'd never trusted. The girl clearly had her own agenda, gods or no gods, and Tommi had no doubt that whatever scheme was in play, it offered no benefit to Hunter, to say nothing of her own welfare. Pele had just been leading him on, using his body, like a conniving woman might do, for her end purposes, and judging by the seriousness on his windblown, hardened face, and how he puffed his chest, it looked like he believed everything she had told him.

Shifting to a more comfortable position in the raft, Tommi looked ahead to their destination.

"What are those?" she asked, believing she could identify the forms on the sand.

"Bodies," answered Hunter, cold and empty.

"Some of those bodies are moving," Tiki noticed, and stopped bailing as they entered shallow water.

46

Hunter felt like no hero, no god, but if he was one, he was an angry god. He could not decide if he felt damaged or invigorated as he tried to wrap his mind around the surge of his changing body. Far more quickly than Tommi trying to process all that had happened, he accepted at face value that there were two worlds co-existing; he had to acknowledge that for him, all truth began at the moment when he believed that Pele was indeed what she claimed to be. Nothing written or preached in times past could be trusted; it must all be attributed to superstition created to allay the fears of the unknown canonized by the human beast.

A new world. A woman who could enter his dreams, a statue that could come alive, gave evidence that he was entering unknown territory, and like an explorer he would try to react favorably to new vistas. What he could not abide was betrayal, and as for Tommi, Tomoe Jingu aka Judith Chen, he saw how she had misled him, had used him to advance her own cause.

And what cause was that? Being paid well for access to bomb secrets? No, she already had a small fortune accumulated. He had to believe she wanted revenge for her parents, for the Japanese people, against the U.S., for Nagasaki. His American loyalty saw her as the enemy, while his loyalty to a friend, if that's what she once was, could lean towards forgiveness considering the angers she must feel over the death of her parents. He was just mad at her because she hadn't confided in him, even knowing he would refuse to allow it. But more importantly, she had to see the threat she had unleashed. The Russians were up to no good, and without a doubt she had aided and abetted.

The landing party exiting from the compromised raft saw that the Russian trawler crew lying on the sand were all alive, merely wave-shocked, and slowly regaining their senses.

"Where's Baran?" Hunter shifted his anger away from

Tommi, whom he decided to ignore from now on; he would go after this furniture store spy.

Tiki Shark found him still hiding in the bunker.

"Why, he's totally dry."

Baran exited, shielding his eyes against the sun's glare, staring out into the lagoon, where fewer ships could be seen, several in various stages of sinking.

"I ran to the bunker and fell in when the blast occurred. Barely made it."

One of the Russians cursed at him, and Baran responded with an angry declamation.

"If I were to guess at the translation, Baran," said Hunter with a sneer, "seems like you bolted for cover first, leaving your comrades to be drenched with this radioactivity. Hope they understand what you did for them."

Hunter turned to Tiki and in doing so had to deal with Tommi since she was standing by the boy's side.

"When we get back to the *Clipper*, I want you and her" — he pointed to Tommi — "to take hard soap showers with fresh water from the jerry cans. You've got to purge yourselves of this poison in the air and for sure it's in the ocean."

"Save enough water for you?" The question came from Tiki, not from Tommi, who stayed silent, knowing she had hurt him.

"No, something has happened to me. I can't explain it, but either I did not get irradiated by the stuff bouncing off my new skin, or I did absorb it, but it's like a tonic…"

"Rejuvenation?" Tommi tried to enter the conversation.

He stared at her, a hard stare.

"Re-birth. I can't go back to what you wanted me to be — the drunk. Call it rejuvenation or reincarnation; my eyes have been opened."

Tommi felt like crap.

"What about cleaning off our Russian friends?"

Hunter had entered a brutal phase of this new life: it was them or us.

"No, let them figure out what they got themselves into."

"One small point," offered Tiki Shark, staring out into the empty ocean.

"How are we going to get back to the Clipper? Our rafts are destroyed, and it seems we have lost the radios."

Baran joined the tail end of the discussion.

"No, I kept mine."

"Good," said Tommi reasserting her control in the situation. "I will contact the plane to bring the remaining life rafts."

Taking the radio from Baran she walked off , not wishing to witness what she knew was coming between angry men.

"Who is that?" Baran pointed to Kū.

Hunter and Tiki exchanged furtive glances, then looked to

Tommi to supply some form of rational answer, but she was down the coral beach barking orders for their rescue.

Finally, Tiki Shark took a shot.

"He's Pele's boyfriend."

"No, he is not," yelled Pele.

"Well, let's say, like a rock he dropped in, and we rescued him."

Hunter wanted to cut to the chase, throw out the accusation he knew was hanging there. To Baran: "Did you get what you came for?"

"What are you talking about?"

"The more I revisit the set up for retrieving a heavy statue, the more I can see all our trip logistics could handle the movement and heavy load of storing a bomb onboard the *Clipper*."

"Bomb?" Tiki uttered in astonishment. "This was an atomic bomb heist? Wowie!"

Baran held open empty hands.

"If that's what you wish to believe. As you see there was a missed opportunity." Baran would not deny what could not be proved in a court of law. Besides, the truth revealed here was not going to upset his future plans.

"And if you could not get the bomb, what was your plan; to do some sabotage?"

"A choice of last resort, if someone was that diabolical. As we saw the components were encased, no explosion would prematurely set it off . Perhaps some well-placed dynamite, might have destroyed the delivery boat, the wiring, caused weeks of postponement, and embarrassed the U.S. government to the world."

"Well, at least you did not get that chance," Hunter was surprised at the man's forthcoming answer.

"No, the chance was there. We just discovered that someone had sabotaged the saboteur, and taken out the wires of the detonator timer for the dynamite." The two men, fencing with words, absorbed what had been revealed; both turned to look at Tiki Shark, who in turn stared innocently seaward.

"Wonder how long it's going to take our guys to get here?"

47

One hour to be exact. In the noon time heat everyone had moved to the shady side of the bunker except for Tommi, who strolled the sand spit caught up in her own thoughts.

Two rafts approached one skippered by Captain Lang, the *Clipper* pilot, the other by Ishirō, the Japanese ex-POW. There was room for everyone, but the rafts were cramped, and messy as one of the Russian crew was throwing up his last meal into the water before boarding. Another crew member, perspiring heavily, looking sunburned, climbed aboard lugging a salvaged canvas container.

Cameras, realized Hunter, those sneaky bastards. The Russkies had taken photos of the bomb up close; that had to have lucrative espionage value. Hunter couldn't let that happen. And then he saw Ish with his hand held movie camera strapped around his neck, taking a panoramic swing of the lagoon. 'Damn', thought Hunter, 'this Ish probably, from a distance, has taken film of the bomb blast itself'. If he worked for Tommi, and he did, she could probably sell copies of the footage to the news people before the U.S. government raised their censorship curtain. Hunter gave a hopeless smile to all that was devious around him. So what could he do to set matters right; what could he do with the new powers Pele claimed he had gained?

A high pitched scream would give him one answer.

Tommi, still in peripatetic reverie, tried to come to grips with Tiki Shark's far flung tales of mythical history being no longer myth; maybe that naval historian, what was his name — Jim Michener — maybe he could better place sequences in order, move fiction to non-fiction, make it more palatable. The red tiki statue, which she had seen with her own eyes, had disappeared and been replaced with a living man, or rather the alleged god of war. He looked war-like, the man looked, manly. He sat on the beach, his legs folded like an American Indian's, watching and listening. Like watching prey. Several times he glanced her way, but he likewise watched Pele, who from time to time would say a few words to him, words only they could understand. Perhaps she was telling him who was the most tasty to try first.

And then, there was Hunter Hopewell. Tommi saw a different man in looks and attitude. Kū looked the handsome warrior, whereas Hunter, who had been attractive, now showed a worn and rugged facade, rock-like: a statue who could move. And did he not despise her? That's what she wondered; it seemed so apparent in his face. Over her washed a new feeling: guilt for being cruel, for belittling a man, destroying him by capitalizing on his faults, sapping his strength, just so she could create profit for herself. Was this really who she was? No, she was not a bad person. Guilt hurt her inside. She did not know how she could undo all the harm that she had done to him.

She tripped over a sand pile of dead coral and seaweed, and caught herself.

No, the seaweed caught her. Not seaweed. A coral claw, the size of two fists, gripped her ankle, and from the sand a creature began to emerge.

She screamed her heart out.

Everyone turned and gaped, not believing, least so Pele and Kū. They were indifferent, as in 'no big deal', or 'seen something like that before'.

"God — " swore Tiki Shark.

"Zillah!" cried one of the Russians, religiously crossing himself.

"Gorira!" [Gorilla] shouted Ishirō, grabbing for his camera.

At first focus, he corrected himself, "Kujira!"[Whale], and then, not knowing if the beast was of land or water, blended the two into a chant, over and over, "Gojira! Gojira!"

The beast was neither gorilla nor whale, nor a forgotten dinosaur of the Mesozoic Era, but a monster standing at least twelve feet tall, covered in pimple-like boils, head like a moray eel with mouth of spiked reticulated teeth, stubby arms with claw graspers, and a large tail, thick to thin, that flicked with a snap. It looked at the unmoving crowd, held Tommi upside down, shaking her, and began shuffled crawl steps to the ocean...until it was flung back, hit low in the stomach by the onrushing Hunter, a linebacker tackle, definitely a punch with a lot of force.

Tommi found herself launched in the air, and — *oof!* — when she landed, not gently but with a heavy splash into breaking waves, she struggled and ran from the water towards the other humans, then stopped when she realized it was Hunter going fist to claw, who had saved her.

The creature lashed out with its claw and made a chomp at Hunter's head with a snapping jaw. Missed. It was a punch drunk fight, as Hunter quickly noticed in his dodging and weaving. The monster, this 'Gojira!', the name he kept hearing shouted in the background, was like him: too new to its body, for it made awkward lunges, easy to parry. When one swipe raked across Hunter's back, there was no pain, just a scraping sound like across hard sandpaper, and with anger, he felt his body harden even more, armoring itself.

Hunter dodged again as Gojira made a charge, lunged to the side and under the beast, then jumped on its back, reaching his arm around the neck, beginning a choke hold that he knew would bring this vicious thing to its knees, if not its demise.

Suddenly, Hunter found himself yanked away and thrown to the beach, unhurt but definitely surprised.

Kū stood there in a wrestler's crouch, yelling at this Gojira. The beast gave off no hint at understanding the war god's language, and took a clawing one-two swipe which Kū easily side-stepped. Kū stopped in wonderment as if seeing the creature with new perspective. Hunter could only guess that the war god had expected to be responded to, given deference in honor of his exalted position. And when this did not happen, Kū's expression went from cautionary commands unanswered to anger, and with a quick movement, which Hunter saw in a whirled rush, Kū fastened upon the creature's tail and swung hard in a circle, like an Olympic discus athlete. The beast was, to its animalistic surprise, flung far out, a hundred yards into the ocean, from where it disappeared into the deep.

Hunter responded first.

"You imbecile! Why didn't you kill that thing?"

Kū offered only a death-look sneer to Hunter, as if baiting him to take one more step in his direction. Then, seen in his eyes the sudden realization that he was among mere mortals, and he turned his back on them all and walked to one of the newly arrived rafts to inspect this strange canoe.

Hunter saw Baran's surprised look at this recent fight, glancing first at Hunter, then at Kū, the Russian's mind possibly calibrating the muscular strength of each of them, trying to categorizing that his must have been some secret underwater creature the Americans created as a 'stealth weapon'.

At all this, Hunter could only shake his head with the frustration of having no clue of what he could do, except mutter to the survivors of the bomb blast, "Okay, people, let's scram this party." As if on cue, another siren sounded from the far side of the atoll, certainly an all-clear signal, but moments later as the rafts motored away from the shore, it was apparent to most that the events of this morning were not that clear at all.

48

T
hank you," said Tommi quietly as she leaned into Hunter, feeling his rock arm against her, no warmth, yet he did not flinch away.

The Russians in the other raft, with Captain Lang guiding the way, were all in muttered but animated conference, every once in a while looking to the sea, fearful of the monster's return. Another Russian was heaving his guts out over the side.

"Okay," Tiki Shark, the brave, directed his question to Pele. "What was that?"

"I do not know," she said in all sincerity.

Hunter, no longer needing to prove anything to anyone, was himself surprised by his quick-thinking hero response, as he was no hero. He had acted intuitively, and yes, he marveled, he had moved like lightening to her rescue — *faster than a speeding bullet.* That expression came to his mind.

"I could have taken that — -," he paused, seeking the precise word to what that indeed was.

"Gojira!" laughed Ish, motoring the raft, shaking his camera.

He prattled on fast-clipped, ending in glee with "Toho! Toho!"

"What did he say?"

Tommi smiled, her first of the long day. "He says he's sure to be re-hired by his old company when he gets back to Tokyo. Toho Studios. And with what he has in his camera for the photos of the bomb, he will call himself *Mushroom Man* and be famous. And since no one will believe him about the *Gojira*, he will have to make a science fiction film of his experience and mint piles of yen."

"I'm glad somebody sees a happy future and financial success in what just happened," Hunter griped, still upset at his presumed loss of victory. "I was the one doing all the fighting. If old Kū here had not interfered, I would have torn Mr. Gojir-ee apart."

Pele spoke to Kū, who, in turn, grunted huff y words and gave a sadistic grin at Hunter.

"What did you say?" Tommi still mistrusted the goddess.

"I told him Hunter would have defeated the monster and Hunter then would say to Kū, 'if you get in my way again, I will defeat you'."

"Hey, I did not say anything of the kind. I don't start fights."

He smiled at his growing bravado. "Of course I could finish one."

"Watch it Hunter, she's baiting you. She's going to egg Kū on, until you two are like the top contenders for the world domination championship."

"I can lie very well," said Pele with her school girl charm.

"Don't you see, what just happened?" Tiki was eager for his interpretation of the event to be heard. "If Hunter had killed the Gojira, we would have had a carcass to show to the Navy, display it to the entire U.S., go on a nationwide tour; they would've believed us then. 'The monsters are coming! The monsters are coming!' That would stop these god awful bomb tests." He scratched behind the ear of the goat he held in his arms. The goat, in some kind of animal shock, offered a mild bleat.

"Perhaps so, young wizard," said Pele, almost maternal. "But don't forget your painting." Another surprise to digest.

"Wowie, I did paint two creatures fighting on the beach in front of a sunbathing beauty."

"It *was* a Tiki god," exclaimed Tommi, understanding the farseer implications, and she pointed to Hunter, "fighting the Gojira — and Tiki's painting did have similarity, though as usual, wildly exaggerated."

"Shit," agreed Hunter, "Tiki Shark sees one step ahead of what's coming. We need to go back through everything you've been sketching recently."

Tommi was coming around, edging towards a reluctant belief. She had seen, with her own eyes, a Tiki man fight a sea-land beast. All things were possible now.

Pele spoke seriously, "What you all don't understand is what you did not see when watching the battle."

"Huh?" asked Tiki Shark.

Pele clarified. "Kū looked into the creature's eyes and did not see one of the devil spirits of his realm which would answer to his commands. This creature is of the sick earth, not from the breach in our heavens. Kū did not try to win; he prevented Hunter from killing your Gojira, as you call it, by flinging it far away, so that he would on another day come back and find it when he would know how to make it answer only to him and follow his will; to rule over that creature and all the others who arise from your bombs or descend from our world."

Tiki Shark turned his mental light bulb on.

"Jesus H. Wowie — So, this tattooed guy sitting in our raft and smiling at us is going to create an Army of Hellions?" He looked to Hunter. "What are you going to do about that?"

Gojira

49

H unter," Tommi called to him. He went forward from the lounge area of the Clipper to a private cabin. He could hear the Russians yelling at the back of the plane while the bladed noise of the propellers began to kick in, goosing the RPM, readying for departure. Tiki Shark was in the lounge area tearing through his sketches, trying to create a workable story board of what might be coming in their direction from his inked prophesies. In all the strangeness of strange, Pele flipped through her screen and fashion magazines, showing the photographs to Kū; like a boy with his first girlie magazine, the super-warrior definitely was bowled over by what he was seeing. It had to be a strategy of Pele's, perhaps to give him a reality check that the current civilization was as powerful as he, though if he saw any movie magazine stories on the Marx Brothers or the Three Stooges, Tiki Shark thought, better give Kū the keys to the world and step aside. Maybe Pele, even with her most ardent enemy at her side, felt that after hundreds of years being a stone giant, Kū deserved a little R&R, that it might make the god homesick for his own castle in the sky, or wherever he had sprung from.

"Help me wash my hair, please." Tommi, speaking to Hunter as he entered, was wrapped in a blanket with her shoulders bare, leaning over a bucket, with several buckets of warm water nearby. He knew this was her third hair and body washing today, but a girl could not be too careful when it came to unseen atomic bugs in her scalp.

With nothing better to do and wanting to find a comfort zone away from the others aboard, he began working in the shampoo, wondering if this was such a good idea. He was no longer mad at her. Hell, even the Russians gave him no cause for immediate reactionary alarm. His challenge — to save a small part of the world — was mind boggling and of such a grandiose scale that he could not seem to get his hands wrapped around the best response. He agreed with what Tiki and Tommi had not said but expressed in their worries. He could not take on Kū, mano-a-mano; he just wasn't that sort of superman. The guy was a killer, a slayer of giants, a plague on any army that went against him.

Tommi understood the silence, enjoyed the hardness of his hands, kneading in the soap yet trying to be gentle.

"Hunter, I'm sorry I helped create this mess. I will do anything to make amends. If what Pele says is even half-way true, this past world war would be dwarfed by what that guy could do if he really got hold of a marching horde, of human soldiers, or flying ones."

He smiled, which she could not see, as he began the first rinse. He longed for the past times with her. No, not really, not anymore. Not back to his drinking; those urges were gone. And he had never enjoyed his strong arm military cop act that kept her in check, the pushy threat of deportation that was not really him.

Hunter enjoyed the moment, the touching of her wet hair, smelling of fresh coconut. He wanted to start over, a new slate, but what could he now offer? He did not see a way clear of the approaching climatic end game; where he had changed and the world might do so as well, perhaps not to a good finality.

Having rinsed her hair twice he took a towel and began to shag it dry; she began to sing, something in Japanese, but a modern tune, maybe, it sounded like, yes, it was that Johnny Mercer tune, *Ac-Cent-Tchu-Ate the Positive*. What were those lyrics? He found himself singing in English to her Japanese chorus. *You've got to accentuate the positive —*

Eliminate the negative — Latch on to the affirmative — Don't mess with Mister In-Between. They laughed together: had that ever occurred before? He realized that in this moment he did not think of her as a past enemy, nor care about her nationality; he touched her as a human being, let his fingers linger in the drying of her hair, touched her as a man touching a woman. She turned to look at him, longing, as he felt, but so awkward. Beauty and her Beast, yet — .

"Hey guys, you got a minute? Like now?" Tiki Shark's high whine broke the moment. She tied her hair into a towel bun and he followed her out.

Everyone was there, but it was the Russians holding firearms, pointed at them, that gained their immediate attention.

"There's to be a change in the flight plan," stated Baran, waving a German Luger pistol. "Everyone nicely put their hands up. No tricks." And they all complied except Pele and Kū, who Baran came to expect were exceptions by ignorance to the rule.

Hands went up and Tommi's blanket covering fell to the deck, revealing her demure body, clad only in a bra and thin cut panties.

"Bi-kini," said Kū, his first word spoken.

Pele shrugged her shoulders.

"I was showing him the latest Paris swimwear fashion."

One of the Russians, leering, started to step forward. Hunter balled his fist and moved in front of Tommi, protectively.

"Careful, Hunter," Tommi placed a hand on his arm.

"Now's not the time. *Don't mess with Mister In-Between.*"

Baran waved his gang back and with his gun as a pointer, directed everyone else to take their seats as the plane began its take-off roll across the ocean.

50

The sea rushed passed the *Clipper's* viewing ports, the plane so close to the white caps that Tiki Shark could have sworn he saw frolicking spinner dolphins. One of the Russians up on the flight deck held a machine gun on Captain Lang, the Japanese co-pilot Shiggy, and the Navigator-Engineer Spenser as they obeyed the new compass bearing at a nervous 500 feet above sea level to avoid radar.

Baran spoke with menace. "Now that our course has been set, act with caution, obey my orders, and no one will get hurt."

"Why do I feel like I'm in a flying movie version of *Petrified Forest?*" Tiki Shark's mood was morose, his idea of a lark adventure past saving.

Baran ignored the complaint.

"All right, a little truth, and remember I'm the one holding the loaded pistol."

Tommi, Hunter, and Tiki were in over their heads trying to figure out how to tell the truth without getting shot for making any story sound so false as to encourage torture.

Pele stepped in and began, and those who had spent the most time around her in these past days noticed she had slipped her voice up an octave, back into the teen girl motif, rather than the goddess who could sound like the crack of doom descending.

"The truth is this: the world is not as it seems. What you've seen this day has many views where science has become too powerful."

"Talk to me plain girl," growled Baran.

"My father was a powerful scientist from Germany who came to the islands in the early 1920's and married my Polynesian mother. For most of his life he worked for the German Government, the last ten years for the really bad guys, in secret experiments."

The prisoners under the threat of the pistol were enthralled, and somewhat relieved. Here was a whopper of a fib any bad guy just might swallow for its audacity.

"Two years ago, he created some chemical formulas, but after seeing what they produced, he decided that the Nazis should not get ahold of his 'new medicines', which were based on something he called 'splicing of genes'. So he hid a cache of the medicines and the formulas, but told me, before he died, and yes, he is dead — heart attack — nothing sinister, just keeled over one day in his laboratory. One of his last acts gave me the responsibility to undo one of his earlier mistakes."

She paused for the dramatic effect, pulled a lukewarm Coca-cola out of a nearby Scotch cooler, and began to sip the sweetness.

"Yes, go on." Baran was listening, but was he buying this stretched spiel?

"My father had created a Super Soldier, one with great powers, but after the creation, felt it was a great evil. Think what would have happened if Herr Hitler could create a division of such mighty soldiers. So, my father put him" — pointing to Kū — "into a state of hibernation, he called it 'suspended animation' and encased him in concrete in the form of a statue."

"So, that's how he got in there," said Tiki Shark with a paint-by-numbers understanding. Tommi had to look at Hunter and not let an expression of 'oh, brother' escape her lips. Their hep young buddy had been shown the secrets of great mystical power of the gods but was gullible enough to believe that any new version must be a corrected update.

"That's about it. I retrieved two vials of my father's serum. One I gave to Hunter Hopewell after we had made wild, passionate love and he was exhausted in sleep. I needed someone who would follow me as I asked."

Hunter did not look at Tommi, but could feel angered eye darts piercing.

"And the second, when aboard the ship I injected into the statue where Kū dwelt captured to bring him alive, as you see." Kū was turning pages of another magazine, entranced by the photos of semi-dressed women and, for comparison, bringing his eyes to settle on Tommi, glad she had been allowed to fully dress in khaki shirt and pants.

"I think this is too far-fetched," said Baran with a half laugh of dismissal. "Certainly, the newspapers are now revealing the Nazis did horrendous experiments on concentration camp prisoners, but creating a modified type of being, this super soldier, as you call him: no, not believable."

The gambit had failed. Hunter feared rough stuff would soon follow. He saw Baran take a hard look at the dark-skinned man who seemed child-like but then could throw a monster the length of a football field? Hunter thought he could see Baran's mind wondering: if what the girl had said contained any speck of truth. Hunter's body tensed, his temper raging; he might have to act on his own.

Pele was not finished with her drama.

"If I give you proof, will you let us go, unharmed?"

Hunter could see by Baran's expression that the Russian's mind was churning. The spy had not been put in such a position before, trying to codify the unknowns, and if her story were true, Hunter had to believe, the man was thinking of the gigantic fortune about to fall into his hands, for the secrets would be sold (not given in patriotic fervor) to Stalin himself.

Let the dictator conquer the world. Peter Baran would become a rich man. Let the masses be the fools.

He waved the gun at her.

"Prove it and I will let you all live. I am not a bloodthirsty man."

Pele smiled, a smile of gotcha, which Tommi feared bore no morality. If her first story of gods and goddesses was true, with Kū rising to first destroy the world of man and then conquer the heaven of the gods, then Pele would do anything to advance her end goal of saving her heaven; the earth was secondary.

She pointed at Hunter.

"Shoot him."

Four people, included Baran, yelped, "What?!"

"Shoot him in the stomach."

Baran, against what he had asserted earlier, could find violence acceptable, but not for wasteful results, not for any psychotic thrill. He laughed at her.

"Why not let me just shoot native boy over there? Wouldn't I get the same test reaction?"

"Kū would pull your bones from your body while you watched and then melt your eyeballs."

That gave the Russian pause, so he shot Hunter Hopewell in the stomach.

51

N o! No!" Tommi shouted hysterically. The Russian ship crew came in, not in panic, but armed and ready for action. Tiki glanced from Hunter who was leaning over and clutching his mid-section, to the bloodshot eyes of the Russians, fearing their itchy trigger fingers. And they were itching.

Baran held them back and looked at his victim. Tommi, crying leaned in to help him to the floor, to soothe the dying man she now knew she cared for.

Hunter pulled back his hands, unclenched his teeth, and stared down to find the back end of the bullet, sticking out of his stomach. He tugged at it and it slowly came out, surrounded by his skin, or rather embedded in a layer of fish-like scales that over-lapped, having absorbed the impact of the high velocity round.

Baran walked over, took the scale encased bullet from Hunter's hand, and examined it.

A Russian voice shouted from the cockpit. The Clipper had started its descent. Tiki Shark looked out the window and, then, shielding his eyes, looked harder.

"Hey, there's a ship down there."

"My ship," said Baran, his smile widening at this new miracle, at what he might do with such power. "That is the communication vessel that was at Pearl, now at my bidding."

"Aren't we all flying back to Hawai'i?" Tiki asked lamely.

Ah, our misled artist, thought Hunter. Tiki sometimes cannot see the big picture. The bad guys don't let valuable cargo or witnesses go.

With Tommi still cradling him, Hunter slowly recovered from a not so near death experience, although certainly a bruise would form on his non-penetrated stomach. That was it; he was no longer enamored with Pele, if he ever was. The girl, concluded Hunter, was a mean bitch.

Baran twirled the gun back into Pele's face. "Ah, that is the question; so back to our unfinished business. Where *is* your Father's formula and these super soldier inoculations?"

The plane made a hard water landing and started to taxi.

"Shoot me and Kū has been told to boil your brains, or I could do that. Want to take a chance? But to save time, if you are letting us go, let us go, and I will show you the way. I don't need such drugs. Kū, Hunter and I, and yes, I also was Daddy's little experiment, we have some immunity to your threats, and a few tricks of our own to protect us."

"Okay," said Baran, with the firmness of wanting to play the tough guy. "I don't trust any of you mystical charlatans, or whatever you are. But I still need to make a point of who's in charge here." Baran shot Tiki Shark in the shoulder.

Tommi and Hunter ran to the boy's side.

"Owie," Tiki mumbled in shock, as blood spewed out. "Ouch. Ouch."

"You bastard." Tommi shouted at the Russian, their pact now null and void. "Where's the first aid kit?" She shouted the demand again in Japanese. Shiggy, the co-pilot, shouted from upfront and above, and he could be heard opening metal cabinets.

A banging on the Clipper passenger door signaled additional conspirators, who had approached the plane in a long boat. Russian voices were heard and the exterior door unlocked and opened.

"Now, miss," Baran barked out to Pele. "Where are your father's formulas?"

"There are some government cabins near the top of Mauna Kea on the Big Island of Hawai'i, a place called Hale Pohaku. My father used one cabin for some of his experiments. He needed clear air and cold temperatures, and only there on the island can be found both in combination. Inside the cabin there is an old ammunition case, tucked away in a rafter. Everything you seek is there."

All of a sudden, the attention of everyone in the passenger space was drawn to Kū, who had walked over to Tiki Shark, leaned down, touched the boy's bloody shoulder, and then probed the wound. Tiki Shark screamed in pain.

"Stop that!" Hunter pushed Kū away, but the warrior god was rising anyway. He walked over to Baran and touched the Luger in his hand, sensing the heat on the barrel. His smile, if one could call it that, was an understanding of powers on the earth he had not seen before.

"What's he doing," asked Baran, making sure that the pistol was not yanked out of his hand.

"He wants to learn from you." Pele's dry observation.

"Now, that is something we can all agree on." He spoke to several Russians, one of whom then stood guard as Baran left to talk to the trawler captain, and to stow their equipment and camera gear for the short ferrying over to the mother ship. Even Kū trailed along behind, in curiosity. The violence held attraction.

When they were alone except for the guard, Tommi had to curse at a goddess.

"You had him shoot Hunter!"

"Hard proof sells the best. I was surprised that the bullet did no damage."

"Surprised?"

"Please understand I have not seen a man-god created in over a thousand years. I don't know all your hero traits."

"You were experimenting with me." Hunter's shock and disgust was obvious as he held Tommi's hair towel to Tiki Shark's bleeding wound. Shiggy arrived with the first aid kit and quickly sprinkled Sulfa powder over the entry point.

"You could help him," Pele said to Hunter.

"By doing what; is this more experimenting?"

"Put your hand directly over his wound." He did so, somewhat reluctantly. "Close your eyes, and think only of the bullet, imagine it, give it direction, ask it to come to you." Hunter stared at her, but seeing the pain in Tiki's grimace, he complied. Eyes closed he concentrated.

Within seconds, more hurt rose from Tiki's clenched cries, and then a huge relaxing sigh. Hunter turned over his hand, a spent bullet had fallen into his grasp.

"Move aside." Pele went to Tiki, bent down and put her hand on the wound, and Tiki again cried out, and the smell of burning flesh wafted through the cabin. Her hand, her touch, had cauterized the wound.

Tommi shook her head in numb disbelief. "Absolutely amazing."

To a moaning Tiki Shark, and to all, she explained, "We will have to monitor you for internal bleeding and perhaps infection."

Hunter tried to give the boy reassurance. "I know an Ambassador's son who can get us this wonder drug called 'penicillin'... when we get back... and out of this mess."

52

Baran returned, and at his shouted orders, all the plane's passengers, not Russian, were shoved in together into the first class lounge.

"Time for travel. I am taking the two natives with me to retrieve her Daddy's medicines." He pointed to Pele. "If, little girl, there is nothing there that creates these super soldiers, then we may just have visit our own scientists where they might just want to dissect your friend Kū, and maybe you next."

"He's not my friend, nor will he be yours," was Pele's threatening reply.

"Oh, and I nearly forgot, by sign language our native boy here has asked a favor, and how could I say no. Seems he has been lonely for so long, he wants us to bring Miss Tommi along."

Baran motioned to Kū and the war god grabbed Tommi's arm and yanked her to his side.

"No," she cried. "Hunter, help!"

Hunter started an angry lunge, but Baran's revolver went to her head.

"Now, now. Take it easy and back off. And for the rest of you, I am a man of my word. You will be left alive."

The sound of smashing was heard above them on the flight deck.

"Of course, you will be left aboard with no working radios,"

Baran announced with a sardonic grin, before calling out to pilot Lang.

"Perhaps you could taxi all the way to the closest land. I believe that is Bokak Atoll about fifty miles away."

Shiggy, the co-pilot, became animated. "Bokak. Taongi."

"Yes," said Baran. "I do believe during the war you guys called it Taongi."

Outside the *Clipper*, machine gun fire popped against metal. "Naturally, you will have to taxi on two working engines. No flying anymore for this crate." Both pilot Lang and Engineer Spenser looked shaken, devastated at their coming abandonment. They were to be left alive in a floating coffin.

Baran laughed.

"Save me, Hunter," Tommi's cried out softly.

"I will," he replied. It was more prayer than promise.

"That I would like to see." Baran laughed, flourished his pistol — a warning to stay put — and departed, but not before Pele intoned her own prophecy. "He will save her."

Baran smirked and pulled Pele along with him.

A god, a goddess, and a war profiteer boarded the departing boat, headed towards the Russian trawler. Hunter stood at the plane's door and watched them move away. Seeing Tommi's expression nearly broke his heart. Kū's hand on her shoulder, holding her down, infuriated him, and he felt his chest rising, his scales cracking as they expanded at his internal wrath.

"You will," called out a weak and bandaged Tiki, trying himself to understand his role as an aero-castaway.

"Will what?" Hunter returned to comfort those he could.

"Save her." And he showed Hunter one of his color drawings: a Tiki god carrying a beautiful island girl, who looked more Japanese than Polynesian, across a sunset bay towards an A-frame hut labeled, 'Tiki Lounge'.

Hunter sighed at insurmountable odds that this farsight of a seer had created. He leaned over, and checked Tiki's wound, a quarter-size scar, nothing more.

"Tiki, my oracle, you may have only painted a false hope. Here we are stuck in the middle of the ocean on an aerial bus that won't fly and probably barely will taxi across the waves, if at all."

"My painting is the future, I'm sure. You will find a way out of this predicament, Pele said so. It has to get better."

It didn't.

53

Pilot Lang brought them the news. "One of the engines they shot up is smoking. I don't want it to get to a fuel line. So we need to haul water to the wing and douse it out. And Spenser got a weather report before we landed: a storm will hit us tonight. Not quite a typhoon, but a strong gale. I'll have to run the engines at the waves, accelerate at the top crest. It'll eat up a lot of fuel and it may blow us away from Bakok Atoll."

Hunter could, with a twist to that song, only seem to *acceuntate the negatives* into a headache. *Do gods pray to other gods?*

Everyone tried to make Hunter feel better as he rode in the belly of the beast, through the shadow of the wet valley of death, but he feared all sorts of evil fatalism.

Even engineer Spenser, taking a break as the plane shifted and rolled to the whims of the storm, tried in his own way.

"Naw, this is not so bad. The worst was flying the Hump over the Himalaya Mountains between India and Kunming, China. I was with the Fourteenth Air Force back in '43. We would fly the A C-87 Liberator transport, and that guzzler consumed three and a half tons of 100 proof-octane gasoline just to cargo over four tons. Before they'd let a bombardment group go on a single mission in their B-24 Liberators, we had to fly the Hump four times to build up base supplies."

In the morning, they woke to overcast skies but no rain, and one could see the storm's darkness moving off to the north, following the track of where Hunter thought the Russian trawler was sailing. If on target, the storm would hit them by evening and he worried for Tommi's safety. Up until this point, their relationship had never reached intimacy; it was a compact of mutual business needs carried out with mutual distrust. Looking back, he saw they were more alike than he had noticed. Both of them were doers, get-things-done people. If and when they got back together, back to Honolulu, he could make a go of the detective agency business and Tommi could run her businesses, drum up clients for him. He could steer legal but questionable opportunities her way. There could be a beautiful partnership in the future...maybe more… if only...

Tiki Shark had a quaint way of destroying the blue bird of optimistic happiness.

"I didn't want to bring this up, but I'm worried for Tommi's sake."

"So am I, Tiki. So am I."

"Well, not just that Kū character. Pele probably can keep him in control. And Baran wants Tommi to keep Kū in line, and pressure on Pele to take them up Mauna Kea. Boy, it's going to be a frickin' long walk on top of that epic mountain."

"What's your point?"

"It's the other crew members that came along with us. Those Russian sailors. Did you see they were getting sick? They weren't looking good at all. And I think they're going to get much worse."

"And you are saying?"

"Zombies. The radiation poisoning will turn them into zombies and they'll go crazy with their sickness."

54

Hunter's growing anguish, his concern for Tommi, even Pele since he did not know what Kū was capable of, should have pushed him into a high gear, but the ocean and the damaged plane would not give him respite.

The storm had damaged one wing, actually shorn off a part, so the *Clipper* leaned. The working propeller strained and Engineer Spenser worried that it would overheat, so every four hours they took a one hour cooling off break. The salt spray would not help the motor, so the plane had to be angled away from the breaking waves, swells still high, residual from last night's blow.

On top of the frustrating boredom of letting the hours drain a speck of sand at a time in an imaginary hour glass, they had to put up with co-pilot Shiggy's enthusiastic Banzais, pointing to the map and telling them their destination had to be Bokak Atoll. Yes, everyone agreed that would be their destination though uninhabited according to military reports, but after they established a secure base there, what next? They would continue to be stranded, just on land, and Hunter had no confidence that Baran would notify any authorities of their plight until he was on Mother Russia's soil with his prize — if he notified them at all. Hunter felt the expectation of their final fate was to run out of food and water and perish.

Still, depressed at all things, he had to consider what Pele was up to. Her plan, whatever, was a mystery, but he could see some reasoning, from her goddess point of view. Her 'my daddy was a mad German scientist' was pure bunk [Tiki had shown him his 'Superman vs. Nazi' comic book she had read earlier], but Baran had latched onto this fable in his blind greed. So, they would land on the Island of Hawai'i. Yes, that would build up her Mother Earth power. Closer to a volcano, more hoodoo strength, would she then drop a volcanic meteor from Mauna Loa on Kū's thick skull and fry him? Hunter analyzed her situation. Kū was the enemy and she had tricked him before, somehow placing a magma shell around him and carving him into a Tiki, encasing his power. But on the loose, their powers were equal. No, not heat. He saw it: she was going to do something with the cold. On

Mauna Kea, nearly 14,000 feet high, one could find snow most of the year. Pele would lead Baran and he would follow. Pele would tell Tommi to follow her, and Kū would follow both Baran and Tommi, keeping a watchful eye on Pele. The more he learned of the 'modern ways' from Baran, the more dangerous Kū would become. And what powers did Kū the War God typify? Strength — they had seen that, but how was he going to control this horde to do his bidding? Hunter wondered and then guessed.

A good god would ask for loyalty based on a righteous cause; a bad god had to use mind control, something like hypnotic persuasion. Yes, Hunter saw it in the man's eyes, a deep pooling that seemed mesmerizing, drawing one in, but so far, with all the rushed events of escape and flight, he had not been in a position to be transfixed. Perhaps Pele and Hunter of the gods can't be suborned by trance inducing trickery.

Baran would be susceptible, so would Tommi, certainly Tiki

Shark and so would the world.

Slaves to the War God, Kū.

Tommi will be on that mountain top. Pele will have to act. Try not to look into his eyes, Tommi. Hunter cursed at himself. He was here and he could do nothing to save her.

"Ah-loo."

What was that?

55

They were into their second day, and at this point drifting, the plane's two remaining engines idling.

"Ah-loo."

"What was that?" Tiki heard it too.

From the flight deck, they could hear Captain Lang shouting out the side window of the cockpit.

"And hello to you!"

They ran to the windows: a ship. Hallelujah! Not a ship, not a big boat, but a small sailboat. In the middle of the South Pacific?

Hunter ran and threw open the plane's passenger door.

"Thank you for saving us. We crashed. We are marooned."

"Ah-loo, United States."

Hunter turned to Tiki.

"I'll be damned. I think we're are dealing with the League of Nations. That guy barely speaks English."

The sailboat had tacked to parallel the course of the plane. A woman, young, attractive, and very tan, went to the tiller, while the bearded young man with long stringy blond hair ran forward to loosen the fore halyard and drop the head sail.

"Break out the small raft; I am going over to pay my respects."

Tiki put up a stop-sign hand. "Perhaps Lang, I or Spenser should go. You still have that granite look. They might see you as a swarthy pirate." Hunter, with a grumble, acquiesced.

From the broken English dialogue, Hunter and Tiki learned that the sailors, Thor and his wife Liv, were Norwegian, sailing back to Panama. Thor had spent several years as a beach bum on Fatu Hiva in the Marquesas island chain, and later wrote a book, *På Jakt etter Paradiset* (Hunt for Paradise), published in 1938. Such a creative spark made him an immediate kindred spirit to Tiki Shark. Thor's background in zoology and geography left him keen to do an anthropological study of the Polynesian people, how they traveled from island to island, their historic migration.

Thor and Liv did not have a shortwave radio aboard their sailboat so, in response to Hunter's gentle prodding, they agreed to make a detour and sail the sixty or so miles to reach Bokak Atoll. There was no way Hunter or his group could wait the next two to three weeks until Thor's sailboat made the next official landfall with communication. Arrangements were made and sealed with handshakes of gratitude, across the wide ocean where few friends were to be found.

Pilot Lang and Engineer Spenser would stay with their company's property and keep motoring to the island, expected to reach it in two days. The others — Hunter, Tiki with his nervous goat in tow, and the two Japanese employees of Tommi J's enterprises — would sail with Thor and Liv, sleeping on the deck and acting as crew. Hunter had to speak slowly to explain the presence of former POWs to their new hosts. Upon arriving at the atoll, Hunter would choose the best spot for a base camp and direct its setup while awaiting the arrival of the *Island Clipper*. The Norwegians, whenever they arrived back at civilization, would notify the authorities to send a rescue as soon as possible. The *Clipper* had enough food rations to last two weeks, but not three. They had to be saved before then.

And so here he was again, reflective, his eyes closed, recalling a sailing excursion on Chesapeake Bay, years ago. Sail boat speed of light breeze, eased rolling motion as the bow surgically sliced the waves. If only his god-like powers could take him back in time. A sudden thought struck him: he would want Tommi by his side, his arm around her.

At this moment with the stars above, the world looked tranquil, like it fit well within the scheme of the cosmos.

The two Japanese were asleep; the shakes of the previous storm would have worn anyone down. Both of them seemed to get along well, but he noted that Ish tried always to cheer up Shiggy. The aviator kept silent; said little, no doubt, a lot was eating his insides, to believe in the omnipotence of one's Empire and be disillusioned so harshly to find one on the losing side. In Japanese culture, Hunter knew from battlefield scenes he bore witness to, to a soldier or a pilot, the loss of face would lead to ritual suicide, Seppuku, stomach cutting, disembowelment. Not a pleasant thought on an evening such as this.

Tiki Shark and Thor sat in the sailboat's cockpit attempting a disjointed conversation limited by the language barrier. Thor did speak English of sorts, but it did not go far as Tiki was trying to make his points about the origin of civilization.

"The Chinese took sampans, you know, small boats, and crossed over into Alaska territory, and they came down, and settled all along the West Coast into South America and then they wanted to go back to China, so they sailed west, but found all these islands. So they peopled them."

"No, no," said Thor. "Chinese come down to Southeast Asia, canoe to Borneo, Sumatra, become the island people. Dark skin people come from Africa go to India then travel east, go to Australia, and become small black people."

Tiki tried to make his host understand a concept that the young artist did not himself quite grasp, but the conversation bore marks of creative stimulation, so he plunged ahead. "I believe Chinese Indians, the Incas, the Aztecs, build rafts, look for a better home — like Columbus sail to America — they like the trade winds so go east to west but find islands instead."

Thor laughed. "Maybe both ways the wrong way but they came anyway. Could not find way home." Tiki Shark laughed. Friendships formed. Tiki had an easy way about him, trying to always please, even dismissing his bandaged wound to Thor as 'suffering is required in any masterpiece yet unfinished'.

Later, when Hunter began drifting off to the light slapping of the ocean currents against the hull, he heard his name mentioned.

"He is big man — stor; is there problem with skin?"

"Yes, skin problem. Bad rash." Hunter smiled at Tiki's explanation as being a reasonable answer. "But he is very strong. Good man. Will save us all. He is like a Tiki god."

They laughed.

Thor from his travels knew the word, and pointed at Hunter's sleeping form.

"Kjempe Tiki," said Thor. "Big animal with such strength.

Kjempe Tiki. Like huge hairy ape in Hollywood movie, but he ape with funny skin instead of hair."

"Oh, you mean like King Kong? Yes, he is like that, strong, but a wild animal only if he is provoked. A King Kong Tiki," laughed Tiki Shark, musing that it was an apt description.

"King Kong Tiki," repeated Thor with a chuckle. "Kong Tiki."

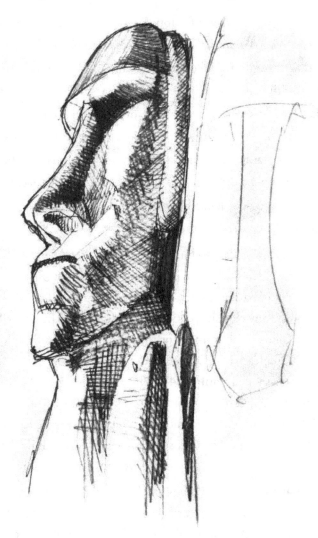

As a parting thank you gift for Thor and his wife, Tiki Shark created one of his 'vision' sketches. "Be wary, it'll be in your future," Hunter assured the mystified Norwegians.

56

Her first day of captivity blended the mundane with pangs of desolation. Tommi had access to most of the trawler's open spaces, but always followed by an armed guard, a new one from the ship's company, with a menacing sneer offset by a smoker's cough from the Turkish cigarettes he smoked incessantly. She dubbed him Boris and never gave him a second glance of consideration or emotion. At night, Boris locked her in her own cabin, postage stamp small with a metal bunk and a mattress befouled with sweat odors and stains she did not wish to guess at. The toilet facilities were down the hall, but with the door locked they gave her a honey bucket; she was in charge of disposing of the contents in the morning.

The ship, Danish flagged but christened the *Altair Beria*, had no Danes aboard, though Tommi saw a few fake passports lying in what she perceived was a purser cabin. The main mast nest sprouted communication radar and radio antennae that would not pass any close inspection by a U.S. vessel. The *Altair Beria* had been on her way to Bikini Atoll to monitor the next atomic bomb explosion [fortunately, they would later learn that Operation Crossroads radioactivity was so severe, future testing was postponed until 1954]. When Baran radioed the ship from the *Island Clipper* to say he had film to place into the hands of Russian Intelligence as soon as possible, the ship made the mid-ocean rendezvous. In quest of the super-soldier serum they would make a quick stopover at the port in Hilo Town, near the base of Mauna Kea, before sailing on to the western Soviet Union port of Vladivostok.

Where along this route Tommi's life would be most at risk she could only guess, and secretly, she was afraid. Her life never had brought any heroes to come to her rescue, and though her thoughts dwelt from time to time on Hunter, she did not see him in the role of the cavalry charging to the rescue of the damsel-in-distress.

On board, she, Pele and Baran were the only other English speakers, though the Captain had a good handle on pidgin English and British sailor slang phrases.

And in the Captain's questioning of Tommi on the second night, as she ate a cold dinner of meat soup in her cabin, she came to discover that the Russians who had accompanied the Clipper in its rendezvous with the Baker blast were quite ill, and the ship's doctor had no clue what might be the cause, or if it were contagious. She could provide no answers, wondering to herself if this might be the same 'atomic sickness' that those in the cities of Hiroshima and Nagasaki, destroyed by only one bomb each, were now experiencing.

At 1 am, she was awakened by the first rifle shot, followed by several others. Along the corridor outside her cabin, she heard footsteps, a scream, then shuffling footsteps, and her door was unlocked and opened. She backed to the corner of her room where no escape existed; before at the door stood, weaving with menace, a living horror.

One of the Russian sailors looked at her with anguished hatred. In one hand, he held an half empty bottle of Vodka which he spilled into his mouth and poured over his ravaged face, crying out like a wounded, dying animal. He had no nose; his mouth visible through a hole in this cheek, most of his hair had fallen out; large scabs covered his head and hands. He was holding a metal wrench, wildly swinging and waving it at her.

"Sooka! Bliad!" Without a dictionary, she translated the shout as a curse, maybe "Die, Bitch Whore!" Tommi started flinging anything she could find at him and jumped on top of her bed, which immediately, collapsed tumbling her to the floor right towards him and his raised swing.

Kū rushed in behind the crazed, tormented ghoul.

"Thank God!" Tommi cried, trying to scramble out of the way.

Kū grabbed the dying man's head and ripped it off his shoulders.

Tommi screamed at the geyser of blood spurting, and darted past both the corpse and the victor admiring his trophy. Into the hallway she ran and down the corridor. She had to leap over the collapsed body of a Russian crew member who, by his startled dead look, had earlier met up with a skull-caving weapon, probably the steel wrench.

Around another corner she screeched to a halt, as another crew member, another ghoul with a fire ax, charged at her, until his head exploded. Behind that falling body stood the ship captain with an odd looking gas-operated carbine, its muzzle leaking expended smoke. Tommi couldn't care less that this was a prototype rifle (codenamed AK-1) designed by an inventor named Kalashnikov, out for field tests; relief swept over her when she saw affixed to the weapon a large magazine clip for man or ghoul stopping power. When the Captain motioned her to follow she clung close behind.

The survivors, and it seemed there were a lot of them, congregated in the bridge. She saw men she hadn't seen before, young ones; not the rough sea-worn crew sorts, but intelligent looking, definitely the handlers of the communication array equipment, they were radio spies and scared to death, unaccustomed to the insane, destructive world she had just come from.

Baran entered holding his Luger pistol, Pele behind him, and an armed guard behind her.

"I think we got them all." He spoke in English to calm

Tommi, who was clutching herself and shaking, not sure if she was more afraid of radiated monsters or of Kū the Ripper who could easily end life with his bare hands.

Baran spoke to the captain in Russian, the latter responding in anger.

Back to Tommi he said, "He lost six crew members, not counting the five sick ones from Bikini who we have finally tracked down and dispatched. Seems they broke out of the infirmary and into the ship's liquor cabinet, hoping the alcohol would save them, or at least deaden their pain. They feel no pain now."

"Why aren't you sick like them?"

"I heard over the radio what Hopewell wanted us to do and took shelter; they did not. I made it to the bunker in time, they did not. Also, I followed Hunter's orders to you and the boy, and washed myself on the plane several times. Those crew members are not used to washing." He gave off a smirk, smug at his cleverness. She only saw the evil he manifested in outwitting the less swift.

The ship's doctor spoke to the Captain and Baran, and again, Baran translated.

"The good doctor wants to collect the dead bodies of the sick and do autopsies on them to understand what drove them mad, what disfigured them so horribly."

"If you really cared for your shipmates, you might tell them to wear gloves, and face masks if you have them. And use any equipment these scientists have on board to measure this thing called radiation."

"You're right, Miss Chen. Not only for safety — our entire trip, even up to the top of the mountain, will be for science. By the way, where is our native warrior?"

Said Pele, "If I know Kū of old, he is probably eating the hearts of those he slayed."

"Eeww." Tommi felt her stomach churn. "Tell your captain buddy that I am bunking in with my girlfriend here, and I will even sleep on the floor, if you find a mattress without blood on it, and a clean blanket."

"I am not your girlfriend," said Pele, though she did squeeze her face into a scrunch and stick out her tongue. Tommi rolled her eyes in exasperation.

57

The next morning, the entire crew, except for the on-duty radar-radio spies, did an entire wash down of the *Altair Beria* with high pressure hoses using sea water. Tommi thought this might be overkill, as a glance to the skies saw a turbulent darkness of clouds, following them and gaining. By evening the storm was upon them with a fury.

Whether from the bucking ship, the howling wind, or a subconscious fear, she awoke in the middle of the night to find Pele's bed empty, and a dark form standing in the doorway, highlighted by stabs of lightning flashing behind him: Kū.

He came to her, leaned down, and in one motion scooped her up and plopped her onto the vacant bed.

Tommi knew what was coming. She had seen his stares at her during the past days, knew from all her dealings with the male species what they wanted when seized with lust, and knew that all but one or two of the most despicable would not act on that desire because 99 per cent of them had a sense of honor to hold them in check, a consciousness of what was right. Not so the unregulated warrior caste, in any form, human or spirit deity, life and bodily satisfaction were theirs for the primeval taking. She had thought he might be different, might respect her as an individual. But no, he came from the ruthless past, and what had happened the previous night, that was not protection of her, that was sated blood taking, filling a deep need to conquer all living things. Tonight she was on his altar of sacrifice. She prayed that she would survive the night. A sudden thought struck: how many of her sisters of war had sacrificially allowed such violation just to hope they would live, or debased themselves to feed their starving families? Tommi Jingu was going to be raped by a god, but she wasn't going surrender without a fight.

Flailing her fists at him she yelled, 'no! no!' along with a few apt sailor slurs about his manliness, and cursed the pedigree of all his ancestors until he held her down in a vise-like clamp.

He then slapped and shook her, and said harshly, "Tommi!" That stopped her struggling; he had personalized his actions by calling her name; she looked at him, and that was her mistake — she looked at him, it was into his eyes. And she fell in.

They were standing on a lava ridge with the ocean as a backdrop; a light breeze blew through her hair. He stood before her naked. She met his desire by unbuttoning her blouse, undoing the side buttons on her slacks, letting the pants fall to her feet. He drew her close.

Crack! The sound rocked the ship as a luminous discharge of plasma struck the ship's mast, exploding all the listening apertures; a blue light scoured the ship with jumping ionization; a crackling fire of electrical charges sought out all metal points within the cabin where the couple lay entwined, and the blueness pierced behind her eyelids. Consciousness came to her of knowing who she was, what she was made of, and what was happening to her.

Another lightning bolt cut the night's blackness and the momentary brilliance filled the cabin. This one broke her trance. The aura of the flashes put electricity into the air around, him, he staggered back. She took advantage and in reflex kicked him the balls, realizing it would be minimal discomfort, and she fled the cabin.

Running, looking back, he did not follow. Some type of violet glow with a buzzing noise encased the door, menacingly.

58

ommi stumbled along the ship's walkway, letting the stinging rain purge away the foreign body smells. Such a close call, would he come at her again? He had that power.

She swore aloud her familiar wartime mantra, which she now doubted: *I will survive.*

Easily she found Pele at the bow of the trawler, her arms raised to the heavens, chanting. Tommi recalled Tiki Shark's lecture on Polynesian mythology — no longer myths. The fact hit her. Pele was, after all, the goddess of thunder and lightning.

Dropping down next to Pele's feet, and let the rain wash the off her skin, cool the bruises on her face and body. She didn't care if anyone came upon her in this disarray of nakedness.

"Why did you not save me from him?" she shouted above the roar of the storm's fierceness. "You are a woman somewhere inside your cheerleader facade; you, the Mother of Earth, Overseer of this violence of Nature, you should understand what he was trying to do to me!" She sobbed for understanding.

Pele kept up her chanting for a few seconds more and then looked down at Tommi.

"Did he take you, did he destroy you?"

Tommi bit her lip, and spoke with force. "No, he did not."

"You are strong for a mere woman. I presume you did not pleasure him as he might expect from a slave girl, and yet he did not kill you for your failures."

"If he gets his jollies off ravishing a dead mackerel; no, I can say, I did not try to please him." And she washed herself gently, even though he had not penetrated her.

"Did you not see a blue light? Within that light did you find a god to help you to escape his lust?"

That gave her pause, remembering in the attack she had superimposed Hunter's face, over the war god's sneers of dominance. "Yes, I did. Hunter's presence helped, yes. Was that blue light of your doing?"

"Sailors who worship the nailed god on wood named my fire after their blessed priest. It has always been my fire. Depending on your need, they say it is a good omen."

"It was a good omen, a saving one."

"From now on I will protect you from any of his further advances or touching. Knowing him, I am sure he will direct his anger against those he can control, namely Baran and the crew."

"How can you protect me?"

"He sees you as unimportant in his plans, but you are important to me. Through you and Hunter I hope someday Kū will be vanquished."

The rain still pummeled Tommi's face and it was hard for her to speak without shouting out each word in her questioning.

"And your chanting?"

"I need this storm to go before us and hold fast on Mauna Kea, and let the rain become snow and ice. I have summoned a favor from one of my sisters, Poliahu." Her teenage persona returned. "I'm basically chanting, 'Keep it snowing, sis.'"

"So you have a plan to defeat Kū?"

"Not really, no."

"What? All this for what?"

"I had to get him back on dry land, on my home soil, where I will have equal power. But sometimes even the gods must seek out miracles and put trust in the hands of the Fates. As I told Hunter, it must be mankind, not us, who fights Kū's allies and destroys these atomic beasts."

"And how can you be so certain we have a chance to win?"

Pele patted the top of Tommi's head, gently with a school girl grin of knowing a scandalous secret no one else in the class might have learned. From the pocket of her pants, she pulled out a crumpled piece of paper and handed it to Tommi.

Unfolding it, Tommi saw it was one of Tiki Shark's drawings.

She stared hard.

"By the grace of all you gods, how will that be possible?"

Tommi could see she held hope in her hands as the rain washed the ink from the sketching paper.

Part Six

The Plane

59

After much protestation from Thor and Liv, who felt guilty about re-marooning Hunter and his band of misfits, the four of them plus one goat, waved off the sailboat after encouragement to send help as soon as the two Norwegians found a radio.

And so here they were, waiting on the *Island Clipper* to arrive tomorrow, and then all waiting for rescue, with Hunter dejected at their circumstances since he was in no way close to finding, and by writ, saving Tommi from the clutches of Commies and Demons, a bad combination of malevolent characters.

They stood on Bokak Atoll, though the Japanese naval pilot Shiggy kept mumbling *Taongi* as in Taongi Atoll. He seemed more interested in his surroundings, more upbeat and refreshed, to the surprise of his stranded colleagues, who earlier in the adventure had thought they may have to take turns on suicide watch.

With renewed vigor, first Hunter, then Shiggy, reviewed their only map, out of *National Geographic*, circa 1920, though it was apparent that maybe war and more certainly scouring weather had altered the stark landscape. There it was: a pinpoint. Bokak Atoll. No one really wanted to settle here; there was no water, no lush vegetation. It was the driest of all islands in the South Pacific, yielding not even one measly hill of guano (bird shit as nitrates/phosphates became a sought after fertilizer) that would have attracted any money-grubbing explorers. A true passed-over orphan, the atoll and its six small islands were discovered by Spain in 1565, and left undeveloped until the German New Guinea protectorate took control in 1906, in turn relinquishing it in 1914 to the Japanese who during World War II, had established an aerial reconnaissance communication outpost and a seaplane tender with a small runway cut along the beach on Sibylla, one of the atoll isles, 4.5 miles long by 333 yards wide, the longest piece of land in the crescent of this drowned, extinct volcano. Even the stoic Japanese could not handle the nothingness and left in 1943; the Americans bombed the abandoned facilities in 1944. After the war, they made a couple of sweeps around the Marshall Islands, including stopping at this atoll, seeking Japanese soldier stragglers. None were found and no searchers wanted to linger.

The group broke into unassigned duties void of leadership.

Ish snapped a few vista shots of where they were with his still camera. Tiki Shark found shade under beach Naupaka shrubs to begin doodling; Shiggy took their Geographic map and their small raft, waded down the beach, and crossed the shallow reefs to explore the smaller islands of the atoll, Kamwome and Bwdije. A rarity, Shiggy was singing as he departed.

Hunter gathered driftwood and wood from dead Heliotrope trees to build a lean-to shelter for all, as well as an emergency cord stacked for an emergency fire signal in the slim hope a would-be rescuer might be spotted. Their absent floating shelter, *the Island Clipper*, should arrive sometime late tomorrow, and with the added help of Lang and Spenser, they could take stock on how to survive for the two to three weeks until rescue, perhaps lasting a little bit longer by supplementing their diet with fish and birds. There seemed to plenty of avian species available: whether they had edible meat that tasted half-way like chicken or squab that was the mystery to be tested.

Shiggy returned less exuberant. With hand signals he conveyed in mimic that he had found the old Japanese communication hut, but whatever equipment there (his hand to his mouth) was broken (cracking a stick in two). That night they sat in front of a fire they really did not need; the moon was out, the air hot and muggy, no ocean wind. The two Japanese men conversed quietly among themselves and then moved off to sleep apart.

"What do you think that's about?" asked Tiki Shark, still working at a drawing in his sketch pad.

"We're being ostracized, for what reason I don't know."

"I was just thinking Ish was getting comfortable with my drawings."

"You do make one of those modern art painters, like a Picasso, come across as Norman Rockwell."

"From what he can convey to me by his pointing and waving, my art to the Japanese is like a cartoon; they call it manga. Very Asian: you read it right to left. I think he wants me to do a manga type book, like a comic book, about monster

Gorija. He will make the film and I will sell a book. I thought we had a partnership in the making, you know a cultural one, postwar buddy buddies, all that."

"The war is over for most; some of us are letting the bias and animosities go," (he was thinking of his own feelings, thinking of Tommi, concerned about her) "but for others the war was the blackest of hells, and being 'buddy buddies' is not yet palatable."

"Well, the war is over. People gotta grow up and move on."

Not quite so.

60

In the morning, a bayonet pricked Tiki Shark awake.

"Hey, what the — ." He looked up into the face of a very determined Japanese soldier and into the barrel of his rifle.

"Take it easy, Tiki," Hunter was rising slowly, putting his hands over his head, and Tiki followed suit, getting his bearings.

There were three soldiers surrounding them, all in unkempt, tattered and stained uniforms, wearing beards of various lengths, mean-spirited and shouting at them with deadly determination.

Hunter was about to say something like 'we friends, mean no harm,' when Shiggy began ranting at the soldiers, loudly, moving towards the bayonets pointed at himself and Ish. It was an authoritative voice the soldiers had not heard in years, and the bayonets lowered but only against their like kind, and now all three rifles pointed at the Americans.

"Keep it steady, Tiki" said Hunter talking calmly through his teeth. "Nothing silly, please, no false moves. Remember, bullets may not hurt me, but Baran didn't try a head shot on me either, and you may catch a stray. Let's see how this plays out." He had been talking while Shiggy informed the soldier who seemed to be of rank, corporal perhaps, but not high enough to outdo the bluster of Shiggy who seemed satisfied to be taking over command.

They all marched down the beach, Shiggy and the corporal in the lead exchanging remarks in animated conversation, both of them flailing arms for emphasis. Ish behind them, then Hunter and Tiki Shark, their hands now behind their heads, subservient prisoners, prodded by the two trailing guards using their bayonets.

"Ouch," said Tiki, with one poke. "I have the feeling that our supposed good friend Shiggy has told these Japanese Army rejects that they're winning the war."

Hunter received a thrust now and then to keep him moving.

"I'm getting mad. We better get somewhere soon or I may wrap these rifles around their necks."

"You know," said Tiki, talking as if it were a Sunday stroll in the park, "I've noticed, as it is happening now, that the angrier you get, the more expansive your body and the more prominent your scales, as if they are multiplying under your skin to form protection. Totally pissed off, I'd guess you could be invulnerable. When you are at peace you revert back to almost all human normal. I'm thinking that maybe you need to learn your on-off switch. Maybe find a monastery — Ouch — where they do that meditating."

Shiggy turned to them and began a pantomime. Airplanes wheeling in battle, rat-a-tat of machine guns, crashing planes, survivors swimming — waving his arms around — to this island.

Then Ish gave them the secret wink that everything might just turn out okay.

Hunter translated the gestures.

"Ish will be a great visual storyteller some day. Seems like what pilot Shiggy is telling the head soldier here is that we were in a great air battle that his side won, but his plane was damaged and he and Ish crashed in the ocean where they found us, and captured us, and made it to the island. End of story. That's why we are prisoners. They won the battle."

"Those without rifles cannot write the final history," spoke Tiki, wide-eyed at his own profound mouth.

They all had approached the reef between where they were on Sibylla Island and the smaller but more square Bwdije Island. The soldiers began to wade into the water.

"Whoa," said Tiki. "Look what they've done. They built a small causeway across the reef to the other side." He and Hunter began carefully watching their steps as they waded.

"Made with coral to be invisible from the air," Hunter took note, even admiring. "And wide enough that a jeep could have made it across without getting your gas pedal wet. Ingenious. Well, they had years of garrisoning this island with really nothing to do except fight boredom."

On Bwdije Island they hiked into more dense undergrowth until they reached several small buildings, all but one bombed and destroyed. In that still standing structure was the remnant of the communication headquarters, looking as if it had not been touched for years, with a bulky military radio set off to one corner.

As the corporal was giving the tour to Shiggy, his new leader, Ish went to inspect the radio and shook his head, suggesting 'not working'. Then, he ran his fi nger along the top of the radio's metal cabinet, and behind his back, held up his finger, so both Americans could see.

"What's he trying to tell us?"

"Of course. That's why Shiggy came back yesterday, not depressed, but confused. The radio set, left for years, had no dust. Someone had been here, and recently. One of these jokers probably keeps the transistor and bulb components clean, waiting for parts that have never arrived."

To the surprise of the prisoners, they and the two Japanese 'brave airmen', Shiggy and Ish, were marched out and along the side of the hut to cellar-like doors that when opened led down into the darkness.

"Bomb shelter," said Hunter, "hopefully nothing more devious, but I am trying to figure out how to make myself intensely angry, just in case."

In the damp cellar, against a wooden wall, a small latch popped a spring, opening a small door that could only be entered by crouching. Once through, torches were lit and the procession began a long-distance walk.

"My god," Hunter murmured in disbelief, "We are walking under the reef, going back the direction we came from. They must have started constructing this tunnel back when they took over from the Germans, over 30 years ago."

One of the Japanese soldiers yelled at him, and Hunter could translate mentally as 'Shut up'.

Soon the tunnel opened to a large room. Hunter estimated 200 feet in width but much more in length, perhaps two football fields long. And it wasn't a store room, it was an underground hangar… with airplanes.

"Their secret seaplane base," Tiki comprehended. "Who would have thought to look below ground."

"Sadly, for them, I think their radio broke and their Naval air force forgot to come back and get them."

Tiki agreed. "We must have killed all the ranks up the totem pole who knew of its existence."

They watched, even smiled, watching Shiggy confidently reassume the mantle of full air commander, but like an excited school child on Christmas, he went rushing among the planes to see what was and what worked.

"Hey," Tiki Shark whispered aloud, "We might just be able to get off the island."

And go and find Tommi. Hunter prayed it might be so.

There were four planes, two of which had been cannibalized for parts. The other two received Shiggy's endorsement as he patted their undersides with approval. The corporal nodded in the affirmative.

Hunter, from his service and intelligence work in the Solomon Island theatre, recalled his airplane identification. He pointed to one of the two serviceable planes. "That's a Nakajima float Fighter-Bomber. Navy called them 'Rufes'. Two machine guns mounted on the forward fuselage, two 20 mm cannons on the outer wings. Jeez! It has a bomb mounted on the underneath carriage. It looks pristine and ready to go!"

"But no pilot...until now." Tiki looked at Hunter, each realizing a strange dilemma was raising its head. "What's the other plane?"

Hunter gave it once-over from where he stood under guard, the soldiers wary, alert, fearful of sabotage by their prisoners.

"Wait. That's not Japanese. It's decaled with Jap insignias but that's American."

"Well, it looks like it's ready to go, and it's big enough to hold us."

61

N ot all of them.

The hangar's exit was a gradually sloped ramp that ended with a wide door to the surface, on the ceiling, wooden, angled like a skylight, but hidden under sand. A winch system with an electrical generator would be operated for the hangar roof ramp to open. If the door was not to be opened, Japanese personnel still could exit via a concrete bunker and chimney smokestack type climbing ladder with metal rungs that exited to the surface through a type of manhole cover, likewise hidden by sand and shrubs and only a hundred yards from where Hunter and friends had pitched last night's camp — and the access used by the soldiers to take them by surprise. This is the way they all went out.

Back on the surface, in the broiling sun, an argument ensued between the army corporal and navy pilot Shiggy. The corporal kept pointing to the two Americans, and emphasizing his point by counting on his fingers: one thru seven, take away two leaves five. Shiggy countered emphatically, holding up one finger and pointing back towards the hidden hanger where two prepped and ready airplanes have been awaiting a pilot and a mission for more than three years.

"If I understand basic math," guessed Tiki, definitely acting nervous, "soldier leader here believes the larger plane can be flown with only five passengers, out of here back to Japanese held territories. Shiggy is arguing he can take the smaller plane and go for help.

Tiki continued, "My first concern is that if Shiggy flies off by himself, what's going to happen if he either decides not to come back, or the plane sitting here all these years just can't make it at all, and he is left floating in the ocean like the *Clipper*. Second, if only five can make it on the second plane, then two people are odd man out, and my subtraction says that's us."

"And," Hunter finished the boy's concerns, "the Japanese are not going to want to leave any Americans alive to tip off the location of this secret base. And telling them now that the war is over and we won would make us immediate pincushions for their bayonets."

"Hunter, any chance you can get good and mad? Do some demi-god headbanging?" Tiki raised his voice. "Hey, Hunter, your mother wears combat boots; your father wears dresses! — Working yet?"

"No, my parents are deceased. And you are a clown offering humor in a time of crisis. Wrong effect."

The Corporal believed he had all the authority to solve the problem, permanently. He grabbed a bayonet rifle and marched towards Hunter.

Tiki Shark backed up and moved away from his friend.

"Hunter, duck."

"Won't help."

"No, Hunter, dammit, really duck!"

Hunter threw himself to the ground. The Corporal, looking startled, glanced to Tiki, who had thrown himself to the ground, and then looked to where Tiki's eyes led. Too late.

SWOOSH! A loud banshee scream. SCREEEECH.

The talons of the black dragon dug deeply into the corporal's body, lifting it in a swift swooping motion, like an eagle grasping a lake trout, and the flying beast ascended back into the skies, beginning a looping arc.

The two Japanese guards stood frozen, deer in the headlights, bringing up their guns too late, too shocked to know what else to do except in numbness prepare to be the next unwitting morsels with the dragon's second diving pass.

Hunter yelled at Shiggy and Ish and pointed to the Japanese soldiers. They nodded and went running to grab the men and drag them towards the underbrush, gently removing their rifles, ceded without protest.

Hunter and Tiki took off racing down the beach, then cut into the foliage as the dragon came at them, spewing out a stream of fire like an army flame thrower on an enemy bunker. Above them the greenery burned and they ran the other way, this time with purpose, towards the manhole cover and safety in the subterranean hangar. Just in time, as another belch of flame incinerated the beach, turning sand into glass.

Almost safety.

"I can't fit," came Hunter's surprise.

"Well, now, you decide to get mad!"

Hunter had become the rock warrior.

He heard a noise, metal whirring, and turned to the beach.

"They're opening the hangar door. I'll head that way."

The screech of the dragon was matched by another noise: the sound of an airplane propeller.

As he approached the opened hanger he had to step over the half discarded body of the corporal. 'So close to going home', Hunter muttered, 'like we all wanted to do and then this'. He felt his arm muscles ripple and his shirt tear. 'Damn, going to have to figure out how to avoid ripping clothes every time this happens.' Tommi could design a malleable costume, and with that thought he ran down the ramp.

At the bottom he saw something no American had seen up close, if at all. One of the soldiers was in the cockpit checking instrumentations, monitoring the engines' RPMs. Shiggy had found a discarded pilot's jacket to put on and was wrapping around his head a hachimaki headband with the rising sun. One of the soldiers handed him a senninbari, a "belt of a thousand stitches" sewn by a thousand women who made one stitch each. He was doing a quick ritual of sake, a last Shinto prayer, a wish to be remembered at the Yasukuni Shrine in Tokyo.

Shiggy no longer, the man who entered the cockpit of the Rufe was a determined Lieutenant IJN Pilot Shigeru Mori. One last mission.

Speaking to Mori would not have changed the pilot's mindset, so Hunter raced up to Tiki Shark, standing as witness to the most amazing sortie to be flown.

"He's going to commit suicide going after that thing."

Tiki shouted back over the engines' mounting propeller whine, "Yes, I think that is his purpose."

"But the war is over, the Empire dissolved. His sacrifice would be useless."

"No, it won't. He punched me on the chest and said, "Tommi" twice. He's not trying to be heroic for Japan he's doing it for the woman who saved him as a POW, who allowed him to find a purpose to redeem himself for a new good."

"What new good?"

"To save you so you can get to her. He understands his death will now have value. Creating that value, Mister Hunter Hopewell, is now your burden."

Indeed through the cockpit window, Pilot Mori's grimness faded for an instant into a quick, knowing, and a gritted teeth smile to Hunter. The man was going to die with inner peace. His fellow traveler, Ish, bowed to his friend, knowing duty.

"Well, nothing will change, if the fire breather gets to him first. The dragon will torch him before he gets in the air."

"Yep," agreed Tiki, "I guess you probably figured out by now — and he put on a movie role accent — "of all the islands in this big ocean, this flaming serpent just happened to find ours, and his first attack was aimed at you, not at that soldier."

Hunter got the message. "The creature is one of Kū's allies. From the other side."

"Maybe they have a mental homing device aimed at you. Get rid of Pele's human god, and the bad guys win. Ok, Hunter, go play dodge balls — yours — with Dragon Breath and be the distraction not the appetizer."

Hunter understood what was expected and ran from the hangar slope not looking back, searching the sky for the next attack. In the distance he saw the dragon making its target run. He headed down the beach huffing at full speed, away from the hangar entrance but right at the beast, its two claws extending towards him. He could have ducked, but no, he was the distraction.

Like a freight train hitting an immovable object the dragon's claw struck, not impaling him but encircling with a suffocating squeezing, jerking him from the ground. He was not all god; the impact knocked the wind out of him. The talon was closing like an anvil vise. Act now, he shouted to his brain, and he pushed with all his might, squirming, and slipped under one talon, using it as a stepping stool, and bent another talon back until he heard it snap.

The dragon spit flame and throated pain, and dropped

Hunter.

Holy shit, he was a hundred feet above the middle of the atoll. This would be an Olympic-event belly flop, and it was.

Splat.

Wind knocked out of him for a second time, his head broke the surface and he started swimming back towards shore, satisfied, for he could see Pilot Mori's plane reach the water and on its pontoon skids begin accelerating for lift-off .

Fins were circling him: Grey Reef sharks. 'You gotta be kidding, back to being the appetizer.'

One shark came at him and he punched it hard on the snout before it had a chance to bare its teeth, the impact knocking cartilage into its brain, killing it, and its death thrashing drew more finned predators to an anticipated meal. Another shark hit his back but even with its jaw open could not break the scaly skin covering Hunter.

Their attacks only raised his anger level, a good thing at the moment.

He had forgotten about the black dragon, and when he turned in the water, there it was, some sort of toothy glowering, hovering, within striking distance. Was he susceptible to being boiled? He couldn't take the chance. Hunter reached out and grabbed a passing reef shark by the tail and fin, dug in his own finger nails until they ripped into the fish's leathered skin, an almost impossible fabric to tear, and twisted the shark around to use it as a shield, just in time, for he was consumed in roaring flames.

The dragon stopped blowing fire to survey its carnage. Hunter dropped the crispy critter he held, and turned and paddled as fast as he could until sand was under his feet. He stood, accepting that there was no quick shelter to run to; the foliage was too far away. The hangar door had been raised and closed.

Alone, against one of the bad god's devils, Ku's pet. No atomic blast could have spawned this fire-breather so quickly. If he could get to the beast's underbelly he might be able to do damage, but it was a long shot. Then, he heard the plane's approach.

Pilot Shigeru Mori, four years ago, had been escort wing commander, with his Zero division, assigned to protect the bomber squadron making the attack on the aircraft carrier *USS Lexington*. He excelled in battle tactics. If he'd more time he would have made his approach in a steep diving descent.

But the dragon's presumed acute animal hearing would have detected the engine's high-pitched whine, so he made his approach above the water across the atoll with flight speed pushed to maximum.

"That's a Nakajima float Fighter-Bomber. U.S. Navy called them 'Rufes'. Two machine guns mounted on the forward fuselage, two 20 mm cannons on the outer wings. Jeez! It has a bomb mounted on the underneath carriage. It looks pristine and ready to go!"

The dragon did hear the unusual noise and turned, starting to flap its wings to rise back into the sky, but too late; the last thing the creature saw was an intent face, satisfied, then the propeller hit, followed by the bomb's explosion.

For Mori's ultimate sacrifice, Hunter said solemnly,

"Banzai!" then threw himself into the shallows, where part of the disintegrating carcass crashed down upon him. When he rose from the frothy red water, he was laughing, his rock-hewn body size diminishing.

Tiki Shark was running towards him.

Hunter felt buoyant. "We can defeat these monsters. They are not infallible or indestructible. I just need to bring a bigger war club to the party."

Later that afternoon, they heard the *Island Clipper* enter the lagoon. Ishiro sat on the beach with the two surviving Japanese soldiers. They were listening to his stories, sad to them, that the war was over, that the Americans had the power of atoms that could destroy entire cities. They heard him tell of Hunter, the scaly god who fought and defeated the Gojira (or at least it went away). The soldiers would give them no problems. They had seen the human god fight a sky dragon and survive. If the Americans had such samurai warriors as Hunter who became armor clad when angry and transformed from man to god, Japan could not have possibly won the war. Both men, youths actually, merely conscript draftees, with no lofty ideals, cried unashamedly, only wanting to go home and see their families, to rebuild their lives.

In the dusk, Hunter stood staring at the lagoon, smelling the oil smoke of the destroyed plane mixed with the odd odor of burned creature flesh. Tiki Shark walked up to him and, guessing his friend's reasons for silence, said simply, "He died because of the way he was raised; *bushido*, in the end, he could not fail his Emperor."

"Yes, but he found a cause he could die for: saving others, saving people like his fellow soldiers and you and me, those with white skin. I think he understood the world had changed and it was not his world anymore. But he did show me that the humanity of doing what's right still exists."

Later that evening, men became brothers, sitting around the fire, a bottle of the late corporal's sake passed around, Mori's heroism toasted, strange cigarettes smoked, some weird kind of tobacco Tiki Shark had bartered from a Maui gift shop owner ('Wowie,' said Ish, mimicking Tiki Shark's drifting appraisal of the inhaled smoke).

The dragon steaks were not bad either. Tasted like chicken.

62

The gunfire, its unrelenting staccato, unnerved Tommi and she covered her ears. Every waking moment she had sought to avoid, put distance between herself and Kū. When they did see each other by chance there was a mutual ignoring of each other. It was not mere target practice with these new

Kalashnikov rifles, they were holding a training session for Kū, and the sailors seemed eager to obey his wishes, to move as he commanded. Pele explained that in the hundreds of years he had been a statue, weapons had gone modern, machine guns versus *pololū* the long spear and *Lei-ʻO-Manō*, the shark-teeth club. Kū had once used those weapons so bloody to start a rivalry, brother-against-brother, in a war history never recorded.

He was merely learning the new tools of his ancient craft.

"Kū will not only try to conquer by creating his armies," Pele continued, "he lives by absorbing the destruction of war. If he merely helps to launch a war, bring hostile parties together so that they do battles unto themselves, he is happy. In the end, war and anarchy, the breakdown of humanity, will overwhelm everything. You all call it…," she thought for the right word, "an apocalypse. When he does, his army will be so strong the gods of heaven must come to do battle, to save themselves, and frankly, they are soft. They have always been muses or creators. Being brave and fearless does not wear well on most of them."

That conversation had taken place the night before in their cabin, with the door locked on both sides. This afternoon, Pele found her to announce, "Tomorrow morning we dock in Hilo. We must find warm clothes before we advance to the top of Mauna Kea. The weather report, I heard from their communications officer, says there has been an extraordinary weather system over the island, and the top of the mountain has received a record amount of snow and ice. How lovely."

"Any ideas on your battle plan yet? Kū learning how to shoot does not seem god-like yet any weapon in his hands has me worried."

"Haven't got a clue. Baran will certainly be pissed when he discovers Super Soldier serums don't exist. Something will have to happen before then as you know. Just be ready to act."

"Any tingly feel or heavenly voices as to Hunter's whereabouts?"

"Yes, I do get, what would you say, 'vibrations', that scientists call 'seismic'; it is said when I yawn the earth has tremors."

"Oh, please."

"My brother and sister were able to slip through the void. I do believe my fellow gods saw Kū recruiting allies, and wanted to make the battlefield equal, if at all possible."

"Aren't your siblings only sea creatures?"

"They can be many things, a school of fish, or a good size fish. What did you call them, call me?"

"Shape changing, personality shifting. I saw that at the Red Tiki when we first met. Polynesian native, naïve, to jive teenager, immature know-it-all. I just don't know how you do it."

"Someone has to die for me to become someone else. We gods are tricky."

The gunfire having resumed, a chill of worry brushed through Tommi. "I hope Hunter is okay, but how is he going to get here?"

"I sense he fought a battle yesterday."

"What? You didn't think to tell me that? Is he alright?"

"I sense he is and there is one less demon to oppose us." The question Pele now posed pushed Tommi to cross a mental line.

"Are you that concerned for him?"

Tommi hesitated, but what did it matter, if there was a time to stake one's claim, then... "Yes. I want him here with me and both of us safe, to be back in Honolulu, dancing the night away at the Red Tiki and far from this madness."

"You two are forever entwined with this 'madness'. The Fates have decreed."

"How can anyone speak with certainty? For Hunter to reach us in time he would have to fly here, and by tomorrow."

"Yes."

"But the Clipper is damaged. And I did not see him sprout wings. It would take a miracle."

"Or the will of the gods. "

"To save the world, can't we have both?"

Lockeed Electra 10E

63

He finished his inspection.

"It's a miracle," spoke Captain Lang, mystified. "But they kept that plane in top notch condition. Except for the under struts, large pontoons instead of wheels. Yes, it's flyable. With little to do, this must have been their pet hobby."

Hunter Hopewell and Captain Lang considered the last remaining airplane that could fly.

"Tiki Shark said last night, he was going to pray to all his known spirits to get us out of here. This may be the ticket." He looked hard at the pilot. "I need to get to Hawai'i as soon as possible. Do you think you can do it?"

"If we top off the tanks, the distance is 2,300 miles, well within range. The only thing that might be a bother is her weight on the pontoons, since she was never originally configured for them."

"Does Engineer Spenser know anything about this plane? Who it once belonged to? Tiki Shark, I know, has no idea."

"Naw, Spense sees a working machine not its pedigree. The Japs, I mean the Japanese, had six years, or whenever they got hold of the plane to do the modifications. And with the Japanese markings, he didn't pay it much attention. I've been sending him to scrounge radio parts for the *Clipper*. He thinks he might be able to build a composite transmitter with the Japanese equipment. It would get us a rescue plane or ship, hopefully within a week."

"Not soon enough. Can we depart within the hour?"

"Give me two hours. Who do you want to go with us?"

"He can't fix the *Clipper* to fly but Spenser needs to stay and fix the plane's radio. I don't trust the two Japanese soldiers not to have some second thoughts about revenging the homeland, so Ish stays to keep them company. And I can't leave Tiki Shark. Believe it or not, his flakiness kinda grows on you. Besides, he's my prophet sidekick."

"What?"

"Private joke. Obviously, Tiki Shark is going to have leave Mr. Billy the Goat behind. No room and I can't stand the bleating ba-ahs. He'll be heartbroken but he'll get over it. It should survive here."

"What do you want to do all about this?" Lang pointed to the American plane. "We could tell the world."

"Considering the way I've been seeing the world go, I think some mysteries should remain buried. Literally."

"What do you think happened here? How this got here?"

Hunter laughed out a silent thought. 'Right. After all I'm a former Intelligence officer whiz, or was.' Hunter put his hand on the cold fuselage. "Well, Lang, in a nutshell, they were trying to make Howland Island, 2,500 miles from Lae, New Guinea. They couldn't get a radio bearing, decided to turn back and aim for the Marshall Islands, and something happened; a wrong bearing in the navigation, whatever, they overshot the upper Marshalls, ran low on fuel, and crash landed in the lagoon here. Ripped out their undercarriage. There's no water here, nothing to sustain them. If this underground hangar was already built it was well hidden and was there a garrison on Bokak Atoll during... 1937? I don't know. They died — how I could only guess — and no one knows the true story. Do you?"

"I knew Fred Noonan," said Lang, somber to the moment. "He worked for Pan Am. Helped lay out the China *Clipper* routes in the Pacific. Later taught navigation for Pan Am's San Francisco to Manila run. He wouldn't have gotten lost so easy."

"And the graves we found, there were three Christian crosses among the other 'Asian' burial markers?"

The two surviving Japanese soldiers had given everyone the grand tour and pointed out casually the small grave yard in a side tunnel. Keeping the gravesites underground was a smart move and maintained the stealth of staying out of sight. The soldier, in telling Ish who gave his own hand signal translation said it was all like this when he and his fellow troops arrived in 1942. He said and pointed to where they had buried two soldiers since their arrival, one from beriberi, the other, shark bite from swimming in the lagoon. Chomp, chomp, the obvious hand gesture.

There were 18 gravesites in all, though many might cover only cremated remains. Since construction began nearly 35 years ago, each grave had been maintained religiously and with reverence under mounds of coral rock, except for the three graves marked with stick crosses.

"Wild guess: the plane was found first. Over time and typhoons and heavy seas, they found the bodies later in the sand. Somehow they knew they were foreigners, and a decent Christian burial seemed proper."

"The third cross?"

Hunter shrugged to mysteries that would never have answers.

"Maybe a stowaway like Tiki Shark on our flight. A shipwrecked Allied sailor during the war? No, I would hazard another wild guess, that one of the soldiers was a Christian and he handled the internment. And then he later died and his fellow soldiers treated him as he did others, regardless of creed."

"They just should have let everyone know back in the U.S. whenever they found the plane."

"And what? Have American newspapers hound them, fly in teams to scour the atoll? Reveal a secret airbase when war clouds were looming? No, tell Spenser to shut it up after we leave. No one the wiser. This is a shrine of past dreams unfulfilled."

They both looked again at the modified float plane, seeing past the Japanese decals and camouflage green-brown stripes, to when it once, in its glory of silver metal sheen, was identified by the now removed tail number *NR16020*.

64

In drizzling rain, as the *Altair Beria* spy-ship eased into the Hilo harbor, Tommi found Pele at the railing looking towards the town, viewing the devastation that was still apparent. The central district of the town at the harbor's edge had been obliterated four months earlier by a tsunami in a series of 15- 30 feet high wave surges. 159 people died in the Hilo tsunami, generated by an underwater earthquake in the Aleutian Island chain. Tommi who now knew Pele's power, accepted the goddess had caused this destruction, and indirectly, the deaths. Was Pele admiring her work, appraising her own force of nature? And was this merely collateral damage when Pele first came looking for Hunter Hopewell?

The steel rail track of the Hawai'i Consolidated Railway twisting, its route across the many gulches along East Hawaii's Hamakua Coast had been totally destroyed; only truck traffic thereafter would be used to deliver sugar cane to the outgoing ship carriers to the U.S. mainland. The roads they would be traveling were not in the best condition, beaten to ruts by military traffic during the war years.

Could there by anything worse than a tsunami when you are standing on the shoreline?

Yes, much worse: Tommi noticed it immediately upon debarking.

The twenty or so Russian sailors and technicians who left the ship did so in a lock-step trance. No ribaldry of being on shore, no ogling the shop girls or singing drinking songs. They all walked like heavy-footed soldiers, but even more so, what was Tiki's word...like zombies, definitely under a hocus pocus spell. Especially frightening were two observed revelations: they were taking hand signals and one word directions from Kū, and more terrifying, Peter Baran, spy extraordinaire, also saw what was going on, that he had lost control of the situation, and Tommi could see when she and he exchanged glances that Baran feared for his life.

Not a good sign. Baran (mistakenly) now knew the power of the Super Soldier, and if he had any doubts about Pele's made-up stories of Nazi secret experiments and the formula hidden away in some abandoned lab on top of Mauna Kea, he made himself a believer, mobilizing the expedition to buy warm clothing, for although it was currently 70 degrees at the harbor, all reports indicated a snow storm at the summit. Next step, rent heavy duty vehicles to transport their party up the mountain and sufficient firepower to ward off any ambuscade adversaries. Tommi saw it in Baran's fervor. Not under Kū's hypnotic trance, Baran was insanely determined, she deduced, to find the Super Soldier formula, inject himself, and take back control from Kū, oblivious to the god's true unworldly powers. At the moment when Baran discovered Pele's story was a sham, she felt sure, he would turn homicidal, and in his blind rage would seek out the person, the one frail, prick-and-she-bleeds human, who has no super powers, and Tommi would become the first to die — in an unthinkable and horrible and excruciating torture.

Chikushō. Her time had run out.

65

N ot a good sign."

"What?" Hunter asked of pilot Lang above the vibrating noise. Cotton swabs stuffed in ears did not help.

"I've got an oil pressure gauge dropping."

Hunter looked out the co-pilot's window back at one of the two Pratt & Whitney Wasp engines, seeing nothing out of the ordinary, considering he was watching the propellers spinning to 600 horsepower efficiency.

"That one looks okay to me."

Pop. Pop. Like an auto backfire.

"Guess it was the other engine," replied Lang, very calmly.

Hunter went back into the stripped down passenger cabin. Tiki Shark, as usual, sat sketching. He wore a black rubber mask that covered his entire head, with the face cut out.

"What's that?"

"Tommi made it for you. If we are heading somewhere cold, this could add some layer protection. Trying it on for you."

"You look like seal." Hunter looked out the window to the starboard engine. He kept his expression neutral.

"Everything OK?"

"Yeah, but keep that seal thought."

Back in the cockpit, he informed Captain Lang. "Oil spewing out that engine."

"Damn those — -. They repaired everything, but without a pilot I bet they never air tested the engines, put them through some maneuvering. In fact, this might clear up one of the mysteries. Not a navigational mistake, nor low fuel. They had a blocked oil line."

"What's that do?"

"Engine loses lubricating flow, or — ."

The engine popped a few more times, and then the propeller rotation slowed.

"Or the engine could conk out."

"Critical?"

"We can fly awhile, but we might overheat with just the one engine."

Tiki poked in his black rubber head, slightly nervous.

"Is an engine stopping, is that some sort of planned maneuver, like resting it for a while?"

"Tiki," said Hunter, "nothing so far to worry about. Go locate where the life jackets are and make sure the raft is at hand."

"Not a life raft again." Tiki Shark went off with a hustle.

"How far are we from The Big Island?"

Pilot Lang stared to the horizon.

"I can see land ahead, but I can't promise you I can cross the island to land at Hilo."

"What's our choice?"

"Well, they were experimenting with this Lockheed Electra E as a pontoon scout plane, but it still flies like a Douglas DC-2. Again, I bet they never even lifted it in the lagoon. But, Hunter, keep in mind, my specialty is Clipper water landings. How bad can that be?" He gave a weak smile. "I'd go check on Tiki and make sure he doesn't inflate the life raft inside our plane. Besides, once again, we can taxi for a while on one engine. The closest place is the old whaling village of Kawaihae. I'll aim for that."

"Not literally, please."

At that moment, the second engine started popping sparks.

"Okay, get back there. I think we might have to find a wet runway."

Back in the passenger cabin, Tiki Shark was charging around trying to throw non-vital items into a canvas bag. He handed Hunter a pile of rubber stitched together.

"What's this?"

"Like my headdress. Didn't you see Tommi make this for you? It's a one piece bathing suit made out of this rubber stuff. It's supposed to keep you warm... like if we're swimming in a cold ocean or up on a freezing mountain. You can put your clothes over it, and best of all, it will expand when you do and hide your family jewels when your clothes are ripped off. Please, for propriety's sake."

The plane started descending, more gliding.

"Okay, it can't hurt anything, can it?"

One minute later, the second engine quit; the ocean came up fast. Tiki Shark and Hunter braced themselves, and all seemed like a safe but rough three point landing, with a little bouncing, as the front pontoons hit the tops of the small waves. Unfortunately, the Japanese pilots were used to the balance pontoons under the entire length of the Japanese Scoutplane, the Rufe. With the Electra the Japanese mechanics had sought to add a back skid pontoon to balance the weight, and the innovation functioned to the point where a wave caught that skid and broke it partway off, creating drag, shoving the plane, still at about fifty nautical miles airspeed, to swerve in a fast loop, a u-turn, hitting another wave at the wrong angle and the Lockheed Electra flipped over.

The water filling the cabin brought Hunter conscious. Everything was topsy-turvy. Tiki Shark floated in his life jacket sputtering, trying to hold his painting supplies and waterproof kit over his head. Hunter noticed the air pocket diminishing; the plane was sinking. He tried the door but it was stuck, a lack of pressurization.

"Get mad."

"Goddamit, Tiki, I'm just trying to open the door." This quick pissed-off snap did the trick; the door did not open as much as Hunter broke it open.

"Swim out. I'll push the raft out to you to inflate."

"Where's Captain Lang?"

"Jeez, the cockpit is lower than we are. You, get moving. I'll get Lang."

He swam towards the front of the plane, now nose down under water. Diving down and making his way to the cockpit, Hunter found an air pocket and Lang floating in his harness, unconscious, a nasty cut over his eye.

Hunter dragged the captain back underwater with swiftness he did not know he had in him. He dove and exited, found Tiki floating in the raft, and made his own grand entrance, pulling the pilot with him, still out cold.

"He may have a concussion. Let's just keep his head up. Where's the paddles? Looks like we have about a good four miles to shore?"

"What paddles?" The Lockheed Electra slid under the water and disappeared.

Hunter looked at Tiki and felt his body starting to huff.

"Don't get mad, we might not be able to handle any more weight."

Hunter took a breath and smoldered. He could see the island of Hawai'i, but still a ways off, a long ways off. The raft drifted as did his mind. It was a beautiful day where they floated and yet beyond the distant shoreline up the hills towards Kohala, Hualalai and Mauna Kea, the skies had closed in with the turbulent darkness of a vicious storm in progress. If that wild Nature could only slow the Russians down, give him time. 'Ok,

Pele, you got me into this fine mess... is this all you got?'

"Tiki, call on your fellow tiki spirits? Prayers or chants, I don't care. We need some serious assistance here."

Thirty minutes later, *Bump.*

"Did you feel that?"

Bump.

"Hunter, there's something underneath us. Think it's a monster, from Kū?"

"Ac-cent-u-ate the positive, lad. Pray again, just be more specific. Like for an American submarine." Hunter was keeping his tone light, for if anger turned him into a weapon, and he fought out here in the ocean, there would be little chance of his reaching shore in one piece, and none for his companion.

Tiki Shark threw himself to other side of the raft, petrified.

"Don't look now but it is an animal, a fish, a large one."

The raft half rose out of the water onto the back of a large creature, there was no attack.

"Thank your gods, Tiki. We are being carried and we are heading towards land."

"Hunter, don't get mad. But I did pray. I prayed to you to save me."

Hunter hadn't expected that. Responsibility for someone else. He shifted away from what those ramifications meant, and peered over the edge of the raft. "Looks like our rope line has hooked the pectoral fin of a whale shark. The biggest I've seen, must be over 40 feet long. And the good news is they are filter feeding sharks, not meat munchers like the Great Whites."

Tiki Shark stared, surprised to find the raft half out of the water on the shark's upper back, wedged against the dorsal fin. Gulping his Adam's apple, he bravely patted the fin with a lame, "giddy-up," then turned with amazement.

"Hunter, don't you see? This is the spirit fish, *Ka-moho-ali'i*.

He is the brother of Pele. In Hawaiian mythology, when ships are lost at sea, he is known to guide sailors back home. Hunter, Ka-moho-ali'i will take us to land. And Pele sent him."

"All I know is, if and when we do land, you have to get Captain Lang to a hospital. I have to go up Mauna Kea."

"Your destiny awaits."

"I don't know about that, but this day, I have some sixth sense somebody is going to die, and I will make sure it's not me." He thought of Tommi, worried about her, believed he would die if need be to save her. No, think only positive thoughts. Again imagining Tommi, smiling at those few good memories and wishing for more, he took note of his black neoprene underwear expanding as well, snug in the loin region, keeping the body heat in and the chill off as a light rain began to fall.

Part Seven

The Mountain

66

ropical rains with muggy humidity two hours ago, and here snow is falling and looks worse up the mountain, which I can't even see. And this cart path road ends here, hardly half way up, I'm guessing. How did your father get his equipment in?" Baran gave Pele a suspicious inspection. His dour mood had been set in place back in Hilo when Pele spent her (delaying) time shopping for wardrobe to make the trek. The goddess looked out from under the parka hood of her stylish Hawaiian blizzard outfit. The fact that they found a store that offered winter clothes seemed surprising, more so to learn that during the winter months people actually hiked up to the summit and could go skiing on the top of the 14,000 foot high mountain, higher than Mt. Everest, if one did the measurement from the sea floor.

Strange that this was late summer and Baran had yet to grasp that they were heading into a freak summer snow and ice storm bound to break meteorological and historical records, going as far back as when glaciers had formed on the mountain 3,600 years ago.

Pele, dismissively, responded without courtesy to the furniture salesman-atomic spy.

"There are only cattle and wild pig and goat trails to the summit, but I know there are buildings up there. They were built before your kind started a war and offended the people of this island. My mountain is sacred."

He was disgusted at her singsong litanies.

Baran pointed to Kū and then pointed up. Kū nodded in the affirmative, and he, followed by obedient soldiers, started up a trail, many of the men openly carrying rifles, others bearing food in knapsacks. "Okay, then, we hike. I swear you better be right about this."

"You certainly will find your reward," she said. He turned from her teasing smirk, and yelled at those men who hesitated with second thoughts of what they had volunteered for.

Tommi, standing nearby, likewise attired as if she were skiing in St. Moritz , wondered how Baran had not yet added up all the odd occurrences and deduced that something was amiss in the world. She fell in step beside Pele as they joined the procession, trailed from behind by a grump guard assigned to them.

"Why is Kū coming along? What's in it for him? He has to be wary of your — charms."

"Gods are not all knowing, especially if they have been out of circulation. Kū sees the modern world, knows he knows less, especially about modern wonder drugs, so for the time being he is buying into Baran's hope for untold power from a Super Soldier syringe. Plus, if you noticed, he does have his following. He is practicing to define the limitations of his powers. Mentally and physically atrophied from years inside a statue, the hike will do him good."

"What is your strategy to snare Kū? You have an idea by now?"

"No clue. But it will come to me if all the right circumstances align."

"Why can't you blow the mountain? I looked it up in the gift shop. It exploded 5,000 years ago. Do that again. You do have the power to bury them all in a lava avalanche?"

"Destroy this whole end of the island? Kill thousands of people? Why, certainly. But no, Kū is on to my last trick; in fact he has been haughty with boasting, believing that he can defeat any fiery thing I throw at him. He sees the heat of earthly fire as my strong suit. The storm is not a threat but only an inconvenience. Come, let us tread carefully, the rocks are slick, and the snow will become deep where we are going."

67

The ambulance, siren wailing, tore off to the County Hospital with wounded Tiki Shark comforting injured Captain Lang who had starting recovering amidst groggy mumblings. "His girlfriend, I think," said Tiki before departing. "Keeps saying, 'Sorry, Amelia, I lost it.' If he starts talking about giant lizards fighting tiki gods, doctor definitely will say concussion."

Hunter had no choice, being in a hurry, but to stand out in the pouring rain, and try to thumb a ride, to what, save the world? To where? *Oh, the top of Mauna Kea, if you please.*

Cars flew by him, many enjoying the meanness of splashing puddle water all over him. And his appearance did nothing to invoke sympathy or slowing of cars. His latest navy khaki look had rips, oil smears, and underneath, a seeming black t-shirt, in the upper tropics, definitely out of place.

Only those would stop who could sympathize with a husky man down on his luck and out of pocket change, nevertheless standing, in a rain-purifying attitude of beach bum rakishness with his thumbing finger upraised, proud in humility.

Who? What good Samaritans? Teenagers with no cares in the world, no prejudices yet formed, knowing the poverty of the allowance, they best understood the forlorn and would welcome those who seemed helpless. And he was right.

The old beat up pick-up truck clanked to a halt next to Hunter. He started crawling in the back of the pick-up bed, but it was stuffed with two tied-down surfboards whose owners made room for him in the cab. They were now three pilgrims squashed together, no heat, one windshield wiper not working. You could see the moving road through a hole under the driver's gas pedal. Hunter felt blessed for the rescue. He sensed he had little time left.

"Thanks for the ride."

"Where are you headin'?" Two young teenage boys, the outdoors type, dark skinned, one lighter than the other, queried him.

"Mauna Kea."

"Somewhere up on Saddle Road?"

"No, on the mountain, somewhere up from there. I'll know it when I see it." Both boys gave him a quick glance as to sobriety.

"They say it's snowing as far down as 6,500 feet. Guessing it could be two feet at the top. Craziest thing we've heard. Rain and waves cut short our surfing day," said the kid in the middle seat. "Real freak weather. So bad today even the pig hunters are coming off the hills."

"I need to find some warm clothes. Even hiking boots."

"Are you military?"

"Use to be." Why lie?

"On Mauna Kea, what's happening?"

"I'm going to kick some trespassers in the butt all the way down to Hilo." A little lie could not hurt.

"They're defiling Mauna Kea?"

"Something like that."

"My father is kahuna nui in our clan. He can tell the stories of the second migration on my grandmother's side going back 30 generations when Pili first came to the islands. He says Mauna Kea is first-born son of sky father Wākea." Hunter did recognize the Hawaiian features in the surfer boy's face.

"Well, I can tell you if I were Pele I'd be pretty upset at them. Sacrilegiousand all that." He laughed to himself. Did he just now speak the truth or a lie?

The pick-up pulled to the side of the road, and Hunter thought he was going to be ejected, but the Hawaiian teen passenger excused himself, pulled out his surfboard from the pick-up, and scurried up the hill towards a small turquoise house sitting on cinderblocks: company housing for sugar cane employees.

Hunter and the other teenager were alone, the boy driving down the highway squinting out the window seeking visibility through the sheets of rain; travel progress was at a crawl. Not fast enough. Hunter wanted to encourage speed, but he saw the dirt highway road was mud.

Trying to hide his anxiety, he took a quick glance at the pick-up's interior. Teen trash of an empty soda bottle, an *Argosy* magazine, and something odd, a set of spurs on the floor, jangling at each bump.

"I'm Hunter Hopewell," he offered, breaching the lull in conversation.

"Danny. Danny Gonzalez."

"Is that your girlfriend?" Hunter pointed to a high school annual photo of a pretty Hawaiian girl clipped and held, probably with chewing gum, right under the dashboard, above the radio.

"Was. Chrissy Iolani. She died."

"Oh, I'm sorry to hear that."

"Accident. Just a month ago. She talked brassy but she was great fun. In the groove."

"Car accident?"

"No, lava. She was on a summer school field trip. She fell into the ocean at the lava fields, scalded to death. Never found her body. Broke my heart."

Hunter did a double take. Working his way back through the past events of his meeting with Pele, enlightenment came. To do the best for the world, a sacrifice had been made. The girl's face in the photo was not the face of Pele, but he'd bet Pele held the child's soul, her knowledge of present society and manners; as he had come to realize, she was a 'hep cat'.

That was the Pele he knew. But definitely also a woman, all the way. Wait, was this Chrissy a virgin? Was a virgin required for sacrifice? Was Tommi a virgin? Pele was not after him; maybe she and Kū needed Tommi for some human sacrifice. How were they going to kill her? Not lava, not boiling water? Not on Mauna Kea. Suffocate in snow? He agonized; he'd be too late.

"Are you alright, mister?"

"Oh, yeah. Just was thinking about catching the bad guys."

"You know I was thinking. I'm working at Parker Ranch, up the road, that's where I'm kinda heading. It's right outside Waimea. Largest cattle operation here or on the mainland. 250,000 acres. Anyway, they just shut down the military training camp there."

"Military camp?"

"Camp Tarawa. Yeah, it's on the ranch. The 2nd Marine Division trained there, and later, preparing for dry terrain, hills and cave fighting, the 5th Marine Division practiced combat, invasion stuff , before they landed at Iwo Jima. Met some marines, about a year or two older than me and we hung together. They promised some of the girls at my school they would be pen pals. Girls never heard from them again. Guess they didn't make it off the rock."

"I was in the Solomon Islands campaign." Bonding talk. He didn't say if he fought there.

"Anyway, I know there are a half dozen soldiers at Camp Tarawa doing an inventory of what they're going to surplus. I bet we could scrounge up your clothes. They owe my boss, Mr. Carter. His father and he are the ranch managers."

"And what do you do for them?"

"I'm a paniolo. Hawaiian for cowboy."

As the pick-up still slogged over the drowned road and to drag out the talk between grown-up and juvenile cow puncher, Hunter mentioned he was testing a water suit (revealing the affixed skin-tight black rubber) for his good friend back in Honolulu, surfing great and movie star Duke Kahanamoku. Thereafter, the floodgates of adulation and surfing stories poured forth and by the time they reached the gates of Camp Tarawa, Danny and Hunter were close as possible to being blood brothers. Awkward, since Hunter's conscience bothered him somewhat with a moral dilemma: did he have sex with Pele's body or Chrissy's mind? And what should he expect at the climactic battle; did it really matter?

68

ure thing, Commander," said the sergeant, turning, barking out an order to a bored supply clerk. Five clerks, in the large Quonset hut were in tedium going through boxes and counting one by one whatever, then resealing. "I think I have what you need. After Iwo, we were going to take the marines up to northern Japan, invade Kuril Islands, then the war ended. Just when I knew I was going to see some action." Hunter had flashed his old I.D., looking more authentic from sea dunkings and dragon close combat showing in its current state, hard used and battle worn. The sergeant at the supply depot had examined it carefully and noted that the man in front of him was an officer with Navy Intelligence. He, being from Texas, a late joiner in '45, and only recently stationed on Hawaii, never had run across that job description.

"Somebody jump ship?"

Why lie.

"After some Russkies. They left their ship in Hilo and headed this way. I'm worried they might chug too much of their potato vodka and steal one of our mothballed ships at Kailua."

"You gonna arrest them?"

"Long enough to stop any thought of piracy and turn them around and send them home. Don't want to make an international incident with the Bolsheviks. They're still our allies."

"I never trusted them. Dance all funny. Talk funny," the sarge said in all seriousness with his west Texas drawl.

"Couldn't agree more."

A supply clerk arrived with an arm full of fleece — gloves, heavy windbreaker coat, thick cotton army pants, all oversized to everyone's curiosity. Setting them down on the counter, the clerk asked, "What shoe size?" Hunter told him a 13 and the clerk gave him a strange look.

"I might grow into them." Not a lie.

In departing the supply depot Hunter only spent one minute in concern over his transportation, or lack thereof, before he saw Danny, sitting in a large Ford stake truck with an ancient, dinged-up horse trailer in tow. Two horses inside, quarter horses, blanketed were neighing and snorting. An old Stetson-wearing codger, had to be in his eighties, with a rifle propped between his legs, opened the pick-up cab door, beckoned, and smiled wickedly. "I heard, son, we're going after some cattle rustlers."

Hunter said nothing. Let the new lie lay.

After an hour of bumpy, sloshing, axle-deep snow and icy roads, the old man, the Parker Ranch manager A.W. Carter, said they were near 6,000 feet and approaching a switchback that the truck would not be able to make, so here was the place to unload the horses.

"This is far as I go. Altitude puts a hammer on my chest. I'll be your back-up if the skunks head down this way. I put a Model 70 Winchester in your saddle scabbard. They say, 'never take a knife to the gunfight', hell, you military men should show up with bazookas or howitzers. Take this." Mr. Carter handed over what looked like to be an old World War I Army issued Colt. 44.

Hunter, growing up in Colorado, though a Denver city boy, had ridden dude ranch mares. Hunter was not a 'paniolo,' so he let Danny take the lead, the snow up past the hooves, a new sensation for the equines, but they endured, an icy wind lashing their heads and glazing their coats; Hunter pushed his own face into his jacket and, whether it was working or not, wished Tommi could sew and wrap him up in a neoprene mummy suit.

They tried to talk as they rode, the wind too fierce, snow stinging. When he could, Hunter seeking to take his mind off the troubles ahead, yelled at Danny, "Should have brought your surfboard. You could surf snow like on the ocean."

"Never thought about that, Mr. Hopewell. Might be a blast; better to try it on a mainland mountain. More snow." They kept moving, slowly trudging, the horse hoofs breaking frozen sleet to make a trail.

Over the rise of another ridge, they met two wild pig hunters tramping downward, quite lucky to not be frostbitten on the extremities.

"Got caught." Both were in hunting gear, dressed for high elevation, but not a freak blizzard. The hunters exchanged recognition with the young boy.

"Say, Danny, We saw a steer, to the south, over the next ridge line. From the distance I couldn't tell if it was Parker beef or a wild one."

"Which is the fastest way to the summit," Hunter asked, impatient, close to his destination, pushing.

"Several ways," said one of the men. "I'd go this way, or where we last saw that steer, it was following a trail."

"Then, there's that way," said the other hunter.

"Are there buildings up there?" Did Pele know what she was talking about?

"Sure, Conservation Corps back in the 1930's built some shelters."

"Any might pass as a work building?"

"Can't say. A couple I think are bigger than just huts."

Hunter turned to Danny. Which way do you suggest we head?"

A whir of snow, a sudden darting past the four men.

Hunter's horse reared.

"What — -?"

"Damnedest largest boar hog I've ever seen." One of the hunters tried to unsling his rifle, but his hands could not get a grip in the cold, and the pig disappeared into whiteness.

"Where'd it go?" The other hunter looked upward, seeing nothing except snow blowing sideways.

"Danny, you follow the hunter's trail and look for your steer. That's all you need to do, and if you see a bunch of men don't try to meet them, don't talk to them, just see which way they're heading and relay the information to Mr. Carter. Let him call the military authorities."

"Where are you going, Mr. Hopewell, sir?"

"I'm going to follow the trail up the mountain left by our oinker friend."

The two hunters, to keep blood flowing, would follow the horse trail down to A.W. Carter and the warmth, if any, of the ranch's pickup truck.

"That's a record one for sure, Harv. Did you see that pig's size?"

Hunter flicked the reins and nudged the horse to the left. They stepped along the broken snow path left by the pig, the same animal he had seen before — in the bar at the Red Tiki — looking for him.

Pele's ex-lover turned pig: Kamapua'a

69

Five of the Russians had turned back and started down even in the face of Baran's threats and cajoling.

"People try to climb the mountain but get sick instead," said Pele.

"They call it 'altitude sickness', something to do with the pressure and oxygen as we go higher. Some can take it, others can't." Tommi let Baran understand why these men might get fatally sick as he still called them cowards and warned he would deal with them later. Interesting that, as she saw it, their sickness somehow broke Kū's spell and his hold over them.

And she saw the war god's confusion. She filed away that tidbit of information, hoping she would have use of it later, if she survived this ordeal.

The climb had become so treacherous they were unsure if their steps traversed any correct trail, when Tommi sensed the storm abating, the wind ebbing. That might not be the best news. Across a small, rocky moraine valley, above the alpine level, the mountain was all crushed lava, windblown and eroded. Four small buildings could be seen.

Baran seemed amazed. "You were telling the truth."

No, Pele wasn't, and Tommi strategically began to assess her chances of escape, seeing that as her only option. As she looked, Nature provided a partial answer. Baran's party with their prisoners had walked away from the storm. It seemed the true summit, 10 square miles, lay several hundred yards across, and still 5,000 feet higher, and to everyone's surprise it was perfectly clear, a gorgeous view under a bright sun, the mountain top like an island above the cloud sea.

The four stone buildings were right at the edge between bright sharp clarity and storm obscurity, the latter a cover of security, a chance to run for help. They had about another hour's hike to reach those buildings; within that time she had to make her move.

Side by side, she whispered to Pele, "To escape we need to run down and back into the storm. I will start slowing down, creating a gap from the others; watch for my signal. I will push the guard down and we both run."

"No, just you run. I'll be fine. It is you that must be saved."

"What? What about Kū? We have to stop him."

"Yes, but where you humans always make the mistake is that you live for your pocket watch, your bell tower clock. The gods blink and eons pass. We measure time by when stars are born and die."

"Cripes lady, I may die and other millions of people may die, just so your fucking time clock is punched to your schedule. Thanks a million." Tommi was really getting tired of god stuff .

"Well, yes, we could stop your Armageddon, this end of times your religious texts preach of, sooner than later. However, this battle is up to you and Hunter and your kind." The goddess shrugged indifference. "But don't worry about me, you go and do your escape plan."

"Don't worry, I won't and I will."

After ten more minutes of fuming, she noticed the clouds were dipping lower, the storm clouds burning off, but the wind not letting up, frigid and biting. She would have farther to run. Oh, screw this all. Rounding a corner on the path, she stopped without notice, bent down as if to tie her shoe, and then slammed the guard, sending him sprawling down the steep slope, watching his head thud hard as he rolled.

Tommi ran back up the trail, a few seconds out of sight, and then moved downhill, jumping from rock to rock, skittering down the steep slope, sliding at times, and then rising to run; fifty yards to reach the cloud haze.

Ping. A nearby rock chip popped near her, followed by the crack of a rifle shot. Though she tried, Tommi could not run any faster; she slipped once, and felt stabbing, sharp needled pain to her hip; keep moving. Another shot, but she heard no ricochet nor felt a bullet hit her body. She glanced over her shoulder; in the fog, three of the armed sailors were scrambling after her, rifles slung. Did Baran want her alive or were they just trying to get close, move in for the kill? She sensed the moisture of Mauna Kea's clouds on her face, even within the misty mantle hiding her. The race to safety was far from over.

Hunter heard the echo of gunfire, though where it came from he could not tell. He urged the horse on, afraid to canter, afraid to slip into a collapsed lava tube crevasse with one false step. *Craaack.* The next echo. Damn, where to go, what to do? The frustration ate at him; he was angry at himself for being so impotent. His body started bulging, his skin cracking as a new layer of scales broke the surface, then another. I feel shitty mad.

"Ok. No more Aloha for you."

70

Baran had broken into the first three buildings, and was on to the fourth, his men tearing the place apart. When Tommi broke away and ran down the mountain into the clouds, he sent three men after her to bring her back. That was a stupid thing for her to do. There would be no place to hide on this barren mount. He put two guards around Pele taking no chances. She had pointed at the fourth building and in duress he completely ransacked the structure. Nothing. There had never been anything. Was the formula real? Had he been deceived? She would tell him everything, one way or the other. He came out of the building with his Luger pistol gripped tight in his hands… to find the two guards on the ground… dead. What?

One of his men hovered over the bodies, staring back at him with a strange expression. Baran inspected the dead men, their faces contorted, black skin to one side of the face: burns. No other marks. Like they were touched by, what? Fire? How could that be? Yes, she said she had taken the formula her Father had prepared. Super Soldier, yes. But if that formula did not exist, then there would be no Super Soldier. How do you explain Kū's powers; how did these men die except by something or someone who could cause such damage? If not Super Soldiers, then what had he found?

Peter Baran turned. Kū stood near him, staring at Pele's handiwork. At least he had this native freak, and he had seen firsthand the Super Soldier powers at work; his Russian bosses would pay a lot to get hold of Kū as a specimen… to dissect him… to see how he ticked.

Kū walked towards Baran.

Yes, I have this Super Soldier, affirmed Baran to himself, regaining the mental strength to think of the next strategy: how to get back to the *Altair Beria*, to get Kū to the Russian doctors. Did he have to bring him back alive? No, they could dissect a corpse.

When he began to raise his Luger, he made the mistake of looking into Kū's eyes.

Within the white invisibility, Tommi continued her hasty scramble downward, the storm quieting, the clouds breaking. They would soon be able to see her movement. She heard shouts: Russian voices, and not so far away. She heard a yell, another apart, and another, over there. She understood. They had formed a line moving downhill; like the quarry she was, either they would come upon her or, driven forward she would soon be in the gun sights of the hunters. She had no choice. She slowed her running, cautious zigzagging, peering into the lifting clouds, the pockets of fog, trying to see in front of her, voices edging closer.

She tripped, then slipped, no, slid. On ice, under snow. Could this be a lake? Or some gulley depression filled with water, flat, but frozen solid?

She sought to regain traction when a clamping hand grabbed her arm yanking her up with bruising force. She knew not to look at him.

From nowhere Kū had appeared; would the inevitability be her head torn from her body? She winced in anticipation, finding herself being dragged back, as a captive. She had to look at him.

It was Baran instead, his eyes wild, strong as Kū.

Then they were rolling, bowled over, sliding across the ice. Three of them.

"This is where you say, 'thanks for saving my life for a second time.'" Hunter helped her up.

Baran on his knees, shot Hunter twice, sending him sprawling.

"You haven't saved me yet."

"Yeah, I noticed." He flicked a bullet from his chest. "You know, your black suit works well, but doesn't stop a bullet."

"Maybe I'll add some Teflon to the next version." She gave him a goofy smile while she tried to scramble to some nearby boulders for cover.

"Teflon?"

"Something new from DuPont."

Baran, frustrated, pointed the pistol at the fleeing Tommi.

He no longer needed her. He shot at her pointblank and Tommi prepared for the velocity shock of being killed.

Hunter held up his hand and let the two bullets drop to the ice.

From behind a protective boulder, Tommi shouted at him in disbelief. "That's a new one." The bullets had to have made a mid-air turn, drawn to Hunter's power.

"Granite magnetism, I guess." Suddenly, he had the whoompf knocked out of him as Kū, from nowhere, sent him reeling across the ice. His anger grew as he got to his feet.

"Ok. No more Aloha for you." Hunter raced towards Kū, who did likewise and their mid-lake collision reverberated up the lake's valley, a shock wave sent a small snow and rock avalanche down the hill that swept one of the sailors off his feet, burying him and his muffled cry.

They walked towards each other, Hunter and Kū, bent on destruction. Tommi could only think of the movie, *High Noon*, the showdown. No drawn pistols. Fist blows. The slugfest began in earnest and as much as she wanted to watch the entire battle, trepidation set in as she saw Baran advance at her readying his kill shot, Hunter too absorbed in his fight to notice her peril.

She saw his face, a feral snarl. She had seen that once before… but not on Baran.

"Die, you mo — ." he began.

Craack. Tommi heard an echo, but not the sound of a close-in pistol shot. Baran grabbed for his shoulder as the Luger went flying. Tommie turned to see a whole bunch of people standing on the ridge above the lake valley, most of them armed. Some old man with a rifle stood up from his sniper position. The Russian sailors saw this also and as they employed their new-fangled 30 round magazine clips, the whole side of Mauna Kea erupted into a crescendo firefight.

After, ten or fifteen minutes of heavy gunfire, Baran grasping his shoulder, returned to the protection of his sailors amongst the rocks. Not really trying to kill anyone, they were simply providing cover fire to allow for the Russian spy to reach dry ground and move back into the fog patches. Not expecting opposition, their superiority vanished; they were sailors after all, not combat infantry. Retreat had become their valor.

Tommi sensed a presence behind her: Pele and some young boy carrying a rifle. They crouched with her behind the boulder, keeping clear of the stray bullets from the sailors versus the shooters on the ridge line.

"Can you believe it," exclaimed Pele, in the voice of precocious, perky youth. "This boy wants to save me, protect me from all those bad men."

The boy looked to Tommi, a complete stranger, for support.

"Ma'am, this girl is just walking around in a storm as if she has no cares in the world."

"And you are just big, dark and handsome enough to do the job," Pele teased. "Now, I got two personal heroes."

"No," said Tommi with her own strong intent. "No, this John Wayne can be your hero. I've got the other one." She returned her gaze to the fight on ice, the Brawl on Mauna Kea, as it might someday be called.

The brawl, battle, duel, whatever, was equal in strength and a draw at the moment, no one able to gain advantage. They were gladiators of good versus evil. One must be victorious, the other dead in his blood in this ice frigid coliseum.

Tommi, out of the corner of her eye, watched Pele slide over to where the large boulder edged into the frozen lake. She placed her hand on the ice, then withdrew it as if testing.

"Danny, can you hit that snow overhang at the end of the lake?"

"Yeah, sure." He was smitten. "If you think it might help."

"Miss J, tell your new boyfriend to launch Kū, that way."

She pointed where she had directed the teenage boy's shot to be placed.

Tommi smirked. "If you think it might help." She rose with an attention-grabbing shout.

"Hunter, out Gojira him to the end of the lake!" She demonstrated with a tossing motion.

Kū, distracted by the woman's command, paused for half a second, enough time for Hunter to duck under a shoulder, dodge a swing, and grab the wrist, yanking in a large swinging motion to pull Kū off his feet in a 180 degree leveraged toss ...and let loose... not before Kū said in plain English... "Who... are... youuu?"

"Now," Pele said to Danny as Kū sailed in mid-air, and the rifle barked twice at the high ice-snow overhang. Pele placed her hand to the ice, a motion the boy did not see as his eyes were focused on what his shots had accomplished. A zipping line of steam, like a hot snaking rope, shot across the ice, to spider web under the falling man.

Kū hit with a thud, cracking the ice, his eyes startled, and then the ice broke, or actually dissolved, like a quick melting; and with a flailing grasp to find some hold, Kū went under. Pele removed her hand. Liquid became cold solid. From above, Danny's rifle shots, or its echoes, released a heavy duvet of slush ice avalanche sliding down slope and covering the hole in the ice on the re-frozen lake. Silence came back to Mauna Kea until it was broken by the cheers of the people on the ridge.

Tommi ran to Hunter sprawled on the ersatz iced boxing ring.

She ignored the heavy breathing of his effort to catch his breath, and covered his face and mouth with apparently healing kisses.

"I am totally out of shape to fight demons and their hordes."

"I'll whip you into shape," she laughed. "Maybe even find your detective handcuff s to keep you in one place."

He saw that he had nothing to worry about; two friends moving past the friendship.

He thought he might as well be blunt. "I wonder if one of those huts at the summit has a mattress? And an inside lock on the door."

"You are going to have to take a snow check, my demi-god. You are the winning general and here comes your stalwart army." Tommi stared at the diversity of characters. "Who are these people anyway?"

71

They arrived in groups.

Hawaiians in native ritual war garb, the Kao warriors, sporting colorful feathered outfits and spears or battle axes seemed oblivious to the cold. Standing next to his son, whom Hunter had met with Danny, their leader, the Kahuna, said with hands raised high, "The evil spirits have been exorcised from the mountains of the gods. They will never return. Our island shall prosper."

The Supply Depot Sergeant whooped, surrounded by his armed posse of clerks, wide-eyed and no longer bored. "Showed them commie bastards not to tread on Hawai'i or the U.S. Marines."

"Didn't know I still had that shot in me," grinned A.W. Carter, taking in deep breaths, years younger in expression.

"Any of you folks see which way that pig went?" asked a hunter, eager to pick up the trail.

"We'll go and see if there are wounded. None from our side." A doctor and several medical corps people sought out any surviving Russians. All the bad guys seemed to have faded into the mists including Baran.

"I asked them to come," Tiki Shark beamed, "I was worried you might get hurt, Hunter. By the way, Captain Lang is A-okay. Told me to tell you, 'Never again.'" Hunter and Tommi agreed with vigorous nods, each holding the other.

The sun awoke the valley into glistening colors, the summit sharp and clear.

"Hunter, maybe we could stay the night, and see the stars. I was told down in Hilo, the summit is where heaven and the stars meet the earth."

"Yes, I'd like a more peaceful repose." He kissed the top of her head. She liked that, a fresh start.

"Hey, guys, look here," Tiki Shark yelled to beckon them over. With his foot he was shoving away the slush ice and gravel from the mini-avalanche.

Hunter and Tommi tested the iced lake. Danny had told Hunter this was Lake Waiau, highest lake in the Pacific basin.

As they walked towards Tiki Shark, Tommi's eyes searched the snow-covered ice.

Tiki jumped up and down. "Looking for cracking? This thing is frozen solid."

Tommi did not see what she was looking for. "Everything from now on will be a little bit strange."

"Yes," Hunter said with a sigh of resignation, "yes, that will be my... our future... if you want it."

"I do," she replied, laughing at the prematurity of that type of answer.

Tiki Shark was on his knees, scraping away, standing back, pointing down at the glassy view.

A tiki statue of gigantic proportions stared back up at them from under the ice. The mud-carved visage looked mean and very ugly.

"That's not the Kū I was fighting," Hunter stared down. "It's a statue."

Pele smiled. "There can be containment, encasement, when the power is stripped. Looks like my sister wanted to try her artistic talent."

"That's exactly what I drew," Tiki Shark, muttered in shy, self-deprecating amazement. "A tiki in a snow storm in a block of ice. I sketched it a week ago on the Clipper but haven't seen the drawing since."

Tommi, to herself, recalled Pele showing her that drawing.

"Tiki, please," Hunter said in mocking jest. "From now on show me all of your art works the minute they're completed so I can adjust my work calendar accordingly."

Tommi regarded the ice-encased statue.

"It looks nothing like Sheftel's Red Tiki, but it's larger and there's a new tiki scowl in place. I would bet Lyle will take it as his replacement without a second thought. Besides, so far the cost to him has been minimal. For us..."

"How are we going to get it out?" Tiki Shark's question found an answer when Pele and Danny walked-slid over, his arm protectively around her shoulders, to Hunter's observation a picture of teenage angst and hormones in full flower.

Pele hugged her new man. "Danny says he can get a Parker Ranch crew up here in a week, and they'll cut it out. I asked to keep it in a block shape. If hell freezes over, a devil can't get you, and it looks like it did."

"Are we shipping it over to Oahu?" Hunter wondered aloud. He wasn't at all sure that he wanted that thing to be near him in Honolulu.

"Oh, first, we'll do a warming stop at Mauna Loa, sprinkle a little of my hair over the statue. Danny's friend is going to bring his dad and a few elders to do chanting. Can't hurt. Kinda lock everything in place for all time."

"Let's all get down to Waimea," beamed Danny, eager to celebrate with new friends, "I know a steak place that's the best."

"You gather the rest of the 'army'." Hunter put on his military airs as their 'general'. "Steaks are on me". A quick glance to Tommi suggested a rethink on who would run any bank account for disbursement. "And Tommi."

Tommi accepted her continuing role as the money manager.

"Tell your restaurant he and I will be by to settle up tomorrow."

"Where you are going?"

"Tonight may be chilly, but it's time to be one with the stars," and Hunter again hugged Tomoe Jingu.

"Not going to be chilly," said Tommi, considering this new adventure, knowing perils and battles remained. She had looked at the snow on the lake and seen nothing, and that was the problem. Peter Baran had been shot, but she found no drops of blood; nevertheless, she would not think about it tonight when the universe would be opened for just the two of them.

He handled bad account collections Tommi passed onto him, and did the odd process service from Sheriff Duke K's office. A reputation had gone out that Hunter was good at solving domestic abuse cases in favor of any battered wife; his intolerance of aggressive husbands, convinced them to tone down the violence, beg forgiveness. Well, and letting a little of his anger drip, and puff up his arms and chest, resulting in a broken jaw or a fist through a door were powerful persuaders.

72

A romantic interlude too short and three days later, Hunter found himself sitting at the bar of the Red Tiki, alone, nursing a Coca Cola supplied by Dutch Leonard, the temporary bartender, who made a good try at cheering him up.

"Look at the positives; you found Lyle's Red Tiki. He's happier than a pig in shit. He's going to make a big splash of its return. Wants it unveiled on Halloween, throw a real costume shindig."

Hunter smiled weakly. "Yeah, everything's just swell." It wasn't as bad as what he felt. He did have an official girlfriend, though they'd had their first disagreement of sorts upon their return to Honolulu.

"If you're going to be fighting monsters," Tommi had said, halfway lecturing, but more out of care than bitching, "You are going to have to learn how to fight. All kinds of ways; learn every trick."

He tried to make light of an unknown situation. "I can throw a few hard punches and then pull out a pistol, finish them off with a couple of rounds."

"Think so, like that boxer, Mister Hard Rock-o Marchegiano? I know a few instructors, and you can start taking karate and ju'jitsu lessons." That was a command, not a suggestion, and Hunter bowed to the inevitable. He would be forced to start a regimen of fitness, but if it could provide endurance for the love-making he had enjoyed for the last few nights, he could stand the sweat and strain of a few push-ups.

But then, Tommi had been caught up in some emergency social volunteerism and had run off to cries for help, leaving him behind. He was visibly upset. *No, I'm really confused, not mad. What is our relationship? Great nights of passion, days of talking like good friends. But where are we going? She rushes off but not before giving me a really weird going-away gift, and a deep kiss with the gift. A thoughtful yet vexing woman whose parting words to me were 'Stay safe'.*

"What is that?" asked Dutch bringing him a Coke and eyeing the curved leather package, thin and long like a small golf club bag, sealed at the top.

Hunter shrugged and pulled out the black veneer scabbard.

"Katana sword." Only slightly did he reveal the blade. Intricate flower designs were ornately carved into the steel.

"From the battlefield?"

"Don't think so. It's a sword like those Japanese samurai guys in their silk bathrobes used to carry around for fighting duels. Tommi called it a *Sukenao* blade. Bought from a destroyed museum."

"Destroyed? Where?"

Hunter hesitated before answering. "Hiroshima. Recovered in the ruins of the city. She gave me a strange look when she gave this to me. Said she heard about this sword going into a fundraising auction and, to help the city rebuild, bought it sight unseen. Said I needed this can opener more than she did."

"Are you going to hang it on your office wall?"

"Naw, supposed to learn how to cut off dragon heads with it."

Dutch laughed at the ridiculous answer. "Where is Tommi?"

"Off on one of her good deed missions. You know about the sugar strike?"

"Yeah, I just read about the details in the Honolulu *Star*. 25,000 union employees out on strike, 33 of 34 sugar plantations shut down. If the strike lasts long it's going to be a major economic impact on your island economy. Luckily, back in my home of Detroit, we have the auto industry, and going from war to peacetime our economy should be strong when I return."

"You are more of a book reader than an assembly line worker, Dutch. You should look into office work, what about an advertising career; they'll be pushing car sales hard to vets."

"Good idea, I'll look into it." Dutch however was a temp bartender and hence the listener more than the talker; he enjoyed studying all the characters he had met, how they spoke and acted. Hunter Hopewell, if he was a writer, thought Dutch Leonard, would provide a colorful sketch in extremes: from drunk to teetotaler, once saying little, doing nothing, animated in mood swings, happy on arrival, now morose. "So, where is she?"

"Tommi has gone off to set up the food banks for the out-of-work plantation workers and their families, putting up a tent city for those who have been evicted by plantation landlords; she's working with that lady attorney, Harriet Bouslog. Even Tiki Shark is helping. The union set up an aid camp over near Mililani Town, next to Wheeler Air Field."

Hunter paused before continuing, "and she's spending the nights out there." He did not know what to think about that, or if he liked it.

Dutch saw it differently, as just a good cause. "Well, good for her." He went back to washing and drying bar glasses, before Hunter could find a way to say aloud, *'yeah, good for her, but I miss her.'* He held the leather encased sword in his hands. *Now, what good is this really? Who'd use a sword in this day and age?*

"Commander Hopewell! Hunter Hopewell!" He looked up from his reverie to see a tall, lanky woman striding his way, a bubbly smile on her face as wide as the room. She was pulling along a man by the hand. She did look familiar, out of his past.

"Of course, you don't remember me," she said, laughing. "We only met once. R&R cocktails in Madras. I went off to a Ceylon posting and they shipped you to Australia, then unspoken parts east into the South Pacific."

Her accent was strong and a faint glimmer of recognition spread across his face. Was that so long ago? "Julie — ."

"Julia McWilliams." She pulled up a chair at his table, and beckoned her companion to join her. "We were on our way back home, and got waylaid in Honolulu. Seems our flight out of Wheeler Field was grounded, some aircraft accident or what, and they told us it might be a few days. Heard you were wounded and sent here, so I did the inquiries — you know how we OSS brats can be — tenacious. So, here we are."

An incident at Wheeler Air Field? Hunter had just said the name earlier, hadn't he? Wasn't Tommi out that way?

Julia waved Dutch over for two beers, and looked to Hunter.

"No thanks, on the wagon."

"Good for you. Oh, and by the way, let me introduce you to my fellow co-worker, Paul Child" — she gave a lopsided grin — "and my fiancée."

"Congratulations," said Hunter, exchanging a handshake with Paul. "Drinks are on me." Yes, thought Hunter, it was nice to see people happy, in love, and not a care in the world. It would be nice, someday.

"You know we heard about this Red Tiki dive," said Julia, "even when I was on station in China."

When the drinks arrived, they clinked bottles, he with his Coke. He offered Julia and Paul a toast to their upcoming nuptials, and asked when the happy occasion might arrive.

"Sometime next year I think," said a beaming Paul, a nice sort of fellow, Hunter concluded. "I'm being transferred back to Washington, D.C., while Julia's job, her OSS job is no more."

Julia jumped in. "Soon as the war ended they stamped my separation letter: 'position terminated'.

"One of the reasons I wanted to track you down," Julia continued, "before this whole show closed down and the tent folded up, was to give you a personal 'thank you'." She turned to Paul. "Commander Hopewell wrote the best field reports during his coast-watching assignment, with such clarity and brevity of words." Again addressing Hunter, she continued,

"When I was first posted to Ceylon, they used your reports as the guide on how to convey information without the trappings."

The beers arrived and Dutch was putting them down, when Julia said to all: "Write for clarity, that was what was in Hunter's reports: leave out all the stuff the top brass are going to skip anyhow." Glasses clinked between the happy couple.

Julia was not to be stopped. "When they stationed me to Chungking [China] I missed those stories. I tried to write like that, even as a lowly "Administrative Assistant,' the label I got stuck with, me, just an ordinary typist-filer at the queenly sum of $2,980 per year."

"No one in the OSS did 'ordinary' work," corrected Hunter.

All three laughed to the private joke, the mirth dying back to quiet drink sipping, as they realized with fond sadness that the glory days of intelligence gathering and clandestine work were over. To Julia and Paul, no more worldly enemies were left to conquer. Not so for Hunter and trying to shake off those recent adventures, he asked them both. "What civilian work will you be looking for?"

"Prior to the war," Paul answered, "I was a teacher at a boys' school. I'm very East Coast, while Julia is a California girl. Where we might live is up in the air."

"I am, or was, as they say, bi-coastal." Julia gave a smile unconcerned as most young people were about the future. "I did graduate from Smith College, though before Pearl Harbor I wrote newspaper ad copy and did Junior League volunteer work in Pasadena. If Paul can find a good job, I guess I will play at being the dutiful housewife." Her expression was glum. Hunter could sympathize; the world war had indirectly enchanted so many Americans by shipping them off to every compass point of the globe.

"So, you don't know what you will do, or where you will live, East Coast, West Coast, or be world explorers?" Hunter empathized with their lack of a game plan, wishing it would be so easy for him. For all three of them, he needed to put a positive spin on the unknown. He was tired of being led. He gave off a laugh. "I've got the perfect solution."

Hunter got up and walked over to a dart board, secured two darts and returned to his seat. "See that world map over there?" He pointed towards the crowded message board behind them on the side wall. Patrons heading toward the restrooms would pass by an unfolded *National Geographic* 'Map of the World', thumb tacked to the wall. "For the last five years that was a tactical map where everyone here could follow the battles across the globe.

Places we never heard of before: Tobruk, or closer to home, like Tulagi. I guess Lyle Sheftel, the bar owner, will take it down some day. Maybe not. World's grown smaller. I should know."

Julia and Paul, their expressions curious, waited for him to continue.

"Okay," said Hunter, his spirits rising.

"I do not believe in fate, but let's just say there are gods out there" — here he let loose a mysterious chuckle — "who might be willing to give this young couple a helping hand in their decision-making, who will use me, little power that I have. I call on the island gods to give me strength, and in doing so to guide my aim, and where this dart point lands shall be your future."

As if an omen, a strong breeze blew open one of the plantation shutters. The coupled laughed nervously, but gave their supportive pledges — why not? In the humor of the moment he could decide the rest of their life; it could do no harm.

Hunter exaggerated his aim, faked an intoning plea to the heavens (the bar's ceiling), and finally gave the dart a strong toss. By some act of whatever, the blasted thing stuck on the wall, and into the map. Dutch, the bartender, who had been leaning on the bar reading one of Lyle's worn Zane Grey paperbacks while sideways watching his customers play at this strange antic, walked over and squinted at the projectile's landing spot.

"You missed the United States altogether. Let's see, seems you hit France, looks like close to… yes, that's it, Paris."

Julia and Paul looked to each other, amazed.

"That is a strange coincidence," said Julia, in slight awe. "Paul, after graduating from Columbia College, studied in France and Italy. He speaks both languages fluently."

"How odd," agreed Paul, "I had given thought to the Foreign Service. Paris would be ideal." He turned to Julia with a lascivious grin. "A perfect place for a honeymoon. And the wine and the French cuisine. You would love it, darling."

"Well, what would I do in Paris?"

"What we both do so well: eat."

"Speaking of this 'believe-it-or not' strangeness," said Dutch to the couple, "tonight's special is French, if you consider Viet Nam colonial French. Our Filipino cook has prepared shrimp and lobster cooked with lemon grass and chili peppers."

"Fate or luck, it sounds good; how is this dish prepared?" asked Paul Child, the now recognized food expert at the table.

"I don't know exactly all the ingredients, but he puts it in a large metal bowl he calls a 'wok', he shuffles it over a wood fire, 'stir fry', they call it… and he uses plenty of butter."

Holding hands, Julia and Paul ordered another two beers. Their flight out would not leave until tomorrow, if then, so why not enjoy an evening at the Red Tiki.

"Your turn," said Julia to Hunter but nudged Paul, smiling, her boyfriend rose to retrieve one dart from the game board. Paul handed a dart to Hunter.

"Oh, you've got to be kidding," Hunter brushed her off. "I have a feeling circumstances may just keep me tied to the islands."

"A girl no doubt being the best reason," smiled Paul, both to Hunter and to Julia. "But if you're on a roll with the island gods and the fates, certainly your aim will hit Hawaii."

Bowing to the light-hearted persuasion, Hunter picked up a dart, made a careful aim at the Hawaiian Islands, and let the missile fly.

"Off the mark, for the U.S. or Hawaii," said Julia, walking over and staring at the map. "Now that is a mistake, I'm sure," said Julia, pulling out the dart for closer inspection. "Korea."

Hunter laughed it off . "See, the gods only favor those in true love. Not for your life do I have plans to visit Korea." He shrugged good-naturedly. "If the gods want, they know where to find me."

The pay phone on the wall rang. Dutch answered. "It's for you, Commander Hopewell."

Seeking some privacy, Hunter retrieved the earpiece, and whispered, "Yes?"

It was Lang, the pilot, himself recently released from the hospital, for his injuries aboard the crashed 'Amelia' plane. He sounded rushed and mysterious.

"You still doing your private eye shtick?"

"Well, you know the times we've had. Just haven't gotten back into the flow, as of yet."

"Got something you might want to see. In fact, I know you need to see this. Right up your talent, if you know what I mean."

"I don't know, Lang. I am really trying to not find trouble, if you know what I mean? And where are you by the way? What's that noise I hear in the background?"

"I'm out at Wheeler."

Wheeler Air Field having been mentioned three times in the last hour or so went beyond mere coincidence. His earlier mention of Tommi's proximity to Wheeler now spiked a true concern.

"I'll be there as soon as possible. Give me your location." He begged off to Julia and Paul, mentioning an emergency and wishing them well. For some unknown reason, except it gave him a strange comfort, he brought along the leather case that held the sword.

73

W hat's that you're carrying?" asked Pilot Lang, looking at Hunter's leather case. "Looks like a pool stick case for Willie Mosconi?"

Hunter ignored the question.

"Okay, tell me, what is going on?" Hunter and Pilot Lang were racing in a jeep across Wheeler Field towards the jungle end of the runway. Lang spoke loudly as wind raced around them. His soft cap covered a bandaged head.

"I was out at Wheeler this morning to do some training on the new Lockheed Constellation. Seems like no one has heard of my recent plane crash, and Transcontinental Airlines is changing its name to Trans World Airlines and wants to start a long distance passenger service to compete with Pan Am and has hired me as one of their pilots." Before Hunter could throw out a 'congrats', Lang continued, "While I was here, they locked the whole placed down. I know the Army chief and got some of the scoop, and that sounded like something you might run into. So, I mentioned your name as one of the Navy's top investigators. I guess the Army military police are little stymied at their discovery and are willing to swallow their jurisdictional pride and let us take a gander."

Hunter could yell his frustration at not having a specific idea as to what was going on, they had pulled up to the airplane.

Hunter jumped from the jeep, amazed at the size. He had never seen one up close.

Lang provided the details. "It's a B-29 Superfortress, a special Silverplate modified version. You know what got me thinking you had better be called in: this plane is part of the 509th Composite Group, that's the unit involved in Operation Crossroads. Hunter, the sister of this plane, *Dave's Dream*, dropped a 'Fat Man' type atomic bomb in Test Able on 1 July 1946. Jeez, Hunter, we were there for the next blast. Wha'd you think are the odds?"

Hunter would not try to figure odds or coincidences. Something was in motion.

The plane was roped off, with heavily armed soldiers guarding the perimeter. An army military policeman, a senior officer by the name of Lieutenant Jeffries met them under the plane at the boarding ladder. Introductions were made. Lang put on the heavy syrup that Commander Hopewell was one of the Navy's best and Hunter realized it was being suggested that he was still in the service and operating with both the Navy's JAG office and OSS clearance. The Lieutenant did seem impressed.

As they crawled into the plane and headed to the cockpit, the Lieutenant began the story.

"The plane flew in, normal approach, and landed like all the daily traffic, but what went weird is it turned and taxied to the end of the runway. Those in the tower saw it weaving back and forth, then it stopped, engines idling. We sent fire and rescue equipment out to the plane when the tower couldn't raise a response from the crew. Emergency folks called for us. And this is what we found."

He pointed to the cockpit where a sheet lay draped over a body.

"The pilot," said the Lieutenant. "Dead when he was found, but the body still warm."

Hunter hesitated. He did not need to be drawn back into a military investigation with all its bureaucratic levels. And yet, the greater unknown had been a central part of him in recent months.

The Lieutenant drew back the sheet cover. The pilot's face grimaced a horrid death; part of his scalp had been sheared off and dangled to the side. Hunter noticed the first odd element of the 'accident scene' and spoke slowly as if trying to fit pieces into the mosaic.

"Look at his hands. Death grip on the yoke. I would guess he was trying to land the plane and shut it down when he died."

"Our interpretation too. But look here on the neck." The Lieutenant, showing little respect for the dead, for someone who had died inconveniently on his watch, turned the pilot's head. A hole the size of a fifty cent piece showed dried blood and some sort of white fluid coagulation.

"We think," said the Lieutenant. "That this was caused by a stabbing instrument."

"And your suspect?" asked Lang, unhappy at the fate of a fellow pilot.

"This was only a three crew supply ferrying operation. The co-pilot and flight engineer are missing. And I guess you'll want to see this." He led them back to the belly of the plane. The cargo area looked like a disaster, with crates and boxes thrown everywhere. The bomb bay doors were opened half-way.

The Lieutenant pointed to a small pool of blood.

"What's your hypothesis, Lieutenant?" Hunter wanted to play careful, not step on toes, and give the impression he would defer to the military police investigation.

"Seems apparent," said the Lieutenant, somewhat cocky, ready for center stage, more so to test his observations of what was definitely some sort of crime scene.

"The plane was on automatic pilot. The crew, back here, got into an argument. The pilot either killed or otherwise disabled the co-pilot and threw the body out the bomb-bay opening, but not before he was stabbed. He was a walking dead man. The pilot returned to his seat and did all the proper procedure for landing, not realizing he was bleeding out internally. His autopsy should confirm that."

"Mind if we look around for a bit?" said Hunter, "We won't touch anything. And will let you know if we find the 'murder weapon'."

"Yes, well, quite, alright. Yes, don't touch anything. We have taken photographs, but haven't really collected any evidence, as of yet." The Lieutenant hesitated and then departed, shouting commands to someone outside the plane.

When they were alone, Lang, looking around, made the comment.

"You don't buy that plot of a co-pilot gone mad scenario?"

"No," replied Hunter. He began walking carefully through the scattered pallets of boxes.

"Definitely looks like the cargo," noted Lang, "might have taken a wild ride in the sky. Turbulence?"

"Maybe," said Hunter, his eyes searching. "But you wouldn't expect the ropes securing it would be torn apart, ripped. No," and he paused. "Something... something moved violently in this area. Perhaps it made a noise and the co-pilot went to investigate and the *Whatever* attacked him. Maybe the co-pilot screamed and the pilot came to find out what was going on and the pilot was stabbed."

"But why is the bomb bay door open, but not all the way?"

Hunter reached in between two boxes and pulled out a piece of fabric, torn and somewhat transparent. He fingered the material.

"Maybe what the pilot saw, what attacked him, so terrified him that he thought he might flush the *Whatever*, let it drop out the cargo hold like a sprung trap, but somehow the door jammed. If you look here, this bolt and screw was sheared and then wrenched apart. Perhaps when the plane hit the runway, the door opened more." Hunter bent down on his knees, reaching against a corner of the bomb bay door. He picked up another piece of the flimsy fabric. "And maybe the *Whatever* was able to escape... after the plane was on the ground." He looked at the two pieces of fabric.

"Lang, where did this plane originate from?"

"Let's see. The Lieutenant told me the manifest was for spare parts on the Able and Baker Tests."

"But from where?" Hunter felt rising agitation, reaching toward his own horror of discovery.

"From New Mexico."

"Of course. From the White Sands testing grounds at Alamogordo. The first atomic bombing sites in the United States, the Trinity Project, what, July, 1945." To himself, either an earth monster or something from a tear in the fabric of the heavens.

"What did you find?" Lang looked, wondering.

"Look at this." He handed over the two pieces of torn material and Lang considered it.

Not canvas, more like a rubber tarp, transparent, and with — it has a design — It almost looks like — .

"Snake skin! The *Whatever* is a snake, a giant one, mutated by an atomic bomb blast. The pilot wasn't stabbed he was snake bit and the venom killed him."

"A giant snake?"

"It's these damn coincidences. I think it must be a snake, and it has a purpose, a direction. Some unholy power is causing this aimed migration to Hawaii."

"What? You think this snake traveled all the way here, to what, come after you? Like a homing device?"

"Yes, the bad gods stop me, who else is there to fight them?"

"So where is this giant snake? It just slithered out the bomb bay door and into the jungle?"

"Tommi! She's nearby. And the snake is out there." Hunter fled the plane.

Tommi, this snake monster came for you. I may be a demi-god but you did something to be placed on its menu.

74

He raced the jeep he had appropriated from Lang. His swerving, accelerated ride took him along the fringe of the runway until he spotted what he thought might be apparent, the bent grass trail heading towards the military fence, into the jungle. He followed the trail until he came to the 'Off Limits', the Military Reservation's high fencing. The barbwire topped fence had been, not torn down, but bent over, crushed. That's one big snake, considered Hunter. It must be gigantic. He paused, backed up the jeep and took a running charge at the laid down fence. Catching the barbed wire in the wheels, causing one tire to go flat the jeep bounced out of the wire entrapment. He tried now to navigate through the narrowing vegetation.

Stupid. That was his conclusion when he overcame his concern for Tommi's welfare with his own rationalization of his present circumstances. *What am I doing in this undergrowth with a slithering serpent... and now my jeep stuck... and I'm on foot? Stupid.*

He stepped out and began his pursuit, but paused. Returning to the jeep, he extracted the leather case, opened it, and pulled out the black lacquer scabbard with the Katana blade inside. *Oh, what the hell,* he considered, *even if it will probably only be good for machete chopping vines out of my face.*

He listened. He had been in jungle settings before, but here there was an eerie silence... no bird or animal noises... except in the distance he could hear people, not talking, more like shouting. He picked up his pace, running but with wary footfalls.

As soon as he made an open clearing, he found himself facing the muzzle of a deadly-looking rifle.

"What do you want here?"

Before he could answer, try to figure out, why he was there, what he was searching for, he heard the shrill voice of Tiki Shark.

"He's with me!"

Hunter found himself standing in a small group of people, most angry, a few of them armed with rifles. There were about thirty tents and an awning covering of space where picnic tables seemed to be set up for feeding the on-strike workers. Around the clearing were the sugar cane fields, the main industry of the islands, laying untouched.

Tiki Shark herded Hunter away from the suspicious crowd.

"They're upset. They thought you might be a scab sent by the owners. One of their people walked into the jungle this morning and hasn't returned. The people here are on edge."

"Missing? Where's Tommi?"

"I'm not sure. I think I saw her heading up the road a while back. Hey, what's that you got there?"

Tommi sat on an outcropping of old volcanic rock, colored sienna brown in contrast to the red-iron soil. She could see the valley below, the air field, from her view on the side of road with sugar cane stalks tall below her and a burned off field up on the mountain side, tilled and ready to be replanted. She was there to think.

I know I like — love was too strong a word — *Hunter. The feelings must have been there all the time we've known each other, a love-hate relationship, the hate slowly dissipating like an early morning cool fog and a hot sun rising. And being with him, touching him, evokes emotions, tender ones, memorable, to off-set that nightmare night aboard the Altair Beria. But do I want to change my life, open myself up to be hurt? What if something happens to him? All this fighting of demons. It was so unreal. I don't know if I'm ready...*

She heard a sound on the makau side, up the hill. A noise in the jungle that bordered the cut sugar cane fields. *No, nothing,* she supposed. *A flock of birds, perhaps.*

If we were together, would he ask me to stay at home, or go to an office and be a real bookkeeper? I could not do that. That is not me. I don't know if I am ready to be with this man who has changed so much.

She heard a noise, makai, toward the ocean, down the hill. A man running towards her, carrying — .

"Hunter! What are you doing here?"

Surprised to see him, not unhappily so, she was even more shocked when he grabbed her and held her tight. He kissed her hair, her head. Tommi's wonderment turned to tenderness.

This is nice, so unexpected. She listened to his heavy breathing.

What is he doing here? Indeed I could grow to enjoy him in my life.

"We have to get out of here, now," he said, starting to pull her along. "Something evil is coming this way."

"What's up?" Tiki reached them, totally out of breath

"I can't leave these people." She pulled away from Hunter.

"We have weapons, if they're necessary."

"We can fight the plantation rent-a-cops." Tiki bristled.

"It's not about the strike. It's an atomic bomb creature."

"Oh." Tiki lost his verve.

"What can we do?" Tommi, use to having a plan, needed more information.

"What's that?" Tiki looked around nervously.

What?" Hunter yanked his head. He listened. There was quiet... except... that noise.

Rattling. Like shaken gourd maracas, but deep bass tonal, growing closer.

"It's a fuckin' snake!" shouted Tiki Shark. "Sort of. I've never drawn that before!"

Moving from the depths of the mountainside jungle into shorter slash grass, moving in undulating gyration, a snake-like creature emerged.

"It has the form of a Diamondback desert rattler," said Hunter, trying to calm them with a clinical look. "Gigantus size. Look, the head is deformed."

And as Tommi glimpsed it, the one head divided and four beady, narrow eyes looked upon its prey. "It's split. Two headed."

"And long as a sugar company train and as big!" Shouted Tiki Shark, frozen in place. "Perhaps we should run."

"I think it could out slither us." Hunter quickly deduced, though with Tommi they slowly started backing up, moving away from the creature, down the hill towards the dirt roadway path. With their movement, the rattling increased in ferocity.

Tommie gave thought. "I have a theory to prove. Tiki, run down and grab a rifle from one of our people; don't bring anyone back. Bring it back to Hunter. Please, make sure it's loaded, and bring ammunition. Lots."

Tiki did not need further explanation and sprinted away. The snake turned its head suddenly at the running human, but then focused its attention back to Hunter and Tommi.

"I thought so. This creature has picked its target. You, Hunter."

"Hold on, I have my own detective theory." He moved away from her, not behind her, or running away, but to the side, moving towards the snake. The creature paused looked at him with two swinging heads, and then returned its gaze to Tommi, who had not moved. Hunter moved back to stand in front of her, shielding.

"I don't want to belittle your great mind, babe." Hunter gave her a sideway grin. "This snake monster came for you. I may be a demi-god, but you did something to be placed on its menu."

"News to me, no idea why. But we need to keep away from *It* until Tiki returns."

Hunter drew the blade from its scabbard.

"You've got to be kidding, Hunter. You need years of training. And besides, that was an expensive gift, not a toy for creature poking."

"If I can use it like a baseball bat, and baseball I do know," said

Hunter, taking a few practice swings. "Maybe I can keep it from biting. And by the way, I have come to believe those fangs are highly poisonous." As if cued to respond, two heads of the snake hissed with open mouths, devil-forked tongues spitting at them.

"Tommi, dearest, start moving to the road. I will do my best to attract *It's* attention."

'Dearest', huh? I can get to like that." She gave him a smile, a nervous one, keeping her eyes focused on the threat uphill and taking small shuffle steps backwards, needing to, but not wishing to leave Hunter.

He, simultaneously, at the same time, stepped forward to do battle, totally unprepared. If he recalled correctly the snake would — and there it did — start to coil, preparing to strike. Hunter only hoped that he was keeping himself between the creature and Tommi's position.

Both man and creature were digging their eyes deep into the others to guess movement.

The snake struck out: Hunter dove, hitting the ground to scramble to the side, the tail whipping at him. Taking a chance, he extended the sword, and instead of sticking the snake, as he ran back against its length he felt the sword slide down the skin, flaying it.

He paused in amazement. This sword is razor sharp. I never knew. He looked at the blade startled to see the snake's blood, not evaporating or running off, but steaming, boiling off, leaving the silver metal gleaming again, as if it had never been used. Even more surprising was the snake creature's reaction. A snake is a cold-blooded reptilian; it should not feel pain, but with a loud hiss, the snake must have felt its flesh sliced, and instead of squirming after Tommi, it turned on its aggressor.

Hunter backed up, preparing for another lunge from the snake, breathing heavily, not knowing if he could keep up this dodge 'em game. The rattling grew louder as the snake moved into its striking coil. The time had come.

A shot rang out. One of the snake's heads lurched and shook, an eye splattered. Hunter looked to the far part of the field. Not Tiki Shark, but Tommi pulled the rifle away from her shoulder, bewildered, her expression: *How the heck did I hit that monster?* She would not tell Hunter it was pure luck. She fired again. *That's more my style, a miss.*

The distraction of the bullet hitting, another fired, gave Hunter an opening. He ran back at the snake and ducking under the two heads before they could focus back their prey, Hunter swung as hard as he could, yelling, "It's a hard hit to the outfield, it's going, going, gone!" The two heads of the snake and a long section of its tapered body fell to the ground. Both sections of the body writhed in final convulsions, which Hunter made several jumps to avoid.

The blade looked pristine as he Hunter inserted the sword back in the scabbard.

"I don't understand this thing," he said to Tommi and Tiki, waving his gift, the lethal weapon, in their direction as they walked closer, but not too close, to the dead beast.

"Considering all of the unreal mysteries that have become part of our lives," guessed Tommi, "your samurai sword came from the ashes of Hiroshima. Atomic fire against this snake from atomic fire, definitely mystical powers at work."

"But Wowie, man," Tiki commented in critique of the fight. "You sure don't know how to use that as a weapon. Jumping all around, thrashing at Mr. Rattler. You need lessons, man."

Hunter and Tommi exchanged an understanding glance.

"Yes, I agree, Tiki. All the lessons and instruction I can take. Still, that rifle came in handy. I might have to become a big game hunter in the future."

Tommi tried to hide her relief that he was safe by offering a new plan. "What you need, if there are more evil things coming out of the sand or out of heaven, is a team of fighters who can likewise fight this creature; especially, if you're not running to the U.S. Military with a wild story of gods and demons." She did not say further that a team would be protectors for him.

Tiki walked around the snake, very carefully, to look at the two heads, thinking of drawing them. "That would be good, a fighting squad. And maybe every one could learn this Kung Fu and how to fight with all sorts of weapons, even be sword masters. I like the idea, Tommi. But what do we call them? They need a battle-born name, like 'The Big Red One', or the 'Fighting Seabees'? How about 'The Demon Killers'? Or, if you are sword fighters, how about?…" he thought… "'The Five Samurai'? No, something more American. 'Fists of Aluminum.'"

"No, make it more international," laughed Hunter, going over to hug Tommi. "This probably will be a world-wide battle." He looked into Tommi's eyes, concerned, desiring. "I still don't understand why this thing came after you, and I am now sure it was looking for you."

Tommi mused to herself with a thread of an idea, more an internal feeling, but kept silent.

"Anyway, I think," said Hunter, reasserting a male persuasive stance, "I think we need to stick together more closely."

Tommi could accept that and nodded at such manly wisdom, wondering however where the next beast might arise from. The future caused her great fear.

Tiki Shark kicked the snake. "You know we could cut this thing up and cook it for the folks down the hill. Wonder if it tastes like dragon?"

"No," said Hunter, turning serious again. "I need to bury it as soon as possible to keep the islanders from raising questions we don't want to try and answer." He looked grim. "Besides, see those three lumps at the tail end of this Gigantus Snake? I just solved the case of missing persons — one of your strikers and two airmen. One fell from the sky and hit the other is as good a conjecture as the military police might accept. I tell that to the authorities, why, I might become the greatest detective on the islands.

"So, you both go back to the camp. I'll take care of this. Three bodies to recover and a snake to disappear."

Eew," gagged Tiki Shark, no longer thinking of food.

Here are two of my best friends; they put the tiki back into Red Tiki.

Epilogue

Halloween, 1946

A perfect night, a blood red full moon scraped by finger nail silvery clouds, an apt celestial tapestry for the dedication of a grotesque looking, unworldly creature.

J. Chen Shippers and Forwarders delivered the crate and installed the statue, secured with a bath of cement on a surrounding new pedestal which had been anchored into the ground. Only an atomic bomb could move the thing, said Red Tiki Lounge and Bar owner, Lyle Sheftel, which brought awkward laughter from his friends, and they were good friends, since they had gone after the statue and returned with a bigger and uglier one.

Whether it would bring the Red Tiki Lounge good luck only time would tell, or rather this night, since Lyle was going to go high card wins all against Donn Beach, who was in town. The bet, if Lyle won, meant the West Coast restaurant owner would postpone opening one of his Don The Beachcomber restaurants in Honolulu for two years. To his bookkeeper's ears only did Lyle reveal he had learned, going back as far as his Chicago grade school days, how to fast-shuffle and cut cards. All fair in love and pupus.

Still, Lyle told Tommi, "Not that I am giving anyone notice.

There's time. If I win, it will be at least two years before I have to decide to fight the new kid on the block or close up shop and take my banked profits" — he winked at her — "and try something new. I've got old friends who are talking about opening a class joint, maybe with a few slot machines. I hear it's near the California border, in Nevada, where they've had open gambling for ten years. Dusty village called Las Vegas. My friends have named their hang-out the Flamingo Inn and Casino. Funny name: a water bird in the middle of the desert. Might look into a future there. Maybe open a tiki motel with a restaurant and bar. Maybe a show lounge. Maybe burlesque. Let's talk about a possibility like that over the next year." Tommi agreed to run some number scenarios.

On All Hallows' Eve, The Red Tiki Lounge had a rip-roaring crowd gallivanting, most patrons in costumes. The theme, creatures from old monster movies, suggested by Tiki Shark, the ever entrepreneur, who just happened to have set up a palm thatched booth outside the Red Tiki where he would be seated, ready for quick ink portraitures of Lounge party-goers, inserting their faces into stand-up pre-printed monster movie lobby cards.

Tiki was giddy. He had received a short letter from Ishiro Honda of Toho Studios, in blocky English, about wanting to see his drawings; could he sketch a manga drawing of a Gojira in skyscraper size, tromping through downtown Honolulu, or better yet, for his planned audience, Tokyo? Ish would consider any other ideas that Tiki might create from his fertile imagination. Reliving adventures in his mind, he thought to reconstruct an invulnerable man who became hard as a rock whenever he got angry. He had sent off one sketch to that comic book contact in New York City but had heard nothing back. No matter. Things were looking positive. Maybe new adventures would bring new art ideas, so he planned to stick close to Hunter Hopewell and his girlfriend, Tommi. Yes, thought Tiki, I will volunteer, but not at the front lines, to serve in any battle group Hunter forms. Did they decide on a name yet? The Five or Six Samurai, yes, could be a catchy name. But not the one Hunter liked — 'United Nations Fighters'. Drabsville.

While waiting for his next client to receive a Tiki Shark face, he stared at a blank sketching page, hoping for a muse of inspiration to land, smoking some good pakalolo stuff, allowing his mind to float, waving off a large moth attracted by the spotlights centered on the fabric covered tiki, soon to be unveiled, the cover cloth provided by J. Chen Fabrics.

Near his side, his tethered goat, 'Bikini', nibbled on Maui sativa hay.

Tiki Shark started sketching the fluttering moth, exaggerating its size, drawing it flying above a city... *Doing what?...perhaps off to fight Gojira.*

Tommi, filled with mixed feelings, didn't feel ready to sort them out. One she would be facing soon: though she did not consider herself a 'girlfriend,' she knew she was in love, and experienced any long absence from Hunter's side to be heartache. She was proud of him, his self-confidence strong since his detective income out of *Hopewell Investigations* had risen into profitable black ink. No wealthy clients, but enough walk-ins. He handled bad account collections Tommi passed onto him, and did the odd process service from Sheriff Duke K's office. A reputation had gone out that Hunter was good at solving domestic abuse cases in favor of any battered wife; his intolerance of aggressive husbands, convinced them to tone down the violence, beg forgiveness. Well, and letting a little of his anger drip, and puff up his arms and chest, resulting in a broken jaw or a fist through a door were powerful persuaders.

Tommi wondered, *Does that vocation of wanting to protect women indirectly suggest Hunter's concern for my welfare? Am I being too self-centered, seeing him as a protective knight, my knight?* Of course, to her concern was the fear of what lay ahead, for Tiki had sketched Hunter as some sort of paniolo-samurai warrior, an island cowboy with a sword.

She had been in the Red Tiki earlier in the day, finding it a better field office than her bookkeeping storefront as a place to hold meetings. She saw a friend, a client.

"How did your California surfing trip go?"

"I think the West Coast is going to explode with enthusiasts," said Duke K., showing her a packet of color photos several fans had taken. "Wish I was twenty years younger. You know some are using smaller boards, sharper for turning. Tried my skill at under wave runs they call 'a pipeline'."

"How did the water suit fare?"

"Strong possibilities. Make me a new one. I left mine with two brothers back in California, Manhattan Beach. They may send you an order. They have some ideas for improvements."

"My pleasure. With J. Chen Fabrics, business is booming."

Duke K. had always liked Tommi's hutzpah, her sharpness and was pleased to notice her somber sharp-pencil all-business persona had abated, or at least been toned down. Was it caused by this relationship with the owner of Hopewell Investigations? He could work with both of them, but being in law enforcement, sometimes his mind drifted to unfounded suspicions.

"You know, I heard you took over the business of Baran Furniture. Did he sell out?"

"No, more like a fire-sale. You knew the courts had to step in when he disappeared?" Her face remained neutral, a cool demeanor, as if merely responding to a general conversation.

"You know where he went off to?"

"No idea. I just stepped in, covered past due employee salaries, and got a great deal on assets, pennies on the dollar. Couldn't pass it up."

"What are you going to do with it?"

"Well, after some late-night brainstorming here at the Red Tiki, I decided there seems to be a big interest in everything 'Polynesian', from all the servicemen returning home. The market for Asian swords has fallen off precipitously. Baran-Jingu Furniture is starting to crank out what I'm calling the tiki den look. Rattan furniture, palm thatch rumpus room bars, that sort of stuff ."

She turned to Lyle, who was in the process of jamming the bar with extra bottles of liquor for the Halloween festivities.

"Hey, Lyle, show him your new tiki barware."

Lyle, dressed as Bela Lugosi, even with fake plastic teeth, proudly displayed glazed mugs with tiki faces.

"Maitais will be half off tonight!" Lyle half-choked on his own generosity. "And a new drink: *The Island Clipper.*"*

"Tiki Shark did the mug designs," Tommi beamed proud about her new consulting client, "He gets a royalty on every dozen sold. The way I think they'll go out of the stores when shipped mainland, you could have one rich hepster on the Honolulu streets very soon."

"Civilization," mused Duke K., as he rose to take leave, "must take heedful warning of Tiki Sharks." To Tommi he bid a farewell with, "See you tonight. And may the island gods bring you and yours peace."

"Tonight yes, see you then; gods and peace I don't know about." She was thinking of the early evening meeting she and Hunter were to have with Pele, whom they had not seen since the Brawl on Mauna Kea.

She went upstairs to the plain rooms of the Hopewell Investigations agency, to freshen up for the party and dedication tonight… and shut down the office early. She took in the destitute looking setting. *One of these days, I must start the subtle hints at finding... joint housing. Am I dreaming to wish for a bungalow on the beach... for both of us?*

"We're doing what?" asked Hunter, exasperated, looking up from office paperwork that he always sought to postpone, but bills had to be paid. He bet Sam Spade never had to deal with accounts owing.

"You need relaxation methods to keep your anger down."

"You already have me running the beach every day, lifting weights, and doing that, what again — -?"

"Daitō-ryū aiki-jūjitsu."

"And now, I'm training in this new style — ?"

"Taekwon-Do."

"Those leg kicking exercises are stretching my legs past their breaking point. Probably someday I'll be able to wrap my feet behind my head."

"Yes, you might, but before we go meet up with your ex-girlfriend, let me show you how I can do my own feet-head gymnastics." And she locked the office door.

Even in the midst of party prep in the Red Tiki Lounge, only to the initiated, Lyle Sheftel particularly, could one define the rhythmic bumping noises upstairs. Smiling, he began to mix:

*The Island Clipper
2 ounces Calvados or other apple brandy (applejack)
1/2 ounce fresh lime juice
3 dashes of absinthe
1/2 ounce pomegranate grenadine
Shake with cracked ice. Strain into cocktail glass.
Thin strip of lime zest for garnish.

A beautiful young girl, dressed in a long, gloss green trench coat, sat on the dock behind them,
her feet trailing in the water. No, not her feet, her tentacles.
"I can't wait to join the party tonight," she said.

Hand in hand, they walked to the quay and down an abandoned dock to where they found Pele sitting dangling her feet, her toes not quite reaching the harbor water. Though dusk had come and gone, early evening offered no cooling from the heat, even in October, but it was to be expected.

"I have come to say goodbye," the goddess said.

"Hey," said Tommi, "you have a new accent? It sounds like… what?… French?

"A school teacher drowned on vacation, in Martinique. I needed a more worldly view."

Both Tommi and Hunter looked at the young woman dumbstruck, while she continued.

"I am leaving, for a time."

"But aren't you... of the earth?" Tommi's reluctance to accept her departure was sincere even if begrudging. She had enjoyed the bantering strangeness of this 'person'.

"I have put in motion the major events I was asked to."

"What about Danny? How's he going to take it?" Hunter was curious.

"Oh, we split after a month. I broke his heart, for a week. But gave him a thrilling rodeo ride; character building, boy to man; he will be better for it, a better rider for sure."

"That's nice to hear," deadpanned Tommi; even in a French accent, the girl's flippancy so annoyed her. "Will you send him a love note from the other side?"

"No, of course not, but that's why I wanted to see you both. Revelation time for everyone."

"What are you talking about?" Hunter's queried, wary.

"Hunter, I am pregnant," said Pele, the goddess of Mother Earth.

When shock hit disbelief, she added, "And the child's yours, Hunter. Not Danny's. Girls know these things. Usually. And before your jaw drops off or Tommi bursts a blood vessel, here's what's going to happen, just to get the rules straight."

She had them trapped to hear her next proclamation, a dire command as it seemed. "I will be gone until March of next year. Seems like there's going to be an inventory taken in the spirit world. More atomic bombs are being dropped. They're talking about hydrogen bombs, whatever those are. You know, your friends the Russians got hold of some Baker Test bomb photos, and had some spies in place in the U.S. Government, and they're working on starting their own atomic arsenal. I'll be back with a list of what's coming and what's here already roaming around. It'll be your shopping list of what to take care of and send back, or better yet, destroy. On my return I will place a child in your arms for you to raise as a proud father. I'm not into changing diapers." She looked to Tommi and back to Hunter. "You have some months to figure it all out."

"Meanwhile, to keep your mind occupied. I have brought you a client."

A voice behind them said a pleasant, "Hi." Hunter and Tommi jumped at this appearance from nowhere.

A beautiful young girl, dressed in a long, gloss green trench coat, sat on the dock behind them, her feet trailing in the water. No, not her feet, her tentacles.

"I can't wait to join the party tonight," she said.

Hunter now in apoplectic alarm, still not having digested the first part of Pele's surprise on him, exclaimed in a confused spurt, "You are coming to the Red Tiki this evening?"

"It is a costume party, isn't it?" Her lovely face bore an innocent expression. "I should fit in, maybe even win a prize for 'Most Original', don't you think?"

"My sister and her wit," said Pele. "She tried to kill me once, but enough of us. Nā-maka, why don't you and Mr. Hopewell talk about his new case? Miss Tommi and I are going to go over there and have a little girl-to-girl chat."

The two women wandered off the dock and sat on a bench under, appropriately, a tentacle-dangling banyan tree; they could see Nā-maka waving her appendages for emphasis in her story telling to Hunter, quite an animated project, whatever it might turn out to be.

Pele looked intently at Tommi, provoking a shy uncomfortable blush.

"Do you know you are also pregnant?" queried the goddess.

Too much information. But she had known, had that feeling, the morning feelings.

"How the hell do you know?"

Pele gave a shrug to suggest female deity all-partial knowing.

"Have you told Hunter?"

"No," admitted Tommi. "Compared to what you just sprung on him, my problems are insignificant."

"No, they are not. Will you be truthful and tell him?"

"With what you hit him with, I can't very well be the icing on the cake."

"Perhaps not, but such events must be spoken of. The point is: what sort of man is Hunter? Will he be a good father?

Tommi did not respond.

"The way I see it, you tell him the truth and let everyone know you will be the mother of 'twins'." Motherhood being a foreign word to her, Tommi reeled at all the overpowering implications yet to calculate. There was one choice. "I could lose the child, for it is not a child yet. There are many trained women in Chinatown."

Pele frowned and Tommi felt an aura of heat come over them both, making her shift uncomfortably.

"That will not happen. I have my hero and he is cured. I will not let anyone hurt him, physically or mentally. He has a destiny. If you interfere, Hunter will be shown a Tiki Shark drawing before your abortion; it will show you hemorrhaged and dying from such practice. Would your death placate Hunter's conscience, or would he see himself as the cause of your destruction? Would you be willing to destroy him with grief, drive him back to his downward spiral drinking?"

Tommi recoiled from such a vision; that she could be so selfish just to solve her own problems and that with her absence by death, Hunter would presumably go on, find other happiness. No, she believed, she could never hurt him. He had become so happy, until now. What should she do?

"You forget one minor aspect."

"Oh, Pele, come on, hit me with your wisdom. It can't send me over the edge any faster."

"Sarcasm?"

"Yes, loads of it." Tommi felt the emotional burden cascading inward.

"Your children are to be of the gods; they will be raised to have extraordinary powers. While mankind tries to imagine the future with all these silly comic books of fantasy and outer space paioles, or the superstitious religions of ancient peoples, you all still can't comprehend what this tearing of the heavens is to mean for your world and ours."

As an afterthought Pele threw out her attempt at support.

"At the right time, I will send you, what do they call them, a nanny, to help raise your children. One of most extraordinary abilities. Give you freedom to stand with Hunter against the demons. That's all I have to say." She walked away, not looking back, a pig suddenly appearing at her side, as dutiful vassal companion.

Tommi slumped; the future of two worlds bore down on her, like Mauna Kea pressing down on her shoulders.

At the appointed hour, the Lounge closed for the planned forty minutes of outside ceremony, the audience standing in one large gathering of camaraderie, boisterous, attentive through short speeches, including one from the Mayor of Honolulu.

"We need to talk," said Hunter, still numb.

Later," came her only response. She feared to face the discussion, the outcome: will he stay, propose marriage, or leave, and never return to her? She was losing the courage to what made the right decision. And a new truth had been revealed when she had her girl talk with Pele: the Atomic two-headed snake, as Hunter had surmised, was after her, to kill not her, but the embryo inside, a future threatening god child. Tommi saw the tragedy that lay ahead: she must cling to Hunter as much for protection as love.

Hunter, nodded to her silence, and accepted her postponement for that talk, a prospect he also did not relish.

At the end of another speech, the Honolulu Chamber of Commerce gave Lyle a 'Better Business' award.

They whispered over the oration.

"Tell me what Nā-maka wanted? Something for us to be involved in?" She left the 'us' hanging, a temptation, a riddle to her thoughts.

"A posse of black devil banshees is headed this way. From the other side, not mutated like Gojira or the snake. They seem to be homing in on me or you or the both of us."

"Speaking of Gojira, what's Nā-maka know? She's of the ocean. Where's Gojria?"

"Growing, in the deep. Someday, I — we — will have to face him — it."

At least they were talking, Tommi considered. Maybe we could talk things out, not let emotions overwhelm us. She might as well get out her hypothesis. "I think we need to consider other monsters still unaccounted for."

"The ones from the other atomic bomb blasts?"

They listened as a youth choir from the Kamehameha School were singing standard Hawaiian songs, "Aloha 'Oe" and "Malama Ia Me Oe' led by a young soloist, a Chinese-Portugeuse boy by the name of Donnie Tai Loy Ho. In this land of mixed bloods, Sheftel never had been prejudiced against any race or their money.

Tommi leaned in, her voice at Hunter's ear, her head resting on his shoulder, liking the feeling. Wanting it to continue, forever, but... "More like Kū on the loose."

"Aren't we doing the Kū dedication at this moment?" He looked at the cloth covering.

"Are we sure? Try me on this. First, Kū controlled the sailors. But in the end it was Baran who fled with the soldiers guarding him, not Kū, who was still fighting you. Second, no blood on the snow. Baran was not bleeding; a man shot leaves a crimson trail, even if only droplets. None. Finally, when Baran came to kill me, he shouted,

'Die you — .' And then he was shot, his last word hanging. I'm thinking he was not going to say 'bitch' or something like that. I think his formed words were 'Die, you... mm... mortal.'"

Hunter's eyes widened as he put past pieces of a puzzle into place. "When I was tossing Kū, his last words were very well spoken... Who are you?" Kū knew what I was, but Baran thought I was a soldier with an unusual look and a few muscles, nothing more."

"Whatever happened, happened on Mauna Kea?"

Hunter mulled.

"What Pele did with Chrissy — "

"Who?"

"Later, part of our 'later' talk. I think the word is something like 'transference' or 'transformation,' 'trans' something. Kū got a hold of Baran's body and took over his knowledge, but still has the soul of Kū."

"Then, what are we dedicating tonight?"

"The husk of Kū, with the leftovers of Baran, what Kū did not think important."

"Then out there somewhere is Kū looking like Baran. Kū is now educated to the modern ways, far more dangerous, wars with devil gods, war between men. Kū -Baran fomenting them."

"Yes, I'm am afraid you could be right."

"I had my suspicions. Here's the clincher. Lyle handed this to me off the message board. Addressed to me." She had not meant to show him the postcard of a pagoda-styled temple among pine trees. The other side was inscribed: "Having a wonderful time. Hope you drop in and see me soon. Bring your friend... and family. — B"

"Where's this card from?"

"Korea."

Hunter froze. Too many coincidences were foretelling action he was fated to take. He tried to comfort himself, believing it was not to be, yet he did say, "But nothing is happening in Korea."

"Unless Baran- Kū will start it."

"Is this why you wanted me learning this Taekwon-Do? That's Korean martial art." He gave her a comforting smile of it doesn't matter, suggesting a future.

Tommi took in the ceremony around them.

"I wonder if Pele knows Kū is on the loose and not that tiki statue at the front door?"

"She fooled Kū the first time and captured him. Perhaps Kū now has tricked her. These gods are powerful but not all knowing; they have flaws, they can make mistakes."

"Yes, Kū did not know about firearms; Pele came first as an innocent native girl and later as a high school cheerleader type. Not the brightest light bulbs."

Tommi bit her tongue at this put down, realizing she still smoldered with jealousy, of how easy Pele manipulated the role of temptress.

"Well," Hunter saw beyond the personalities, understood the greater fall-out and sighed with reluctance. "When she finds out, she will be one pissed off goddess, and will expect me to fight Kū and save the day, if not the universe."

She was going to answer, pleading him not to go for her sake, for their child's sake, when she heard Lyle Sheftel call their names to join him up front. "Two of my best friends, who unselfishly helped to put the tiki back into the Red Tiki."

The three of them simultaneously pulled on the drawstring ropes and the cloth curtain fell from the statue — the applause resounded, as the doors of the bar were flung open, greeter Mister Manaa stepped aside, and tiki mugs clinking halfprice maitais drew in the monster-vampire-witch costumed and thirsty patrons to one of the most renowned drinking establishments, west of San Francisco, east of Hong Kong.

The Red Tiki Lounge and Bar.

Hunter Hopewell and Tomoe Jingu, left alone, stared up at the massive tiki overseeing all who might enter, both with mixed thoughts, their dreams unfulfilled, uncertain futures dangerous and as powerful as an atomic bomb, out there somewhere, on a countdown. Still, they held hands and stood close to each other, seeking comfort and happiness.

Tiki Shark came running out, breathless. "Come in, you gotta see her. Just gorgeous. Great costume. That tentacle thing." He giggled. "My Mona Lisa octopus. I want to paint her. And she wants to dance with me. Can you believe that!? Wowie!"

All three, each with their own private wish for luck and good fortune, patted the tiki and, arm in arm, walked in to join the celebration.

THE END... not quite

Tiki Shark's view of All Hallows' Eve, 1946, at the Red Tiki

Quest Mystery Quiz

Now that you have finished Atomic Dreams, take this quiz, and see where these people found their fame in history. And don't be misled by those who are merely fictional. Answers at www.spgrogan.com

____ Head circling sharks and 35th

____ Got a frog in your throat?

____ Tiny bubbles

____ Hawaiian store named after singer

____ Surfing Legend

____ Pilot, died in the Ba_ le of Midway (supposedly)

____ Directed first Japanese giant mutated lizard movie

____ 1930's — what to do with old kimonos

____ Overcame handicap #1 — infield rule

____ Overcame handicap #2 — vote for me

____ Interviewed T.E. in the desert

____ Fictional Hippocrates

____ Fictional grandfather of famous Big Island artist

____ Man (Spanish) before ge_ ing short

____ Lost at sea

____ Bad guy

____ Hurricane leads to a Pulitzer mutiny

____ Lovely biz babe

____ Wrote about fear of atomic weapon danger

____ Tiki eatery

____ Too Hot to Handle*

___ Lots of butter for cooking

___ Friend of author, website: RockComedyFilm.com

___ From here to forever (something like)

___ Musical tale, or a bridge, or some islands

___ Friend of author, retired bar owner from Central City, Colorado

*Bonus question: What is the significance of the 9 months surprise?

Place a letter in blank for your answer

A. Hunter Hopewell

B. Lyle Sheftel

C. Tommi Chen

D. Jim Michener

E. Private J. Jones

F. Doctor Lundell

G. Doctor Heimlich

H. Tiki Shark

I. Peter Gray

J. Pele

K. Daniel Inouye

L. Donn Beach

M. Donnie Tai

N. Peter Baran

O. Hilo Hattie

P. Duke K

Q. Shigeru Mori

R. Ishiro Honda

S. Lowell Thomas

T. Aloha Shirt

U. Dutch Leonard

V. Dr. D. Bradley

W. Exec. H. Wouk

X. Amelia Earhart

Y. Julia McWilliams

Z. LTJG of PT 59

Mahalo nui loa
May the Tiki Spirit be with you always
Mista G & Tiki Shark

Other Books by S.P. Grogan

Vegas Die

Captain Cooked
*Best Food Novel 2022 Gourmand International Cookbook Awards
Atomic Dreams at Red Tiki Lounge

Lafayette: Courtier to Crown Fugitive

Cookbook Passion by Pamela Kure Grogan
Edited by S. P. Grogan
*Special Award Winner 'Best in the World
Gourmand Cookbook Awards
*Bronze Special IPPY Cookbook Award

Crimson Scimitar: Attack on America

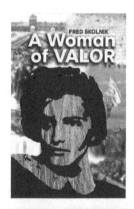

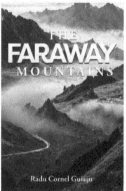
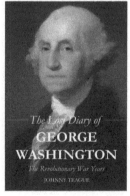